Critical Acclaim for *A Press of Canvas*,
Volume One in the 1812 Trilogy

*"Sailors everywhere will rejoice in the salt spray, slanting decks and high
adventure of this lively yarn of the young American republic battling for its
rights at sea."*

Peter Stanford, President, National Maritime Historical Society

*"A great read . . . a very engaging story with believable, honest characters
. . . taught me a lot about this period of history . . . just fabulous!"*

John Wooldridge, Managing Editor, *Motorboating and Sailing*

*"The Age of Fighting Sail has been well portrayed by C.S. Forester, Patrick
O'Brien and their followers. But all of these writers saw the world from the
quarterdeck. Now comes William H. White with* A Press of Canvas *to
present the same conflicts on the same ships from the viewpoint of a
fo'c'sle hand. It is a worthy effort, well executed, and thoroughly engaging,
and all of us who love the subject matter are in his debt."*

Donald Petrie, author of *The Prize Game, Lawful Looting on the High
Seas in the Days of Fighting Sail*, Naval Institute Press, 1999

Readers' Comments:

"A real page turner . . . couldn't put it down."

*"The book disappears — you find yourself right there watching the action
unfold."*

*"The characters became my friends. I hated to finish the book because now
I have to wait until next year to see what they're up to."*

*"I found myself wondering about my friends on those ships while I was
gardening or doing chores. They became part of my life for a while."*

"Professionally done — and accurate. I especially enjoyed the ship action."

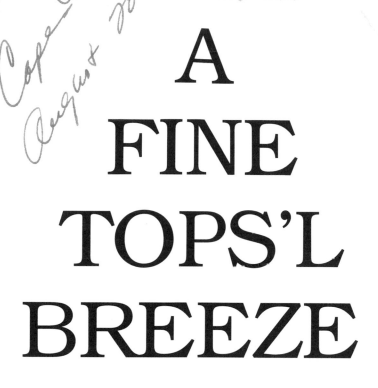

A FINE TOPS'L BREEZE

a novel by

William H. White

Volume Two in the
War of 1812 Trilogy

PUBLISHING
St. Michaels, MD

Cover art: "The Liberators"© 2001 Paul Garnett
Illustrations © 2001 Paul Garnett

Graphic design and production by:
Words & Pictures, Inc., 27 South River Road South, Edgewater, Maryland 21037

Printed in the USA by:
Victor Graphics, 1211 Bernard Drive, Baltimore, MD 21223 USA

Questions regarding the content of this book should be addressed to:

TILLERPublishing
605 Talbot Street, Suite Two
St. Michaels, Maryland 21663
410-745-3750 • Fax: 410-745-9743
www.tillerbooks.com

DEDICATION

My sister, Linda White Wiseman, has always been there for me. She is as enthusiastic about history as I am; her different focus and specialization has worked to compliment my own efforts. In addition to actively promoting the finished product, she has encouraged me, supported my effort, and helped with research. Her relentless pursuit of a detail has inspired me, and hopefully made this tale more accurate. Thanks, Lin.

ACKNOWLEDGMENTS

During the course of researching and writing this novel, a number of people in two countries gave freely of their expertise, wisdom, and time to the author. I would be remiss if I did not publicly thank them.

In the United States:

Don Marshall, Ph.D., and Rick Guttenberg, Associate Director of the Peabody Essex Museum in Salem, Massachusetts, for providing copies of early nineteenth century charts of the Salem/ Marblehead waters and harbors.

John Mooshian, a banker with a major New York institution who supplied a steady stream of reference materials stemming from his habit of haunting second-hand book shops and keeping my needs in mind. And for the occasional lunch in New York.

Linda Wiseman, an independent scholar specializing in the field of 17th-, 18th-, and 19th-century culture and decorative arts, for her help with some shore-side detail and wisdom.

William Martin, best-selling author and historian, for his unstinting willingness to share his knowledge of the world of agents and publishers, and provide a read of the manuscript with helpful comments.

John Hattendorf, Ph.D., the Ernest J. King Professor of Maritime History at the United States Naval War College, Newport, Rhode Island, author, speaker and renowned maritime historian, for his ready availability and amazing depth of knowledge — even of the little, seemingly insignificant, details.

Karen Markoe, Chair of the Humanities Department at SUNY Maritime College, Bronx, New York, for her generosity of time, and willingness to share her knowledge and wisdom. And for her splendid foreword to my story.

In Canada:

Beverly Richard, a descendant of a 19th-century French inmate of Melville Island who helped with research in Halifax, Nova Scotia, and arranged for introductions to others who participated in my research in that beautiful city. And for giving up an entire weekend to ensure I saw and understood those areas of importance to my story.

Jim (JB) Byrne, a transplanted American with a fondness for history and a willingness to share his knowledge over a pint, for showing me some marvelous and rare photographs of Melville Island when the prison was more in evidence.

Other members of the Armdale Yacht Club, Melville Island, Halifax, who all shared their historic site and many of its secrets with me, for their warm welcome to an outsider on a cool Friday night in October.

Dan Conlin, Curator of the Museum of the Atlantic, in Halifax, who opened that wonderful facility's library on a Saturday for me, for providing materials and copies for my study, and suggesting sources for investigation that I had not dreamed of. And for allowing me to use his local historical knowledge as a sounding board for some of my plot ideas.

To each and every one of you, and probably others whom I have neglected to mention, I thank you; any success this effort enjoys is partly yours, for without your assistance and availability, it would have been very difficult to attain the accuracy of fact and, hopefully, the realism in the following pages.

Of course, I must acknowledge the support and love of my family: Ann, Skip, John, and Joshua. Each of you aided and abetted this project with constructive criticism, encouragement and good humor. And I thank you most sincerely for that. And especially a thank you to John for taking time out of his incredibly busy life to create and manage my website, www.1812trilogy.com, and answer all the silly questions that flooded out of my barely computer-literate mind with patience and wisdom.

Last, but certainly not least, I have to mention the help provided by my editor at Tiller Publishing, Jerri Anne Hopkins. Your patience and facile skill with the written word has made me a better writer as well as provided my readers with a tale that flows more easily.

William H. White
Rumson, NJ

FOREWORD

We are inclined to read historical novels from the vantage point of history. The history in *A Fine Tops'l Breeze* is that of the War of 1812, peopled with historical figures, notably the controversial James "Don't give up the ship" Lawrence. Real vessels, such as the *Chesapeake* and the *Shannon*, sail among the ships created from the fertile imagination of author W.H. White.

Ask Americans to name wars that were controversial and divided the nation, and surely they will name Vietnam. One has to probe (and often supply the answer) before the War of 1812 surfaces. Ask Americans to name a war that the United States did not win, and only the most astute will name the War of 1812 — one, by the way, that the United States did not lose; the war ended *status quo antebellum*. Ask Americans to name a war fought for freedom of the seas, and they might name the War of 1812. However, ask them to name a war in which impressment was an issue, and surely the War of 1812 would surface.

This war, while certainly involving land issues, was precipitated by events on the high seas. A nation whose orientation was then eastward towards the Atlantic depended on unimpeded coastal and transatlantic commerce for its very existence.

On the front lines to insure the free flow of people and goods were merchant seaman, generally young men, white and African-American, full-time sailors and part-time farmers. When hostilities with Great Britain escalated into war, these men often signed on to privateering vessels to win glory and treasure — or if the engagements went badly, to exchange freedom for incarceration in a British prison for life, or for death. Some of the sailors we meet in *A Fine Tops'l Breeze* are imprisoned on Melville Island, Nova Scotia, site of a real prison then, a tourist attraction 200 years later.

The novel's descriptions truly reveal life aboard ship, the feel and language of the sea. A seafarer's life in the early nineteenth century was gritty and dangerous. While American seamen were generally treated better than their often-flogged British cousins, they also suffered bad food, terrible living conditions, and, not rarely, brutal shipmates and officers. Theirs was a hard world made harder by the absence of civilizing feminine hands. Women were on the periphery, whores and girlfriends left in port.

The seafaring tradition, so important in the early history of the United States, can be understood by reading *A Fine Tops'l Breeze*, meticulous in its rendering of life at sea. Real sailors will marvel at the nautical detail; armchair sailors will also surely be drawn into the salty spray and learn and enjoy.

Karen E. Markoe
Chair, Humanities Department
State University of New York
Maritime College

SAIL PLAN OF A SQUARE-RIGGED SHIP

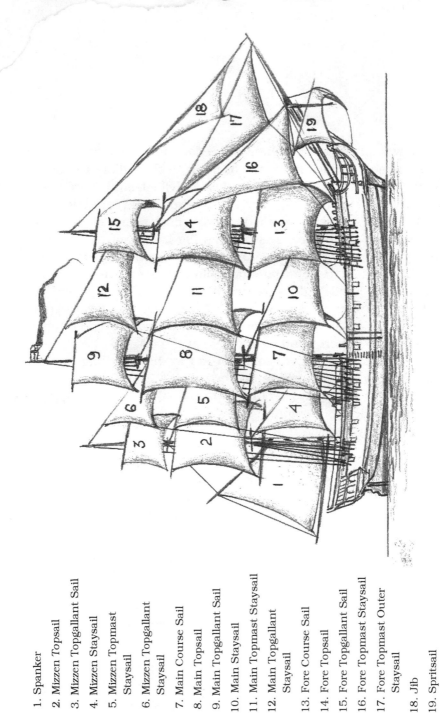

1. Spanker
2. Mizzen Topsail
3. Mizzen Topgallant Sail
4. Mizzen Staysail
5. Mizzen Topmast Staysail
6. Mizzen Topgallant Staysail
7. Main Course Sail
8. Main Topsail
9. Main Topgallant Sail
10. Main Staysail
11. Main Topmast Staysail
12. Main Topgallant Staysail
13. Fore Course Sail
14. Fore Topsail
15. Fore Topgallant Sail
16. Fore Topmast Staysail
17. Fore Topmast Outer Staysail
18. Jib
19. Spritsail

APPROACHES TO HALIFAX – 1813

1. Halifax Harbor
2. Halifax
3. Melville Island
4. Point Pleasant
5. MacNabb's Island
6. York Redoubt
7. Purcell's Cove
8. Citadel Hill

A
FINE
TOPS'L
BREEZE

CHAPTER ONE

February, 1813

Percival 'Butterfingers' Dunn raised up his lanky form and warmed his big hands for a moment over the galley camboose. Then he hitched up his canvas trousers and offered his messmates a grin. His face was mostly hidden by a brown beard specked with gray, and his mouth displayed a number of holes where there had once been teeth.

"Hang on to your story, Isaac, I got to go to the head. . . though it'll surely be a wonder if me arse don't freeze where it sits, har har."

"Watch yerself, Butterfingers. You don't want to go fallin' into the sea here. You'd not make it past the stern afore you'd be an iceberg. And we likely couldn't get the barky wore around in time to drag your frozen arse out'n the sea." Ebenezer Stone, foremast hand and captain of the top, winked at the third mate, Isaac Biggs, as he cautioned his shipmate. "'Sides, we ain't got time to be comin' after the likes o' you. Cap'n Rogers seems in an all-fired rush to get on with this cruise an' take us some prizes up yonder." His face was serious, only his eyes giving away his amusement, as he watched Dunn move toward the ladder.

General Washington, a brig of 300 tons burden with a dozen nine-pound long guns and four carronades, labored under reefed foretops'l, spanker, and single jib as she slogged eastward on her second day out of Salem, Massachusetts, one of the ports left open by the blockading fleet of British line of battle ships which had, since the end of the year, effectively closed the Chesapeake and Delaware Bays. Why Britain had not run the blockade northward to include New York and Long Island Sound puzzled many, but they surely weren't about to question the wisdom of His Majesty's Navy. Salem, Boston, and a few waterfront towns in Connecticut had become homeport to many private armed vessels, or privateers, which, with large crews, sallied forth to harass British merchant shipping.

In response, Royal Navy brigs, sloops and sixth rate frigates were being assigned convoy duty, taking them away from the blockade and action with American ships.

Dunn stepped out of the companionway hatch; the icy wind hit him just as a wave broke on the windward side of the bow, sending freezing spray over him. Each wind-driven sheet of spray froze as it hit the ship, leaving a growing coat of ice on everything — decks, rigging, bulwark, and the watch on deck. The footing was treacherous. He pulled his tarpaulin coat tighter around his neck, shrinking himself down inside the protective canvas, then, clapping on to the ice-covered lifeline, he inched his way toward the bow and the head.

Butterfingers clung desperately to the slippery line. *Hope me arse don't seize up, hangin' it out in this Gawd-forsaken weather*, he thought as he ducked an ice-flecked sheet of spray and tightened his already death-like grip on the safety line. He looked aloft and spoke aloud, more for his own benefit than anything, as there was not a soul within fifty feet of him. "God awmighty. Would you look at that? Wouldn't want to have to get up there anytime soon. Ice on ever'thin' an' slick as ever it could be, I'll warrant." His seaman's eye took in every detail, from the ice-coated pin racks at the foot of both masts to the shining yards and topmasts, each with a layer of ice which could bring a topman down or, should it get thicker, create a dangerous instability aloft from the added weight. The decks, bulwarks and boats were likewise glinting in the weak afternoon light, their individual blankets of ice catching the rays of what little sun poked through the racing overcast.

Dunn saw a figure approaching him as he eased his way carefully back toward the hatch, thinking how good the heat of the fire in the camboose would feel warming his backside after its recent exposure to the elements.

"Dunn! That you? What in the name of all that's holy are you doing out here. Ain't your watch below?" First Mate Jack "Starter" Coffin squinted his eyes down even more tightly than normal, his face screwed up in a grimace. The ice on his beard and the white scar over his cheek gave him a look even more grotesque, and the gravel in his voice, the result of a stroke from a belaying pin many years before, had caused many a poor landsman to go rigid in fear.

His towering height added to their fear; indeed, Coffin was about the only man aboard who could look Dunn straight in the eye. "You'll be comin' on deck soon enough to enjoy this dandy weather, I'm thinkin'."

"Aye, Mister Coffin. Headin' back below right quick, I am. Just payin' a call to the head. Surely hope we ain't gonna be shortin' down on my watch. God alone knows what that ice yonder is doin' to the top hamper. Hope the ol' *Gen'l* can take it."

The mate smiled, his voice laden with sarcasm. "Why, Butter-fingers, you been aloft in worse 'n this. 'Sides, why would Cap'n Rogers want to shorten down, this bein' such a fine tops'l breeze? I'd warrant we'll have this all the way to Canada — just like last time." As the mate spoke, an outsized wave smacked the bow, causing the ship to shudder, and sending a gout of ice laden spray over both men. Coffin laughed as the wind-driven spray hit him and waited until Butterfingers straightened up from where he had ducked away from most of the icy deluge. "*Gen'l Washington* sails right fine in a nice breeze o' wind like this'n. When I was a foremast jack like you, I sailed in her 'round Hatteras in the wild weather — that was back afore the war — an' she behaved like a perfect lady. You don't need to worry none 'bout her. She'll outlast all of us." With that, Starter Coffin turned and made his way aft, moving with more caution than one might expect given the tone of his words, and Dunn returned to his mates below.

"Right nasty it is out there, lads. Worth a man's life to tarry up for'ard. I'd warrant even the quarterdeck ain't noticeable better." He pulled off his coat, the ice falling from it and melting quickly on the warm galley deck, and ran a huge paw across his beard to comb out the ice that had accumulated in the few minutes he'd spent topside.

"I hope you didn't go on with your tale, Isaac, whilst I was top-side. I'd not want to miss any o' that yarn."

Biggs looked up at his shipmate, his wide-spread, penetrating eyes studying him briefly, and shifted his compact frame into a cor-ner of the galley, both to provide a backrest and minimize the motion of the ship as it beat its way east into the steep, icy seas.

"No, Percival, I waited on you. . . where was I? Oh, righty oh. My ship, *Glory,* and them other two, *Bill of Rights* and *Freedom,* had just got into Baltimore — that was afore the Brits closed the Bay. As it was, we had to take it real careful headin' in toward the

Virginia Capes; they had a third rate sittin' outside sailin' off and on and stoppin' anything they could catch. Wasn't many sharp built schooners they catched, though; I ain't never sailed on anything what could sail like that, on the wind or off. I'm tellin' you boys, she was some fine swimmer and, under a press of canvas, ain't nothin' afloat, Brit or American, what could outsail her.

"After we was paid off an' got our prize tickets cashed in, I headed off to Mrs. Wright's for a real hot bath an' a full night's sleep in a honest-to-God bed . . ."

"Aye, and a honest to God doxy to share it with you, I'd wager." Ben Stone voiced what each of the men were thinking; Isaac merely smiled at his shipmate. A slow blink and a hand pushed through his curly dark hair were the only indications of his annoyance at the interruption.

"Not then, Ben. Sleep's all's I was thinkin' on there. They was other nights . . . well, I guess that's another story for another time. Right now, I'm tellin' you coves 'bout gettin' in and me back home again. Anyway, now where was we? Oh yeah, in Baltimore. Well, Cap'n Smalley wanted me to come back aboard *Glory* an' stay on as third for the next cruise, and mebbe permanent-like, but I had to get meself up to Marblehead to see my kin. You collect I ain't seen 'em in two years an' more.

"Ol' Coleman, Brit though he was, took our second, Clements, and the Irishman, Conoughy, down toward Annapolis to see 'bout signin' onto a Navy frigate. Likely he thought they'd be better off on a bigger vessel, him bein' a topman an' all and Tim Conoughy bein' a gunner. Tried to talk me into joinin' 'em, they did, all the time we was waitin' for our prize tickets. Couldn't make me change my mind 'bout headin' up here, though by the Almighty, they surely did try. Surely do hope those boys are takin' care, and that they found 'emselves a Navy ship to sign into. Coleman was dead-set on that right from the start. Called himself a 'man o' warsman', he did, and while he surely was grateful 'bout bein' took out o' Haiti on *Glory*, he pined for a frigate or line o' battle ship. Mister Halladay — he was first mate on *Glory* — he told ol' Coleman the United States Navy didn't have no 'line o' battle' ships, alls we got is frigates and a few brigs, so Coleman, he says, 'well, that'll 'ave to do then. I bin on a frigate most o' me life, I 'ave, an' make no mistake.'" Isaac mimicked the English sailor's accent quite accurately.

He continued. "I didn't have an idea in my head 'bout how I was gonna get myself up here to Massachusetts. Didn't know even if I could do it — they was talk 'bout the Brits bein' ashore in some places I'd have to go through, but I figgered I had to try, so I bought me a horse right there in Fells Point and tied my belongin's onto its stern end. Climbed aboard and headed north — didn't have no idea where I was going. Seemed like I was makin' course corrections at every turn of the glass. Good thing I didn't have to worry 'bout a bunch o' foc's'le Jacks handin' and settin' sails — they'da mutinied like as not with all the changes I made. Findin' a place to lay up at night proved a bit of a worry to boot. Most of the time, I stopped aside the road and slept in some ol' barn or, should one not show up, in a field. Had to belay that after I'd made a little northin' — it started in a gettin' downright cold, and they was snow on top of it. So then I'd have to get myself into a tavern, get some hot vittles an' a real bed. I didn't like to do that 'cause I didn't want to part with my money".

At this, Ben Stone and Tight-Fisted Smith nodded sympathetically, both notoriously parsimonious. Isaac continued.

"But when they wasn't no barn I could fetch up in, seemed like a fair course. Sometimes bein' in a tavern wasn't the safest place to be neither an' I recollect one time when I'da been better off, damn sight better off, if'n I'da stayed away." Biggs paused in his narrative to take a drink from his coffee cup.

"What happened, Biggs. The Brits catch you up?" Ben Stone couldn't resist another opening to interject a comment and steal the attention of his mates; it backfired.

"Let him tell it, Stone. 'Course the Brits didn't catch him up, else he wouldn't be here spinnin' out this yarn for us. Don't pay him no mind, Isaac; just go on with the story."

Biggs continued. "Well, on this particular night I was sittin' in a tavern — The Whistling Pig, I think it was — likely in Pennsylvania somewhere — mindin' my own business — don't pay talkin' to the likes o' what's inside most o' those places — when this cove comes over and sits hisself down like I'd invited him, an' without so much as a 'howdy do', says 'That your horse out yonder?' 'Well,' I said, 'Aye, he's mine, bought and paid for'. 'Well', he says, 'I'll give you five dollars for him right now.' 'Why would you want to buy my horse?' says I. 'I'm in a bit of a jam,' he says, 'an' I need to move along. What about it?' 'No,' I decide. 'I can't sell you that horse or how'll I ever get myself to Marblehead?' The fellow gets up without another word and sets full sail for the door. Movin' smartly he was. I didn't think nothin' of it right then. Next thing I hear is a horse runnin' down the road, an' I dash over to the door; I can just make out someone ridin' a horse hell-bent down the road, and my horse ain't tied where I left him. In fact, ain't no horses at all tied to the rail. Clear as a West Indy dawn it was, I was afoot, and most o' my slops gone in the bargain! I figgered they wasn't nothin' I could do 'bout it right then, since I couldn't chase him down afoot, and went back inside to finish my supper and enjoy the bed I'd already paid half a dollar for. Which I did, and come the morning, I had a word with the innkeeper. He didn't seem like he was much interested in my problem, an' I didn't hold much hope in findin' either that plug of a horse or my gear.

"Innkeeper mentioned they was a stage stop 'bout fifteen miles up, but I could take the troddin' path and save myself some miles, if'n I had a mind to. Course, he said, I could tarry there — eatin' and drinkin' up more o' my cash money should I desire, an' maybe the bastard what stole the horse might come back. I surely didn't think that would happen, what with him bein' in a hurry an' all, so I set out afoot.

"After I'd been walking a ways, I realized, all of a sudden, that this was the first time since I sunk Fells Point astern that my arse wasn't hurtin' me. By now, the weather was mostly bad and it was while I was hoofin' it that it really turned against me, and wasn't fit for walkin' or much else — snow ablowin' around and causin' one to squint down they's eyes like Starter Coffin just to see the road a few feet in front of me. Some kind o' ugly, it was."

"So what happened, Biggs? Do you catch that cove or walk on up to Massachusetts?" Stone was becoming impatient to hear the rest of Biggs' tale before they had to take the watch at eight bells.

"Well now luff up, there, Ben. Don't go gettin' ahead o' me here. I got to tell this the way it happened."

"Aye, but don't make the story take as long as it did for you to get yourself to Marblehead. We got only three or four months for this cruise! Way you're headed, we ain't gonna hear the end afore we's back in Salem; spread some canvas on this tale!"

Ebenezer Stone was not known for his patience, most of the old hands on *General Washington* having felt the brunt of his impatience both aloft and on deck when tasks were performed less quickly than he felt appropriate. This trait was encouraged by both

Captain Asa Rogers and Starter Coffin, to the continuing dismay of the hands, and many of them felt an accident was inevitable.

Biggs had signed the articles only a few days before sailing, when his predecessor had summarily signed onto a Navy frigate as a warrant officer, and had yet to learn the personalities of his shipmates. Even though he technically "outranked" all but a few on board, there was on most privateers a casual camaraderie which, except in times of crisis, put most of the men on an equal footing, always excepting the captain, of course. In the fo'c'sle, one earned respect with his fists and his ability to hand, reef, and steer. Biggs, while not a resident of the fo'c'sle due to his status as third mate, had early on shown his natural leadership, and the men were not the least grudging in their respect and liking for their new ship- mate. Well seasoned for his barely twenty-three years, Isaac knew that the real test of his leadership would come when *General Wash- ington* faced enemy cannon fire, something many of the new men aboard had yet to experience.

As he was about to continue his tale, the ship, without warn- ing, heeled well over, responding to a sudden blast of the arctic gale, and the men heard a sharp booming report followed by a crash over their heads. "All hands to shorten sail! Foretops'l's blown out!" was shouted down the hatch almost immediately by an unseen voice, punctuated by a torrent of icy water driven below by the rising gale. The half-dozen snatched up their oiled tarpau- lin coats and hats, donning them while they surged together to the ladder. A blast of cold hit them as they emerged from the galley. Immediately one of their number, Tight-Fisted Smith, slipped on the ice-slick deck and slid to the lee rail before he could catch a safety line. The ship momentarily regained an even keel as the helm was put down to ease the strain on the rigging, and it saved him from being washed right over the side to certain death in the winter Atlantic. Smith staggered to his feet, holding the bulwark and the leeward safety line for support, and looked at his mates, his face ashen. There was no time to blow and fuss; Starter Coffin was right there, using the short hempen quirt which gave him the nickname, urging the men aloft to salvage what was left of the foretops'l and bring the shattered yard to deck before the rest of the rigging was destroyed by its flogging.

*   *   *   *   *   *

"Stand by to up anchor. Let go the foretops'l. Mister Clements, you may bring her to short stay, if you please." First Lieutenant Jervis Lyon, second in command of the United States' thirty-eight-gun frigate *Constellation*, craned his neck to ensure that his new warrant bosun could handle this simple responsibility. They had not sailed together yet, and a new man, particularly one not brought up in the Naval Service, bore some checking before receiving the complete confidence of the officers, most particularly First Lieutenant Jervis Lyon. Clements had come aboard just as the year ended, and between the ice in the harbor, a lack of orders sending *Constellation* to sea, and a delay in the completion of her refit at Baltimore, there had been no real opportunity to check his bona fides. He boasted service as second mate on a rather successful and recently notorious privateer, *Glory*, and seemed, so far anyway, to be what he claimed.

Aye, safely to anchor he's all he claims, thought the first about his new bosun. *Some sea time and the first engagement, with all its thunderous noise, chaos, shot, and splinters'll tell the tale, not only about Warrant Bosun Clements, but also the dozen and more new hands we shipped, 'specially those Britishers. It'll be a cold day in Hell afore I'll give those coves my confidence.* He glanced aloft at the men working on the foretops'l; one was a former Royal Navy topman who came aboard with Bosun Clements, and Lyon included him in his short list of uncertains.

Captain Charles Stewart, on the other hand, was grateful for the additional crew, and was of the opinion that most any man could be shaped into a worthy addition to his ship. And if a man was English, that could not be helped; at least he had had the wisdom to "see the light" and sign the Articles of War in an American fighting ship.

"Anchor is hove short, sir." Clements' voice carried easily aft the one hundred forty feet to the break of the poop where Lieutenant Lyon stood. Lyon again glanced aloft and, seeing the foretops'l yard two-blocked and the sail itself out of the brails and ready to drop, bellowed forward to the sailing master.

"Mister Warren, you may drop the foretops'l, if you please. We'll be getting under way directly." Raising his voice slightly to be heard on the fo'c'sle, he waved at his bosun. "Bring it aboard, Mister Clements, quick as you please." He turned aft, and in a lower voice, ordered the crew at the stern to "Haul out the spanker and trim for a larboard tack." Then, "Helm, put your wheel to starboard."

Showing the deliberate majesty consistent with her class, *Constellation* paid off and, with her dripping anchor safely secured to the starboard cathead and the foretops'l and spanker drawing nicely in the frigid early February breeze, she headed for Fort McHenry and the open Bay.

"Mister Warren, we'll have the main tops'l and the fores'l now. And trim for a close-hauled larboard tack." The Sailing Master nodded and made a half-hearted attempt at a salute to his superior, accompanied by a contemptuous look.

"Him tellin' me what tack we're paid off on — why I got more time passin' through stays 'n that little pop-in-jay's got at sea." Mr. Warren muttered aloud, turning to execute his orders. While he directed the heavers in the waist and motioned the topmen aloft, he warmed to his anger and continued, though more under his breath. "By my lights, Cap'n oughta give me that piece of weevily sea biscuit for a couple o' watches; I'd teach him about bein' a sailor-man, aye, that I would." The thought delighted the sailing master, and his crusty, sour face split onto a grin — short lived though it was. His pleasant thoughts were over-ridden by the incompetence of the landsmen in his crew, and he directed his full attention to their activities.

The sailing master's lack of regard for the first lieutenant echoed the low esteem most of the officers and warrants felt for the man. Lyon's orders rarely received the response one would expect on a trim and well-respected frigate in the American Navy, and Lyon, acutely aware of his general unpopularity in the wardroom, let it be known that he was unmoved by it. He knew his job — he had learned it at the side of then Lieutenant Stephen Decatur, when, in the year four, they had sailed a captured Tripolitan ketch into Tripoli harbor and successfully destroyed the American frigate *Philadelphia* which the Bey's limited navy had taken. Decatur was jump-promoted to captain; Jervis Lyon, a midshipman, received some cash reward, and a promotion to lieutenant. *Aye*, he thought, *I cut my teeth fixin' the messes caused by others, and learned from the best. These bastards don't appreciate that it'll likely be me that pulls their chestnuts from the fire.*

He attributed his subsequent success and promotions to his unswerving attention to duty and the demands he placed on those subservient to him. A constant source of annoyance to him was the relative lack of flogging as punishment in the American Navy.

Those Brits got it right, he thought as he watched the debacle of sloppy sail handling and seamanship taking place in front of him, seemingly in spite of the best efforts of Sailing Master Warren. *A good layin' on of the cat'll straighten out a bunch o' lubbers quicker'n kiss my hand.*

The fact that he was hard on both the officers and men did not signify for First Lieutenant Jervis Lyon; he felt sure it would pay off with a faster and more precise response when the splinters started to fly. He also was convinced that he had to be tougher than most because of his height; he stood barely five feet two inches in his shoes and had a natural dislike for anyone who was significantly taller. This included a large majority of the officers and warrants on *Constellation.* A grudging acceptance, not to be confused with friendship, was accorded to those who were taller but had proven themselves as capable seamen in Lyon's close-set eyes.

Seeing that the vessel was headed fair, he turned the quarterdeck over to a junior lieutenant, the ship's third, and a midshipman, and headed forward to ensure that they were ready for sea with no loose articles on deck, and all of the thirty-eight cannon and four carronades properly secured in their breechings. And to check on Bosun Clements as well, who should have seen to securing the deck already, but who Mr. Lyon could see chatting with a sailor — who he couldn't yet make out — at the foot of the foremast.

"Well, Robert, here you are back to sea, and in a vessel suitable to your talents. We could have been back in the Indies by now had we stayed where we was on *Glory,* 'stead of freezin' our arses off here in Baltimore." Jack Clements tightened the muffler he had tied around his hat and under his chin and shivered as he spoke to the British topman, late of the private armed vessel *Glory,* and prior to that, the Royal Navy frigate HMS *Orpheus.* The two had stopped to gam for a moment — Clements on his way to ensure the ship was secured for the potentially rough water they could encounter in the Bay, and Coleman just down from the foretop.

"Aye, it's off to sea again we are. And if'n you be thinkin' you're cold down 'ere on deck, scamper aloft yonder to the foretop, and see 'ow you like it there. 'Twill be warm soon enough, I'm thinkin', if it's the Indies we be 'eadin' for. By my lights, I reckon I can stand a few more days o' this numbing cold with the Indies just over the 'orizon." Coleman smiled at his old shipmate, thrown together quite by accident when Clements' privateer *Glory* took as a prize a merchant vessel which itself was a prize of Coleman's Royal Navy frigate. The two men, along with another Royal Navy crewman, a gunner named Tim Conoughy, and pressed American topman Isaac Biggs, had become great friends during the balance of the *Glory's* commission and, try as they might, the three had been unable to convince Biggs to join them in signing onto a Navy frigate. Coleman looked around the frigate, sizing up her sailing qualities, and making the inevitable comparison to both the sleek Baltimore schooner and the British Navy frigate *Orpheus*. Remembering both ships reminded him of their shipmate.

"What do ya 'spose ol' Isaac'll be doin' 'bout now, Jack? Do ya think 'e's gotten 'imself onto a ship up there in Massachusetts? If'n 'e 'as, I'd warrant it's a damned sight colder there than 'ere. Mayhaps 'e's froze in somewhere, warmin' 'is backside by a galley camboose, yarnin' and drinkin' coffee."

"Knowin' Isaac, my guess is he's either at sea or headed that way. Said he was gonna visit his kin for a spell, but I'd reckon he ain't gonna stay on the beach any longer 'en he has to." Jack Clements was reasonably certain their friend would not swallow the anchor and, while he didn't say it, thought it likely that Isaac had signed onto a Navy ship in Boston. "Mayhaps we'll cross tacks with young Isaac out on the blue — or down in the Indies, should we be headed there, as some have said." He looked sharply at the British topman who claimed to have an early insight as to the destination of their new home. Over the man's shoulder, the bosun noticed the first lieutenant heading their way, and under full sail. He gestured surreptitiously, both with his hand and his eyes, to his friend, using Coleman's bulk to shield his motion from Lieutenant Lyon; his efforts were too late.

"If you two have nothing more pressing to do than stand around like a couple of landsmen chatting over a fence, I'll see to it that you're given more jobs of work. This vessel is bound for the war, and there's plenty to do afore we find the enemy. Look lively there, now and get on with it." Lieutenant Lyon was not pleased to have found two of the new men, especially this Brit, visiting when there was work to be done. He expected more of a warrant bosun, and said as much.

"Mister Clements, time for socializing is after the work is done and you are off watch; unless you have instructions for this man, I would suggest you let him get on with his duties, and you with yours."

"Aye, sir. I was just on me way to the quarterdeck to report the vessel is secured for sea, sir. I guess you bein' here saves me the trip. I reckon we'll be encounterin' some ice gettin' out o' here. I'll mention to the carpenter he might keep an eye on the well in case she starts makin' water." Clements had handled officers like Lieutenant Lyon before and was not put off by this one. His response caught the first lieutenant all aback, and he looked at his bosun in silence for a moment before he blustered a retort.

"I'll worry about issuin' orders to the carpenter, Mister Clements. You mind your own duties here on deck." Lyon turned on his heel and stepped off briskly — right into a fores'l sheet block which took him full in the face. He staggered some, brushed his hand across his eyes as if pushing away cobwebs and collected his wits, drawing himself up to his full, but still diminutive, height; then he stepped off again, keeping a wary eye out for recalcitrant deck and rigging blocks. The color rose in the back of his neck, the only acknowledgment of his undignified departure. Clements and Coleman smiled at the officer's discomfort and, with a wink, the bosun turned and headed back to the bow. He intentionally tripped over the breeching tackle of a forward carronade and turned in time to see Coleman laugh aloud at his antics.

USS *Constellation* proceeded through the outer harbor of Baltimore, passing occasional floes of ice, nudging others out of the way with her copper sheathed forefoot, and headed for the Chesapeake Bay, leaving the shoals inside Bodkin Point a wide berth. After turning the Point, she would turn south to make her run to Cape Charles and then the Atlantic Ocean, and whatever the Fates had in store for her and her crew.

CHAPTER TWO

S truggling against the flying spray and the pitching and rolling of the ship, the men climbed up to the fore topmast and out onto the lower yard. Everything they touched was slick with ice. As they moved crab-like on the footrope under the yard, the ice broke off as it flexed under their weight, and what wasn't blown off to leeward by the gale landed on the men below, adding to their misery. The men aloft all knew that one misstep would likely be their last, and worked their way cautiously farther and farther out from the relative safety of the mastcap, where the remnants of the tops'l had become flailing strips of ice-hardened canvas ready to knock the unprepared sailor off the yard. Hands became numb almost at once, faces froze in the icy wind, and even taking a deep breath was painful.

The heavy weather canvas was stiff with the cold, and handing it into some semblance of control took the combined strength of the sixteen men balanced below the sail on the foreyard, as the haulers on deck sixty feet below lowered what was left of the tops'l yard, and the flogging rags of sail with it. Captain of the foretop, Ben Stone, yelled encouragement and instructions to his men; the words, whipped away by the wind, were more for his own benefit than theirs as none could hear him, and it was only through their individual skills and seamanship that the task was completed without disaster. After the sail — or what was left of it — was stripped off the two pieces of the tops'l yard, the yard itself had to be unrigged and sent down to the deck, a job of work not made easier by the coating of ice and rolling of the *General Washington* as Captain Rogers bore off to take the heavy seas on his quarter and ease the strain on the rig.

The wildly swinging larboard end of the yard approached the deck, marginally controlled by the heavers amidships, who struggled to keep their footing on the treacherous deck. Two men, directed and assisted by Third Mate Isaac Biggs, tried to catch the spar as it came within reach of their outstretched hands. The yard swung crazily as the wind, combined with the rolling of the brig, whipped it around behind the three.

Seeing a disaster in the making, Biggs yelled for them to wait; his words were blown away to leeward. As one man stepped toward the flailing timber, he looked away to check his footing and never saw the lethal missile responding to the roll of the ship. With a dull thud, the broken end of the yard hit him full in the back, knocking him to the deck and continuing on unchecked. Biggs and a seaman dove for the injured man, catching him before he slid across the icy deck and through the break in the bulwark to the sea. Watching his chance to avoid the still-unchecked yardarm, Isaac signaled his intention to the sailor helping him hold their injured mate, and when the yard swung clear, they dragged the man into relative shelter and safety under the lee of the chocked longboat.

"Get him below to the gundeck, Mister Biggs. I'll be down directly to have a look at him." Biggs had not noticed Captain Rogers' arrival at the waist and at first didn't react. Rogers grabbed his arm and pointed at the hatch, receiving a nod from Biggs in acknowledgment.

Staggering under the weight of their injured shipmate, they manhandled him to the safety of the lowerdeck. Biggs and the man they called The Prophet could hear the broken spar still flailing around topside. Suddenly, there was a flurry of muffled commands issued in a gravelly voice, some yelling, heavy footfalls, and then nothing but the howl of the wind screaming through the rigging. The spar had been secured under the guidance of First Mate Coffin, and the men below could feel the ship ease up and settle into a more gentle, predictable motion as the helmsmen brought her back onto the northerly wind and she continued her easterly course.

Captain Asa Rogers had followed the two and their burden into the gloom of the lowerdeck and now watched as they eased the injured man to the deck between a pair of nine-pound long guns securely lashed to the bulwark. Biggs and the Prophet stepped back, and Rogers knelt down beside the man, who was beginning to regain consciousness. He came to and, seeing the Captain beside him, tried to sit up. Rogers put a restraining hand on his shoulder.

"Just hold on, son. Let me have a look-see and get a damage report." The Captain gently felt around the man's neck and shoulders, noting that there was no sign of serious injury. "Don't look to me like you're any the worse for wear, son. Go ahead and sit up. You'll be right as rain — no need to worry. Mister Biggs here likely kept you from gettin' serious hurt. You get on up, now, go on 'bout your work." Rogers was not about to let a knock on the head put him down a man this early in the cruise. Having satisfied himself that no serious damage was done, he stood up as much as his height would allow and nodded to Biggs. Then he headed aft for the quarterdeck in the comfort of the lowerdeck, between the double row of nine-pound cannon, six to a side. It was most unusual for a privateer to be armed with two decks of guns — the usual armament was six to twelve nine- or twelve-pounders carried topside on the main deck. *General Washington* was an unusual vessel fitted out much like a U.S. Navy brig, but more heavily armed. Her owner and master was equally unusual.

Asa Rogers had a reputation as a successful man; between 1795 and 1810, he had turned a single ship merchant operation into a thriving fleet of vessels carrying goods between Charleston, South Carolina, and Salem. He and the Crowninshield family controlled most of the merchant shipping business in Salem, and Rogers' operation was structured similarly to that of his large competitor. One son ran the shore side in Salem, and another the operation in Charleston; a third son had learned the art of seafaring and, just before the war with England was declared, had sailed in command of his own ship.

Linda Rogers, the captain's wife and a strong woman in her own right, was not content to merely sit at home; she had run the office in Salem with an iron hand until her untimely death in 1811. Asa, at sea at the time, returned in time to bury his wife and close the Salem operation for a month of mourning. He briefly ran the office himself, but realized that his disposition called for him to be at sea, dealing with men, wind, waves, and stout ships, and it was not long before he found a suitable director to take his place, returning to sea on the *General Washington.*

When the war began, even though he was heartily against it,

Rogers had seen an opportunity and acquired letters of marque and reprisal for most of his ships, sending out several strictly as privateers and the remainder as letter of marque traders. These latter continued in the cargo trade, but were armed and, should the opportunity arise, they could and did occassionally take a prize. Quiet and soft-spoken, Captain Rogers had a commanding presence, not just due to his six-foot frame and great shock of white hair, but because of the aura of control he fairly exuded. He was known as an outstanding seaman, and more recently as a clever privateersman, successfully outsmarting the British warships and stealing their merchant charges from under their noses. To secure a berth on Asa Rogers' brig *General Washington* was considered a stroke of good fortune, and he enjoyed the luxury of picking only the best to crew his ship.

Biggs returned to the deck. The sun had come full out — just in time to set, he thought to himself — and while the wind was still up, its scream had diminished to a moan, and somehow he thought it seemed a trifle warmer. He heard the ship's bell faintly striking 3:30, and moved aft to the quarterdeck to talk with Second Mate Jared Tompkins, whom he would relieve in a half hour, at eight bells.

"This surely ain't for the faint hearted, Isaac. Bet you're glad you ain't sailin' down in the Indies — why you'd be missin' all this pretty weather and these nice, warm, sunny days!" Tompkins, for all his years at sea, or perhaps because of them, was always cheery, and rarely took anything too seriously. A finer seaman couldn't be found aboard *General Washington*, nor a faster wit. He always seemed to find the amusing side of things and had more than once broken the tension of a potentially ugly situation with a droll remark. The men liked him, followed his leadership, and looked to him to intercede with Starter Coffin on their behalf.

Catching the second's mood, Isaac laughed. "Aye, Jared. It surely would be a shame to have to sail down there what with the fair breezes, warm days, an' whole fleets of British merchants to chase. Course, most of the time I got recently in them waters was aboard a Royal Navy frigate, so the prizes I was chasin' was mostly Frenchmen." His face lost its smile, and his eyes took on a distant look as he recalled his nearly two years as a pressed seaman in the British Navy. "Had me a pretty fair prize share on *Orpheus*, I did, but never collected on it, seein' as how Cap'n Smalley and them other privateers catched the prizes we was sailin' to Antigua. But I reckon I can make up for some of that here with Cap'n Rogers. As to the weather, it don't bother me none. I grew up in these waters and fished more 'n once with my father up here on the Banks in the cold months. Now that's some real cold — workin' nets and lines when the weather's up. Ice all over, and days with nothin' hot for the meal." Biggs looked hard at the second for a minute, and then smiled. "'Sides, another month or so and we oughta be seein' a real improvement and mebbe a flock of British merchants comin' in with the spring replacements and supplies."

"Wal. . .that's the way it's s'posed to be, 'cordin' to Cap'n Rogers. I can tell you they wasn't much to chase two months ago when we come in from these very self-same waters. Don't bother me none, though it would help if we got lucky this time out. Things gettin' a little lean at home and some prize shares would truly be a wonderful thing." He changed tacks abruptly, looking squarely at Biggs. "We gonna continue close-hauled to th' east here — likely through your watch — now the wind's startin' to haul 'round to the nor'west somewhat. Cap'n thinks this'll calm down some and we can set some sail afore supper's piped down. Reckon he'll let you know — he ain't shy 'bout lettin' us know, or spreadin' as much canvas as ever he can."

"Aye, Jared. We'll handle it. You go down an' warm up some. You'll be back in no time at all to take her while I get some supper." With that, the second mate knuckled his forehead in a mock salute and stepped off the quarterdeck, dancing a little hornpipe step as he did just to show the treacherous deck didn't bother him a whit.

Isaac stood at the leeward bulwark, watching the water rush by only a scant few feet from the deck. *She surely don't move like one o' them sharp-built schooners*, he thought, and then chastised himself, adding, *Course, Glory'd been rolled on her beam ends in this weather, so don't go thinkin' about what mighta' been. You had to get home to see your folks, an' you done that. An' here you are back at sea in the same business you fell into down south. 'Sides, from everything you heard, ain't no one gettin' out of nor into them southern ports; Brits got 'em sealed up tighter an' ever you please. You'd be standin' on the beach, and not much to do either.* His mind continued to wander, but he was subconsciously aware of every subtle change in the ship and the wind. He returned in his head to the first few days of his arrival in Marblehead, and his parents' home.

CHAPTER THREE

It was cold; the snow under foot squealed in protest with each step, and his breath made a white cloud in front of his face, hanging there momentarily in the frigid, windless air as Isaac stood at the open gate of the neatly shoveled walk to his home. He looked appraisingly at the house; his father had continued to keep the shingles replaced as necessary, and the paint on the trim did not show as much the effects of the harsh Marblehead winters as many others did. A feather of smoke rose from the stone chimney, etched sharply against the bright, cloudless sky, and he recalled the great central fireplace and hearth with its cheery fire, a throwback to the last century when his father had built the house and which his mother would not let him replace with a new iron stove. A picture of his mother tending a pot hanging on the crane over the flame rose in his mind and he stepped through the gate. He noted a figure pass in front of a window near the door, and suddenly the door opened, framing his father squinting into the bright morning light. Isaac thought his father had aged beyond his years, and looked like an old man.

"Isaac? Is that you, boy?" The incredulity in the senior Biggs' voice quickly gave way to excitement as he realized that, indeed, his son was not only safe, but standing on the step in front of him. "Liza, come here. Isaac's come home. Don't tarry, woman — it's your son, back from the dead!" He turned momentarily into the house as he yelled for his wife, quickly returning his gaze to his son, as if afraid the mirage would disappear if he looked away too long. Some of the years his son had noticed on first glance faded from the old man's countenance, and the worry lines and creases smoothed out as he beamed at this vision before him.

Isaac reached for his father and the two men embraced each

other. After a moment passed, Liza Biggs appeared, wiping her hands on the ever-present apron tied around her ample middle. As she saw her son locked in embrace with his father, her hands flew to her mouth, stifling a gasp. Tears immediately appeared in her eyes, and she threw her arms around her son's neck.

"Oh, Isaac! We'd given ya up for dead, lad. Not a word did we hear from ya for all that time. And what with this dreadful war now . . . well, we just never . . . oh, son, you're finally home . . . oh, thank God for your deliverance . . . let me look at ya, now . . ." She stepped back and wiped the tears from her cheeks, giving him an appraising look. Suddenly she realized they were all standing in the snow and cold of a Marblehead December and, in a motherly voice that would brook no nonsense, said, "Come inside and get warm. It's much too cold to be standing out here like a bunch of fools. You look like you've been starved. And you must be cold with just that canvas coat on. Look at you. Let me get you some hot food." She led the group into the great room where a fire glowed and a wonderful smell emanated from the iron pot hanging over the flames, just as he had pictured in his mind's eye only moments ago. Isaac's mouth immediately began to water, and he realized he had not eaten more than a few pieces of biscuit and some jerked beef in two days.

"You didn't get none of my letters, I reckon. I wrote any number of times, but I guess the post from the British frigate weren't any good. Well, it don't signify. I'm here now, and I can tell you all that happened to me. I am sorry you was worried 'bout me, but I didn't come to any harm, as you can see." He spread his arms and turned in a circle, showing his parents that, indeed, their son was intact.

"Cap'n Smalley wrote to us — musta been just before that fool Madison decided to go to war against the English that we got his note. Said you and some other men'd been pressed off'n the *Anne* by a British frigate down there in the Indies. Had no idea where you were or what would happen to you, but wanted us to know you was at least alive, far's he knew. Thought it was real decent of him to let us know. 'Course that set your Ma a worryin' 'bout whether the frigate was involved with their war with the French. An' then when we didn't hear a word from you nor anyone else, we began to think the worst, but we had faith you'd find your way home sooner or later, though, and with the help of the good Lord, here you are. Praise God."

The older man began a torrent of questions that flooded the air, not even giving Isaac the chance to answer, let alone eat the thick, aromatic mixture of venison and potatoes his Mother ladled into a dish for him. Isaac held his spoon at the ready, his mouth watering as he patiently began to answer his father's questions. Liza Biggs looked sternly at her husband.

"Now, Charles, let the boy sit and eat his vittles. Don't make him answer a bunch of fool questions until he's got some food in him. Eat your stew, Isaac, then you can tell us everything." Liza Biggs was back in charge, and nobody was going to argue the logic of her instructions. Isaac smiled and took up his spoon again. He watched his parents beaming at him as he ate; their joy at seeing him not only alive, but here in Marblehead, showing on their faces. He was home!

Charles Biggs sat grinning at his son, his weathered face aglow and his still sharp eyes sparkling, the edges crinkling as the reality of his son's return struck home. He brought a hand up occasionally to wipe away a tear that trickled unbidden from the corner of his eye down the craggy lines in his face. He let his son eat in silence for a moment, but not content to sit idly while there was a story "what needed tellin'," he began again to press his son for his tale. Isaac, around great mouthfuls of stew, began to tell of his odyssey, starting with his impressment from *Anne*, the ship on which he had sailed from Boston in 1810 bound for St. Bartholomew with manufactured goods and produce under Captain Jed Smalley.

"When that frigate, the *Orpheus*, stopped us out there in the middle of nowhere, we knew we was goin' to have trouble. We'd all heard tales of them stopping and stealing seaman from American ships, but I guess no one ever figgered we'd be seein' it our own selves. A British officer an' a midshipman come aboard the *Anne* with a bunch of marines all dressed up in they's red coats and shiny black boots. Had guns, they did, and as it turned out, wasn't afraid to use 'em." His Mother gasped audibly at this revelation, her hand again flying to her mouth. Isaac continued. "Anyway, they made Cap'n Smalley line us all up in the waist and then this officer, his name was Lieutenant Burns, an' I come to know him better later on, walked in front of each man and asked where he was from. I tol' him I was from Marblehead an' was American, but it didn't signify. He picked me and Tyler and Pope from the line and made us stand away. Then he told us to get our slops and had a pair of his marines watch us while we did. When we come up deck, they was a scuffle of some kind — I didn't see just what started it — but one of the marines fired into the Annes and I reckon killed one of 'em. Lieutenant Burns made us get into the boat alongside and we was rowed over to the frigate — *Orpheus* she was named. I never seen so many men on one ship, and guns pokin' out of ports up and down the main deck and even a few on the one above it — called the spardeck. Well, off we sailed, an' me an' Tyler an' Pope was in the Royal Navy. Cap'n Winston was the captain, and it seemed like ever' day he had two or three sailors flogged — a dozen an' more stripes each. More often'n not, it was more. Tyler got into a difficulty with one of the British sailors and was brought up for a floggin'. He fooled 'em all; he jumped right over the side of the ship and we never saw him again. That really got me riled up, I'll tell you, and I began right then to figger a way off'n that ship."

Isaac paused in the telling of his story to ask for more stew, and his father took the opportunity to ask. "Did they make you fight, Isaac? I guess it woulda been the French, then, since we wasn't at war with 'em yet."

"Aye. I was assigned to the maintop and helped out at a gun when I wasn't need aloft. We had more 'n a few battles with the French, an' in one of 'em, we took a whole fleet of merchantmen as prizes. Beat a couple of their frigates in the bargain, we did. Lost a brig to 'em, but I reckon we made 'em pay for that. Cap'n Winston, for all his usin' the cat regular, was a fine sailor, an' if'n I hadn't got off that ship, I'da had some prize money from the French ships we took . . ."

"Mister Biggs, we'll have the forecourse now, and you can shake the reef out of the main tops'l. Might as well take advantage of this weather while we can." Captain Rogers' voice interrupted Isaac's reverie and brought him sharply back to the present.

"Aye, sir. I'll see to it right away." He moved forward to where a small knot of men sheltered from the cold and, sending them aloft, began giving the orders for getting more sail on the *General Washington*. The reef was shaken out of the main tops'l, and the tops'l yard was hauled up and two-blocked. The "heavers" on deck strained against the filled sail, successfully fighting the diminishing gale as they manhandled the yard to its proper position. Next came setting the forecourse, and the men who had most recently been aloft on the mainmast clambered up the ratlines to the cap of the lower foremast, and thence most carefully out the footropes to the foreyard. When they were all in position, Ben Stone, as captain of the foretop, gave the order and the brails were removed. The men on deck clapped onto the sheet and braces, horsing the yard around and trimming the sail to where it filled with a mighty '*whoomp*'. The men, finished with their task, made their way cautiously into the mastcap and then stepped into the ratlines one at a time, returning to the relative safety of the deck. Only one came down the fore backstay; Ben Stone was not about to let some ice intimidate him in front of his men, and he made the dangerous descent without incident.

The ship responded immediately to the increased sail; she heeled and charged ahead, knocking the waves asunder and throwing sheets of ice-laden spray over the windward bow. Biggs returned to the quarterdeck, surprised to see Tompkins waiting for him.

"Time for you to get you some vittles, Isaac me boy. An' I'll be seein' you right back here after the second dog." Isaac nodded his assent and headed for the warmth of the lower deck and his supper, noting that it was just about full dark now, and the next watch would be even colder.

*   *   *   *   *   *

"Ice . . . we got ice dead ahead! Deck there . . . ice ahead!" The lookout in *Constellation*'s foretop was paying attention and pointed at a rough patch of ice extending several hundred yards side to side, only a hundred yards or so away and directly in their path. The few men on the quarterdeck gazed aloft at the lookout. The midshipman on the quarterdeck ran up the mizzen rigging to see for himself and from the cro'jack yard could see a large area of rough saltwater ice, layered upon itself and undulating slightly with the motion of the water beneath it. He hailed the watch officer confirming the report and added, "If we bear off about two points, sir, we'll likely clear it."

When *Constellation* had left the confines of the Patapsco River and carefully turned south around Bodkin Point only a few hours previously, the first lieutenant had smiled and said to the watch officer, "I reckon we won't have to concern ourselves about ice now. We're likely past any worry there." He had then ordered full sail and now the frigate was sailing full and by down the middle of the Bay. The hands had been fed their noon meal, and most of the officers were dining in the wardroom. The ship's work was mostly done, save for the stowing of a few final crates of stores. Usually Captain Stewart would be about ready to send the men to quarters and give them some much needed gunnery practice; today would be an exception since they had just got underway and in the confines of this part of the Bay, he didn't want to risk an errant ball going ashore in Maryland. And it was likely there would be errant balls.

The bosun and first lieutenant, momentarily at peace with one another, were just aft of the mainmast watching carefully the running and standing rigging, ensuring that the tensions had properly been set by the riggers and the bosun's men in the yard. At the lookout's hail, each cast their eyes forward, moving to the rail to get a better look. They did not hear the casual response to the report from the watch officer, the ship's third lieutenant. He had glowered in the direction of the midshipman, now descending the ratlines, and quietly offered a terse "Carry on" to the two quartermasters at the big double wheel.

When the midshipman returned to deck, his unspoken question was all the third lieutenant needed to educate the boy to the ways of the navy. After all, a midshipman barely old enough to shave was ill-advised, indeed, to question the decision of his superior.

"Mister Olson, when you have had some time at sea, you will learn, I should hope for your own benefit, not to question the wisdom of those who have experience and significantly more knowledge than a fledgling. This vessel was just refit. I reckon that new copper sheathin'll go right through a little ice."

Both Mr. Clements and Lieutenant Lyon heard this exchange and quickly separated, the bosun heading forward, and the first lieutenant moving toward the quarterdeck. Neither were prepared for the shudder and screech as the forefoot of USS *Constellation* rode up on the ice, then broke through it. And neither man had yet reached his destination.

Lieutenant Lyon reached the quarterdeck and the surprised lieutenant of the watch immediately after the screech of rending metal and ice was heard fore and aft. He lunged for the helm, snatched it from the two quartermasters and gave it a vicious spin, bellowing, "Topmen aloft! Clew up the fores'l. Braces ease; cast off the bowlines and trim your sheets on the main and foretops'l. Sheet in the spanker. Sailing Master, get those men moving."

A dozen and more sailors jumped to grab sheets and braces; some, in the panic of the moment, grabbed the wrong lines, further adding to the confusion. Many of the heavers and foc's'le hands were landsmen and this was their first venture out of the security of the harbor at Baltimore. The sailing master, in an effort to straighten out the confusion caused by the first lieutenant's bellowed orders, was grabbing some and shoving others, pointing at the appropriate lines as he did so. Only the topmen, experienced seamen all, including Robert Coleman late of the Royal Navy, knew what to do and leapt into the rigging to gather in the huge forward sail and secure it to the spar, as the deck hands hauled on the clew lines. This first maneuver did not go well, and some of the more skeptical among the hands felt it boded ill for the rest of the commission.

Bosun Clements, hanging over the bulwark at the bow, peered down at the cutwater. Unable to see as much as he wanted, he climbed out on the bowsprit, and continued on to the jib boom, turning around when he got to his vantage point to face the ship.

"What about it, Mister Clements? What damage?" Captain Stewart was right there, standing at the bulwark, and alternating his gaze between his bosun and the forefoot of his ship.

"She's not wounded bad, Cap'n. I kin see a bit o' copper bent back and off some, but don't look like they's no holes in her. Probably should get a man down there and finish off that sheet o' copper — have to do her afore the seas take it and maybe more, anyway." He looked squarely at the Captain when he spoke. "Send a man down there to pry her off, I'm thinkin'," he reiterated.

"Aye, Bosun, we'll do just that — as soon as I make sure we're clear." The Captain watched carefully as *Constellation* moved easily through the edge of the ice on a course that would carry her away from the thickest part. Then he headed aft, presumably to the quarterdeck.

"Ah kin git that done for ya, Bosun. Rig me up a sling right off'n the cathead yonder, and drop me down. Have it fixed up quicker'n you kin say it." The bosun looked up as he stepped back on the foc's'le, and came face to face with the speaker, a tall rangy young man with light colored hair sticking out from under the front of his hat, and a grin splitting his face. He looked at him for a moment, trying to place him; he'd seen him on the ship before they got underway, but from his lack of uniform and casual attitude, assumed him to be a shipyard worker.

"And you are . . .?" Clements needed someone with experience down there, and had been contemplating doing the job himself.

"Tate, sir. Jake Tate. Foretopman an' rigger. Come aboard 'bout a week afore we sailed." The young man continued to grin, and Clements looked him over more carefully. He saw a comfortable looking cove, early twenties, he'd guess, tall and wearing clothes that were obviously from purser's slops; his wrists hung out of the sleeves of his tarred canvas jacket, and his blue regulation pants were substantially too short. He wore a dirty regulation hat which had been old before the war started, and his neckerchief could be seen at the open neck of the jacket, wrapped around his throat instead of as custom and regulation required. His light-colored hair hung down his back, tied with a short piece of leather into a queue. Tate continued to smile at the bosun.

"From Maryland, sir, and sailed merchants since I bin weaned." Tate responded to Clements' unasked question and stood comfortably in front of the him as the bosun took his measure.

"Reckon you'll do, Tate. Get you a length of line and let's get it rigged." Clements looked around the foc's'le, picking a few men he knew to be reliable. "You lads, there, stand by to handle a line here — soon's the Cap'n gives the word. You there — go find the carpenter and get me sum'pin' what'll cut the sheathin'. You'll likely find him in the for'ard hold, checkin' to see if we're makin' water. Lively now."

CHAPTER FOUR

"Deck there . . . deck . . . light to leeward . . . 'pears 'bout three, mebbe four leagues . . . for'ard o' the beam 'bout two points." With the easing of the gale to a moderate breeze and the resultant steadiness of the ship, the lookout in the foretop had been re-established, and the sharp eyes of the seaman stationed there had paid off. Even though he knew there was nothing to be seen from the deck, Third Mate Biggs, on watch for another hour until midnight when Tompkins would again relieve him, looked instinctively where he expected the light to be. The fact that he saw nothing but the blackness of the night, which even the limited starlight failed to diminish, caused him no concern. He lifted his head toward the topmast forward and shouted back.

"Can you make out anything else? Another light, a sail? Look sharp, man!"

"No sir, nothing. In fact the light I saw seems to come and go. Must be a smaller vessel gettin' down in the troughs. There . . . there it is again. Can't make a course or nothin' else from it. Just the one light."

"Good eyes, sailor. Keep watchin' and let us know if'n anything changes with it." Turning, Biggs said to a seaman loitering near the small quarterdeck, "Go wake Cap'n Rogers and tell him we got a light to leeward 'bout ten miles off."

It seemed like the seaman had been back on the deck only a minute when the tall form of Captain Rogers materialized beside his third mate, saying quietly, "Hold your course steady, Mister Biggs, until we can know more about our friend to leeward. Let us see what he does, or if, in fact, he has seen us. I assume you have extinguished any lights topside?" The question drew a nod from the watch officer, and the captain continued. "I want to stay well to the weather of him until daylight and we can see what in fact we have. Mercifully, we have ample sea-room and needn't worry about puttin' her on the hard whilst we keep an eye on him. Make any corrections in course you think are necessary to keep him in view, but do not close with him."

Biggs nodded and acknowledged his Captain's orders. He had learned from his service in the Royal Navy that maintaining the weather gauge was critical if one wanted to be in control of a situation, and *General Washington* was positioned exactly right for determining what action, if any, would come with the dawn. He had only to maintain this position and then, when the sun was up, they could close with the unknown and, should an action be necessary to take her as a prize, begin it at their behest rather than at the whim of the other captain.

Rogers stood at the rail for a moment watching his ship work in the easing weather. The worst of the storm was past now and he fully expected the morrow to bring a clear day and a fair wind, perfect for taking their first prize of the cruise if the light to leeward proved to be British or an American sailing under British license. He hated to take American ships as prizes, being an American ship owner himself and knowing what the loss would mean to the owner, but even more he hated the thought of Americans selling their services to the British to transport cargo which ultimately could be used against other Americans. He hoped the vessel would prove to be British and a worthy prize for the *General Washington.*

Throughout the middle and the morning watches, the two ships continued to sail on a generally northeasterly course, Rogers' ship maintaining its distance and, as far as their quarry was concerned, ignorant of the presence of another vessel anywhere in the same ocean. As dawn's fingers of light splayed across the lingering clouds, turning them first pink, then orange, Rogers again came onto the quarterdeck and surveyed the situation. The lookout in the foretop reported that their quarry was now visible, "Tops'ls only, sir," and then "Three masts I can see, sir." Tompkins had again relieved Isaac Biggs on the quarterdeck watch and looked questioningly at his captain, waiting patiently while Rogers decided his next course of action.

After some minutes of study, Captain Rogers spoke. "We'll ease her off a trifle, Mister Tompkins. Start your sheets and let us close somewhat with him. When her top hamper is visible from deck, we will clear for action and see about taking us a prize. Show no colors as yet. We'll let him make the first move there, but have your lookouts keep a weather eye out for another, or any sign of a ruse. It wouldn't do to get caught all aback, as it were, sailing blindly into what could turn into an ugly situation if we're not prepared. For now, howsoever, I shall take my breakfast in the Cabin. Call me should anything change."

With a nod and a tacit salute accompanied by an "Aye, sir," Tompkins watched the captain's tall frame disappear into the aft scuttle as he headed below. He turned back to the men at the wheel. "Bring her off a point, lads, easy now." Raising his voice after turning forward again, he fairly bellowed at the men in the waist. "Ease your sheets, there. We're coming off some. Braces haul . . . tops'l sheets . . . ease off. Mind the sheets on the jibs, you lubbers. Look alive there . . . that's better. She's drawin' now." He issued orders to the two men coming aft to tend the spanker, and saw the brig pick up speed as the new course and trim took effect. Even in the now moderate breeze, *General Washington* made a fine turn of speed, showing her true colors as a fast swimmer, able to outsail almost any vessel she might encounter. Tompkins bellowed to the man standing lookout at the foretop. "Aloft there. Look sharp now. Let me know quick as ever you can when you see her hull up, and keep an eye out for any other ships." He looked at one of the men standing at the foot of the mainmast. "You there, scamper up to the maintop and keep a weather eye skinned. Look smart there, now."

Having satisfied the captain's orders, he moved over to the windward rail and watched as the water rushed by, casting an occasional glance forward and to leeward, hoping to catch a glimpse of the strange vessel, even though he knew it would be most unlikely to sight her anytime soon.

The day continued to brighten as the forenoon watch saw *General Washington* on a more easterly course, gradually closing the three-master under their lee. The shadows of the sails under the thin morning light were perfectly white with their coating of frost; the sun was not yet high enough or hot enough to penetrate to all areas of the brig's deck and melt the last remnants of the ice. The ship's work was nearly done and the day had warmed, allowing the men to repair the damage from the gale of the preceding night. A new foretops'l yard was raised and rigged on the fore topmast, and a new topsail bent on. And while the ice had, for the most part, melted anywhere the sun touched, the lower rigging and some of upper works retained their slick coatings. Sending up the replacement yard and bending on the sail had continued to be difficult in the extreme.

Third Mate Biggs, who supervised the work, could not help but compare the effort of the men with that which he had experienced on both the British frigate and the privateer in the West Indies; working a ship in warmer climes was definitely favored. In a few short weeks, however, the cold would break and the occasional pleasant day would be a harbinger of the coming spring — a better time for all, with ample shipping from which to select prizes and mild weather in which to operate.

"Deck there! I have the top hamper in plain sight now, no other vessels around." The lookout had been changed frequently during the forenoon watch to maintain the sharpest eyes possible aloft. Captain Rogers, on the quarterdeck since finishing his breakfast responded instantly.

"What do you make of her, lad? Does she show any colors?" What's her rig?"

"'Ppears to be a bark, sir. No colors I can see. She's under a press of canvas — looks like she's set to her t'gallants and flyin'."

Rogers wasted no time in heading for the main rigging and, with an agility born of years and years of sea time, climbed quickly to the main topmast cap where he hooked a leg around the t'gallant jack stay and trained a glass on the stranger. The wind whipped through his hair, giving him the look of a wind-driven white-capped wave on the cold gray Atlantic. After several minutes of study, he yelled down to the deck and, specifically, Second Mate Tompkins standing by the brig's wheel.

"Mister Tompkins: bring her off another point, if you please. And we'll set our own t'gallants now." Having satisfied himself that the selected course would close the other vessel, and that *General Washington* would easily overtake her with sufficient canvas, he returned to the deck smartly, though not by the topman's favored route of the backstay, choosing instead to use the windward rat-lines. When he stepped onto the quarterdeck, he instructed Tompkins to have the crew fed early, as "I 'spect we'll be seein' some action early in the afternoon watch." The work aloft continued apace, and the additional canvas was shaken out, adding a noticeable increase to the already nice turn of speed shown by the brig. The excitement and anticipation of action and a potential prize spurred the crew on, and, even before the men were piped to their dinner, preparations were being made to clear for action.

*   *   *   *   *   *

"We ain't seen but a few vessels since we left Baltimore, Coleman. And they was headin' out like us. I'd reckon them schooners we seen was private, an' nary a single warship — not even a brig or a sloop; nothin' save them two gunboats headin' out from Baltimore. I'da thought they'da bin a few ships headin' in, up to Baltimore or mebbe into the Potomac up ta Washington. You s'pose they's all gone in at Norfolk? Don't seem likely to me. Don't feel right." Jake Tate and his fellow topman Robert Coleman were standing in *Constellation's* foretop, having been ordered, along with their fellow topmen, to unfurl the big sail after the determination had again been reached that ice would no longer be a worry; the two remained behind after the dozen others had headed back to the deck.

" 'ow d'you expect me to know; I ain't ever been in this water but once, last November comin' up from the Capes in the ol' *Glory*, with Clements and Conoughy. Mebbe them coves think it's still iced in out 'ere, an' are afraid o' comin' out to 'ave a look. You seen what that ice done to us just yesterday; you was down there peelin' off what was left o' the sheathin'. I'da thought ol' Clements woulda sent a carpenter's mate down there, or done it 'is own self, 'stead sendin' the likes o' you. Seemed 'appy to 'ave your arse hangin' over the forefoot 'stead o' 'is though — 'specially with Cap'n Stewart not 'eavin' to or nothin'. I'd reckon the Cap'n's right keen to 'ave a shot at me countrymen, an' ain't gonna let a wee bit o' ripped up copper slow 'im down none. Aye, an' the quicker we get the barky to sea, and 'eaded south, the 'appier this cove'll be, I kin tell you, Jake, me boy. I am lookin' for'ard to gettin' warm. . . and gettin' some prize shares."

"You 'spose Cap'n Stewart'll go into Gosport down yonder afore we head out, or just leave that copper gone?" Tate, for all his experience at sea, had virtually no experience with the ways of the Navy, and was relying on Coleman's long time in the Royal Navy.

"I ain't Cap'n Stewart, Tate. Ain't for me to say. But I surely wouldn't. 'Ave to 'eave 'er down to do it, an' that'd mean liftin' out the guns an' topmasts. . . probably 'alf the stores inta the bargain. You ever bin inta Gosport? They even got the sheers there that could 'andle the job?"

"I reckon they likely do. That's s'posed to be a yard there like Baltimore. Ain't bin in there my own self. That's just what I heard. Reckon we gonna have ta wait. Cap'n ain't likely gonna share his plans with either of us'n. You had 'bout enough o' this cold? I'm headin' down."

The two arrived on deck as the bell rang the change of the watch, and headed below to the gun deck where it was warmer.

"Wot you two bin doin' up there? Your messmates bin down this 'alf an 'our an' more. What, it's too warm for the likes o' you down 'ere?" Tim Conoughy, gunner's mate, late of the Royal Navy and the privateer *Glory*, was sitting astride a twenty-four-pound long gun with the unlikely name *Momma's Kiss* emblazoned on its carriage. He was fitting a new firing lock on it and stopped his work to greet his former shipmate and their new friend.

"It's all the 'ot air from some Irish cove a'spoutin' off what makes it so warm down here. Give me the open air and fresh smells you kin get aloft anytime. I'm gonna get your lazy Irish arse up there one o' these fine days, Tim, an' you'll never want to come down again, I'll warrant."

Coleman maintained the good-natured rivalry between not only the Irish and English sailors but more commonly between the men who worked aloft in the dizzying heights of the upper masts and those who stayed on deck, dodging the bucking, dangerous, and deafening guns, the real teeth of a man of war. The friendly banter was interrupted rudely; they all heard the insistent beat of the drum as it reverberated down the hatches and were already moving before the disembodied voice followed yelling, "Quarters, man your quarters stations you lazy louts! Get your arses out and up. Lively there. Quarters!"

The sailors tumbled out of the hatches — those with battle stations on the gun deck remained below. The experienced hands went quickly to their stations whether at guns on the main deck or below on the gun deck, or for some, including Coleman and Tate, aloft to shorten the ship to battle sail. The others, landsmen who had not before heard the ship beat to quarters, initially stood dumb and rooted to the deck, looking around wide-eyed. Then almost as one, they began shouting and calling to one another.

"Oh good Christ . . . the damned Brits are attacking us. . ."

"Jack, where're we s'posed ta be . . . ? Whot'd that fella tell us?

"Hey, mate, where's gun three?"

"Gunner said I should be ahelpin' him in the magazine. . . where's that 'sposed to be?"

The gunner, a warrant with service in the American Revolution, stood on the forward end of the gundeck and watched as the landsmen ran in confused circles, bumping into everything from each other to the masts and gun carriages. He calmly discussed with Bosun Clements just how long they should allow the confusion to reign before they waded into the melee to help the sailors find their stations for quarters. Finally, Gunner Jackson could stand it no longer. He stepped into the middle of the gundeck and grabbed a sailor by the back of the collar.

"Where're you 'sposed to be, sailor? I don't think Cap'n Stewart had in mind for you to just stand here an' not help out your mates." Jackson's growl did nothing to calm the sailor's confusion. Indeed, the implied danger from the gunner briefly struck the sailor dumb, and it was only when Jackson gave the man a hearty shake did the words come out.

"Ah don't rightly know, sir . . . cain't recollect what was told me."

The gunner gave the man a shove in the direction of the number one gun and, before he was out of range, followed with a vicious kick aimed at the departing sailor's stern. This was accompanied by "I haven't time to be nursemaidin' you lubbers! Get your arse up there to number one and do what the gun captain tells you to do."

By now, Clements was helping sort out the chaos and handled the confused landsmen much in the same way as his colleague. Between the two of them, and with the help of two lieutenants and three midshipmen who oversaw the confusion on the spardeck and aft on the gundeck, *Constellation* eventually came to quarters for the first time since going into her refit in Baltimore in October, 1812. It was a long and painful process.

The guns were run in, loaded, and run out. Then they were fired. Had not the captains at each gun been experienced hands, God alone knew where the shot would have gone; likely not at the flotsam and jetsam drifting by, and while none of the guns scored hits, some were close. Tim Conoughy, experiencing his first taste of American gunnery, was grim in his determination to have his gun be the first to hit the target, but the lack of coordination and teamwork created havoc with his plan. He couldn't do it all himself, though it seemed he tried.

The surgeons and their mates were given the opportunity to exercise their own skills, and not in "dumb-show"; the steady stream of casualties from the great guns ranged from smashed fingers to amputating a lower leg from a sailor, a landsman, who slipped and fell right behind a gun carriage just as it fired. The recoil rolled the man's leg nearly flat between the hard wheel of the gun and the unyielding deck; his screams could be heard over the cacophony of the gundeck, and many of the grimy, sweating and tired sailors stopped in mid-action — until the gun captains quickly brought their attentions back to the task at hand, and none too subtly at that. Attrition on the gun crews was high in this first drill, and it was a grim-faced Captain Stewart who silently took the reports on the quarterdeck as the midshipmen came aft to tell of mishap after mishap. His only response was an occasional shake of his head and a deeper frown.

They kept at it until dark. Captain Stewart delayed supper, determined to build some fighting capability into his ship. Tomorrow they would clear the Virginia Capes; it was certain that the British would be just beyond, lying in wait for any who dared attempt the run to open water. The letters he had received from both his fellow captains and the Secretary of the Navy warned him of the ever-tightening blockade at the mouth of the Chesapeake, and those same captains went on to warn him of the legendary proficiency of the skilled British gunners and expert ship-handlers fresh from the war with France. A meeting with them would be disastrous unless he could bring some level of fighting trim to his ship.

"Those fools in the rendezvous ought to be drawn and quartered, Cap'n. This crowd they sent us should be plowing their fields or joinin' the militia, not trying to fight an American frigate. I am loath to admit it, but it appears to me that the best of the new men were those Brits we shipped in January. They act like they know what they're doin'. Bosun Clements'll work out as well, I'll warrant. If you are plannin' to put into the yard at Gosport before we leave the Bay, we might pick up a few hands there with some sea time. Might be a vessel in ordinary there." Lieutenant Lyon spoke as strongly as he dared to his commanding officer; as hard as he was on his subordinates, he maintained an air of concern to his superiors.

"I told you already, Mister Lyon, we are absolutely not going into Gosport; I aim to get *Constellation* to sea as quickly as ever possible and get her, and us, into this scrap. I can not let *Constitution* and *United States* do all the work; they need our help." Stewart became incensed every time he read about yet another victory by the young American Navy. Not because he didn't want to win this war — to be sure, no one had ever questioned his patriotism. He was consumed by his own need to fight ship to ship and lived in daily fear that the war would end before he could achieve a crowning victory, assuring his rise to commodore. Just before sailing, Stewart got news of the brilliant victory won by the USS *Constitution* over the HMS *Java* off the coast of Brazil just prior to the turn of the year. Word had also been brought into Baltimore with the news that the hot-tempered James Lawrence had trapped a British sloop-of-war in a neutral harbor. The consensus was that it was only a matter of time before he lured her out to battle and a likely victory for his little *Hornet,* which could easily lead to a greater command and accolades from his superiors. Stewart seethed at the unfairness of it all; he was a captain, commanding a thirty-eight-gun frigate, and as yet had not even seen a British ship. Neither a minor bit of damage nor some ice would hold him back, now that he had orders to sea. And he'd have a crew that could shoot into the bargain. Or kill them in the process.

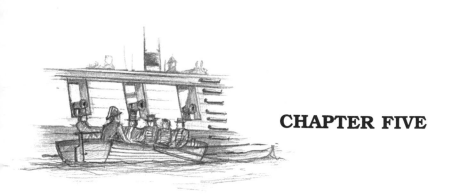

CHAPTER FIVE

"Fire a gun to windward, Mister Coffin. Let 'em know we mean business." Hardly had the words cleared Captain Roger's lips than the air was rent with a thunderous roar from the forward carronade. The crew had been at their action stations, with shot and powder at hand, well before the order to clear for action had been given. Dinner, piped early, was fed and cleared in the space of half an hour. *General Washington* still carried full sail to her t'gallants, in case their quarry decided to run, and Captain Rogers had his topmen aloft ready to clew up the unnecessary canvas and reef the forecourse in the event of a fight.

In the space of three hours the two ships had closed, with *General Washington* coming on with rail under and a bone in her teeth. Now they paralleled the bark's course, about a cannon shot off to weather, and waited to see what reaction their gun to windward would bring.

"Looks like she's fixin' to show her colors, Cap'n. There they go . . . my God! She's run up the American flag. Do you think it's a ruse?" Starter Coffin stared intently at the bark as indeed, the Stars and Stripes whipped out at her mizzen peak.

"No, Mister Coffin, I don't. I think it might be one of George Crowninshield's ships headin' for some port in Europe. Lookee there. On the foremast . . . isn't that the Crowninshield's house flag they just put up? I believe it is." He watched for a moment, then ordered the colors hoisted on *General Washington*. "We'll hand the t'gallants, now, Mister Coffin. Quick as ever you please, and let us ease her up and back the fore tops'l. Just in case I should be mistaken, however, we'll remain at action stations with the leeward guns ready." Asa Rogers was known to smoke a ruse from the best and he was taking no chances that the bark might have been captured and manned by a British prize crew who showed American colors and the Crowninshield house flag to confound the privateer.

Even as *General Washington* slowed from the reduced sail and the backed fore tops'l, the bark was backing her own tops'ls and brailing up fore and main courses, having already dropped her t'gallants. The two ships closed slightly, and the men on the privateer were disappointed that there would be no prize — and a rich prize indeed she would have made. A sizable figure could be seen stepping into the lower rigging of the bark's mizzen with a speaking trumpet.

"That you, Asa? Thought you was still in Salem. Jack Leighton here." The voice carried to windward with nary a word swept away, testimony to Leighton's considerable lung power, consistent with his vast bulk.

"Good day to you, Jack. If you've the time, come aboard for a bite." Rogers bellowed back to his friend, then lowering his voice, turned to his mate. "We'll heave to, Mister Coffin. You may prepare to receive a boat alongside. I must be gettin' old. I should have recognized Leighton's *Salem Lady*. Been a Crowninshield ship since she was built back in the year eight. Jack Leighton's a good friend and a solid seaman. Tried to get him to sail for me, few years back, but he wouldn't have none of it. Came up from the deck in Crowninshield vessels; guess he figures he owes George and is going to stay. Hard to find that kind of loyalty in these times." Rogers glanced aloft to satisfy himself that sails were being furled and backed as appropriate to bring his vessel to a standstill. "And you may secure the men from quarters, now, Mister Coffin."

The bark and the smaller brig lay hove to, rolling easily in the now gentle Atlantic swell, about a rifle shot apart. The General Washingtons watched as a boat was lowered, set off from the merchant ship carrying its captain, and made its way across the water. It occurred to Isaac that Captain Winston of *Orpheus* would have had the boat crew flogged for their sloppy oarsmanship, make no mistake; the British captain would not tolerate so much as a missed stroke in his cutter crew and, whether out of fear or pride, it was rare indeed for the *Orpheus* boat crews to look less than sharp. The boat soon was bumping alongside and, after the man ropes were lowered, Jack Leighton's round head, covered by neither hat nor hair despite the cold, appeared over the bulwark. His ponderous frame followed more quickly than one would expect and the merchant captain stepped onto the deck of the privateer. Rogers was there to greet him.

"I see you're still taking your meals regular, Jack." Asa smiled, knowing his friend would not take his jibe as an insult, but merely as the continuation of a long-standing joke between them.

"Aye, that I am. What surprises me is that you're still takin' ships to sea. A man your age ought to be settin' on his arse in front of a warm fire this time o' year, sippin' a tankard and yarnin' with his mates. Hardly fittin' for an older gent such as yourself to be out here afore the warmth and easy breezes of spring." Leighton laughed and followed Rogers aft to his cabin for dinner. As they neared the quarterdeck, the men standing aft of the main mast heard the visitor say, "Have you heard the news of the *Constitution* takin' another British frigate?" Rogers stopped in his tracks, raising his bushy white eyebrows questioningly as he turned to face his guest.

"Not a word have I heard, and we only left Salem a matter of days ago. The news must have come in after we sailed. What can you tell me?" The men on deck stopped what they were doing to take in the response.

"Aye, I guess it wouldn't have made it to Salem yet. I got the news in Newport just as we were makin' sail. Seems we sunk another one of their frigates — down off South America it was. Word has it Commodore Bainbridge on *Constitution* caught HMS *Java* and they wasn't enough left to sail into a ncutral port — had to burn her where she lay, he did. An' young Jim Lawrence — he's got the *Hornet* you recollect — got some Britisher bottled up in one o' them ports down there. 'Sposed to have a load of specie on board. Now that'll make a right plum prize, you ask me. Only a matter of time afore he takes her into the bargain."

The men around them made no secret of their eavesdropping, and suddenly, one shouted out, "Let's have three cheers for *Old Ironsides*, boys. Looks like she done it again." A chorus of "Huzzahs" went up, and when it died out another sailor yelled, "How 'bout three for a New Jersey boy, Cap'n Lawrence and *Hornet!*"

"Huzzah, huzzah, huzzah" came the weaker response from the few New Jersey men in the crew, and the two captains, smiling, disappeared below.

After the captains had taken their ease and eaten some of the dinner Rogers' steward had prepared, they returned on deck. Captain Leighton nodded to a few of the men on deck as he waddled to the waist and clambered over the bulwark to his waiting boat. The privateer captain leaned over his quarterdeck rail and shouted to his friend below.

"Jack, a safe voyage to you, my friend. And thankee most kindly for the news — both about the *Constitution*'s success, and the British fleet out of Halifax. We'll get together when next I return to Salem."

Rogers watched as the boat landed alongside *Salem Lady* and turned to Starter Coffin, standing by the wheel.

"Mister Coffin, We'll get under way now. Make all sail to the t'gallants, and make your course north a half east. There's some British merchants need our attention, maybe a day and a half's sail. Less if the breeze holds sou'westerly and picks up a trifle."

"Aye, sir. Mister Biggs you may take the quarterdeck. I'll see to gettin' some of the hands aloft and some sail on her." With that, the mate stepped to the waist of the ship and began bellowing at the sailors clustering there. "You lubbers heard the captain. Let's get some sail on her. They's a bunch o' Britishers out there, askin' for us to take 'em as prizes. Topmen, get your lazy arses up aloft and shake out some canvas. You heavers, clap a hand on them halyards and stand by to take a strain. Look like you been at sea more'n five minutes!" Every command to each group came with a vicious swing from the hemp starter landing athwart the slowest man. The starter and the mate's words had the desired effect.

General Washington leaned her shoulder into the diminishing seas and, responding to the trimmed canvas aloft, leapt ahead, seemingly as eager as was her crew to pursue the potential prizes sailing from Halifax, Nova Scotia.

* * * * * *

"Deck, there, deck ahoy! I kin see a light a p'int an' some off'n the larboard bow. Could be more 'n one vessel." The lookout hailed from the foretop and was rewarded with a shouted but unintelligible response from *Constellation*'s quarterdeck. Within minutes, the midshipman of the watch was beside him at the mastcap. Together they peered into the blackness of the pre-dawn night, unable to discern where water ended and sky began. No stars shone to aid their search, and after several minutes of straining, both the young mid and the seaman saw the glimmer simultaneously. And then another, and still another.

The midshipman panted out his report when he returned to the quarterdeck and was summarily sent to announce the discovery to the captain. Moments later Stewart addressed the ship's third lieutenant who had the watch on the quarterdeck.

"Mister Martinsen, even though this breeze appears to be dyin' off some, we'll do well to shorten down and hold a position here until the dawn shows us what it is we've got out there. I would reckon they'll be British, and, until I know the strength of my adversary, I'm not inclined to engage." Captain Stewart looked at his pocket watch, holding it to catch the dim glow of the binnacle light, and went on. "We can expect to have the first light of day in not more than two hours, and they will be silhouetted against the lightening sky. We'll bring her up some and shorten down to top-s'ls and jibs, if you please." The orders were being passed on even as Stewart turned and left the deck.

The dawn showed low clouds and only a gradual easing of the darkness; ugly weather threatened. *Constellation* once again headed toward Cape Charles and the open sea. But there was no sign of any vessel, hostile or friendly. Captain Stewart was not about to rush headlong for the relatively narrow opening, and maintained the shortened sail set during the last hours of darkness. The ship was at quarters, guns loaded, run out and slow matches lit to back up the untried new firing locks on the 24-pounder cannons. The men peered out the gun ports and over the spardeck bulwarks, looking for the enemy. Some, mostly the landsmen, faced the unknown in grim silence, at the same time realizing that they likely could be facing death. Others chattered about the capabilities of the Royal Navy, its ships and its gunners, and, with perhaps some false bravado, came to the conclusion that *Constellation*, even with its less than capable crew, would prevail. All, however, asked each other repeatedly, "Where are them bast'ds? Whyn't they show themselves?"

"Deck . . . deck, there! Sails to wind'ard. I got four . . . no five sail comin' out from the headland to weather. Two p'ints they are off the weather bow." Dead silence followed the lookout's hail. Bravado with no enemy in sight is one thing; five enemy ships bearing down is quite another. Then bedlam broke out on the gundeck and was quickly brought under control by the lieutenants and midshipmen in charge of gun batteries.

On the quarterdeck, the response was completely professional; Lieutenant Lyon grabbed a glass and sprang into the mizzen rigging, scrambling aloft. He perched at the mizzen top with the glass to his eye. Captain Stewart, waiting for his first to return to the deck with an appraisal of the situation, worked on his options for dealing with certainly five and potentially more of the blockading ships. His ego and his common sense clashed. Lieutenant Lyon returned quickly to find his captain standing stiffly at the wind'ard rail, his long glass under his arm, and the knuckles on his hand white with the tension of his grip. He did not turn as the first lieutenant approached his back.

"Well?"

"Aye, sir. I seen five at about seven miles, by my estimate. At least two and quite possibly three of 'em are line o' battle ships; seventy-four's, I'd reckon. The other'll be a fifth rate an' one — keepin' a position closer in — appears to be a schooner. One of the line o' battle ships is showin' a blue pendant at her main truck. They're headin' about south, likely out of Hampton and could string out to Willoughby Bay easy as kiss my hand; I'd say we might have a problem." Lieutenant Lyon's report, for all its completeness, was delivered in a flat, unemotional tone that, while in keeping with his professional demeanor and calm exterior, masked his own inner turmoil. He kept a very tight rein on the uncertainty coursing through his mind, a natural blend of great anticipation and fear. The only action he had experienced personally was in Tripoli in the year four. This promised to overshadow that by a wide margin. And he knew well that Captain Stewart desperately wanted to fight.

Let it not be against these odds, he silently prayed, *when first we do battle. These lads can barely get sail on her and run out the guns.*

"I can not, in good conscience, attempt a running fight through that fleet. It would be suicidal," the Captain decided. "We will come about, Mister Lyon, and set a course for Lynnhaven. And hope what little breeze we have will hold. You may make all plain sail, if you please."

Lieutenant Lyon audibly released the breath he had been holding and issued the necessary orders without delay. Prudently, the men were kept at the guns as the frigate tacked around and set more sail. Aloft, the topmen discussed the situation.

"Them Britishers gonna come in after us, Coleman," Jake predicted. "Lookee there, three of 'em bore off already, and that schooner's makin' some time."

"Jake, I reckon even this crew kin take on a schooner without worry. It's that frigate what concerns me. I spent most o' me life on fifth an' sixth rate ships, and I can tell you, if that one gets her long guns close enough, we're gonna be in for it, an' make no mistake. We can only 'ope that they ain't got no better a breeze than we do in 'ere. Likely Cap'n Stewart's runnin' for some protection somewhere; 'ope we find it sooner than later."

The two topmen shared their views with the other men hanging over the foreyard, each casting a wary eye on the hostile ships to wind'ard from time to time. The view provided inspiration for efficiency in setting additional sail, and all the topmen responded to it, praying all the while that the breeze, what little there was of it, would hold for *Constellation*, but abandon their British pursuers.

Their work done, the topmen stayed at their post aloft and from time to time announced to the deck what the British men of war were up to. They were first to notice that the schooner and the closest frigate, apparently a thirty-eight-gun vessel like themselves, were in fact gaining ground on the American frigate.

"This breeze is close enough to gone as to not matter a lick, Robert. And you watch them Brits, they're still showin' sails full. They're comin', and they ain't a damned thing we kin do about it." Tate voiced the concern that every soul aloft was feeling; no other had spoken it in the hope that their fears would not be realized. Indeed, the two closest enemy ships were gaining. The breeze farther offshore, albeit light and shifty, was still a breeze, and *Constellation's* sails hung limp from her yards, slack in the cold, gray, still Virginia morning. The safe haven of Hampton Roads, though in sight, might as well have been across the Atlantic.

"Mister Clements, we'll have the longboat in the water, if you please. And have a kedge anchor prepared at the bow." The first lieutenant's voice drifted aloft, and the topmen watched as sailors were pulled from their stations at the guns to unlash and lower the boat at the bosun's direction. Still others worked feverishly on the foc's'le securing the heavy kedge anchor to a long cable which was led to the capstan amidships.

"We're gonna drag 'er with the anchor, Jake. I surely do 'ope they kin do it quick enough to keep ahead o' that schooner. She looks nigh on quick on 'er feet as old *Glory* was; you 'member that privateer I was tellin' you about — the one what picked me an' Tim Conoughy off that prize down in the Indies?" Coleman took his eyes off the British schooner and glanced at his new friend for a sign of recognition.

"Aye, Robert, that fast vessel the bosun come off'n, right? I still ain't figgered out why you three an' that other cove what's up in New England didn't stay aboard; she sounded like a right fine vessel, and the prize shares musta bin better 'en you're gonna get here." Tate had listened as the British topman had shared his experiences.

"That's the one, an' I tol' you already why we shipped into the Navy. Ain't allowed for British sailors to sail them private warships. Besides, I'm a topman, an' ol' Tim, 'e's a gunner; warn't no real work aloft on that schooner, and they wasn't but a few guns — little ones at that. Tim wanted to get back to what 'e knows, an' 'e sure couldn't go back to the Royal Navy — they'd a had his arse flogged 'round the fleet for desertion and takin' up arms 'gainst 'is Majesty. An' I ain't never 'eard o' anyone livin' through that. I don't know what was in Clements' mind, but 'ere 'e is an' not doin' bad for 'isself."

The longboat, after a great deal of travail, raised voices, and a few well-placed kicks, was finally in the water, manned and stationary under the bow of the frigate. On the fo'c'sle deck, men were lowering the kedge anchor into the stern sheets of the boat. From aloft, the topmen watched as the boat pulled ahead of *Constellation* and, on signal from the bosun, manhandled the anchor overboard. They rowed clear and waited. On the order of the first lieutenant, a strain was taken by the men on the windlass and slowly the big frigate began to slide through the water in the direction of Gosport and Fort Norfolk. Silently, the men watched, casting their glances occasionally at the British ships to seaward. After a while, it became apparent to even the most casual observer that the wind had played its fickle tricks on the British as well. Now the American frigate, solely through the muscle of her sailors, drew closer to the safety of the Virginia shore.

"You ain't told us why you signed into the Navy yet, Tate. You coulda' bin sailin' them merchants outa' warm ports and made a decent pound in the bargain. Why would a smart cove like you give that up?" With safety within their grasp and tensions eased, the men aloft began to pass the time talking and yarning. Coleman was interested in his shipmate's experiences.

"Robert, the life in the merchantmen wasn't bad as some say. You're right about that, and I likely might have stayed sailin' 'em 'ceptin' the work was gettin' more scarce and more dangerous; your countrymen didn't seem to have no care 'bout stoppin' an American vessel and helpin' 'emselves to her crew. Claimed they was British. Even when we had papers protectin' us from that. Why I recollect one o' those bastards off'n a line o' battle ship even took up the papers we had and tore 'em up — claimed they was false. Took four of our jacks into the bargain, they did, and put 'em right aboard that British ship sayin' the coves they took was British an' hidin' out on an American vessel. Then too, they was precious little shippin' out there. You Brits got the coast pretty well closed up, and they ain't many what get out. Ships lyin' dockside all over — New York to Charleston I'm told. Cain't get a cargo, and cain't get out if'n they got one. If'n we weren't sailin' or loadin', they wasn't no pay, and sailors got to eat too, so I figgered this was reg'lar pay, sailin' or no, and work's pretty much the same. Might get a prize share into the bargain." Tate paused, looking around the horizon and gauging the gain *Constellation's* kedging was making over her pursuers. Almost as an afterthought he added, "And there was Charity. She . . . well, I guess that's all done with now." Tate made a sour face, then shook his head. Coleman and two of his fellow foretopmen sensed a potentially interesting story and pounced on Jake like dogs on a bone.

"What do you mean, Jake, 'that's all done with', an' who's Charity? Why would she make you go to sea on a navy ship?" One of the topmen, Sam Johnson, winked at Coleman as he pestered young Tate for more of the story.

"Well, she was jest a girl I knew once near Baltimore. Ain't nothing you coves need know about. You think we're making ground on them Britishers, looks to me like we might stay outta their range, we keep on kedgin' like we doin'." He tried to distract his shipmates from their quest to find out about this piece of his past.

"Aye, looks like we're not gonna fight this day, less'n they . . ." Coleman's words were cut off by a sudden grinding noise from below, and a lurch from the ship that threatened to dislodge them from their perches.

"I'll be damned, she's took the ground! Lieutenant Lyon's put us on the hard." Johnson grabbed onto the slack clewline to maintain his balance. The *Constellation* suddenly stopped all forward motion. The footropes on which the men were standing swung forward, causing all of them to grab onto whatever was handy to stay aloft. Naturally, once the topmen were again secure on the spar, they looked as one toward the British fleet and were gratified to see that both the frigate and the schooner had given up the chase and hauled their wind to head back to their patrol stations at the mouth of the Bay. The men were called back to their present situation with an order from below.

"Take in all sail! Clew up courses and tops'ls." The sailing master's voice carried easily to the foretop, and the men waited while the heavers on deck hauled the clewlines, pulling the corners of the slack canvas up and into the center of the yard. Then they gathered in the stiff, heavy sail and passed brails around the sail and the yard, effectively holding the sail up. The process was repeated on the tops'ls and the ship sat, "on the hard" under bare poles, a mile off Lynnhaven Bay.

CHAPTER SIX

"What's that mean, Isaac — a ring around the sun? Ain't seen such a thing before." Tight-Fisted Smith, while an experienced seaman, seemed puzzled by the phenomenon that Third Mate Biggs had casually mentioned moments before while he stood with a few men on the deck of the racing *General Washington.*

"I'd say it looks like we're gonna be in for a spell of weather, you ask me. Last time I saw a ring like that around the sun, we had some o' the nastiest weather I ever sailed in — rain so hard you couldn't see the headsails, and lasted for a couple of days, it did. To make it worse, they wasn't no wind to speak of, just rain comin' down like someone was pourin' water out of a bucket. Course, that was down in the Indies, so maybe it don't mean the same up here, but I reckon we'll see somethin' dirty."

"How 'bout it, Prophet. What do you think? We in for some dirty weather — and how 'bout them Britishers — we gonna take us some prizes?" Tight-Fisted Smith wasn't going to give up. He, like the other men in the group, figured what's the use of having someone aboard who can see the future without asking his thoughts on the weighty matter at hand?

The Prophet stroked his gray beard, looked at the heavens, and squinted his eyes down until they became little slits. He claimed it helped him think when the men had questioned him on it in the past. Now they accepted his "pre-prophecy" behavior without question. He had gained his reputation and nickname by a lucky guess made some years previously, and, among the naturally superstitious sailors, the story had grown until he was nearly a legend. Of course, he knew he couldn't foretell the future, but he also knew that even a flogging would never make him admit that to his shipmates. He pondered the heavens, pressing his advantage, and the men waited. The silence was broken only by the *whoosh* of the privateer moving easily through the now quiet seas of the North Atlantic. The men looked expectantly at their strange shipmate, and waited. Finally, he spoke, his deep voice resonated as if from the bottom of the water barrel.

"Mister Biggs is right. We be in for a spell o' weather. Britishers' gonna hurt us some — cut short the cruise — men gonna get 'emselves kilt — others jest hurt some. . . prizes gonna get took." A safe, if somewhat vague prophecy. He stopped and looked at one of the men with a penetrating stare.

"Why you lookin' at me like that, Prophet, you see somethin' more? I'm gonna be one o' the ones kilt, ain't I? Come on, Prophet, tell me if I be the one . . . I can take it . . . mebbe do somethin' 'bout it into the bargain. It's me, right?" Bill Watkins, known to his shipmates as Weasel in acknowledgment of his facial characteristics, was the resident pessimist and whiner, always assuming that he would be the one hurt or killed if anything on the ship went wrong. So far, he had been right, and the men thought of him as an albatross, bringing bad luck. So far it had affected only him, but one never knew. On the previous cruise, he had been knocked senseless by a sheet block inadvertently dropped from the foreyard; had it been dropped from the tops'l yard or higher, it would likely have killed him on the spot. As it was, he was nearly a week in a daze, and the captain thought him probably concussed. Another mischance in the same cruise involved a line which had fouled around his leg through his own carelessness and nearly dragged him overboard. Men naturally avoided him, with good cause.

"I can't tell who, Weasel, and all your whinin' ain't gonna change that. I was you, though, I'd watch my footin', and pay mind to your mates."

"Yeah, Prophet, I know it'll be me. You ain't got to hide it. I can tell right from the way you lookin' at me." Watkins felt that in the light of the Prophet's prediction, and with his own low self-esteem, he was the likely one to bring truth to the words.

General Washington continued working her way north and slightly east. Rogers hoped to be in position to cut off the British merchant fleet as they bore off around the western end of Nova Scotia, or at least catch up to them before they got into the Bay of Fundy. The wind, however, was not cooperating. Lighter and lighter it became, making a frustrated Captain Rogers, Starter Coffin and the other mates pile on more and more canvas — even to the point of jury rigging temporary stu'ns'ls off the windward ends of both the main and fore yards. By dawn of the following day, the wind was non-existent. The canvas hung limply from the yards, not even the wrinkles in the corners were smoothed out. And dawn was a matter of speculation in itself; only by the sand glass and ship's bell did any of the crew know that the morning watch had turned into the forenoon watch. The day didn't seem to brighten so much as merely become less dark.

"Well, Mister Biggs, we done all we can do to get after that fleet; either we are in the right spot or we ain't. I am guessin' they are still ahead of us. That trail of garbage we sailed through earlier had to o' been from them ships, so they's likely somewhere not too far ahead. Short of draggin' the *General* with the boats, I done all I can to get us some prizes. We'll have to wait and see if this wind'll pick up again." Captain Rogers paused in his ruminations, then continued. "Course, if they're anywhere near, they ain't movin' either, so what we got right now is kind of a stand-off."

Isaac respectfully nodded, uttering a quiet "Aye, sir." He looked around the ship, noting the men standing idle in the waist, the lookouts perched at the foretop and the maintop, and the two men resting on the ship's wheel behind him. The captain was right; there was nothing more to do except wait for the wind to return. The gloominess of the day did nothing to add to their spirits, and, with the uncertainty of their position relative to the British fleet and the total lack of wind, *General Washington* was not a happy ship.

Then it started to snow; a few flakes fluttering down, large and wet. It didn't stick to anything on board — the decks and spars were still too salty. It was a novelty, and the men, having little to do to sail the ship, began acting like children, running about the decks with their tongues sticking out, trying to catch the snow flakes. Rogers watched them impassively, his mind on more weighty matters; let them have their amusement now, they'd be too busy for silly games if ever they found the British. Biggs, while not joining in — it was beneath his position as a mate and furthermore, having grown up in New England, snow was not a novelty to him — was amused by the antics of the men. He heard one shout out, "If this is the 'weather' Mister Biggs and the Prophet was talkin' 'bout, we kin take it an' more!"

The third mate laughed aloud as he watched Watkins chase a falling snowflake, trip over the unseen breeching tackle of a forward carronade, and fall full length on deck, face first. He pushed himself up, and immediately the well-known whine issued from his bleeding mouth; he had bitten his tongue, but it didn't inhibit the noise one bit. Of course, the men laughed at his plight. He only increased his complaints, which covered everything from the fool who had not stowed the breeching tackle right (it was exactly where it belonged) to the men watching his antics and laughing.

"Deck, deck there! I got a sail, wind'ard bow — I mean leeward bow — hell — ain't no wind'ard or leeward. Off the larboard bow, 'bout two points. Looks like more 'n' one, but I cain't be sure." The lookout in the maintop was alert, and immediately all the bantering and cavorting on deck stopped. In a flash, Isaac Biggs, former topman, was in the rigging, heading for the cap of the topmast, well above the position occupied by the lookout, and a better vantage point.

"They's more for sure, Cap'n!" he yelled as soon as he reached the lofty perch. "I can count six — mebbe more. 'Ppears they's headed more northerly, but near's I can tell, they ain't got any more wind 'n we do."

"How far off do you make them, Mister Biggs?" The captain was clearly agitated, and impatient for the information he needed to determine a course of action.

"Five, mebbe six leagues — looks like." Biggs responded loud enough to be heard on deck, and then started down. As he passed the lookout at the mastcap, he heard the man mutter, "Might as well be a hunnert for all the good it'll do us. We ain't goin' nowhere without no breeze o' wind."

"Stow that talk, sailor, and move your arse up to the topmast so's you can see them ships. Let the deck know quick as ever you can should they be any change in what they's doin." Biggs didn't know the man, but he was not about to brook any grumbling this early in the cruise. He clapped onto the main backstay and dropped hand-over-hand to the break of the quarterdeck.

"Pass the word for Mister Coffin, if you please." Obviously Captain Rogers had come up with a plan and throughout the vessel; voices called out for the first mate, who hurried on the quarterdeck still buttoning his heavy pea coat.

"Mister Coffin, I'll have the longboat and the cutter put in the water, if you please, and see to rigging some hawsers for'ard; we'll be towing the *General* into her first engagement of the cruise, it would appear, so step lively." Hardly had the captain finished his instruction when Starter Coffin was off to the waist of the brig, issuing orders and reinforcing his word with the ubiquitous quirt across the backs and shoulders of anyone foolish enough to move too slowly. Lifting tackles were rigged to the mainyard and the cutter first, followed by the longboat, were lifted, swung out, and lowered alongside into the calm, slate gray water of the February North Atlantic.

Simultaneously, under the supervision of the third mate, two large hawsers were dragged up from the orlop deck and made fast to the anchor bitts on either side of the fo'c'sle. Their ends were fed through holes in the forward bulwark alongside the inboard end of the bowsprit, and left in readiness for dropping into the boats when the order was given. Snow continued to fall, increasing in intensity; it began to stick to some surfaces on the ship, but was not yet more than a minor inconvenience.

The boats were manned and moved forward to positions under the bows, where Biggs ordered the towing lines to be lowered and made fast in each; then the hard work was begun. The boats rowed out to the limit of the tow lines and jerked to a stop; the oarsmen continued to pull, spurred on by the curses and shouts of both the coxswains and the men on the bow of the privateer. Slowly, the lines again became taut, and the efforts of the men in the boats told; *General Washington* was moving forward. Word was passed up from the captain, and the course was changed a point to larboard, toward the British fleet.

"Mister Tompkins, Mister Biggs, we'll take in all sail, now, if you please. It will lower our resistance and make it easier for the men pulling the boats. I 'spect it will also make it more difficult for a lookout to see us, should one be so inclined as to look."

Within a few minutes, the yards and upper masts of *General Washington* were bare, the sails clewed or brailed up as appropriate, but ready to let go should a breeze appear. The men on deck queued up for the opportunity to relieve the men rowing; no one could long maintain much of a pace, and it was Rogers' desire to close with the British fleet as quickly as possible — and quietly.

"Mister Coffin, we'll have silence fore and aft, if you please. No point at all in letting 'em know we're out here. With this snow, I'd strongly doubt they'd see us at any distance at all, but there's nothing to be gained from lettin' 'em hear us caterwaulin' and jab- berin' afore we're ready to board 'em." He stopped, and seeing Starter Coffin drawing in a great breath, added, "And quietly, Mister Coffin."

The mate let out his breath and motioned for Will Dobson, the ship's bosun, to approach the quarterdeck. In what was *sotto voce* for him, Coffin told Dobson to move up the starboard side of the brig ordering quiet, while he, Coffin, would do the same on the lar- board side. The two men started forward, leaving open-mouthed men, stopped in mid-word, but quiet, in their wake. And the pri- vateer moved inexorably forward toward the snow-shrouded British fleet, dragged by her boats like an unwilling child to church. The Atlantic remained docile; just a rolling swell reminded one that indeed they were at sea, as the surface was glass-like as far as anyone could see into the now heavily falling snow.

* * * * * *

A single curious seagull offered its maniacal laugh to the stricken *Constellation.* It circled, and soon another joined it, then another, and another until a dozen and more were soaring through the rigging, loosing broadsides of ridicule at the earth-bound humans struggling to free their ship. Occasionally, one bird would dive through the cold gray mist to the mirror-like surface and pluck a hapless minnow from the schools of fish swimming in false security around the ship. The success of one encouraged others and soon the great white and gray sea birds were all swooping and soaring and screaming around the frigate.

The sailors, engaged still in lightening the ship in an effort to refloat her, glanced jealously at the birds as they drifted effort- lessly in and out of the heavy mist. Since before the noon meal, all hands had been dragging provisions and stores up from the holds where they had only days before been stowed in anticipation of a lengthy commission. The water around *Constellation* was littered with the bags and barrels, casks, and hogsheads containing the sustenance of the three-hundred-man crew, and a trail of the same gave unnecessary evidence of the still falling tide. The efforts at lightening ship would ensure a visit to Gosport as soon as the frigate was refloated for replacement stores, in spite of Captain Stewart's best intentions. An hour later, new orders issued forth from the quarterdeck.

"Mister Lyon, you may start the fresh water, if you please. We seem to need yet more lightening, if we are to float her off this cursed bar, and I am not wont to jettison our guns, especially since we . . ." Cap'n Stewart's words trailed off as he began to see his career, dull though it had been, cut short with little likelihood of the necessary ship to ship combat he dreamt of. First, the British barred his access to open water with an overwhelming force, and now this. *Ill-starred, indeed,* he thought grim-faced as he instructed his first lieutenant to pump overboard the ship's entire supply of fresh water.

A small boat put out from Lynnhaven Bay and headed for his stranded vessel. The deck watch, as well as the lookout at the fore cross trees, saw it and duly announced its appearance to the quarterdeck. As it approached, a man stood in the bows, waving his arms and shouting.

"Wonder what he's so all-fired excited about. There's little more that can go wrong, unless they're British and plan on taking *Constellation* with that little boat!" Lieutenant Lyon's dismay at their situation transmitted itself to all around him, but this time, his concern was for naught. The man in the bow of the small sailing vessel shouted again and, this time, made himself heard on the frigate.

"I would imagine you're gonna need a pilot to come much further up the bay, Cap'n. An' I'm it, right now. May I come aboard?"

"Aye, and welcome. I could have used your services five or six hours ago, it seems." Stewart's voice lost none of its irony as it traveled to the little sloop bobbing alongside the frigate, its shallow draft allowing it to float easily where the warship was stranded.

"Tide'll be nigh on full in another few hours, Cap'n, and we'll float you right off'n here then easy as kiss my hand." The short, rotund man clambered over the bulwark at the waist, an apparently perpetual smile splitting the gray beard that covered the lower half of his face. His pale blue eyes glistened with glee, either at the prospect of an employment, or merely because of his outlook on life, for he seemed filled, as far as Captain Stewart was concerned, with a most annoying good humor. Then, of course, it wasn't *his* ship stuck on this cursed bar.

"Thank God for that, then. I have jettisoned most of our stores and started the fresh water. I reckon we'll need get to Fort Norfolk to replace what we lost. What news do you have of them vessels off the Cape, sir?" Stewart still hoped for an escape from the confines of Chesapeake Bay.

"It'll be no trouble to take you into Norfolk, Cap'n, and I reckon they'll have plenty o' stores for you; not many needin' 'em these days. You seen the reason right out yonder. Them Brits've had the opening there closed up tighter 'en a Scotsman's purse for the last month an' more, and they've even had the brass to sail right into Lynnhaven and anchor . . . like they was darin' some to come out. No, sir. Ain't no ship got out o' the Bay in weeks. They even chased a few of our gunboats back into the harbor, if'n you can imagine that. An' ain't nothin' we can do about it, neither. Yes, sir. I'd be bettin' you'll be spendin' more time 'an ever you thought likely right there in Norfolk." Even the gloomy news the pilot was offering did not erase the seemingly ever-present smile from his round face, a sharp contrast to the expression worn by the frigate's captain, as he turned and led the newcomer aft to the quarterdeck.

The work of pumping out the remaining supply of the ship's fresh water continued apace in anticipation of the evening's high tide and expected increase in the breeze. The weather had not worsened but continued gray and dismal, a hint of rain showing itself in the hanging mist, making the air seem even colder. The darkness deepened ever so gradually, By the time the men were finished eating their evening meal, full dark had descended on the stranded ship. There was the occasional indication that she soon would float free, however, and preparations were begun to take advantage of the opportunity.

"We'll have the boats in the water, if you please, Mister Clements, and smartly. See that they're equipped with lanterns and have the crews stand by for orders." Lieutenant Lyon had been privy to the conversation between the pilot and Captain Stewart, and was not going to waste a moment in the preparation to get *Constellation* swimming once again. And the crew, remembering the close approach of the British blockaders just prior to their taking the hard, worked through their exhaustion, cold, wet, and miserable.

CHAPTER SEVEN

"Vast heavin' there. Boats come alongside." The hoarse whisper of Mister Coffin was quiet, but none-the-less heard in the two boats. The crews immediately backed their oars to take the strain off the hawsers, and then turned the boats to larboard, dropping the heavy, water-logged ropes as they did so. The fo'c'sle crew clapped onto the ice-encrusted towlines and ran aft, pulling the lines aboard with alacrity, guided quietly by the third mate. The *General* slipped silently forward, its momentum slowly carrying it well past the two boats, their crews now obligated to row up to where the brig coasted to a stop. Nobody shouted, or even talked unnecessarily, as with the nearest British ship less than a league away — or so the captain hoped — the slightest noise would have given them away. The snow continued falling with a vengeance, blotting out anything much beyond fifty or sixty feet away; the wind remained non-existent. Occasionally, a brief break in the snow gave a glimpse of dim ghostly shapes, all that could be seen of the British merchant fleet.

With the last boat crews back aboard and, after giving them time to guzzle their extra ration of spirits, the mates quietly assembled the men in the waist. Captain Rogers stepped forward on the quarterdeck to address them, keeping his voice low enough so that the men standing in the rear ranks had to strain to hear what was being said.

"My intention is to use the boats and execute a 'cutting-out' operation on the merchants. If necessary, we will engage the escort with the *General*, but on our terms, not theirs." The captain's quiet voice held the men mesmerized, both by the audacity of his plan, and the thought of the rich prizes they would have before this day was ended. He continued.

"We will put the other two boats overboard, and the mates will issue hand weapons to each man in the boarding parties and the prize crews. Mister Hardy will captain one of the prizes, and Mister Dickerson the other. The first two boats will move quietly into the fleet and pick a likely prize; the second two will do the same, and each must pick a vessel close to the edge of the formation. You will have to determine where the escort lies and naturally, chose targets as far from it, or them, should there be more than one, as possible, and practical. Bosun Dobson will go with the first two along with Hardy, and Mister Biggs and Mister Dickerson will be in charge of the last two. Once the ships are taken, fire a rocket aloft. And be on your guard for any attempt to retake the ships. As soon as the wind returns, the prize captains will shape a course, first out of the formation by the shortest route, and then for Gloucester or Salem. Once we have evaded, or dispatched the escort, we will attempt to relieve the English of more of their vessels, and then shall point our bow toward Salem. Mister Tompkins, see to getting the two yawls launched, if you please, and Biggs, Dobson, Dickerson and Hardy join me on the quarterdeck. Now let us get to our work and do what we set out to." He watched the men, and seeing them about to shout out a cheer, held his hands aloft, and then placed his finger in front of his lips. The cheer died in their throats, and the silence was unbroken.

"Gentlemen, you must understand that the only chance this task has for success is surprise, and that means quiet — absolute silence. The oars will be wrapped in all the boats, and of course there will be no talking or calling between the boats. While the men will have pistols and muskets, I suggest that to use them will not only draw attention to our effort but, in all likelihood, will cause it to fail. The firearms are to be used as a last resort only, even after you have successfully taken your prizes. It would be particularly pleasant if we could sail their ships out from under their very noses without their even noticing. You will be on your own and, without the wind, I will be unable to assist should you find yourselves in difficulty. Be forewarned. Do you have any questions?"

Rogers waited, looking from one to the other in silence as they absorbed their instructions. Like many other endeavors, the greatest glory usually came with the greatest risk, and this would most assuredly carry a large dollop of risk!

It was approaching that point in the afternoon when dark should be falling — except that the initial change was barely perceptible as the day itself had never really brightened — when the second pair of boats put off from the privateer brig. Isaac and Prize Captain Dickerson watched the first boats disappear into the still falling snow. While they and Bosun's Mate Dobson had agreed on courses to steer and that Dobson's boats would try to locate the escort, there would have been a certain comfort in moving toward the hostile fleet with the boats in sight of one another.

The great tightening in his stomach and his inability to swallow made Isaac realize the importance of what was happening; that for the first time, he, Isaac Biggs of Marblehead, Massachusetts, was temporarily in command of an operation that was to be self-reliant and important to the success of the mission as a whole. Captain Rogers had made it very clear to the crews that the bosun's mate and third mate were to be responsible for finding and taking the prizes, and the prize captains for getting them safely to a friendly port. He became aware of a trickle of sweat coursing down his back and noted that, inside his gloves, his hands were clammy in spite of the cold.

Comforted by the knowledge that he had done as much as he could to ensure the success of his first "command," he got on with the business at hand. He had picked his men carefully; Ben Stone and Tight-Fisted Smith were both in his crew, in fact both were in his own boat. He knew he could count on them if — or more likely when — things began to get hot. And fortunately, he did not have to issue orders in the boat — at least not for a while.

The other twenty-five men split between the two boats were, for the most part, privateersmen of some experience, with only two landsmen, or "first-timers," included. All were armed with cutlasses, pistols, knives, and a few half-pikes and axes added for good measure. All had been carefully instructed regarding the use of their firearms and on the importance of quiet to the success of their effort. To insure that the boats did not become separated in the thick snow, a line of some forty feet was run between them. On they moved toward the English fleet, the heavily falling snow effectively muffling the creak and groan of the already muffled oars and the stirring of the men as they eased their positions on the unforgiving thwarts.

One of the men in his boat pointed over the side, and Isaac looked down at the water in time to see a small collection of garbage, mostly foodstuffs, drifting by their boat. He smiled. And managed to swallow.

"Avast pullin', men," Isaac whispered to his crew, and one of the men tugged hard on the line joining them to the other boat, signaling them to stop as well. He peered into the whiteness ahead of the boat. As they coasted to a stop, the dark shape of a ship loomed dimly, ghostlike in the snow. He watched as the sides of the ship appeared and held up his hand to have the rowers back-water slightly to stop the drift of the boat.

"I haven't any notion of where in the fleet we are," he whispered to Ezra Dickerson, sitting near at hand, "but that sure don't look like a man o' war to me. Let's get us a trifle closer . . . pull easy now." He steered the boat to starboard, trying to get around the stern of the ship so he could study it more closely.

"Ain't real big, that's for sure," one of the men, he thought it might be Ben Stone, whispered. "Don't look like no man o' war I ever seen. What do ya think? Should we try this one?"

Isaac continued to study what he could see of the ship. Stone was right; she didn't appear to be large, and from what he could make out through the densely falling snow and deepening darkness, there didn't seem to be gun ports — at least around the quarterdeck, and for the few feet forward of that that he could see. He looked questioningly at Dickerson and saw the prize captain nod.

"Pull the other boat alongside." Biggs waited as the second boat of his little "squadron" ghosted into position alongside his boat, and spoke to the sailor who was coxswaining it.

"We'll see 'bout this one. You lads go up for'ard and climb up under the bowsprit. We'll go aboard from the transom, and meet at the waist. 'Member, no shootin' — use your cutlasses and pikes. Any crew you find, either kill 'em or drive 'em aft or below. We'll give you a count of two hundred afore we go aboard. That'll give you time to get up to the chains and aboard. Good luck."

Davies, coxswain of the other boat, waved his hand in acknowledgment and motioned to his crew to wet their oars. Biggs and the men in his boat watched as their mates disappeared silently into the snow, an apparition here one minute and gone the next. Isaac began to count slowly, giving the others time to get into position at the bows of the merchantman, as his own crew back-watered their oars and slid the boat into a position well under the counter of the British ship.

Moving with complete silence now, Biggs placed his boat just under the windows in the quarter gallery of the British merchantman; they were about six feet over his head. He reached out his hand and, signaling his bowman to do the same, he grabbed onto a convenient handhold on the looming stern. The boat was positioned so it would be virtually invisible from the deck, and only if someone opened a stern window and leaned out would the boat be seen. Isaac figured that that was unlikely, given the weather. He waited as he continued to count to two hundred and, giving the time a few extra heartbeats, motioned to his men to follow as he began climbing up the counter of the ship, avoiding the quarter gallery windows and the risk of untimely discovery. He sent up a short prayer that the other boat was in position and also beginning their assault. Isaac led the men up to the stern taffrail in absolute silence.

They paused on his signal, as first just their eyes and then their heads cleared the rail, and Isaac peered through the gloom and snow at the quarterdeck. What he saw pleased him; the helmsman was standing by the wheel, lost in thought, likely about warmer climes or soft young ladies in soft feather beds, and facing forward, and the mate — or at least what Biggs assumed was the mate — was leaning on the bulwark, thoughtfully exploring the inner workings of his nose. The men watched amused as he dug his finger into his nose, first the left side and then the right, examining each find with an intense interest, before flicking them over the side or wiping them on his sleeve.

Tight-Fisted Smith, watching the scene in front of them, didn't just smile at Isaac; he bared his teeth in a leer that might put one in mind of a wolf admiring a flock of sheep. At a nod from Biggs, Smith stepped carefully and silently over the bulwark and, with the snow muffling his move, crept up behind the mate of the watch while another of the crew moved to within arm's reach of the unsuspecting helmsman. Simultaneously each stroked a belaying pin across the skull of the man in front of him and was rewarded with not only a hollow thud but also with the complete and sudden unconsciousness of his victim. The rest of the American crew moved onto the quarterdeck now and Biggs cast a glance forward looking for the other half of his team.

A dim shape Isaac took for Cox'n Davies waved from the foc's'le as he moved his men aft; so far no one had given an alarm. He stationed two men on the quarterdeck with prize captain Dickerson to mind the helm and give the appearance of normalcy, motioning the others to move forward to secure the waist and meet up with Davies' men heading aft. He watched for a moment while the sailors began to ease their way forward and, satisfied that his plan was being carried out, Isaac dropped down the scuttle to the main cabin, seeking the vessel's master.

As his eyes adjusted to the gloom of the lower deck, he saw a door slightly ajar which appeared to lead aft. Pushing it silently open, Isaac stepped through. The British captain sat at a writing table, intent on a chart spread out before him. A lantern hung to one side, throwing long shadows over the room, and a candle flickered on his table. He did not look up as Biggs entered.

"Yes, Mister Spencer? 'Ave you a breeze of wind to report?" He looked up, confusion showing on his face as he saw a stranger standing before him, a pistol in his hand. His eyes darted from the intruder to the door, as if expecting the mate to appear. "You're not Spencer. What is the meaning of this? Where is Spencer, and who in bloody 'ell are you?"

"Good evenin', Cap'n. If Spencer was recently on the quarterdeck, he is still there, I'd reckon, and resting quietly. I am Isaac Biggs, third of the American privateer *General Washington*. I have taken your ship. My men are topside securin' your crew right now. I will place a man in your cabin to ensure you come to no harm, and as soon as the breeze returns, we will sail your ship to an American port. Please don't do nothin' stupid, as it will only cause me or one o' the others to shoot you."

"This is an outrage! How dare you? This is a British vessel under the protection of the Royal Navy. HMS *Shannon*, a frigate of thirty-eight guns, is likely within cannon-shot of us and will most certainly get wind of this unconscionable act of piracy. You will surely not get away with this, and the consequences will be right harsh, I assure you. However you got here, leave by the same conveyance and it is likely that nothing further will come of it, since this beastly weather will delay *Shannon* of learning of your American buccaneering, but should you delay, sir, I . . ."

"Enough, Cap'n. We ain't leavin'. You and your crew will be put ashore and sent to a British port when our cap'n says. Right now,

I'm in charge here." Biggs turned and called quietly to one of his men, who appeared in the doorway. "Stay here with Cap'n — 'scuse me, Cap'n. I don't know your name, or the name of your vessel."

"I am Gregory Stephens, and my ship is the *Hopewell*, of Portsmouth. And I assure you, sir, you will most assuredly *not* get away with this outrage. S*hannon* will be on you before you can sail a league."

Unfazed by the outburst and bluster, Biggs continued instructing his sailor: "Stay here with Cap'n Stephens, and don't let him out of his cabin. If he tries, shoot him."

"Aye, Mister Biggs. I can do that, an' make no mistake. The boys topside pretty well got things took care of on deck."

As if to add emphasis to the sailor's point, the three men heard a most distinct scream. It came from on deck, and was followed by a string of curses and the sound of a scuffle. Biggs turned to the door, heading for the source of the problem.

"Thank you. I will see for my own self right quick. Cap'n, you stay here, if you please, and don't give this man any cause to shoot you. I'll be topside." With that he left the cabin and the dismayed captain and his guard could hear his footsteps on the ladder leading to the deck.

When he stepped out into the snow, Isaac was gratified to see that his men had followed their instructions; he had heard no shots fired, and the men under Davies had moved what British crewmen they encountered into the waist with the watchstanders already there. Several of the boarding party were watching them, cutlasses and pistols in their hands. His glance at the quarterdeck was rewarded with a wave from Dickerson, reassuring him that all was still well aft. The only indication of the scuffle he had heard while below was blood flecked snow leading to a large red stain near the pin rail of the mainmast, and one of the British seaman holding a rag to his side while uttering a quiet string of curses. Blood ran from between his fingers, and Isaac stepped toward the man to check his wound.

"Nothin' serious, Mister Biggs; likely only a flesh wound. Fellow thought his fists were a fair match for a cutlass and Jack here had to teach him some manners. Reckon he'll live." One of the General Washingtons guarding the British crew waved his cutlass menacingly at his charges while he spoke.

Davies and Smith, having secured the mate and helmsman,

both still unconscious, were below rounding up the off-watch Britishers and herding them into the hold. Smith shortly appeared on deck, a smile on his face and a cutlass in his hand. There was blood on the sword.

"I'm thinkin' we gots 'em all, Mister Biggs. They was one or two what had a problem with our taking they's ship, but we took care o' that." He looked tellingly at his cutlass, and continued. "Davies checked they's cargo; looks like a lot of uniforms and such, but they's a score an' more o' barrels o' spirits into the bargain. Said somethin' 'bout rifles an' powder too, but I cain't rightly 'member what he said 'bout 'em. Now all's we be needin' is a breeze o' wind to get the barky asailin'. Not a bad prize she looks, you ask me."

Since no shots had been fired and the visibility was still barely one hundred feet, Biggs felt it unlikely that they had been seen from any other ship, and he was quite certain that the escort was unaware of the change in ownership on one of their charges. As Smith had said, all they needed was wind and their prize would soon be on her way to a friendly port. They had but to wait and maintain the appearance that nothing had changed aboard.

Still, the snow continued to fall, though it appeared that it might be letting up a trifle, and the flakes swirled more often, leading them to believe that a breeze might be coming sooner rather than later. It was unusual for the wind to stay this calm for as long as it had, especially in late February in these waters.

"You want to fire this rocket now, Mister Biggs?" Tight-Fisted Smith was holding the rocket they had brought from *General Washington* to let Captain Rogers know their efforts had been successful.

"Let's check with Cap'n Dickerson, Smith, but were it up to me, I'd wait 'til this snow eases some; I doubt anyone on the *General* could see it now anyway." Biggs was staring intently into the whiteness, looking for nearby vessels and, most importantly, the Royal Navy escort. A rocket now might be seen by His Majesty's officers if the escort was even moderately close by and paying attention to their charges. While the lack of wind would likely prevent them doing anything about the capture, it would also prevent Captain Rogers from helping the American prize crew. Dickerson agreed; they would wait.

*   *   *   *   *   *

"Aye, a close one it was. Thought those damn Brits were gonna take us, sure. Cap'n had us at quarters right through it all, but neither us nor them fired a shot. Don't reckon we was close enough for a shot to tell, an' that little schooner was the onliest one what might have gotten into the thin water where we was. I guess even our crew coulda had them without no problem." Jake Tate and some of his fellow topmen, including Robert Coleman, were sitting in a tavern in Gosport regaling the publican with the story of how *Constellation* happened to be anchored off Fort Norfolk, and had been for the past week and more.

"So after you towed her onto the bar, you towed her off with the tide, and then sailed here. You ain't the first what's taken the ground out yonder, and I don't reckon you'll be the last. Ain't catched a Brit on it yet, though we're hopin'." The tavern keeper was smiling at his patrons and pouring ale for them. Business had been good of late, what with half the Chesapeake fleet blockaded in Norfolk or Gosport, and he could afford to buy newcomers the occasional tankard. "Jeremiah Gallant makes hisself a fair livin' pilotin' vessels into Norfolk; piloted more'n a few off'n that bar yonder when the captains didn't figger to need his services. Probably knows these waters better'n anyone livin' or dead; he bin sailin' 'em since he was a boy an' ain't no bar out there he cain't smell. Sailed the deeps for fifteen an' more years afore the war started, and happy to be back home now, sailin' what he calls the 'trickiest water 'tween Boston an' Charleston'. No sir, ain't none better — leastaways, not 'round here."

Coleman nodded, and added, "Aye, and we'd agree with that. Nasty thin, that out there."

"You on that frigate too, young fella? You sound like you might be English. . ."

The tavern keeper's thought was interrupted by the sudden gust of wind and cold which blew in through the open door. With it, like she was blown in by the wind, followed what appeared to be a young woman, wrapped in a heavy cloak and muffler. The door slammed and the figure stopped; she threw off the muffler, shaking out long auburn hair which cascaded in waves over her shoulders as she looked around the tavern, mostly empty at this early hour. The action was completely natural, unpresumptious, and gave an indication as to the upbringing of the young woman. "Would you 'ave a look at that, lads," Coleman observed quietly, and the men at the table looked appreciatively at her.

As her eyes adapted to the dim light, she spied them sitting at the far table, the tavern keeper standing next to them and, under full sail, headed directly for them. Her spectacular green eyes were hard as flint and her gaze never wavered from the men at the table.

"Oh lordy. I got trouble now." Jake cast nervous eyes around the room and made to rise from his seat as the woman altered course to head directly for him. There was nowhere to run.

"Chauncey Tate, you scoundrel! You can not run from me. They told me you'd be here and they certainly were right. I might have known you'd be in a place like this, hiding in the dark like some wicked animal."

"Chauncey? Chauncey?" Coleman couldn't believe his ears. "I thought you said your name was 'Jake'." He laughed, seeing the sheer terror on his shipmate's face. That Coleman knew, and soon most of his other shipmates as well would know, his real name was the least of Tate's problems; the real difficulty was firing chain and grape shot at him from close aboard and showed no sign of offering quarter. Another broadside was coming. He looked around again for an escape and, seeing none, slumped down in his chair, beaten. Maybe seeing that, she'd offer terms. The young woman now stood over him, ignoring his mates at the table, while the publican retreated to his cage, watching from the safety of the bars he stood behind.

"Chauncey Tate, you ran off on me!. Never would I have thought you'd go and join the Navy. Why, we had plans to marry — and you were going to stay with me in Baltimore. What got into you? Why'd you disappear on me like that?" The woman paused for breath, and Tate looked at her, and suddenly the fearless topman was transformed into a boy caught up by his parents in a tale. He smiled hopefully at her.

"Charity, darlin', I had planned on comin' back to you, soon's I got some prize money together. Then I'da stayed ashore with you, just like you wanted me to. But I had to get to sea to get me some money, and they wasn't no merchants what could get out, what with the blockade an' all. Now it don't look like I'm gonna be getting outta here to catch some prizes anytime soon, neither. You shouldn't have come all the way down here. Ain't no place fit for you here, an' I'm on the frigate *Constellation*. I don't know . . ."

"I know very well where you are, Chauncey; I've already been to the ship. It was the men on the ship who told me where I'd likely find you — an officer, I believe it was to whom I spoke. However, it was not he who told me you'd be in this dreadful place; I recall a Mister Conoughy it was who mentioned it to me. I had a most difficult time understanding him at first, so strong was his accent, but eventually he made me understand I would likely find you and your friends in this place. Fortunately, the little boat which sailed me out to the ship waited and brought me back to the shore, then I made my way here. I have gone to a great amount of trouble to find you, Chauncey, and am most disappointed that you do not appear happy to see me.

"It ain't I'm not happy to see you here, Charity, it's just that this ain't no place for a lady like yourself, an' I got to be gettin' back to the ship. It's likely that we'll be leavin' Gosport right soon, and I cain't take you back up to Baltimore as I got to be aboard the ship an' you don't want to be stayin' here without no one to look after you an' I cain't be doin'. . ."

"You said that already, Chauncey — several times in fact. I think you have made it quite clear that you are running off like a coward from obligations that any real man would certainly face up to. I shall return to Baltimore by the same conveyance in which I arrived and I am sure that Papa will have something to say to Secretary of the Navy Jones about your most disagreeable conduct." Her green eyes shining, Charity whirled about, tossed her glorious auburn mane and, without so much as a backwards glance, flew across the room and out the door, securing her muffler over her head and shoulders en route, and slamming the door behind her.

In the ringing silence she left in her wake, the men, including sailors who each had seen their share of terror, and a publican who had stopped more brawls than he cared to remember, could only stare at one another and blink. Finally Coleman let out the breath he had been holding — apparently for some time — and spoke. His delight at his shipmate's discomfort readily apparent.

"So that's Charity. Well . . . Chauncey, I'd warrant there's more to this story than we just seen . . . Chauncey. 'Ow 'bout it, you gonna tell us the whole tale now? I reckon you ain't gonna be able to keep the lid on this one for long." Coleman was clearly enjoying the moment as much as Tate wasn't. The other men laughed — as much in relief as amusement — and sat back to listen.

The tavern keeper had returned and with the prospect of a good yarn, was standing again by the table, brimming tankards in hand for each of the men. As he set them on the table, the door slammed open yet again, causing him to start and, in the process, upsetting both. The spilled ale seemed to be forgotten as the men braced for another onslaught from the severely vexed Charity. But it was not her.

It was Tim Conoughy, petty officer and gun captain of the U.S. Navy frigate *Constellation*. He stopped inside the door as had his predecessor, his eyes adapting to the gloom of the room. He visibly brightened as he saw his mates at the table and headed toward them.

"Jake, you got to be gettin' yerself outta 'ere lad; they's a young miss what's 'eadin' right 'ere lookin' for ye. I got 'ere quick as ever I could, but I'd warrant she'll be blowin' in any minute. Get yerself outta that chair, lad, and I'll take ya back to the frigate." Conoughy grabbed Tate by the arm and started to pull him up. Coleman stood and spoke to his friend.

"You're late by 'alf a glass, Tim. She's already fired both broadsides at poor young Chauncey 'ere, and at the rate she was movin' I'd reckon she's 'alf way to Baltimore by now."

"*Chauncey*? It's young Jake I'm lookin' to save. Who's Chauncey?" He looked from Coleman to Tate and the other topmen to the tavern keeper. Suddenly, his face split into a grin and he grabbed Tate's hand and pumped it vigorously. "Pleased to make your acquaintance, *Chauncey*. Knew a young fella looked sorta like you what went by 'Jake'. Could be your brother, I'd reckon."

The expression on Jake's face never changed; it gave no indication that he even heard the gunner — or his fellow topman. He sat, still stunned. Finally he looked at the new arrival, then the smiling faces of his mates including Coleman, and then the tavern keeper. He stood up. "I got to get meself outta here right quick." He seemed oblivious to the ale which was all over the front of his trousers and shirt.

"Reckon leavin' now won't be much 'elp to you, lad, since your lady friend's already been and gone. So sit you down, and listen to what I got to tell you. Might be just what you need to set you righty-oh again." Conoughy had pulled up a chair and grabbed a tankard from the fresh ones brought by the publican. He grabbed young

Tate's sleeve and roughly sat him down again.

"Earlier this afternoon, afore your young miss come aboard an' raised the ruckus, Mister Clements come to me and a few of the lads tellin' of a plan what Cap'n Stewart cooked up. We might get you and us outta this place right under the noses of them Royal Navy bastards out there. Clements said the cap'n been ordered by the head cove o' the Navy to get hold of a pilot schooner — we could get us one o' them sharp built vessels like ol' *Glory* — and get through them frigates and third rates out there. 'Sposed to warn any American vessels we spy that the entrance to the Bay's closed up tighter than a whale's arse, an' to make for somewhere . . . I forget where 'e said, but somewhere up north, it was. 'E asked me if'n I wanted to go an' who else might be in the crew. Word aboard is that *Constellation* ain't goin' nowhere an' Clements said he 'eard Lieutenant Lyon talking 'bout transferrin' most o' the lads off."

Jake looked at the Irishman, his face completely blank. It didn't seem to signify. Then the impact of what he had been told hit him; his face lit up like the sun coming out from behind a cloud. "When do you think we'll get us outta here? Did you tell Mister Clements I should be on that schooner? What if Charity's still here . . . her Papa's important up yonder in Baltimore and could make me come back up there. Tim, you gotta get me into that crew. It's my onliest chance to get outta here." Jake's words ran together like an unbroken line of waves crashing one after another on a shoreline. The Irish gunner laughed.

"Ye'll be wantin' to ease your sheets some there, *Chauncey* me boyo. I'd reckon Mister Clements'll 'ave room for you. But 'e ain't gonna be in charge; nosiree, he's only a warrant. Mister Midshipman Blanchard, 'e's gonna be skipper o' the vessel, but I'd collect that Mister Clements'll be busy as ever 'e might be tellin' 'im what to do!"

"We got to get us back aboard right quick and . . . oh, lordy, what if she's out there awaitin' on me to come out? Robert, poke your head out there and check for me. Gettin' on that schooner looks like the onliest way I got to save meself from . . ." Jake didn't finish the sentence; he just shook his head, clearing an unpleasant image.

"Aye, Chauncey. I'll just 'ave me a looksee out yonder. Course she might be 'idin' round the corner, she might. Just waitin' to grab you as we walk by, an' drag you off to Papa and 'Secretary of the

Navy Jones'!" Coleman laughed and stood to leave, followed by Conoughy, who hastily threw down the remnants of his pint of ale. Cautiously, Tate brought up the rear, but stopped short of the door as Coleman opened and peered into the gathering dusk.

CHAPTER EIGHT

The storm was ferocious and would be remembered by the locals as one of the worst of the decade. The wind drove the tops of the powerful waves into the air, giving the horizontal rain a curiously brackish taste as it stung the faces of anyone unfortunate enough to be outside. The low sky filled as racing, heavy clouds roiled and tumbled in from seaward, its tone matching that of the sea and Chesapeake Bay. Waves crashed on the shoreline, their white spray and foam the only bright relief in the monochromatic gray of the late afternoon in early March.

As the surf pounded Cape Henry and spilled huge rollers into the entrance of the Bay and beyond into Hampton Roads, a small schooner-rigged vessel, shortened down to a few scraps of canvas, staggered out from behind the lee of Cape Charles and into the maw of the storm.

"I don't reckon them Brits'll be any too anxious to be out here lookin' for the likes of us'n, Mister Blanchard. You likely can set your mind at ease 'bout that." Warrant Bosun Clements smiled as he shouted through the storm into the face of the young midshipman who clung desperately with both hands to the windward main backstay. The water, a mix of rain and salt, dripped off his eyelashes and nose; wiping them would require him to let go of the backstay. A deluge of the same mixture was pouring down his collar, adding cold and wet clothes to his misery. Jonas Blanchard had been the senior midshipman on the *Constellation* and was now in command of this pilot schooner, commandeered by Captain Stewart to sail out and warn any American vessels they saw about the tightened blockade. The bosun's words, if indeed the young captain even heard them, did little to ameliorate his abject fear; never in his short career as a sea-going man had he experienced anything like this. It would be only through divine intervention if they survived this holocaust of raging seas and wind. Never mind the British; they were the least of his worries now. Blanchard remained mute, but it did register in his mind that Clements and some of the other men on this little cockleshell seemed unconcerned about the weather; in fact they seemed to welcome it as a guaranty that the British ships which had effectively closed the Bay would be off station, allowing the American ship to slip through the cordon unnoticed. The storm, along with the rapidly falling darkness, would cloak the little schooner in invisibility, and it seemed likely to most of the seafaring men aboard that as long as this worst of Mother Nature didn't sink them, it was reasonable that the British blockaders wouldn't.

They cleared the Cape and, as the full fury of the storm-driven seas met their sharp bows, Clements again put his face close to his captain's. "I'd suggest that mebbe a lookout aloft for'ard might be a worthy pursuit, Mister Blanchard. No tellin' what we might find out yonder, an' surely better to see them afore they see us'n. I can take care of it for you if you wish, sir, seein' as how you're a mite busy right now."

The midshipman's only concern at the moment was ensuring that no one or nothing caused him to release his grip on the windward backstay. He looked at Clements, at first not comprehending his words. Finally the words sank in and he nodded, opening his mouth to speak. Unfortunately, his dinner rather than words came out and, since Bosun Clements was directly to leeward of the young man, he received most of Jonas' offering. Clements' face darkened briefly, then split into a grin as he wiped the front of his tarpaulin coat with his sleeve.

"You just stay here, sir. You might consider moving to the leeward side if'n you feel that comin' on again." He smiled and added, "or you might go below," knowing that the smells and close atmosphere of the lower deck would surely inspire the midshipman to even greater levels of seasickness. Blanchard nodded again, but remained stationary, and Clements left the quarterdeck, following the lifeline forward.

No sooner had a lookout taken up a tenuous position in the fore crosstrees than a hail faintly reached the deck. "Deck . . . two p'ints ta wind'ard . . . one . . . this way. . ." The words blew away before they reached the deck, but Robert Coleman, topman, heard most of them and waved at the quarterdeck to get Clements' attention. He pointed to windward and jumped into the weather shrouds, heading aloft himself.

"Looks like it might be a brig, but ain't no flag I can see. She's makin' 'eavy weather of it, like us. Looks like she's lost a fore topmast and the yard. She's runnin' off afore it, 'bout a league off. Likely she'll pass astern, and busy enough so's they might not even see us." Coleman thought for a moment, then added, "And if'n they did see us, I don't reckon they's much what they could do 'bout us. 'Ppears they got they's hands full without addin' a little schooner to they's worries."

Clements nodded and ordered the schooner hardened up some, taking the waves more on the bow, but hopefully lessening the likelihood they'd be seen by the brig. He grabbed the rail to steady himself as a green wave rushed down the deck, knocking two men off their feet and continuing on to the quarterdeck. The water swirled around the feet of the watch before running off the leeward side of the deck taking with it anything loose. Midshipman Blanchard groaned and tightened his grip on the backstay.

The brig, still showing no colors and shortened to a reefed main tops'l, was now visible from the deck and, true to Coleman's report, her fore topmast and the tops'l yard swayed drunkenly over the leeward side of the vessel. There were men aloft obviously working as best they could at freeing the dangerous spars before they did more damage to the ship. It was apparent she was running for the protection from wind and seas offered by Cape Charles and had no interest in the schooner heading out, if indeed the brig's crew even noticed it, being as busy with their own problems as they were. The unknown vessel passed comfortably astern of the Americans, and they continued on into the deepening night and the raging storm.

By morning, most of the worst had passed, and while a large sea was still running, the wind had abated and the schooner was showing jibs, a reefed fores'l, and a full main. They had made some southing and tacked at sunrise to gain a further margin of open water between themselves and the British blockade. And Midshipman Blanchard was over the worst of his seasickness. He had not left the deck all night, knowing that to be below would be more than his heaving stomach could stand. Jack Clements handed him a pewter cup half filled with strong coffee.

"Drink this down, sir. It'll likely fix you up jest fine. Gonna be a fine day, good breeze and once she backs around to the nor'west, we'll be seein' flatter seas." The acting first smiled at the young man. The color had returned to Blanchard's face and he no longer found it necessary to maintain his grip on the backstay.

"Thank you, Mister Clements. I'll expect I'll be able to get a sun line presently and work out a latitude for us. We must have made a fair piece to the south during the storm. I collect you have sent lookouts aloft?" A nod from the former bosun indicated he was still ahead of the younger man, but his eyes crinkled at the corners as he smiled at the midshipman's return to command. Clements turned and headed forward to oversee repairs to the minor storm damage the schooner had sustained in the early morning hours. He passed the gunner, Tim Conoughy, checking the vessel's single four-pounder cannon lashed down amidships.

"Everything righty-o with your toy gun, Tim? Surely glad that little fellow was lashed tight last night; woulda made a hell of a mess she'da broke loose."

"Aye, Mister Clements. 'Pears she weathered that recent bit o' unpleasantness just fine, by me lights. I was just awonderin' now we're out, where're we gonna get us back in? I mean, if we're out 'ere to tell other vessels 'bout the blockade, what're we tellin' 'em 'bout where to go?"

"Don't you worry none 'bout that, Tim. Mister Blanchard got it all figgered out. Said somethin' 'bout New York or Connecticut, depending on where we could get in."

"Aye, an' it's righty-oh you are. I guess it ain't for me to worry 'bout. It's surely a puzzle to Missus Conoughy's boy, though, why I can not get meself on a vessel with some guns. Seems they ain't been but a moment or two when I coulda done some good ever since I left the service of the King. Thought I was gonna be righty-oh on that frigate, and now this. What 'appens when we get to New York or the other place you mentioned?"

"Reckon they'll tell us then, Tim. Right now, we got other things to get done. Think that little gun'll fire if'n we need her?"

"Aye, she'll be a firin', for all the good it'll do. One gun . . . and a wee little four-pounder inta the bargain . . . what do they 'spect me to do with this?" This last was under his breath. Tim had volunteered for the berth on the schooner, but was beginning to have doubts. Well, at least he was at sea, and not holed up in Norfolk with all them other coves. And he might get a real warship that might even get to sea when they got into wherever it was Clements said.

The wind backed later that afternoon and, as Clements had predicted, flattened the waves as it filled in from the northwest. The sunset, when it came, was brilliant red, orange, and violet and turned the clouds remaining from the storm into an artist's palette; the colors reflected onto the sea, giving the steady ground swell an eerie, molten appearance.

They sailed to the north, keeping a sharp lookout for any vessels — American to warn, and British to run from; the crew fell into a comfortable routine. And Jonas Blanchard ran a taut ship. He knew he had a fine crew, and looked to this commission as his stepping stone to lieutenant.

CHAPTER NINE

By the end of the second dog watch, the snow had eased considerably. And, while not yet blowing with any enthusiasm, the wind was showing signs of filling in. Most important, it was apparent that the General Washingtons' presence on the British merchantman remained undiscovered.

"Biggs! Lookee there." Captain Dickerson was pointing up to a bright green light shining eerily in the diminishing snow.

"I'll warrant that's Dobson and Hardy firin' off a rocket for Cap'n Rogers. I guess we better do the same. That all right with you, Cap'n?" Biggs received a nod and "Aye, let's get it done" from the taciturn prize master. Isaac called quietly for Smith and gave the order to fire the rocket they had brought for signaling the *General Washington*. With a muted whoosh, the rocket left a fiery trail from the quarterdeck of *Hopewell* into the cold night air; it burst into a brilliant green flare and floated down, leaving behind a shower of sparks, and extinguished itself in the sea astern.

"That surely was quick; you think they seen it on the *Gen'l*?" Smith looked at Isaac, his concern apparent to Biggs even in the dark. It was Dickerson, close by, who responded quietly.

"Sure hope so. And I hope the lookouts on *Shannon* missed it." He turned to his acting first mate and continued. "Isaac, you better ought to figger on that frigate or whatever it is doin' somethin' 'bout them rockets. I don't reckon these vessels would be afirin' off green rockets without they'd tell them Navy coves what they was about. Only question in my mind is whether the breeze'll fill in afore they figger out where they come from. Mayhaps we ought to have a look at them cannon for'ard there and . . ." His sentence ended as he realized the futility of them taking on the Royal Navy with the four puny six-pounders mounted on rolling carriages amidships and on the foc's'le. In actual fact, they were reduced to three, as Isaac had had one of the guns loaded with grape shot and a half charge of powder and aimed into the hold to discourage any ideas the British crew might have about re-taking their vessel. A man was stationed at the gun with a lit slow match and orders to fire should a rush up the ladder be attempted.

"I have an idea might help us out should them Britishers decide to have a look at us." Biggs started off forward, taking Smith with him, and calling for several others to help him. Dickerson heard him sending a man to the ship's magazine for a half keg of powder as Isaac began to shape a plan which might thwart the Royal Navy if there was to be an encounter. And the snow was beginning to ease considerably; the occasional star could be seen peeking through what remained of the overcast. The wind would be picking up shortly, Dickerson hoped. His experience in these waters told him it had been too long indeed, especially in late February, for there to be little or no wind; it just didn't happen that way here. The prize master quietly called a handful of men to get aloft and set t'gallants and stays'ls. He finished his instructions with ". . . and look lively while you're about it. No point in waiting 'til that frigate's smoked our ruse to make sail. We need to get this barky asailin'.

"You men in the waist: stand by the halyards and heave with a will. Soon's them t'gallants are up, clap a hand on them braces. Wind's comin' right soon." Prize Master Dickerson had as much hope as fact in his orders, and, if will alone could have sailed that brig out from under the British noses, she would already be away and gone.

"Ahoy there, 'opewell. Everything righty-oh with you?" The distinctly English voice cut through the darkness and caused absolute silence on the quarterdeck of the American prize. The handful of men there and the others forward looked at each other, wide-eyed. After what seemed a lifetime, but in fact was only a few heartbeats, Isaac responded, imitating a British voice as best as his two years in the Royal Navy allowed.

"Boat ahoy. Everything is quite fine now the bloody snow has nearly stopped — at least it would be if a breeze would fill in. Who are you, sir, and 'ow can we 'elp you?"

"I am Lieutenant 'owell, off'n the frigate *Shannon*. We saw the rockets and Captain Broke thought you might be 'avin' a problem. Did you fire them off?"

"Aye, Lieutenant. We saw them as well, but sorry to say we can't be of 'elp to you; they did not come from us. All is quite well here, save the lack of a breeze. Is *Shannon* far?"

The last question was ignored by the lieutenant from HMS *Shannon* as he continued his own interrogation. "Would you be so kind as to tell me, sir, why you are trailing your boats astern . . ." The question was interrupted by a cry from the window directly below the quarterdeck.

"You damn fools. It's the bloody Americans — they've taken my vessel and . . ." The alarm was cut off mid-sentence by a shot, and the night was suddenly filled with a ringing silence.

Dickerson wasted not a moment before he leaped for the scuttle and the Cabin; obviously something had gone very wrong. Opening the door he was greeted by the acrid odor of spent powder and the sight of the captain slumped on the sea chest under the quarter gallery. The window gaped open, and the seaman who had been left as a guard stood stunned in the middle of the small room. This tableau was lit by a single oil lamp, flickering on the writing desk. Through the open window, the prize master could hear most of the continuing and decidely one-sided conversation with the Royal Navy boat. What he heard was not boding well; in spite of Isaac's efforts to dissuade them, the Navy insisted on coming alongside and boarding the merchantman.

"I didn't mean to kill him honest to God he jumped for that window an' afore I could stop him had it open and was ahollerin' at them coves in the boat I ain't never kilt nobody afore Cap'n I don't know what went wrong I was watchin' him just like you said . . ." Dickerson put up his hand to stop the torrent of words, recalling he was one of the two landsmen in the boarding party; his inexperience had been apparent to the British captain as well. The sailor was not going to be much help for a while.

Leaving the babbling sailor, Prize Master Dickerson moved directly to the side of the ship's captain; he picked up the lamp from the desk as he passed and, holding it high, studied the Englishman.

"He's not dead; the ball cut his scalp, and must have knocked him senseless. Damn fool shouldn't have tried that. But I reckon he'll live — or at least he likely won't perish from this wound." He moved the man so he was sitting more or less erect and propped him up against the corner of the window, which he now closed and latched. "Bind him up so we don't have another problem should he come to his senses afore we're away from this mess. See about some line or rip up that shirt there into strips."

The man was still babbling as he had when first the master had entered the cabin. Dickerson relieved him of the pistol and threw the captain's shirt at him. "Tear this into strips and tie his hands and feet right good now. Better tie one across his mouth so he don't yell out as well. Look lively about it." He hoped that giving the man a job of work to do would be most effective in returning him to his senses; with the short crew he had to call upon, they could ill afford a single man who didn't pull his weight. Dickerson then ran for the ladder, pounding his way up to see if he could regain control over the situation on deck.

Once on the quarterdeck, Isaac greeted him with the news that the British lieutenant had announced his intention of boarding the merchant, and would they be so kind as to drop the man ropes at the waist? Dickerson glanced to leeward; *Hopewell* was making way, though not as much as he would have liked, but from what he could make out through the gloom of the night, the oarsmen in the cutter from *Shannon* were going to be hard pressed to get alongside any time soon, unless *Hopewell* were hove to, something he had no intention of doing. He turned to the men in the waist.

"You men, clap onto that little cannon there. Drag it to the quarterdeck. We'll give those British bastards somethin' to keep them occupied 'sides trying to come alongside this barky. Look lively, now."

The men needed little encouragement; the six-pound cannon was rigged aft on the quarterdeck where the bulwark ended and only a waist-high rail prevented a body from falling into the sea. Loaded with not only a six-pound ball but with some loose bits of iron and nails one of the men found, even a close miss would do damage. A hit would be devastating.

The seaman returned topside from the cabin where he had left Captain Stephens resting in a chair; Stephens had not yet regained consciousness but showed signs that he might come around before too long. The sailor seemed to have returned to his senses. Dickerson looked at Biggs as the group of men gathered around the cannon. Without a word spoken, Biggs answered the prize master's question with a nod and moved to check the tackles and jury-rigged breechings on the cannon. A sailor with a lit slow match appeared. It was Weasel Watkins; even in the dark, his whine made him instantly recognizable and Biggs answered his question.

"No Watkins, we're not ready . . . haven't even aimed it yet." He stood and looked around the faces assembled on the quarterdeck, and not seeing the one he wanted spoke to the closest, which happened to be Weasel Watkins. "Go find the gunner, and get him back here quick as ever you please, Watkins." Seeing that he was about to get an argument from the man, he put up his hand and continued. "Don't give me no fight here. Just do as I told you. Save your fightin' for them Britishers; if they come aboard you'll be a-needin' all you can muster. Now git!" The sailor turned and hurried away, knowing that to whine now would be fruitless.

Gunner Hogan showed up faster than Biggs expected, given the messenger he had sent. The gunner had been finding more powder and shot in case they were needed and instantly took in the situation. He bent down and peered along the top of the barrel. Picking up a hand-spike from the carriage, he levered the cannon forward slightly and then pounded in the quoin under the back of the barrel to depress the aim toward the British cutter. He stood and looked at Dickerson.

"She'll fire, Mister Dickerson. I reckon we might do some damage with this one. When you're ready."

"I doubt we'll get more than one shot, Hogan, so let her go as you will."

The gunner took the slow match and peered again down the barrel of the piece. Satisfied, he picked up the horn of powder and carefully poured a small measure into the touch hole on the top of the antiquated gun. He motioned the nearby men to step back and touched the slow-match to the powder. With a sputter and a flash, the spark burned down the powder and into the breech of the gun, igniting the cartridge within. The gun went off with a surprisingly loud crash, leaping backwards into the jury-rigged breaching tackles, and sending a double handful of shrapnel and a six-pound ball across the water and, hopefully, toward the *Shannon's* cutter, still only barely visible in the profound darkness.

A splash was heard, followed closely by screaming. The privateersmen looked at one another then back through the darkness at the dim outline of the cutter. Isaac spoke what most were thinking.

"Looks like the ball missed, Hogan, but from the hollerin' over there, I'd guess you might have got some of the nails into someone's hide. Maybe that'll give 'em reason to go back to they's ship and leave us alone."

Indeed, as they peered through the darkness, the lieutenant regained control of his boat crew, and, to the men on *Hopewell*, it certainly looked as if they had changed their mind about coming aboard. And the wind was picking up.

*   *   *   *   *

"You didn't have to volunteer for this, you know, Jake. You was in such an all-fired rush to get out of Norfolk and away from Miss Charity. And asides, bein' out 'ere 'as got to be better by far than sitting on our arses wonderin' if ever we'll get the barky through the blockade and into the fightin'. An' this little vessel ain't so bad; kinda puts me in mind of Cap'n Smalley's *Glory*. You 'member my tellin' 'bout that sharp-built schooner what took the two prizes we was sailin' in the Indies. This one don't swim quite as sweet, but she's surely older, an' a damn sight less fine in the lines. I reckon she was all Cap'n Stewart could get 'is 'ands on quick enough to please that secretary cove what kept sendin' messengers to 'im." Coleman paused as he looked around the horizon, still unbroken by mast or hull, friendly or otherwise. They had seen nothing for the past two days despite maintaining a constant lookout, day and night. The men had repaired much of the old pilot schooner commandeered by Captain Stewart, and the work kept them busy during the long dull days when no ships appeared.

Tate smiled at his friend and shipmate. "You know I'd sure rather be out here than back yonder, settin' on my backside and wonderin' when Charity was gonna come back to fetch me up to Baltimore. A determined woman, that. I am surely glad that you and Johnson didn't give me away when she come back aboard *Constellation* with that cove while we was fittin' this schooner out. I reckon that would have put the fat in the fire had she found me out. Why, even on the orlop deck I could hear her stormin' around. Tellin' her I was ashore on a special mission was a truly kind act on your part, Robert. I 'spect that gorilla with her was sent by her Pa to convince me I'd be better off ashore in Baltimore. I collect her Pa's a mighty important cove, knowin' the Secretary of the Navy an' all. I reckon I got myself outta Gosport just in time. I'm tellin' you, Robert, you coulda knocked me down with a feather that day she blew inta the tavern there, comin' in like that storm we went through a fortnight ago. Yessir, I ain't complaining about bein' out here, just wishin' they was something to do save workin' 'round the clock trying to keep this ol' bucket afloat. Any word from Clements when we gonna get in — and where?"

"'E ain't said where, but 'e did show me on the chart that we was off something called 'Long Island'. 'Bout sixty an' more miles off, 'e said. I collect there's places in there to get in. Tim said likely we'd be 'eadin' further up towards Massachusetts — though I 'spect 'e's just makin' noise cause he don't know any more than you an' me. That last vessel we spoke was 'eaded down to the Delaware when Cap'n Blanchard told 'em 'bout the blockade. Reckon they'll be headin' for New York, or mebbe up this way wherever it is we're goin'. Clements said they'd not make it 'round Sandy Hook without they'd get themselves caught by one o' me countrymen. I collect he and Cap'n Blanchard got 'intelligence' from that cove what come down from Washington. Clements said somethin' 'bout Mister Blanchard bein' responsible for tellin' what vessels we see out 'ere, an' where they's bound. So . . ."

"Sail! Sail to leeward! Hull down and showin' topmasts." The lookout in the crosstrees of the foremast was pointing frantically to leeward, and forward. Every man jack on deck looked aloft at the lookout, then in the direction in which he pointed. All any could see from deck was the open and unbroken expanse of horizon; the stranger had to be fifteen miles and more from the schooner. Midshipman Blanchard, a long glass slung over his shoulder, was in the rigging in a heartbeat, heading to the maintop to assess the sighting.

"She's headin' this way, Mister Clements. Under a press of canvas she is too. Let us bear off a trifle to close with her until we can tell what we've found." His voice carried easily to the quarterdeck where Jack Clements gave the orders to ease the sheets and bring the little ship down a point, causing the course to be almost toward the newcomer.

"If this breeze holds true for us, we could make her out before nightfall, Cap'n. We still got us a couple of hours afore it'll get too dark to tell much what she is." Acting First Lieutenant Clements had done some mental arithmetic and was giving the midshipman — and acting captain — a little guidance. He thought it was probably unnecessary; this young man had grown in stature and confidence daily since the storm over two weeks ago, and Clements thought he'd likely make a fine lieutenant when the time came.

"Aye, Mister Clements. I had about the same notion. Let us make the necessary preparations now. Have both flags ready to show, and have that British fellow come here to talk with them in case they are British, if you please. And you might have supper piped down a trifle early. If we have to flee, we'll need all hands working the vessel."

Clements nodded, and smiled inwardly. "Yes, this young cove'll do just fine when the time comes," he mused as he made his way forward in search of Robert Coleman. The schooner moved easily, cracked off on a very broad reach, in the brisk westerly breeze, and closed with the strange vessel heading toward the land.

The hail of the lookout had been passed throughout the ship and now all hands, both on watch and off, were on deck anticipating some level of action. Of course, with only the single four-pounder cannon, there would be precious little "action," but the break in the routine and monotony was most welcome. Men chattered, pointing when they thought they saw the tophamper from deck — their vision enhanced by vivid imaginations as the stranger was still too distant to be seen from deck. They wagered with each other as to the identity of the vessel, and then wagered again as to the action the American schooner would take.

They all had been witness to crossing tacks with three other vessels, not including the wounded brig running off before the tempest as they turned Cape Charles. Except for that one, all three had been American, two merchants, and a Navy brig, USS *Siren*, in route to station off Portsmouth, New Hampshire. The merchants were diverted, one from her intended destination of Delaware Bay, and the other from a course that would have put her right in the middle of the Chesapeake Bay blockade. So far, the crew of the pilot schooner had seen no British vessels, either man-of-war or merchant. None aboard, including Captain Blanchard and Jack Clements, knew what would happen when and if they crossed a British warship.

"Hull up, she is, sir!" The lookout's cry was joined by at least three other voices as the stranger's hull broke the horizon. By now the stranger must see the schooner, and the Americans watched closely to determine what, if any, action the larger ship might take.

The two vessels continued to close each other. Tension began to build on the schooner as the men realized that if this was an enemy, there was little they might do to forestall a disaster. Still no flags appeared on the larger ship, and Acting Captain Blanchard and Acting First Lieutenant Clements studied her rigging intently through long glasses.

"She's close enough now to be about in range of an eighteen-pounder cannon, Cap'n. Mebbe she's American an' her cap'n figgers bein' rigged as we are that we probably are 's'well." Clements spoke without removing his eye from the glass. Before Blanchard could respond, a geyser of water exploded out of the sea a pistol shot in front of the schooner, followed by a dull crack that echoed across the water. A British ensign appeared at the stranger's main truck.

"Mister Clements: you may pass the word for Coleman as quick as you please and let us luff up. No sense in provoking them." Blanchard turned to a seaman nearby and continued, "Get that British ensign up to the main gaff now. Quickly." To some hands watching the other ship from the waist he shouted, "You men there, get yourselves below and out of sight quick as ever you can."

Robert Coleman appeared on the quarterdeck as the schooner came up into the wind, luffing her sails in a cacophony of thunderous cracks, snaps, groans, and thuds as the canvas shook itself and its lines, blocks, and spars.

"Sir? Mister Clements tol' me you wanted me 'ere on the quarterdeck." Coleman approached the young captain who was removing his blue uniform jacket. He handed it to the seaman.

"Put this on, Coleman, and step up on the bulwark there. You just became Captain Coleman of His Majesty's prize schooner en route to Halifax. You are a master's mate off the brig *Narcissus* under command of Captain Westphall and, with a prize crew, are bringing this ship to Halifax. If you need help, I'm right behind you."

"Won't them officers know this ain't a right proper British jacket, sir?" I'd 'ate to 'ave 'em start shootin' if they smoke the ruse you're pullin'."

"Too far off Coleman; now get yourself up on that bulwark with the speaking trumpet."

The British frigate had by now hove to and was laying a long rifle shot to weather of the schooner. A figure climbed onto the quarterdeck bulwark, a speaking trumpet raised to his face.

"You have been stopped by His Majesty's Frigate *Lively*, Samuel Breathwaite commanding. Who are you and where are you bound?"

Coleman hesitated only a moment before responding. "We are the prize of 'Is Majesty's brig *Narcissus*, and I am Master's Mate Robert Coleman, in command. We are delivering this schooner to 'Alifax at the order of Captain Westphall of *Narcissus*." Coleman could see officers on the quarterdeck of *Lively* watching the schooner through long glasses and hoped that he had been convincing.

"Where is *Narcissus* and how long are you out?" There was little hesitation from the frigate.

"Tell 'em the schooner was taken a week ago tryin' to run the blockade at the mouth of Delaware Bay. And you don't know where *Narcissus* might be, as you ain't seen 'em in a week."

Coleman drew a breath and relayed the information. The British captain seemed satisfied with the answer, as he waved his hand, and turned to speak with someone on his quarterdeck. He turned back and raised again his speaking trumpet.

"Mind you watch your contacts, Captain Coleman. There's a fair number of privateers — American, of course — working the water off Cape Cod and on towards Nova Scotia. Wouldn't do to have Captain Westphall's prize re-taken by one of their number." The British sarcasm was undiminished by the distance between them, and Breathwaite turned his back on the American, issuing orders to get his vessel underway.

"Back the inner jib; stand by to bear off on the larboard tack. Put your helm over." Blanchard was wasting no time getting his ship underway as well. The officers and few men topside watched as the frigate proceeded on a southerly heading, rapidly opening the distance between them. He smiled at Coleman as the English fo'c'sle jack took off the blue jacket.

"I guess you convinced 'em, Coleman. Either that or they wasn't thinkin' we was enough to waste time searchin'. That might have been a mite touchy, had they decided to send a boat across."

Clements' words echoed what the young captain was thinking and he nodded his agreement.

"Aye. I'll second that sentiment, Mister Clements. Coleman," he said turning to the seaman and taking the proffered coat, "you did very well. Now let us see about makin' for a friendly port. You may return to your duties. And thank you."

Coleman smiled and stepped off the diminutive quarterdeck, heading back to an area in which he was more comfortable, forward. Some of his mates welcomed his return with a brief round of applause, led by the Irish gunner, Tim Conoughy.

"Ye nearly 'ad me convinced me own self, Robert, me lad. I was just thinkin' what a fine man, and seaman, was the good Cap'n Westphall, an' 'ow much I been missin' that fine vessel *Narcissus*. Would ye be mindin', sir, if'n a poor fo'c'sle jack like me own self shook your 'and an' give you joy of your success?" Tim had his shipmates laughing at once, and Coleman smiled, brushing off the accolade — or was it derision? — without embarrassment. It was likely that the laughter, in part at least, stemmed from the relief each man felt at escaping what could have been a desperate situation.

CHAPTER TEN

"Braces haul. . . ease your sheets. . . mind the stays'l sheets. . . helm down a trifle. . . let's get the barky movin' now, lads! It's only a matter o' time 'til that frigate shows up." Encouraging his men, and escaping from the confines of the British fleet were foremost on Prize Master Dickerson's mind right now. In a louder voice, "You there. . . in the waist; put out that lantern. Don't make it any easier for them bastards to find us." Silence no longer became an issue; the fat was in the fire and getting the most out of his men and *Hopewell* was the only way the American prize master might actually get his prize to a friendly port unscathed. That port had to be southwest of Penobscot Bay, as the folks living north of there along the coast were still sympathetic to the British and God alone knew what troubles they might encounter should they bring their prize into a port between there and the Canadian border.

Neither Dickerson nor Biggs nor, for that matter, any other soul on the brig had any idea where the *General Washington* was, or whether or not Captain Rogers would be in a position to assist them should they need it. Nor did they have any knowledge of where Hardy and Dobson might be, or even if they had been successful in their own cutting out expedition. No, it was better to look only to themselves to get out of this tight spot. Now that the snow had stopped and the wind was gradually picking up, most of the men thought they just might make it.

"Deck there! I think I got a sail to leeward. Hard to tell in the dark, but I'd say they's som'pin out there . . . 'bout two p'ints abaft the beam." The lookout's nasal hail, while not unexpected, caused all heads instinctively to turn aft and to leeward, even though all knew that from the deck, it was unlikely there would be anything to see. Biggs jumped into the mainmast shrouds and headed aloft.

"Point at it, Watkins. Where'd you see them sails?" Isaac was not surprised to find Weasel Watkins relegated to the lookout job; it kept him out of the crew's way, and provided something useful for him to do where his whining would bother no one.

"You don't believe me. I can tell right from your voice. Well, I'm tellin' you I did see a sail right out there." He pointed into the dark, and waited for a reaction from the third mate. "I can still see it . . . there — right there it is." His arm remained outstretched and Biggs peered into the gloom, straining to see the faint glimmer of a sail that apparently was plainly visible to the lookout.

"Aye, there it be. I got it now. Hard to tell whether it's the *Gen'l* or that frigate — what'd they say, *Shannon*, wa'n't it?" He continued to stare, and finally added, more to himself than the seaman, "Looks too tall for the *Gen'l Washington*, and I think I'm seein' three masts. Reckon we'd better figger on her bein' British." He looked back at the sharp-eyed lookout. "Keep your eye on her, Watkins, and let us know quick as ever you can should she do anything — change course or get much closer or anything at all. Got it?" Without waiting for an answer, Biggs was on the backstay and headed for the deck almost as soon as the words were out of his mouth.

As he hit the bulwark, he called out for some of the men who had helped him and Tight-Fisted Smith earlier with the plan he had hatched for just such an eventuality. They gathered around him, and quietly he explained what he wanted them to do, and then headed for the quarterdeck to fill in the master.

From the quarterdeck, Dickerson and Biggs watched as the men loaded some bulky objects into the stowed longboat and rigged a single whip to the main yard. The boat was picked up from where it had been stowed on deck and swung out to the bulwark. The men lowered it so the rail was even with the leeward deck edge and tied off the whip. Biggs turned to his superior.

"Well, if that Britisher gets closer, I think we might have a surprise for 'em. Probably won't stop 'em, but sure as blazes oughta give 'em something to think about, asides shootin' at us. Where do you reckon Dobson and Hardy got to? Since they fired off that rocket we ain't heard nor seen nothin' from 'em. Mayhaps they've gotten away clean if they ain't but one escort and they's comin' after us. Cap'n Rogers oughta be headin' this way by now, I'd think since we got us a breeze." In spite of being battle seasoned, Isaac was nervous. The odds here hardly favored a successful conclusion to their mission.

"Aye, Isaac, that he should. Let's see 'bout settin' the last stays'ls for'ard, and bring this ol' barky up a mite. We might get another dollop o' speed outa her."

Isaac set off forward to see about the stays'ls, turning from time to time as he moved up the length of the ship to check on the position of the British frigate, even though he knew that if he saw her close enough to make out in the dark from the deck level it would be too late to do anything save fire a few puny six-pounders at her. That would hardly slow down a ship of *Shannon*'s size and power. Their only real hope was that *Hopewell* could outsail the frigate — or at the least, maintain enough of the headstart she had to make a stern chase an unacceptable alternative for the English escort.

Even with the brig's course higher, the newly set stays'ls helped and she made a fair turn of speed in the increasing breeze. Returning to the quarterdeck, Biggs stopped to check on the longboat, and ensure himself that all was ready should it be needed. The cry from aloft cut short his stop and he hastened on aft.

"Deck there. I can see courses on that frigate now. Still off the leeward quarter. Showin' a light aloft, she is, an' maybe two leagues off."

"Reckon we're gonna have the devil to pay now, Isaac, and no pitch hot. Better have the lads unlimber what guns we got. Don't fancy much givin' up without we hurt 'em some. But I'm afraid it'd just be a waste of powder an' shot. I'd be mighty surprised if'n this merchant's carryin' more 'an enough for a few shots." As an after-thought he added, "An' you might put a few men aloft with some o' them rifles you found in the hold. It ain't much, but better 'an nothin'."

Biggs noticed the acting gunner, Hogan, standing at the break of the quarterdeck, and discussed with him the master's instructions. He received a nod and a quiet "Aye" and Hogan stepped off to carry out his orders. Isaac stepped to the bulwark where Smith and several others were waiting with the longboat and its curious cargo.

"Looks like we'll be needin' the boat, Smith. Better get a slow match lit and brought back here so we're ready." Isaac climbed into the boat and rechecked his earlier preparations. All was ready. All that remained was to wait for *Shannon* to get almost within cannon range.

"Deck there. She's gettin closer. Maybe a mile, now." One thing about Watkins' whine, it carried easily to the deck. Biggs looked for the hundredth time astern and saw the white glow of the frigate's sails in the dim starlight as she bore down on them, clawing to wind'ard as she gained noticeably, shortening the distance between them. As he looked, he saw a brilliant flash from the bow of the British ship. They had fired a bow-chaser, likely attempting to find the range. A second later, the report of the shot was heard on *Hopewell*. All eyes turned aft in time to see a geyser spout up from a hundred yards astern, just out of their wake.

"Isaac, if you've got something rigged, now would likely be a good time to use it; no point in waitin' 'til they's got the range." Dickerson, while an experienced privateersman who had tasted battle on more than one occasion, had little desire to be on the receiving end of the Britisher's eighteen-pounders if it could be avoided. Biggs shared his feelings.

"Stand by to lower away, Smith. And take 'er slow; remember, we ain't hove to and I got no desire to swim in this water tonight." Isaac was in the longboat, slow match in hand, as he gave the order. The boat easily slid down the vessel's side and touched the water, made easier by the fact that the sea was still flat from the long calm they had all endured. Dickerson watched the proceedings from the rail on the quarterdeck, shifting his gaze between the boat alongside and the British frigate, now visible, even in the dark, from the deck. He saw a sudden glow flare up from inside the boat and then the crew on deck threw down a line to Isaac. As Biggs clambered up the rope, ascending to the deck of *Hopewell*, Smith and his crew paid out the line attached to the bow of the longboat and soon the little vessel, still showing the glow from within, was astern of the bark.

"Bear off, some, if you please, Mister Dickerson. I want that boat ahead of the frigate afore we cut her loose." Isaac's plan was becoming apparent to the master. He nodded, and the ship eased her course. The men watching were startled to see *Hopewell* begin to sail a course that would close them with the frigate.

"Braces haul. Ease your sheets, blast your eyes! Look lively there. You ain't out for a picnic, you lubbers!" Ben Stone's impatience served him well and the sails were properly adjusted for the new course.

Boom! Another ranging shot rang out across the dark water and the splash was noticeably closer this time. It would not be long before the obviously skilled gunners on *Shannon* could fire at the Americans at their leisure. Isaac and Smith watched their long-boat, now at the end of its long tether, as their ship's course took it across the path of the oncoming British frigate. The glow in the longboat was barely discernible but, Isaac commented to Smith, "She's still burnin'. "

"Cut her loose!" The order relieved the tension and an ax swung down on the longboat's painter. The silence was complete on *Hopewell* as all hands watched as the longboat, now free, drifted sideways almost directly in front of the British ship.

"Look to your sheets and braces — we're headin' up." Dickerson's order was slow being carried out; the men were too busy watching to see what effect, if any, the drifting boat would have on the frigate.

"Look alive there, damn your eyes! Helm's down. Get them sheets trimmed." Stone, working on deck since his presence aloft was not required, encouraged the heavers on deck as only he could. The sails shivered briefly, then filled again as the brig settled on her new course, trying to regain the weather gauge and make it more difficult for *Shannon* to get any closer.

Suddenly the air was filled with a mighty explosion, as the night astern turned briefly to daylight, and then a darkness even more profound than before settled over the water. Before any eyes could adapt to the new darkness, a light, growing in intensity, emanated from the longboat; it was burning brightly and from its light, the men on *Hopewell* could make out the entire bow of their pursuer. The ship was clearly going to run right over the drifting fire-boat; there was simply no way they could bear off in time to avoid it.

"What in the name of all that's holy did you put in that boat, Smith?" Ben Stone was clearly impressed with the jury-rigged fire-boat. Whether it would have the desired effect remained to be seen.

"Why Ben, all's we put in there was half a keg o' powder with a fuse made up from a length of line soaked in oil and then powder. The whole thing was covered over with some oil soaked canvas. They's one more half keg in there. Don't think it's caught the flame yet. Reckon we'll know when she does." Smith was clearly proud of his and Isaac's creation and, should the device have the desired effect, it would provide him with a limitless supply of ale and rum ashore in the re-telling.

Only Prize Master Dickerson didn't watch the chasing ship; his attention was focused on keeping *Hopewell* headed fair. He did turn, however, when a second explosion ripped across the water, and in time to see the frigate's forward section apparently engulfed in flame. The captain of the British ship immediately turned his vessel full downwind, ensuring the flames would stay forward and not burn aft, setting fire to his rigging. So far, only the bowsprit and sprits'l were damaged, and almost as quickly as it flared up, the watching privateersmen saw the fire extinguished. However, by turning downwind, *Shannon*'s captain had lost any chance he might have had in catching up to the escaping Americans and their prize. The men on Hopewell cheered mightily and began congratulating each other when they realized they had been spared from the devastation of the heavy guns on the frigate, but both Dickerson and Biggs gained a large measure of respect for the quick thinking British commander who had saved his ship from a potentially devastating fire.

"All right lads. While we got his nice southerly breeze, let's harden her up and see about headin' for home. Trim your sheets . . . braces haul. Helmsman: make your course west, a quarter south. Keep her as tight as you can do, lad, an' give nothin' to leeward. An' Smith, you might check on our passengers. Make sure they's not gettin' into any mischief down in the hold, if you please."

*   *   *   *   *   *

"You may bring her up now, Mister Clements, if you please. We'll head for Newport, unless the British have closed that one as well." Blanchard had intended to put his schooner into New London, but as they approached from the east, having turned the outer end of Long Island the day previous, they found not one, but three Royal Navy vessels, one a seventy-four, sailing off and on across the western end of Fisher's Island, and decided to retreat to the relative safety of Block Island Sound. Now Captain Blanchard was going to try rounding Point Judith and continue into Newport. To tip the odds in his favor, he would do it in the dark of night. Having been at sea now for three weeks and more and warned four Chesapeake-bound ships of the blockade, plus making a narrow escape from a

British frigate, he felt it would be acceptable to Captain Stewart, and for that matter, Secretary of the Navy Jones, were he to put into an open port. It would also allow his crew to be reassigned to fighting ships that could get to sea and confront the increasing British presence. It was with this in mind that he gave the order to acting First Lieutenant Jack Clements to bring the now sea-worn schooner closer to the northwest wind and onto a course that would take her from just south of Block Island to the northeast side of Point Judith and thence to Newport.

"Let us hope that, should the Brits be in evidence there, we can slip by in the dark. By my reckoning, we should be in a position to get into Naragansett Bay toward the end of the middle watch and, should there be a British warship in the area, they just might be less attentive at that hour. Make all the sail she'll carry — and I needn't tell you about showing a light topside."

"Aye, sir. I'd warrant the men ain't got to be told that, 'specially since they know we're headin' in. Wouldn't please anyone to get caught — or have to run back to sea — now. I guess the lads have had enough of this little ship to last 'em a while." Clements smiled at the midshipman and thought, *He's come far, this young man. Not four weeks ago, I'da been tellin him 'bout not showing lights, and runnin' in durin' the dark of the morning watch. I reckon he'll do all right for himself, he will.* Clements made his way forward, rounding up men as he went to add more canvas to the rig aloft, and pleased to be not only heading in, but heading in after a reasonably successful commission. *Hope Cap'n Stewart'll be pleased as well.*

The hours passed and, to the joy of all aboard, the wind held steady from the northwest, allowing the schooner to sail a close-hauled course that would take them past Block Island and across the Sound to Newport. There were few, if any, of the men taking their ease below; extra eyes on deck, and an extra hand when needed would only speed them on more quickly. And quickly they sailed; both the first lieutenant and the captain were wreathed in smiles as the miles fell away under the stern and the log slate showed a consistent eight and more knots. It was during the early hours of the middle watch when a hoarse whisper floated down from the cross trees of the foremast.

"Deck! Deck there! I got something on the weather bow. Two p'ints aft o' the bow, it is, but damned if'n I can make out what it is. 'Ppears mighty big though." Without a word, Clements was in the rigging, heading for the crosstrees with a glass. He wrapped a leg around the backstay and, with the long glass at his eye, perched there for long minutes, squinting into the night. Finally he lowered the glass.

"You keep lookin' Johnson. I cain't make it out neither, but keep watchin' an' see if'n it gets any clearer." The first clambered down the weather rigging. Captain Blanchard waited for him as he stepped off the bulwark.

"They's somethin' out there, Cap'n, but I cain't see enough of it to make out what. Don't appear to be a vessel, and it ain't showin' a light, but it's still five an' more leagues off, I'd reckon." The men on deck, most of the schooner's crew, strained to hear what Clements had reported, and there were whispers among them, "What's he say?" "We got us a Brit?" "We gonna have to fight?"

All were silenced with a hard-edged whisper from their captain. "Silence fore an' aft, you men. Not a sound, hear?" Then to Clements, and Coleman who had materialized out of the night, "We'll ease her off some. Bring her down a point and ease your sails. See what effect that has on whatever that is out there."

"Light. I got a light. Dead ahead, an' above the horizon, 'ppears." Johnson's whisper from aloft stopped all action on deck, and the schooner moved silently through the water, leaving a white feather of a wake astern glowing dimly in the muted starlight. Again, Clements headed to the crosstrees.

After what seemed an eternity, he appeared on deck again, only this time, he was chuckling quietly as he stepped on the deck.

"That's Rhode Island yonder. An' I'd warrant that big shape to weather — that'll be Point Judith. We made better time than we thought, Cap'n; likely we'll be passin' Castle Rock within an hour an' some. Long as they ain't no Brits hidin' along the shore, we're's good as in." He smiled broadly at the young captain, who responded in kind as the first continued. "I'd be lyin' if I said I wasn't glad to be done with this one."

"You don't care much for smaller ships, I collect, Mister Clements. Well, it won't be long and you'll likely be reassigned to a frigate. Perhaps one in Boston or New London."

"Oh, I got nothin' 'gainst smaller vessels, Cap'n. Spent a commission on a private armed schooner out o' Baltimore afore I ever come aboard *Constellation*. And fine it was. Sailed the Indies an' took us a passel o' prizes, I can tell you. But we had a few guns aboard, and hands what could lay an' fire 'em. An' that schooner — *Glory* was her name — could outsail near anythin' she come across. What I cain't get me arms around is havin' to run from anything and everything we see. Ain't my nature, nor I'd reckon, most o' the lads aboard, to run away."

"So why'd you sign on then. You certainly knew in Gosport that we would be unable to fight. *Constellation* was a fighting ship, and well found. You could have stayed aboard."

"She ain't doin' much fightin' I'd warrant. No cap'n would try to get out of the Bay with the Brits what's there. Be suicide. So here I am, an' you, an' them" he gestured forward to the knot of men including Coleman, Tate, and Conoughy, "an' maybe we'll all get us the chance to get back to sea an' fight. I'd 'spect this'll not be endin' anytime soon."

And no one knew how true were Jack Clements' words, as the nameless Chesapeake Bay pilot schooner, commanded by a young midshipman and crewed by a mixture of seasoned American and British seamen, sailed silently, unseen and unchallenged, into the mouth of Naragansett Bay, and past Castle Rock, looming overhead to starboard in the gloom of night.

CHAPTER ELEVEN

Dawn broke, the sky clear and the horizon unbroken by as much as a single sail. *Hopewell,* with her American crew, was close-hauled on the larboard tack, making a course to take them into Gloucester, Massachusetts, in a few days should the wind and weather hold. That was a bit of a gamble in these waters, as a run of fair weather lasting more than two or three days was unusual at best. But one could hope. The deepening cold and a positive attitude permeated the ship, the men still enjoying the success they had experienced during the hours of darkness just ended. There had been no noticeable problem with the British sailors locked below, and Dickerson and Biggs were even now discussing giving them, a few at a time, an airing on deck.

"I think you'll be asking for trouble, Cap'n. We'll be in in only a few days, and they's warm and more or less dry down there. Bringin' 'em on deck in this cold might inspire 'em to try somethin' like takin' back they's ship. Right now, Smith tells me they ain't bein' no trouble, long as they get fed. I reckon they ain't in no rush to risk they's own lives to try an' take back the ship, bein' as how they ain't Navy jacks'n know they gonna be sent home — or at least to Halifax — pretty quick on our gettin' in." Isaac paused, smiling, then added, "Course, some rich English merchant ain't gonna be none too happy, losin' his vessel, an' mebbe another, if Hardy is headin' for home too."

"Aye, you're probably right, but have Smith bring up some o' them, under guard, o' course, if they's a-wantin' to get some fresh air. I ain't heard the crew piped to breakfast yet. Somebody got the galley fires stoked up and fixin' to feed us, I hope? This is hungry work, this time o' year; reckon the men're some sharp-set. And don't forget 'bout Cap'n Stephens. Reckon he's still got a powerful strong headache. Could be he's a-wantin' some vittles as well."

"I'll personally check on the cap'n, 'n as far as vittles is concerned, I put one o' the men down in the galley to see what he could come up with. I reckon we could roust out the British cook if you want. Vittles might be better fixed than us usin' one o' our own lads what don't know a pot from a sheet block. They's plenty o' stores down there, though. Checked that my own self."

"If'n your man don't come up with somethin' right quick, get that Britisher up from the hold. I ain't kindly disposed to lettin' one o' them have run o' the ship, but we could put a guard in there with him."

Biggs started below to see what, if anything, was happening in the Cabin and galley, and *Hopewell* continued sailing for America, close-hauled in a southerly tops'l breeze.

He opened the door to the Cabin to find the British captain awake and earnestly trying to convince his guard to loosen his bonds. Biggs' arrival precipitated a sudden silence and the young sailor who had the watch was startled and stood, knocking over his chair in the process.

"I presume that the Royal Navy is in close pursuit and likely about to open fire. You're here, no doubt, to ask me to speak to *Shannon*, so as to save your piratical hide. Well, you can just save your breath. *Hopewell* 's armament wouldn't last a minute against that frigate, and Captain Broke can take this vessel at his leisure without a thought. You and your gang of American cut-throats will be chained in the hold before very long, I expect." He smiled wolfishly at the thought of their roles being reversed, and his confidence at being rescued by the British frigate was complete.

"'Fraid not Cap'n. *Shannon* broke off last night after we showed her our teeth. Reckon she's back with the rest of 'em headin' for where ever it was you were goin'. You never did tell me where that was, Cap'n. I'm sure curious to know." Biggs was nothing if not ingenuous, and Captain Stephens, slack-jawed at the news, stared at him for a moment, then collected himself and his bravado.

"I'll tell you nothing, you pirate. Where this ship and the others are bound is not your concern, nor will having that knowledge from my mouth advance your cause one iota. I assume you have rooted through my hold like a pig searching out truffles, but I can do nothing about that. Adding to your . . ." He stopped, taken completely aback by Isaac's steady smile and obviously unruffled demeanor. Thinking to rattle the young man, he added, "*Shannon* may have broken off to continue her duties to the others, but when *Tenedos* returns, she is bound to cross your track and will take you quick as ever you please, you may rest assured."

"Aye, Cap'n. And why should we be concerned with this *Tenedos*; we convinced the *Shannon* we wasn't worth the fight." Biggs' calm demeanor was most perturbing to the increasingly riled Englishman.

"A Royal Navy sloop could take this ship, given half a chance, you imbecile. *Tenedos* is a frigate of the fifth rate, mounting thirty-eight eighteen-pounders, and commanded by a most capable officer. You may enjoy your liberty for now, sir, but by nightfall, I'd reckon, you all will be imprisoned aboard a ship of his Britannic Majesty's navy. Those that aren't dead, that is."

"Actually, Cap'n, I came to see how you was feelin', and if you was wantin' any vittles. Likely won't be quite up to your standards, but it will fill your belly."

The bluster died on Stephens' lips; caught all aback by the courtesy Biggs showed, he was again momentarily incapable of speech. Finally, he regained his composure and, this time, he did soften. He smiled. "That would be quite nice, I'm sure. If my steward could be found, he would prepare something for me without undue fuss."

"No, Cap'n. I wasn't thinkin' of lettin' your steward or any other loose. If you be wantin' vittles, you'll eat what the rest of us eat, your crew included. I'll see somethin' gets sent 'round to you." Biggs left the cabin, heading forward to the galley to see if the sailor assigned to cook had concocted something for the hungry men to eat which would not poison them. He could still hear the captain's bluster ten steps and more from his closed door.

The galley was a shambles; the idler from the prize crew, not used to the intricacies of cooking at sea or even working in a galley, had turned the small space upside down looking for the utensils and foods he thought might be necessary. A large pot of something dark gave forth an ugly smell as it boiled merrily on the camboose. Jenkins, the assigned cook, looked quizzically at Biggs, and then smiled.

"This cookin' ain't so hard, Mister Biggs. I reckon my scouse is 'bout done and that an' some biscuit'll keep their bellies full 'til I kin fix up som'pin else for supper. We gonna have a ration o' grog with the meal?"

"I 'spect we might have to, Jenkins, or the men'll never get this foul stuff down they's throats. What did you put in there that makes it smell so bad?" Isaac wrinkled his nose and wiped at the tears in his stinging eyes.

"Just the usual stuff what goes into lobscouse; some meat I found in an open barrel — might be salt pork or beef, which I ain't sure — a bunch o' potatoes, and I even threw in a large measure o' onions. As an added treat for the men, I found some fish — might be cod — and threw that it too. Don't smell too bad, once you get used to it. I been here since the watch changed an' it don't bother me a bit."

"Aye. I'll let Cap'n Dickerson know you got something ready, and we'll pipe the men down. Oh, and have some of that . . . scouse taken to the British captain; he's in his cabin. I'm sure he'll enjoy your cookin'!" Biggs turned and left the galley, muttering as he did, "We're gonna have a mutiny after the men're given this mess for dinner!"

Heading aft on deck, Isaac breathed deeply the clean, cold ocean air, expelling the smell of the galley from his nostrils. Had he not been so hungry himself, he would have been amused by the efforts of a main deck heaver — for that is what Jenkins was — in the galley. The men would hopefully be hungry enough to eat anything at this point, and there would be no trouble.

"Vittles up yet, Isaac?" Dickerson was also hungry. "I want to get the men fed as quick as ever possible. Ain't none of 'em et since we left the *Gen'l.*, and I reckon they're powerful consumed with hunger."

"Well, they's up, and I hope the men're as hungry as you say. With your permission, I'll have the bosun's mate pipe 'em down now. I told Jenkins — I guess he volunteered to cook — to send a bowl of his 'scouse back to Cap'n Stephens. I reckon we'll know when it gets there."

This somewhat oblique remark caused the prize master to raise his eyebrows, but otherwise elicited no response. Dickerson's eyes were riveted on the horizon astern, searching the sea for some sign of the *General Washington*. He turned back to his mate.

"Yes, by all means, get the men fed. And you might send a bucket or two down to the Brits in the hold. They's likely hungry as well."

Biggs nodded his assent and turned forward to find Davies, the coxswain and acting Bosun's mate, when the lookout on the foremast hailed the deck.

"Deck there! I got a sail — tops'ls and t'gallants — a point on the wind'ard bow. 'Ppears to be headin' this way. Cain't make out a flag."

Isaac looked aloft, seeing the lookout pointing at the stranger approaching from windward, and climbed into the foremast shrouds to check the sighting. Davies showed up as he did so.

"Davies, stand by to pipe the meal. I'm sure the men are complaining 'bout not gettin' it yet. I'm just goin' to see about this vessel to weather and . . ."

"Deck there! I am makin' a British ensign on that vessel. Set to the t'gallants and altering to head us. Looks like a frigate." The lookout had been paying attention and now Biggs was in the rigging and moving aloft with the skill of a natural topman, while on deck everything stopped yet again as the American prize crew realized they were not yet out of harm's way.

"Get that British flag up. Smartly now. Let 'em know we're one o' their own." Dickerson would try a ruse first, as fighting seemed a bad alternative, especially if the vessel ahead turned out to be a frigate, as the lookout thought. It was only a matter of minutes before Biggs was back on the quarterdeck confirming that it certainly appeared to be a frigate, and seemed to be under a press of canvas on a course set to cut off the *Hopewell.*

"Sail astern — sail astern!" The lookout in the maintop was pointing and gesturing frantically aft. The men on the quarterdeck could just make out a blur almost directly in their wake. Could be the top hamper of a ship pursuing them or a cloud. Biggs spoke what Dickerson was thinking.

"We surely don't need that right now. A British frigate bearing down on us and possibly one comin' up astern. Mebbe that's *Shannon* decided to come get us after all. I ain't lookin' to spend time on some Halifax prison ship."

Dickerson finished the thought with "Nor swimmin' in this sea. It's the devil's choice we got." He paused, then added, "Hurry the men along with they's vittles and then get some of these little guns rigged out . . . unless you got another plan, like you done last night?"

"Nothin' comes to mind, but we surely will clear for action quick as ever you please. Mayhaps they'll leave us alone, seein' the British flag aloft." He thought to himself, *Ain't likely for that, I'd reckon.* Then added, *Wish this old barky could sail like one of them sharp-built schooners. Wouldn't have this problem then.*

He began to organize the men to action stations, even while some were still finishing what was being passed off as a meal. At least this new threat made Jenkins' foul-tasting scouse seem less onerous than had they had ample time to eat and consider alternatives. A bad-tasting meal was right now the least of their worries, as Isaac reminded the few chronic complainers, Weasel Watkins at the forefront of them.

A shouted curse, including something about "poison" followed by a crash, drifted up from below the quarterdeck in the area of the Cabin. Dickerson smiled to himself, recollecting Isaac's cryptic words about Captain Stephens and Jenkins' scouse. He looked at his quartermaster at the helm and remarked dryly, "Reckon Cap'n Stephens got his vittles. Probably wasn't used to Jenkins' abilities in the galley."

He turned to Tight-Fisted Smith who was on the break of the quarterdeck. "Likely ought to go down there and see that we don't have another problem with the good cap'n like last night. Mister Biggs can help you if you need it, seein' as how Cap'n Stephens knows him. Ha!"

Smith nodded, said "Aye" and departed; he didn't think the mate would be needed for a simple job like securing a man in a chair.

"Good mornin' Cap'n. I come down here to help you keep from gettin' yerself shot again." Smith looked around the cabin, and smiled to himself. Remnants of the now infamous scouse dripped from the bulkheads with a concentration close to the door frame. The larger pieces of a broken pottery bowl lay on the deck along with some of the suspect meat from the repast. "I see you got your vittles. Hope you saved some to eat; we're gonna be a little busy topside, and you likely won't get no more for a while . . . probably won't be much better, neither." This last Smith added more for his own benefit than the captain's. He gestured to the man's gimbaled cot across one section of the quarter gallery.

"Cap'n, would you just lay down there on that bunk? I got to secure you here so's you don't get yerself hurt or cause Cap'n Dickerson no problems."

"Lay in my bunk so you can tie me up again? Not on your life, sailor. You are part of those pirates that took my ship. You can rot in hell for all I care, and I shan't cooperate with you for any reason. You may tell your captain that I aim to see him hanged for the pirate he is, and the rest of you with him . . . unless you might be willing to help me out of here, young man. I am not a wealthy man, but I would see you got a substantial reward for your efforts. If you're going to be busy as you indicated, it must mean there's a British ship — my guess is *Tenedos* — getting close. Were I to be rescued, and my ship, of course, I could see to it . . ."

The bosun's call sounded on deck, filtering below softly, but nonetheless insistently. Smith stepped up to the man and looking him directly in the eyes, said, "Sorry, Cap'n, you ain't given me no choice now. I got work to do and I ain't got time to stand here listening to you carry on." Having said that, Smith swung from his hip and landed a solid right fist in the captain's jaw. The man collapsed in a heap, and Smith picked him up and dropped him unceremoniously on the cot, tying him securely with the line he had brought with him. Finished, he checked his handiwork, winked at the smiling guard and left, closing the door behind him.

By the time Smith returned to the deck, the flurry of activity had increased and, with it, the tension. The approaching British frigate was clearly visible from the deck, and those eyes not glued to this menacing form were focused on the top hamper of the vessel closing them from astern; that ship's course had not varied, and it was clear that *Hopewell* was the stranger's intended destination. Smith watched the ship astern; from its angle, he could not determine its rig, but she was flying everything they could find in the sail locker and gaining ground on the Americans with every passing minute. Biggs happened by and noticed the sailor's stare.

"This ought to prove interesting. I'd reckon we gonna be some busy in an hour or so. Just trying to figger my own self which one was gonna get us in range first. Reckon it'll be that frigate comin' down on us to wind'ard."

"What do you think, Isaac? How we gonna fight our way out o' this? Those little guns we got ain't even gonna get they's attention. By the time they's in range, those eighteen pounders on that frigate'll have pounded this little barky into matchwood." Smith had suddenly realized that this uneven match could have fatal consequences, and Isaac hoped he would not unravel when the splinters started flying.

"I'm sure Dickerson has something planned, Smith. See if you can help out Hogan gettin' them gun crews organized." Biggs watched as Smith headed forward, looking for the gunner, then he turned and moved easily toward the quarterdeck, hoping all the while that Dickerson really did have a plan worked out.

"Isaac, I ain't Asa Rogers; I figgered to bear off and try and run for it if that frigate smokes our ruse of flying the British flag. If that don't work, I reckon we just gonna have to take our lickin'. I know Cap'n Rogers would figger out somethin', but I only once had a prize attacked, and I got lucky; we got into shoal water, and that Brit barky put herself right onto the hard chasin' me. Har har har."

His laugh had a maniacal ring to it. He continued, the false smile leaving his face as quickly as it had come, replaced with the furrows on his forehead that Isaac had seen frequently of late. "Here I don't reckon they's any shoal water for us to run to. And that cove comin' up astern don't sit real good, neither; don't know who he might be. Don't quite make sense they'd be sending two frigates after us, less'n this barky's carryin' somethin' mighty important that we ain't found yet." Dickerson looked ruefully at the ship gaining on them from astern, then to the two masts on *Hopewell.*

"Isaac, put some men aloft an' see about settin' some more canvas. You gonna have to figger somethin' out about where to put it; we're set to the t'gallants now, and onliest thing I can think to add might be some stu'ns'ls, but I'd warrant this barky ain't rigged for 'em. I'm gonna bear off some now an' see if she'll pick up a mite. Surely do hope this wind don't die out on us . . . helmsmen, ease her off a point. . . for'ard, there!" he shouted. "Ease your sheets. . . mind the braces, there. Trim out the spanker. Look lively, men." Further encouragement was unnecessary; each man was acutely aware of the twin perils closing in on their prize.

Biggs rounded up some men, canvas, and line for the additional sail and kept an eye on the two vessels approaching. The British frigate kept coming and, in fact, had altered her course slightly in response to the alteration made by *Hopewell.* The ship astern was still gaining ground, but didn't appear to have changed course. Isaac noted unhappily that he could see her hull now, not just the rig as he had only a short while ago. No one as yet could identify her.

Aloft on the mainmast, Isaac directed his men at jury-rigging some additional sail, realizing that an additional back stay on the mainmast would add some stability to the rig and reduce the risk of the mast going overboard should the wind increase, as all hands actively hoped. As he started for the deck, he glanced for the hundredth time at the ship astern; she looked familiar, and with the changed angle due to *Hopewell's* new course, he could see she was two-masted and likely a brig. While all of this information registered in his brain, it was not until he arrived at the quarterdeck that the implication struck him; it was *General Washington!* He shared this good news with Dickerson, who merely shook his head.

"Reckon that frigate comin' down on us'll take him too, then. What can a little brig do against a thirty-eight-gun ship." He answered his own question; "No more'n us, I'd warrant." He turned back to look astern, and from the slump of his shoulders, Isaac could see he held little hope for their escape. It was worth a fight, though, Isaac thought, and he expressed his feelings to Ezra Dickerson.

"I don't aim to go swimmin' in this water today — or tomorrow, for that matter — so think about this. If us and the *Gen'l* both go after that frigate we might chase him off. I remember once when I was a kid seein' a dog — an' come to think on it, a big one — drove off by three cats. And they wasn't but little ones. I think we could give those Brits somethin' to think on if we was to try, and could get Cap'n Rogers to see what we was doin'." Isaac's impassioned plea stirred something in the prize master; he turned to look astern at the closing brig, then back at the British frigate on their windward bow, still coming on with a bone in her teeth. He again looked back at the brig, then took his glass, purloined from Captain Stephens' cabin, and studied her carefully before turning back to his mate.

"Here, Isaac, have a look-see. I think Cap'n Rogers just might think we's British and lookin' to take us as a prize his own self. He's showin' the American flag on his gaff. Unless he thinks he can outsail that frigate, he must be crazy to think he could snatch a Brit merchant right out from under the nose of a warship! How can we let him know it's us? Think, man. He's got to see that frigate."

Dickerson's frustration gave way to desperation, but Isaac wasn't yet ready to strike.

"I don't know; if we fire a gun for'ard, the Brits on the frigate'll know we ain't British, and if we fire one aft, Cap'n Rogers'll think we surely are British. Hang on, there. What would happen if we bore off even more — away from that frigate? Them Brits might think we was just trying to get away from the *Gen'l*, but Cap'n Rogers would see us turning away from the very guns we should be runnin' under to protect us. That might make him think about it, anyway. Too bad we cut them boats adrift last night after them visitors from *Shannon* came callin'; Cap'n would know for sure who we was then. That's the onliest thing I can came up with, Ezra; just turn her down a trifle more and see what happens. Cain't hurt, anyhow, and might even pick us up half a knot. Or at least it would if this bucket's bottom wasn't so foul with weeds and barnacles."

"Helmsmen, ease her off a point; forward there — look alive! Ease the sheets, we're bearing off some." Dickerson agreed with Biggs that this action might signal Rogers a clue as to their identity, without giving up anything to the folks on *Tenedos*. Both men watched the brig to see what, if any, action their course change might provoke.

CHAPTER TWELVE

"He's going to engage her, Isaac! Lookee there! Them Brits are bearin' off some an' headin right for the *Gen'l.* Looks like they're gonna wear ship to pass to weather of *Gen'l Washington* an' hit her with a full broadside. 'Ppears they've forgot about us. Guess they must of bought that Brit flag we got up there. I surely wouldn't want to be on the *Gen'l* now . . . no siree, not lookin' down the throats of that many eighteen-pounders. Gawd a'mighty, I don't even want to think about what them guns gonna do to the old *Gen'l.* You reckon Cap'n Rogers'll strike, Isaac?

"Not on your life, Ezra. I don't know the man real good, but that don't strike me as somethin' he'd be likely to do. From the things I heard about him, he'll come up with some trick or other to confound them Brits." Isaac wasn't about to quit, and couldn't fathom the 'smartest privateer cap'n in New England' bein' unable to outsail or at least outfox a slow British frigate who's captain had to be burdened with conventional tactics for naval engagements. Never mind he was outgunned by a huge measure, both in barrels and in weight of metal.

Tenedos drew on, unwavering in her determination to cut off the pursuing American privateer from his intended chase, the merchant showing British colors. The alteration in course made by *Hopewell* went unanswered by the frigate and *Hopewell* continued away from the immediate scene of potential horror. Biggs and his captain watched as the play unfolded before them; *General Washington* held her course, continuing on a reach which would have carried them across *Tenedos'* bow, had the frigate not worn ship to open her broadside to the intruder. The tension on *Hopewell's* quarterdeck grew heavy and the silence was testimony to the significance of the drama playing out before the Americans. Finally, Dickerson spoke.

"Lookee there, Isaac. Them Britishers musta fell for our ruse; they's forgot completely about us. Must figger we're safe now from that American brig. I hope to God Cap'n Rogers kin handle a broadside from 'em."

"Don't think he's gonna let 'em fire a broadside at him, Ezra. And I'd warrant he's figgered out who we are and my guess is he's gonna keep that frigate busy so's we can get away. And I don't reckon he plans on losin' the *Gen'l* in the bargain."

"He's hardenin' up, Biggs. Look. The *Gen'l*'s comin' around — looks like she's gonna pass across the frigate's bow."

As the men on the quarterdeck, and now most of the hands on *Hopewell*, watched, *General Washington* bore up with barely a shiver in her sails; it was obvious now that Captain Rogers intended to cross the frigate's bow and likely would fire his own broadside to rake the British vessel from forward. *Tenedos* would be unable to fire little but her bow chasers in response.

Biggs and Dickerson exchanged looks; it was as if they were mentally linked and thinking with one brain. The prize master moved to the wheel, and quietly instructed the helmsmen to bring the brig up closer to the wind — and the pending action. Isaac stepped off the quarterdeck, directing men to trim sails and ease the braces, while at the same time sending Ben Stone and Tight-Fisted Smith aloft with their limited gang of topmen to reduce sail area so Dickerson could more easily control the speed of his ship. Gunner Hogan quickly assessed the situation, and called to the quarterdeck.

"Which side, Cap'n?"

"Larboard will be engaged, Gunner." Ezra smiled to himself, pleased and relieved that his crew — or at least the petty officers — had figured out his plan and appeared to support it.

Hogan grabbed a handful of sailors who had finished heaving on sheets and braces and set them to shifting the few six pounders from the starboard side to larboard. He nodded to one man, who having realized there would not be enough ports for the extras, began to hack away at the bulwark with an ax, making room for the additional guns. As Biggs released sail handlers and Stone's men returned from aloft, all hands got busy preparing to take their ship into action. Powder was brought on deck, along with the limited shot and kegs of nails they had found in the armory. With the light weight of the broadside and the severely restricted resources of ammunition available, all hands understood that there would be only one chance to help their shipmates on the *General.*

The men on deck interrupted their work preparing for battle long enough to handle sails while Dickerson tacked *Hopewell* around, and now the prize master had her headed across the wind on a course that would intersect the frigate's wake at ninety degrees. He could see the privateer holding true a course that would cross the British bow, and hoped the two ships would cross the frigate at about the same time. Through his glass, he could see figures on the British quarterdeck watching his most curious action. Suddenly, one began gesturing at *Hopewell,* waving his arms in an obvious attempt to tell the merchant to bear off and stand clear. Moments later, a hoist fluttered to the *Tenedos'* main yard. The helmsman on the merchant looked questioningly at his captain. Dickerson shrugged and replied to the unasked question from his sailor.

"I'd reckon they's tellin' us to get clear so's we don't get wounded in the fight what's about to commence. Hold your course." The uncertainty and despondency so evident a few short moments ago were gone, replaced by a sense of urgency and grit as he faced the huge odds against him. His jaw clenched, the muscles in his cheeks working visibly, as he thought of the short odds of success in this endeavor. He looked aloft at his own main mast then called out to one of the men nearby.

"Find you an American flag, lad, and stand by to hoist it aloft quick as ever you can when I tell you . . . and get that British one down at the' same time."

He watched the British quarterdeck, particularly the officer who had been watching him, and apparently still was. The Englishman lowered his glass and turned to speak to someone close at hand — might be the captain, Dickerson thought. He watched as both the Englishmen now studied *Hopewell* through their long glasses. Another officer joined them and drew their attention forward, where *General Washington*'s intentions were beginning to dawn on the British officers. For the moment anyway, *Hopewell* was not a concern; all the English eyes were forward.

"I'll take her now. You can help out with them guns for'ard . . .

and send Mister Biggs aft, if you please." Dickerson relieved the helmsman, preferring to drive his ship into the dangerous confrontation himself. It would save time in maneuvering and Biggs would be there to coordinate sail handlers and gun crews.

The young landsman returned with the American flag he had been sent to fetch and stepped to the halyard, looking over his shoulder at Dickerson. Ezra looked at the frigate, the *General*, and his own position, and waved at the sailor; the British flag started down to the deck and, within a few seconds, was replaced by the American flag, whipping tautly in the strengthening breeze.

"Wonder what them coves be thinkin' now, Isaac. They's surely between the devil and the deep blue sea now, they are by the Awmighty." He studied the positions of the various elements in this ballet of ships, then turned forward and raised his voice. "Mister Hogan. Stand by your matches and make your shots count. You ain't gonna get but one try at this; I aim to tack away almost at once you've fired."

The gunner waved from the ship's waist, and Biggs and the prize master could see a lit slow match in his hand. The men at the guns were peering over the bulwark and through the gun ports, watching the stern of the frigate grow larger as *Hopewell* bore down on her. What they couldn't see was the privateer about to cross the British bows at rifle shot range. Dickerson eased his helm a trifle to close the distance at which he would fire his puny broadside.

"I think they've noticed our colors, Ezra." Isaac had the glass trained on the quarterdeck of the frigate and the flurry of activity there seemed to him a clear indication that the officers on *Tenedos* had realized that they were about suffer a raking fire from both forward and aft.

"Aye, I 'spect they might have. I aim to tack quick as possible after we fire, Isaac, so git your men aloft soon as they ain't needed at the guns. This could get a trifle ugly here in a moment or so."

They watched the *General Washington* as she closed on the frigate; their courses clearly about to merge. *Tenedos'* captain tried to bear off some when he realized what Asa Rogers was about, but Rogers countered his move so as to obviate any benefit that might derive to the British ship; the American privateer was unquestionably about to fire a raking broadside into the frigate, a bold move in anyone's book.

"He's gonna be firing right quick now, Isaac. Mister Hogan,

stand by." Dickerson wanted to fire simultaneously — or as close as he could — and he held *Hopewell* firm on her course; they would cross the stern of the frigate in seconds now, and at pistol shot range. No longer was a glass necessary to see the horror and frustration on the faces of the officers on the British quarterdeck. An arm, holding a cutlass, waved, and simultaneous crashes roared from the British quarterdeck and foc's'le, filling the air with lavender-tinged smoke.

Almost immediately, *Hopewell* shuddered as the British iron hit home; one eighteen-pound ball landed squarely between wind and water, holing the hull as easily as matchwood and, although no one on deck saw them, creating a shower of splinters that could easily drive through a man. The other ball cut through the larboard bulwark and imbedded itself in the foremast, six feet above the deck. This ball also created splinters from the bulwark and, unlike the one taken in the hull, there were men close by; injuries and death were common shipmates, and the men noted the carnage and went on with their efforts to prepare their response. The dead would be removed and the injured cared for as soon as time permitted. Fortunately, only two of the *Tenedos'* guns would bear astern, and their crews were evidently not well-trained, as it took some long minutes for them to reload and, at a range of two hundred yards, the relative positions of the ships changed rapidly.

"Fire, if you please, Mister Hogan." Dickerson's mouth was unspeakably dry, as were several others on *Hopewell,* and his command, though easily heard, seemed to him more a croak than a shout. Eagerness to inflict hurt on the enemy mixed with dread of the likely retaliation infused the minds of most of the crew, but their training to duty held sway and the words were barely out of Dickerson's mouth when the guns erupted in a rippling broadside — if 'rippling' can be ascribed to only four guns, and six-pounders at that. As the smoke blew to leeward, Dickerson and Biggs watched the frigate for signs of hits from their 'broadside'. Almost at once they were rewarded with screams and chaos on the *Tenedos'* quarterdeck; the home-made canister shot had done well, wreaking havoc and confusion in the British sailors and officers standing aft. As they watched, the Americans saw *General Washington* fire, and were again rewarded with the sight of the fore topmast on the frigate falling, and then hanging by some halyards, as the privateer's chain shot did its job.

"Get those men aloft . . . stand by to come about . . . Bosun, mind your trim and keep an eye on that foremast. Mister Biggs, let's get some sail on her, if you please. We need to stand clear if we're not to take some punishment which we can ill-afford." Dickerson had made his statement against the English and now, realizing there was little else to say, wanted to get clear as quick as ever possible.

Hopewell tacked around, passing smoothly through stays, and cleared to the west on the larboard tack, her crew crowding on as much sail as they could hang on the yards, and the devil take the wounded foremast. The bosun was doing his best to get some planks nailed on the mast to support it where the ball had entered, and every man knew that his very life depended on the repair holding until they were in the relatively safe waters near Massachusetts.

Ben Stone, having finished with his men on the mainyard, stayed aloft to watch *General Washington.* After he had fired a raking broadside, Captain Rogers held his course and then tacked, again crossing the frigate's bow. In the course of opening his other broadside to the British ship, he exposed himself to another volley from *Tenedos'* bow chasers; this time, he was not as lucky, and Stone could see the privateer take the several shots aboard. One dismounted a cannon. Another seemed initially to pass clear; then the jib boom on the American ship sagged and went by the board, taking with it the foremast stays, jib, and stays'l. *General Washington* slowed perceptibly with the loss of canvas and the timber hanging over the side, but continued on.

Tenedos, in the meantime, had her own problems and, in the confusion on deck, Stone could see even the red-coated marines lending hands on lines and sheets. The hanging fore topmast threatened to foul other rigging, and a crew was busy trying to clear it along with its yard and rigging. The American guns, puny though they were against the might of a thirty-eight gun frigate, had taken their toll, and *Tenedos* bore up, heading for her fleet, instead of coming after the two American ships. A cheer went up from *Hopewell* as they watched the frigate and was echoed from across the cold Atlantic by the men of the *General Washington.*

CHAPTER THIRTEEN

Two days later, on the first of March 1813, an American private-armed brig and her prize sailed into Gloucester and dropped anchor in the protected harbor there. The war was still young enough to cause the townspeople to turn out to witness the event; some were vocally thrilled and delighted, while others were equally vocal in their pro-British attitudes. Needless to say, altercations between the two factions were loud and frequent but, fortunately, none were fatal. None of this mattered to the men and officers on the two wounded ships sailing slowly under greatly reduced sail into the inner harbor; in fact, most of what was going on ashore was unknown to them. It was not until the privateersmen showed up in the local waterfront ale houses that these political differences manifested themselves.

"I see you coves had a successful commission. It must have been miserable out there in that storm what passed through here not long ago." A sympathetic patron of the Fouled Anchor Tavern was buying tankards for his new friends from *General Washington*, and seemed interested in their doings. He was rewarded with a detailed, if somewhat garbled, version of the cutting-out of "not one, but two" British merchants and the subsequent challenge by "not one, but two" British frigates.

"They coulda had us, they kept on. But after Cap'n Rogers showed 'em his metal, they run off, like a bunch o' dogs run off by some birds."

"Lost a few men on both ships, we did, and make no mistake. It wasn't without its cost to us. Some good men, indeed." Davies, late-acting bosun's mate on the *Hopewell*, raised his tankard, managing to spill only a little in the process, and continued his lament. "Here's to some good men — even ol' Jenkins wasn't a bad sort, you keep him outta the galley. Weasel too. I reckon we'll miss even the Weasel. Not his whinin' though; I don't reckon no one gonna miss that noise. He's probably chasin' after the Prophet up there in Heaven whinin' that he 'tol' you I was the one gonna get kilt . . .' an' the Prophet, he's jest lookin' at Weasel and strokin' his beard an' thinkin'."

"Aye, Davies, you're probably right on the mark — 'bout Weasel anyway. Don't pay to speak ill of the dead, though." Ben Stone was, like most of the *General's* crew, not overly fond of the Weasel, but he was a shipmate, killed in battle, and as such, deserved a certain amount of respect. "Strange how he was kilt though, you ask me. What he was doin' down in that storeroom when the ball from that frigate hit us I surely got no idea. Wa'n't he 'sposed to be in a gun crew?"

"Aye, that he was, Ben Stone, that he was. Hogan didn't have time to go lookin' for him afore we fired them little cannon, but he surely was 'sposed to be on deck. Reckon if he'da been at the gun, he wouldn't caught that ball between his own wind and water. Holed the *Hopewell*, and holed ol' Weasel Watkins as well." One of the men had joined the group a bit later and, as a result, was still moderately sober. "Where do you coves reckon is Hardy and Dobson? Kinda figgered they'da been in by now. Biggs tol' me we gonna be gettin' the *Gen'l* back to sea right quick. Soon as the knottin' an' splicin' gets done. Wouldn'ta been in even two days if Cap'n Rogers hadna wanted to ship the rest o' the crew. We still got another two months an' more in this commission. Cain't take prizes swingin' to a hook in some harbor somewhere."

"We ain't goin' nowhere 'til I can lay yardarm to yardarm with some young miss, and get me some . . . well, you coves know what I'm sayin' — don't need to be drawin' it out for ya . . . though I think I mebbe gonna draw it out my own self, or better, let the young miss draw it out for me." Davies laughed heartily at his crude play on words, joined by a few of the others at the table. He clearly had more than a drink on his mind, and his own words must have sparked his memory, because having spoken, he stood, albeit unsteadily, and tacked toward the establishment's front door, leaving rocking tables with spilled drinks overflowing the tops and at least one fallen chair in his wake. He almost made it to the door when one of the tavern's patrons took exception to Davies' rowdy behavior and stood up, wiping the ale off his waistcoat and blocking Davies' way to the door.

"Just who do you think you are, sailor? Spillin' me drink like you did makes me think you should be standin' me to a fresh one, it surely does. You got no call to be comin' in here and braggin' of your exploits against His Majesty's ships. Your kind is what gives us Yankees a bad name. Probably from down south somewhere, ain't ya? Stirrin' up trouble and bringin' Mister Madison's war up here where we don't want it or your type."

Davies looked at the man through bleary eyes; he rocked slightly on his feet, as if he were still at sea, and remained mute. Not satisfied with this response, the pro-British patron redoubled his efforts.

"Don't they teach you coves to talk down south? Didn't no one tell you it ain't po-lite not to answer your superiors? Or are you so drunk you cain't talk?" With each question, the patron moved closer to Davies, finally placing a hand on Davies' chest and pushing him. Davies reacted.

Without a word, he stepped back from his antagonist and visually measured the distance between them. Suddenly his arm flashed across that space, much faster than one would expect from his drunken state, and his fist landed squarely on the man's nose; the crunch of the bone audible at the table occupied by Davies' shipmates. They stood, ready to join the fray should one develop. None did; the British sympathizer crumpled backwards to the floor, the blood from his broken nose mixing with the ale on his waistcoat. Davies, without a look back or left or right, stepped over him and staggered on his way out the door. He muttered "Stuff that!" as he stepped over his fallen antagonist.

The General Washingtons remaining at the table roared with delight and revisited the scene throughout the remainder of the night until it had taken on a life of its own, making Coxswain Davies larger than life in the process. By the next morning, a legend had been born.

Also by the next morning, news flashed through town that a British-built vessel was making the point, but showing American colors. Those General Washingtons whose heads would permit came on deck and peered painfully through the bright morning sunshine at the ship's top hamper, visible over the point. Breathing deeply of the still frigid air was akin to choking down knives, but as their heads gradually cleared of the rum and ale-induced fuzz, they saw the stranger gradually round the corner and make for the inner harbor and the anchorage. Captain Rogers and First Mate Starter Coffin watched from the taffrail on the quarterdeck.

"I'd warrant that's them, Cap'n." Coffin growled his thought, pointing with his chin at the now visible bark-rigged ship. "Can ye make out any faces there on her quarterdeck?"

Rogers studied the ship thoughtfully through his long glass, saying nothing in response. After a moment, he snapped the glass shut and looked at his mate. "Reckon you're right, Mister Coffin. Looks to me like Mister Hardy standing there at the wheel, and Dobson for'ard. Don't 'ppear they had any trouble from the look o' their rig 'n' hull. Lookee there, Hardy's easin' her up toward us; reckon he's seen us and will drop his hook nearby. Then we shall find out where they've been. Seems to me they shoulda been in afore us, not three days after us."

"You men, there. Look alive! Stop standing around like you was sleepin'. Get a boat in the water for the Cap'n." Coffin minced no words in his orders, and even though they were growled in that gravelly voice, they were loud enough to cause several of the men to wince in pain. But the boat splashed into the water a few minutes before the new arrival's anchor did and Captain Rogers was over the bulwark and into the boat before all the sails had been clewed up.

Isaac Biggs stood with the first in the waist of *General Washington* and watched as the captain climbed aboard the prize. Hardy and Dobson greeted him at the rail, smiles and good cheer written on their faces. Biggs and Coffin could tell how the conversation was going, even though they could hear not a word, just by the expression on the prize master's face. Obviously, Captain Rogers had asked after their whereabouts. All they could hear was the incredulously explosive retort from Rogers; "Portsmouth?"

Later, Rogers, his mates and prize masters dined at the American Coffee House on the Gloucester waterfront. Over dinner, Hardy told their tale.

"Aye, sir. We had no trouble at all taking the barky. Seems like they was so surprised to see us, climbing over they's rails in the middle of nowhere, and in a blizzard on top of it, that they just quit. Didn't have no problems roundin' 'em up and lockin' 'em into the hold. Turns out we was well to the leeward of the escort ship — that was the *Shannon*, in case you lads didn't know, and we was glad not to have made her acquaintance — and when the wind come up, we just bore off and later wore around behind 'em all. Headed right for Gloucester, like you said, Cap'n." Hardy paused to swallow some ale, and Coffin leapt into the silence.

"So how'd you wind up in Portsmouth? Lose your way, Hardy? You been sailin' in these waters most o' your life. You ought to know better." Coffin stopped his gravel-voiced jibe and smiled; his eyes, slits only, sparkled with glee. "Wait'll this gets around the waterfront in Salem. Won't nobody hire you on. You'll be runnin' punts out to the fleet at anchor while all the real sailormen laugh and point at you." Starter couldn't resist the opportunity to gain the upper hand in the good-natured competition that existed between himself and his shipmate.

"Nah, Starter, you got it all wrong. We was comin' right along toward Gloucester when we spotted a sail comin' up on us from astern. Figgered it might be one o' them Royal Navy ships lookin' for us, and bore off to get some speed out o' that old bucket. A day later, we sailed right into Portsmouth pretty as kiss my hand, figgerin' that was good's Gloucester, but the good folks there, why they just threw us out, lock, stock, and barrel. Claimed they didn't want no part of 'Mister Madison's War up here in these parts' was the way they put it. Said they had no beef with the English and wouldn't be a party to stealin' they's ships. I didn't have no choice but to cut 'n' run and skeedaddle out of there. I don't know if they'd astarted shootin' at us, but I didn't want to find out. So we got out, and come here, like you said back on the *Gen'l*, Cap'n. I didn't figger to find you here, though; figgered you'da already gone back to sea, or down Salem way."

"Aye, here it is we are, and we'd be makin' sail by now had you not shown when you did. I will wait only until my agent acknowledges that we brought him another prize to get condemned and sold, then it's back to sea. This cruise's got itself another couple o' months to run, and they's more prizes out there askin' for our attention." Asa Rogers smiled at them, enjoying the early success of his cruise, and the company of good men, and fine sailors.

CHAPTER FOURTEEN

Late April, 1813

"Aye, that be so. And I've heard it said HMS *Orpheus* has been seen more'n once offshore towards Block Island. Wasn't that the vessel you was on, Robert?" Jack Clements leaned back in his chair and took a deep draught from his tankard. The table was small, the tavern crowded and loud with sailors and workers from the Charlestown Navy Yard. The three shipmates who gathered 'round it leaned forward, both to avoid being jostled every time the publican or a barmaid went past and to better hear the answer from their companion, formerly of the Royal Navy.

"That was the last English one I were on, Jack, aye. That was the frigate what young Isaac learned 'bout the Royal Navy on. And one what I got no wish to see again!" Coleman's whole face changed as he recalled the ship and her oft-times brutal commander, Captain Winston; his eyes became hard, his jaw muscles clenched tight, and his mouth formed a thin white line across his face. "Anyone say who 'ad 'er now? Was it still Cap'n Winston?"

"No, I recollect some cove named Pigot was what they said. Heard he took her over when she come north. Leastways, that's what was bein' said over to the Navy Yard. No mention 't'all of your Cap'n Winston."

"Pigot! A flogger, that one, just like 'is daddy before 'im. One o' me mates on ol' *Orpheus* sailed with the father afore 'e come aboard. Wore stripes on 'is back like I never seen afore. Claimed Pigot had 'im flogged more'n' once along with some other topmen 'cause another ship was faster swayin' up a t'gallant yard. Poor sod was kilt by a nine-pounder ball square in the chest first time we fought the Frenchies. 'E don't got to worry none 'bout the cat,

Pigot's or anyone's."

"I guess you're right glad you ain't sailin' with them, no more, eh Robert? I heard the 'Merican cap'ns don't flog they's crews hardly at all compared to them Brits. An' when a cove gets a little soft, that's the time to make a change, eh?" Jake Tate joined the conversation with a quick grin and a wink at his shipmate, now bosun on USS *Chesapeake*.

Coleman caught Tate's wink at Clements and immediately got into the spirit of the taunt. "Chauncey Tate, you'd not last a minute with one o' them bastards standing up there on the quarterdeck all 'igh an' mighty while some cove the size o' Jack 'ere swings the cat across your bare back. First stripe an' you'd be running off to find sweet Miss Charity. 'Ceptin' she'd not be there, 'aving run off with some farm 'and what wasn't goin' off to sea an' leave 'er waitin' at the altar." Tate cringed visibly at the reference to his one-time love, the Maryland girl who still appeared frequently in his dreams.

"You 'spose Johnson and Conoughy got the troubles on *Constitution* we got on *Chesapeake*? Jack, you been around. You ever seen such a mess on a ship — never mind a navy ship?" Tate, changing the subject away from his love life, brought up something that had been on all their minds since reporting aboard the frigate *Chesapeake* with Midshipman, now Acting Lieutenant, Blanchard.

Ever since Captain Evans had brought *Chesapeake* into Boston, barely a week before the four men reported aboard, there had been desertions and theft running rampant throughout the ship. A major contributor to the problems aboard was the lack of a commanding officer; Captain Evans, already blind in one eye and seriously ill, had been taken ashore to the hospital and ultimately excused from further duty in the Navy. His officers, warrants, and senior petty officer did little to quell the unrest aboard and, in fact, actually contributed to it. Questions concerning back-pay nagged at the officers, and the many crewmen who moved ashore during the limited overhaul repeatedly refused to return unless they were paid. Drunkenness and whoring prevailed, with the men bringing the women right aboard under the very noses of their officers. Little was being done to ready the unfortunate frigate for a return to the sea.

"Aye, Jake. By my lights, I'm beginning to think thems what says she's a jinx ship might be righty-oh. Cain't see us gettin' out o' here any time soon. Course them two Royal Navy frigates out

there beyond the President Roads ain't gonna let us jest sail ourselves out an' by 'em. Likely to have somethin' to say 'bout that,
you can bet. That is if ol' *Chesapeake* could be got under way in
the first place. Mister Blanchard tol' me jest today that one of the
officers — one that ain't run off yet — said something 'bout a new
cap'n and gettin' under way in less 'an a month. Said *Chesapeake*
would be on the briny afore the end o' May. I'd be willin' ta' wager
a fair piece o' change that that'll not happen. Not unless the new
cap'n brings a new crew an' a new mainmast with him." Clements
laughed ruefully and shook his head at the sad state of affairs on
board his ship. Even on the privateer, with a high-strung crew with
larceny in their hearts, he had not witnessed the total lack of order
extant on this Navy frigate. He swallowed the dregs of his tankard
and, signaling the publican for another round, continued.

"I've heard it said by some aboard that she's already got the reputation of bein' 'unlucky'. It ain't no wonder them sailormen ain't
willin' to crew her, what with men fallen out'n her riggin' and only
four prizes, an little ones at that, on her last commission. The carpenter told me she even stuck on the ways when they launched her
back in '98. Twice in fact. An' runnin' aground from time to time,
as well." He shook his head. "An' that set-to with the *Leopard* down
off Cape Henry in '07. Heard it said that they wasn't none o' the
crew could show they's faces around Norfolk when she come in
after that. Hard to believe she's sister to *Constellation*. Now there
was a fine vessel; too bad she couldn't get out to fight. We wouldn't
be settin' here in Boston an' assigned on that other un."

"Jack, what 'ave you 'eard from Conoughy? He an' Johnson 'ave
not shown they's faces ashore that I've seen since we come up 'ere.
I'da thought they'd be at least turnin' up for the odd tankard. Can't
be that *Constitution* is gettin' ready to go to sea; she ain't even got
all 'er decks back in yet. Men're livin' ashore." Coleman was concerned about his Irish friend. They had shipped together for many
years; in fact, this assignment was the first time they had been
posted to different vessels since their first duty together in 1801.

"Heard from some cove in the Navy Yard that Cap'n Bainbridge
hadda send more 'n' a hundred n' fifty souls off to someplace in
New York to fight up on the Great Lakes. Probably right short-
handed on *Constitution* 'bout now, an' ain't no time for any of 'em
to be sky-larkin' with the likes o' you. I reckon he'll turn up sooner
or later. Drink up, lad, an' do your worryin' 'bout gettin' ol' *Chesa-*

peake refit and out to sea."

The bosun gave good advice; down to less than half her crew and a third of her officers, *Chesapeake* would need the attention of all hands if ever she were to fight again. It was not that she was badly wounded; indeed, though she had been at sea from mid-December until several weeks ago, there had been precious little action for the frigate, and she had suffered minimal damage from enemy guns. Her main topmast had gone by the boards while working into Boston in an April gale with the loss of three men and her mizzen head had been sprung at the same time adding further fuel to the vessel's "unlucky" history. Word was circulating aboard that the Secretary of the Navy would not allow them new masts, and was pressuring the first lieutenant and acting captain to get back to sea as quick as possible. Of course, that could not happen until a new commanding officer was assigned, and none had as yet been named.

"The way things is goin', what with the officers leavin' and none o' the crew about, might be Mister Blanchard an' us'll be takin' the barky to sea, Jack." Young Jake Tate laughed as he spoke, and the others joined in, relishing the absurdity of the notion. But their laughter had a hollow ring to it.

Two weeks later, a topman on *Chesapeake* and Coleman were talking in conspiratorial tones on the spar deck. "I heard it again last night, Coleman. I knowed it wasn't real, but I 'bout soiled my hammock when I heard them screams. Woke up covered in sweat, I did. You ever heard the scream a man makes when he's fallin' out o' the top hamper? I'm tellin' you, this barky is jinxed. I aim to get off'n here quick as ever I can. No more goin' to sea on this ship for me, I can tell you. I know, you say the same as everyone else — 'men fall from the riggin' all the time. That's one o' the hazards 'bout working aloft' — well, I kin tell you, those coves went right by me, they did. I was on the main yard tyin' in a reef when that top-mast let go. They was good men. They wouldn'ta fell but for that damn weakened topmast and that squall what come outa the gale we was in. An' ain't jest we lost a spar an' some good men; damn ship is jest unlucky.

"Last commission we was out nigh on four months and we only found us four prizes. Look around you. Most o' what's left o' the foremast jacks're drunk or pokin' some dockyard whore or both. Officers — what's left of 'em — cain't do nothin', and the mids, 'cept that young 'un come aboard with you — what's his name, Blanchard? — are as helpless as if they's still at they's mama's tit. You got any sense 't'all, you'll get your slops an' follow me right off'n this ship. Only a matter o' time 'til somethin' really bad happens an' I don't aim to wait around for it. You comin'?" William Hawkins, able seaman, and main topman on USS *Chesapeake*, watched his new British friend for a sign of acquiescence to his impassioned plea to desert. None was forthcoming. Coleman shook his head, and smiled.

"Guess I got to see it for myself, Will. But if I was gonna get, I'd do it now. I 'eard one o' the officers sayin' we got a new cap'n gonna show up any day. Some cove named Lawrence, if I 'eard 'im right."

"Well, you can stay 'til somethin' even worse happens. Me, I aim to get gone from this ship and Boston quick as I can. I heard o' Lawrence; he got hisself a bunch o' prizes on his last ship — *Hornet*, it were — including some Brit filled with gold an' silver. But he ain't gonna change the luck o' *Chesapeake*, you mark me well." Hawkins turned and walked away from the foot of the mainmast where the two had been talking. He took ten steps and stopped, casting a glance back to where Coleman stood. "Last chance, Robert. You gonna come with me or get your own self killed on this bad luck barky?"

Coleman waved to the American sailor, "Good luck to you, Will. Perhaps we'll meet up again." He turned and headed aft, leaving his friend in a stunned silence.

As he neared the quarterdeck, he heard Midshipman Blanchard and First Lieutenant Page talking. Actually, what he heard was Page giving rather explicit orders to the young, but seasoned, midshipman.

". . . those women out of the gun deck. If Cap'n Lawrence sees that, he'll have those men flogged to within an inch of their rotten lives and we'll have no crew to work the ship. And find Mister Ludlow, if you please, and have him see to those stores the good citizens of Boston seem so reluctant to part with. My guess is that, when Cap'n Lawrence comes aboard, he will be most anxious to get underway, assuming we have the same good fortune as *President* did just the fortnight past and are able to slip out past His Majesty's frigates that seem fixed like barnacles to the entrance to President Roads."

The midshipman saluted Lieutenant Page and, with a confident

"Aye, aye," departed to carry out his orders. Coleman continued below to find Bosun Clements and pass on this latest intelligence.

When he got to the lower deck and his eyes adjusted to the gloom, he made out several pairs of legs, some obviously female, protruding from beside a few of the eighteen-pounder long guns. Grunts, groans, drunken mumbling, and a variety of other sounds gave evidence that several of the crew were involved in activities other than what is normally associated with a man-of-war. Further confirmation, if any were needed, came from more than a few petticoats strewn carelessly about, over gun breechings, rammers, and indeed, the deck. Several others of the crew were apparently passed out drunk on, beside, and, in one case, partially under, the gun carriages. He saw Midshipman Blanchard moving through the deck placing well-aimed kicks in exposed backsides and urging the men to get back to their duties. His reception would have been considered mutinous by most.

". . .get on with you lad. Can't you see I'm busy?"

"Ooof. What'd you do that for?"

". . mind your knitting, youngster. ."

"You . . ."

Midshipman Blanchard had not recently commanded his own vessel — even though a nominally armed schooner — for nothing. He picked up a bucket of water near one of the guns and unceremoniously dumped its contents on the nearest of the copulating couples. They rose, sputtering and grabbing for clothes, stunned to see a lowly midshipman standing by the gun carriage; his hands held the upturned bucket and his face a frighteningly hard stare. Their sobriety returned quickly and the sailor staggered forward, hitching up his trousers as he went, and muttering drunkenly under his breath. The woman beat an equally hasty retreat toward a ladder leading to the spar deck. Blanchard saw Coleman watching, and smiled.

"Well, that's one, anyway." Turning back to the supine sailors, he added louder, "All right you lot; the same for each of you less'n you get back to work."

It was as if he had never spoken, so little was the impact of his words. Jonas Blanchard shrugged at the British topman and stepped to the ladder recently vacated by the dockyard whore. "I'll be right back," he muttered.

Coleman smiled inwardly, knowing that it would take more

than these loutish American sailors to get the best of Mister Blanchard. It wasn't just anyone who could pull off a successful deception on a Royal Navy frigate, and this minor action just didn't signify, he thought. *Blanchard'll get 'em.* He dropped down another deck, finding Jack Clements, Bosun, about to ascend it.

"Mister Clements. I just 'eard Cap'n Lawrence'll likely be showing up aboard any day now. Mister Page, sick as 'e is, is tryin' to get the ship in order. Seems like it might be more'n 'e can 'andle. What 'ave we gotten ourselves into 'ere? I thought this was the American Navy. This crew would have been flogged 'round the fleet were they in the Royal Navy. I surely 'ope we don't see action anytime soon; why those coves yonder couldn't find the guns, let alone fire them."

"I wouldn't let it worry you, Robert. Them two British frigates beyond President Roads ain't gonna be lettin' us out o' here anytime soon, and 'sides, we ain't got stores aboard or that replacement topmast. An' God alone knows what we'll be doin' for a crew. Ain't enough men aboard to fill one watch right now." Seeing his English friend about to speak, Clements anticipated him. "*President* got out on a fluke. Just lucky that little storm blew through and them Brits hadda get offshore some. Wasn't nobody watchin' when she made it out. Don't mean we can do it, just cause we got us a famous cap'n." He saw the quizzical look on Coleman's face.

"Aye, an' famous he is. Was him what took that Brit — *Peacock* — it was. An loaded with gold an' coin, I hear tell. Why, when he came back to port here in America, he was a real hero. Promoted to captain on the spot, way I heard it. Near as famous as Cap'n Bainbridge was when he come back on *Constitution* from sinkin' HMS *Java* down there off Brazil. He'll whip this crew into shape or die tryin', be my guess. An' then go out yonder an' show them British frigates that it ain't just *Constitution* what can take they's men o' war. You mark my words, Robert. Your gonna see some real changes in the barky when Cap'n Lawrence comes aboard. Unlucky ship, my arse. He'll change that, for sure."

It was the very next day that a tall and quite good-looking officer in his early thirties, wearing the two epaulets of a captain, strode up the brow to the spar deck of *Chesapeake,* followed by a lieutenant and a midshipman. The senior of the three stopped in the waist, flanked by his two subordinates carried with him from his previous command, and surveyed the spardeck; a look at once sour and angry settled on his handsome face. His lips were pursed and his brow became furrowed as he visibly darkened. After a brief conference with his juniors which included much nodding and more concerned expressions, the trio stepped to the quarterdeck of the frigate, taking no notice of the curious glances cast by the few seaman on deck. A midshipman noticed the entourage and ran immediately for Lieutenant Page, who appeared on the quarterdeck looking for all the world as if he were ready to die.

"Captain Lawrence?" His barely audible question merely caused the captain to raise his eyebrows and shift the shiny new bugle he carried from one hand to the other.

"If you are my first lieutenant, muster the crew if you please. There is much to do and precious little time in which to do it. This, by the way, is Lieutenant George Budd, and Midshipman William Cox is next to him. Both are reporting aboard as well and were with me on *Hornet* in our recent actions in the South Atlantic. Assign them quarters and duties."

"Aye sir. I am Lieutenant Page, first lieutenant as you correctly surmised. Captain Evans is unfortunately unwell and in the hospital ashore." Page stopped and, turning away, sought the bosun and a midshipman — the former to call the crew to muster and the latter to escort the two new officers below. He would see to their duties shortly.

CHAPTER FIFTEEN

"Men, I am James Lawrence, and now in command of the frigate. There is much to do and precious little time in which to do it. The Secretary of the Navy wants us to sea and after the British as quick as ever possible, but first we must put *Chesapeake* in fighting order. It will take all hands working watch and watch to manage this. We will also begin recruiting new hands to assist us. My lieutenants and midshipmen will be working with equal vigor and I expect all of you to do your duty. But first," and here, Captain Lawrence held up the bugle he had been holding, "is there one among you who can blow this thing?"

Silence reigned on the spar deck. Suddenly a black crewman, fascinated by the shiny bugle, stepped forward and sang out loudly, "Yes sir. I kin blow dat jest fine."

"Then it shall be yours, and you shall blow it when we board the enemy ships." Captain Lawrence did not bother to find out if Seaman Brown could, in fact, play the bugle.

The men were subsequently dismissed, and the lieutenants and midshipmen moved throughout the ship, organizing work parties and beginning the task of returning the frigate to fighting shape. Lawrence personally handled the merchants ashore, leaving the dockyard workers for the sick and failing Lieutenant Page to manage. In spite of all efforts to the contrary, relatively little was accomplished either by the still unruly crew or the inept dockyard workers. Frustration in the Cabin and wardroom grew daily in the ensuing week.

Rendezvous were established at several taverns and rooming houses ashore in an effort to recruit sailors, though with the reputation of *Chesapeake,* and the fact that so many seamen had signed on with privateers to make their fortunes, results were indeed sparse. Boston's merchants, generally unwilling to support 'Mr. Madison's War', were difficult, claiming insufficient stores, and charging outrageous prices for what they did sell.

And Lieutenant Page was finally sent ashore with what would prove to be a fatal disease of the lungs. Two other officers were coincidentally on the sick roll as well and Captain Lawrence was reduced to temporarily promoting midshipmen to acting lieutenant status in order to complete his wardroom.

In desperation, he paid a visit to his old commodore, William Bainbridge, seeking men and officers from *Constitution*. A small contingent of men was sent, including a topman named Johnson and an Irish gunners' mate named Tim Conoughy, both late of USS *Constellation*.

Late in May, reports began filtering into Boston that the British blockade was being tightened around New England and Royal Navy frigates, brigs, and sloops of war were actively patrolling the waters between Nova Scotia and the mouth of Long Island Sound. A merchant sloop arrived in Boston with news that she had narrowly escaped two British frigates, HMS *Tenedos* and HMS *Shannon*, which were now closely watching President Roads and Boston. It was likely that more would be joining them, since it was apparent that the British were aware that both *Constitution* and *Chesapeake* were in the harbor.

It did not appear to any on *Chesapeake* that either vessel would be going to sea anytime soon. Lawrence however, remained confident that if anyone could get *Chesapeake* to sea, it would be he. And to that end, on May 30th in a strong southwesterly breeze, Lawrence had *Chesapeake* unmoored and sailed out to President Roads.

"Who does he think he's kiddin'? We ain't gonna be able to sail the barky outta here, any more'n we coulda from up to the Navy Yard. An' at least there, we could get our own selves ashore from time to time." Jake Tate was clearly put out and echoed the sentiments of most of the crew after the *Chesapeake* had been brought to her anchor in the Roads.

"Aye, Jake. I 'ear you, lad. But think on this. If you was fixin' to jump ship, you might think twice afore you did, considering that now you got to swim for it." Conoughy, fresh aboard from the now famous frigate *Constitution*, smiled at his young friend. "Cap'n

Lawrence just orders up 'is gig or the cutter, an' off 'e goes as 'e pleases. So bein' out 'ere don't prove any 'ardship for 'im, by all the saints. I'd warrant that 'e's planning to get the barky outta 'ere quick as ever 'e can once that frigate yonder — I think it might be HMS *Shannon* — moves off enough. An' Cap'n Lawrence wants to 'ave as many of the men aboard as ever 'e can, which they would-n't be ifn we was still up in the Navy Yard.

"On *Constitution*, we didn't 'ave much problem with jumpers; ship wasn't thought unlucky. But I reckon I might jest do the same thing my own self if I was commandin' such a vessel as this." The gunner's philosophical answer to young Tate's complaint did little to put the Maryland topman in a better frame of mind, but Jake did acknowledge that the Irishman was likely correct.

The two had been idling on the fo'c'sle watching a fleet of small fishing vessels making for sea. The little boats handled the chop quite nicely and their crews, to a man, waved happily as they sailed past. The men on the frigate waved absently back. The bosun joined them, at first silently, then he turned to Tim Conoughy.

"I'd reckon you'd rather be back on *Constitution* and in the Navy Yard right about now, even without no decks or spars, eh Tim? I'd bet we're gonna be sailin' outta here in the dark o' the moon right quick. I don't imagine Cap'n Jim moved us out here cause the view is better. I'd warrant he's got himself a plan. He told Mister Blan-chard and a couple o' the other officers he was fixin' to head up Nova Scotia way and take some prizes — mebbe some of their whalers what's working them waters up yonder. An' he said he'd fight his way out if it come to that."

"I can not be a gunner on a vessel what don't go to sea, Jack, an' by all that's 'oly, I'd rather be on whatever it is what's 'eadin' out. An' from what I 'ear, Cap'n Jim is the man to get us out. 'e's quite the fighter, 'cordin' to what I 'eard 'round the yard."

"Aye, that be so, Tim." Tate joined the conversation. "I've heard it said below that his last cruise — on the little *Hornet* it was — was so successful they had a parade for him in New York. An' o' course, he did take that British sloop what was carryin' all that money, *Peacock*, wa'n't it? Mebbe he thinks he can turn *Chesapeake* into another *Hornet*. I wouldn't bet on it my own self, seein' what we got for crew aboard this barky. I'll tell you, boys, I gots me a bad feelin' 'bout this ship."

"Oh, Jake, you been listening to too much o' that fo'c'sle talk.

Some o' these very lads was on the *Hornet* with Cap'n Jim when he took all them prizes. I don't reckon they'll be standin' by all ahoo when the fightin' starts and, with a week or so to train some o' the landsmen we got shipped, we'll be in fine shape quicker 'an ever you'll know. You can mark my words on that, lad. You'll see." Bosun Clements tried to shore up the young topman's spirits, but it was clear he didn't completely believe it himself.

The next afternoon one of the topmen, while working aloft, noticed a tall rig standing off the headland and hailed the deck with the news. Immediately, acting Lieutenant Augustus Ludlow and acting Lieutenant Jonas Blanchard were in the foretop, glass in hand, and studying the new arrival.

"*Shannon* would be my guess, Jonas. I'd reckon we ain't gettin' outta here anytime soon now. Word is she's crack; one o' the top frigates o' the Royal Navy. Unless she heads offshore or moves on, Cap'n Lawrence ain't gonna sail us outta here. Be a damn fool to try, I'd say." Lieutenant Ludlow, who at the age of just twenty-one years, had taken over as first Lieutenant with the transfer ashore of Lieutenant Page, scowled at the British frigate and demonstrated his superior knowledge to his junior comrade. Blanchard, who had commanded a ship at sea, merely nodded his head. He wasn't sure about Ludlow yet, and had learned that silence is frequently the wiser course. He did, however, offer a suggestion.

"You oughta send someone to fetch the cap'n. He'll be wantin' to know that the Brit's that close in."

"Good idea, Blanchard. Get you down to the deck quick as you can and find Cap'n Lawrence. I believe he's dinin' ashore with friends. Tell him 'Lieutenant Ludlow's respects, and there's a British frigate standin' to just over a league away.' An' don't tarry."

The captain returned with Blanchard in his carriage just in time to see the English frigate pass smoothly through stays and retrace her course to the north, gathering speed under easy canvas in the westerly breeze. Obviously, she was in no hurry.

"We must find out if she is truly alone out there. I will not be drawn into a fight I can not win, and should there be another frigate, or for that matter, a brig, out of sight behind the headland, we would be in dire straits, I fear." Cap'n Jim stared through his glass and muttered to himself as the two young lieutenants hovered close at hand.

It was not until the next morning, just before a fiery dawn had lit the eastern sky, when Lawrence was able to ascertain just who was out on the deep taunting him. A fishing vessel came by and sailed close aboard, obviously having a look at the towering frigate gently tugging at her anchor. Lawrence, on deck, hailed the little boat to come alongside.

"Since you boys're headin' out past the Roads, it would be considered a favor to me and the Navy for you to have a look around. There's a British frigate yonder and I need to know if she's alone out there. You boys have a look and sail back here quick as ever you can to let me know."

The men in the little craft waved an acknowledgment and bore off, heading for the open sea with a strong following breeze. Lawrence watched them as the vessel took the seas. His face gave nothing away as he turned to William Cox, promoted only the day previous from midshipman to acting fourth lieutenant, and spoke.

"Mister Cox, put a man in the crosstrees to keep watch on that fishing boat. Kindly inform me when they return. I wish to hear their report first hand. I do not wish to waste a moment should an opportunity present itself to us." Lawrence turned and strode away, leaving the young and most junior lieutenant stammering out an "Aye, aye" as he hastened to do his captain's bidding.

The morning of June first moved on apace; the crew performed their usual tasks and lookouts kept watch for the return of the fishing boat. Lieutenant Cox glanced again at the day's newspaper which an harbor craft had delivered earlier in the morning. He still thrilled at the words about his captain, quoted in the paper from President Madison himself as he reported the success of *Hornet* on its recent cruise.

". . . continuation of the brilliant achievements of our infant navy, a signal triumph has been gained by Captain Lawrence and his companions in the *Hornet* sloop of war, which destroyed a British sloop of war with a celerity so unexampled and with a slaughter of the enemy so disproportionate to the loss in *Hornet*, as to claim for the conqueror the highest praise and the full recompense provided by Congress in previous cases . . ."

And young William Cox had been there, alongside his beloved commander, and he fairly glowed with pride at both the fact that he had commanded one of *Hornet*'s batteries and at his recent acting commission as fourth lieutenant.

He was jerked from his reverie by the cry from the lookout

assigned to watch for the fishing boat. He saw Jake Tate coming down from the maintop and was about to send him to find Captain Lawrence, when Lawrence himself appeared.

"Now, Mister Cox, we shall learn of our fate." He watched with the young lieutenant and Augustus Ludlow, Acting First Lieutenant, as the craft drew nigh.

"She's out there, Cap'n. Like you said. But ain't but one o' them what we could see. She was standin' 'bout six or seven miles off when we seen her. Big one, too. If'n you're goin' out yonder, we wish you every success," the little craft's captain waved his hat to the men on the frigate as he tacked and continued back into the harbor at Boston. No sooner had she moved away than a lookout again hailed the deck.

"Sails on t'other side o' the island yonder. Tall. Likely be a frigate, an' a big one, it appears."

"Mister Ludlow: muster the crew in the waist; we're going out." And Lawrence stepped to the ladder heading below.

Shortly, Ludlow knocked on the Cabin door, announcing the men were assembled, and added, "They's a bit of grumbling and complaining. Cap'n. But they're all present an' correct."

When Cap'n Jim appeared on deck, he was resplendent in his best uniform, carefully brushed by his steward, and showing the two epaulets newly earned by his recent promotion. He joined his officers on the quarterdeck and addressed his crew.

"Men," he cried, "a British frigate is just beyond that island yonder and I mean to sail out and bring her to action. We will not dishonor our flag and we will prevail. Remember the old *Hornet* and our great triumph over the *Peacock.* We'll 'Peacock' her, lads, we'll 'Peacock' her."

He fully expected the men to pick up his newly-minted battle cry, but to his dismay, he was greeted first with silence, then more grumbling, and finally a man — one of Lawrence's old crew — cried out, "Aye, Cap'n. We remember *Hornet.* Do you remember our prize money? We ain't been paid."

Another, obviously drunk, joined the cry. "Give us our money."

And yet another added, "We got debts to pay too, you know."

"You earned it, lads, and you shall have it. Mister Ludlow, have the men go to the pursers' office and see that they are paid. Then get these women off the ship and we'll have the hands to stations for unmooring the ship." He went below.

The young officers did their best to chase out the women still hanging around on the gun deck, but were embarrassed by the complete disrespect shown them and the mutinous mutterings of the sailors.

Robert Coleman and his old shipmate, Tim Conoughy, watched from the fo'c'sle as the midshipmen and officers, so recently midshipmen themselves, herded the unruly and drunken women to the waist, many accompanied by their shipboard lovers, and shook their heads at the sight.

"Can ye imagine this on ol' *Orpheus,* Robert lad? Why I reckon Cap'n Winston woulda 'ad most o' them coves strung up to the grating an' flogged 'alf dead by now. I don't know what it is we gone an' gotten ourselves into, but it surely don't give Mrs. Conoughy's boy a good feelin'." Much of the gunner's optimism seemed to have faded as he realized there would be no training before the frigate saw action.

"Aye, Tim. But we're 'ere now, an' ain't a thing to be done about it. You see that group over yonder? Might be Mister Blanchard could use a mite bit o' 'elp." Robert paused, then added, "An' it wouldn't be at the grating, my friend; I'd wager a gold guinea that Cap'n Winston would 'ave them sods strung up to the main yard by now. Grab young Jake there and let's 'elp them ladies over the rail." Coleman laughed, picking a belaying pin out of the foremast pin rack as they passed. Joined by topman Jake Tate, the three headed toward the struggling and red-faced Lieutenant Blanchard as he half dragged several women toward the rail and the waiting bumboats below.

Topside they could hear Bosun Clements calling all hands to stations for unmooring, and the two topmen left their shipmate to help the beleaguered young lieutenant and headed for their positions for making sail.

CHAPTER SIXTEEN

Word went through Boston like a summer squall; *Chesapeake* was making for the open sea. No one had any trouble guessing what was coming next. It would be an opportunity of a lifetime; a major frigate battle would take place, not miles and miles at sea, but right here in the coastal waters of Massachusetts Bay.

Heretofore, the people of the United States had only been able to read second hand accounts of the great naval engagements of the preceding twelve months. *Constitution*'s smashing victory over *Guerriere* had occurred well out to sea to the north, *United States* had taken HMS *Macedonian* some six hundred miles off the Canary Islands, and *Constitution* had triumphed over HMS *Java* in December down off the coast of Brazil. Now Cap'n Jim Lawrence, the darling of the American people, was going to give them their fourth frigate victory right here off the shores of Massachusetts! And within easy view of anyone who cared to find a high vantage point from which to witness the spectacle.

In no time, hills, rooftops, church steeples and any high point that people could get to filled with cheering citizens shouting encouragement to, but unheard by, the men on *Chesapeake*. A spirit of gaiety and eager anticipation prevailed. Few among the thronging citizenry had any doubt that once again, the American warship would prevail.

Boats of all sizes, from small harbor craft with only oars and human muscle for propulsion to fishing vessels and a few small brigs quickly filled and, each decorated with bright flags and buntings, sailed out in the wake of *Chesapeake*, carrying cheering spectators, waving and shouting to the men on the big frigate. These good citizens were going to be right there when it happened, watching from close at hand as the battle began and iron flew. A few tried encouraging their skippers to get closer to *Chesapeake* so they would miss nothing of the spectacle.

On a hilltop overlooking the sea, a young family watched as *Chesapeake* sailed, not as gloriously as some might have hoped, but to those on the hills around Boston none-the-less regally, into the Atlantic. The day was sparkling, and the white sails on the frigate soaked up the sun, growing brighter and brighter until they seemed to glow, giving off their own light, dazzling in its brilliance and cloaking the ship in an aura of invincibility. The beauty of the spectacle far overshadowed the inept sail handling and sloppy seamanship exhibited by the inexperienced crew.

The young man, the left sleeve of his blue midshipman's jacket pinned to his shoulder, noticed and commented to his pretty wife who held a sleeping child in her arms.

"There's going to be some sorrow come to that ship, and this town, before the day is out. Cap'n Lawrence ain't had but two weeks to put a crew together and get that vessel fitted out for sea. He ain't fired a gun or set a sail with them misfits he's got aboard. You mark my words, Elizabeth, there's going to be . . ."

"Oh, Philip. You have become so wearisome since *Constitution* returned. Perhaps had you not been wounded so terribly you would feel differently. You can not assume that just because that ship is the *Chesapeake* and not your beloved *Constitution* she won't carry the day. I am sure that Captain Lawrence is equally as competent as Commodore Bainbridge, and the men can not possibly be as bad as you say or, I dare say, Captain Lawrence would not have gone out. He had to know the British ship was waiting for him out there. Can you hold little William while I spread out the blanket?" The young woman carefully handed the baby into her husband's good arm and shook out the blanket she had brought to sit on while the spectacle unfolded before them. "And besides," she added when they had sat down, Philip still holding the baby, "Captain Lawrence, it is said, was positively brilliant during the engagements he had while on *Hornet*. Did he not entice that British sloop — *Peacock*, was it not? — to come out of a neutral harbor and engage him? And then beat them so mercilessly that ultimately he had to sink what was left? No, Philip, I think you are mistaken; this will be a wonderful victory and yet another feather in Captain Lawrence's cap. You'll see."

"Look how sloppy she trims, Elizabeth. Her sails still ain't set proper and some of her guns are already run out. When that British frigate comes after her, that ship is gonna come apart. I heard just the other day that even without a full crew, Cap'n Lawrence was goin' to sea. Most everyone thinks the ship's unlucky on top of it, and some say that's why she can't get men to sail her. There's a passel of sailors off *Constitution* aboard her on account of Lawrence needed some sailormen to teach all those landsmen to set sail and fight the ship, but I'd warrant they ain't trained yet. I got a bad feelin' about this one, Elizabeth. I hope I'm wrong, but the past year an' more on *Constitution* taught me some lessons I learned good. An' that ship ain't ready to fight."

Elizabeth busied herself with the baby, and ignored her "worrisome" husband. Soon she was caught up in the excitement and spirit of the crowd around them, and forgot about his dire misgivings. In the distance, the people could see the sails of the British frigate, dingy and sea-stained as she headed on a southerly course to cut off the American. The fight could only be a few hours away, and people excitedly pointed out various features of both ships, and spoke most positively of the anticipated results of the conflict. A few of the people on the hillside opened hampers, and spread out picnics on their blankets, making a festive atmosphere even more so. Of course there were ample spirits flowing as the men wagered on the rapidity with which Captain Lawrence would bring the British to heel.

*   *   *   *   *   *

Robert Coleman and Jake Tate, both aloft on the main tops'l yard, watched the chaos on deck as landsmen and seamen from *Constitution* tried unsuccessfully to merge with the Chesapeakes of the last cruise to make a cohesive, functional unit. Confusion reigned and Bosun Clements, along with the freshly minted lieutenants and the few midshipmen, harangued and bullied them without regard to their backgrounds. Ahead and to the north, the topmen could see quite plainly their adversary, some fifteen miles off, and sailing south on the starboard tack.

"Robert, I got a real bad feelin' 'bout this. Cap'n Lawrence is a-strainin' at his lines to take on that frigate yonder. I can't figger how this bunch of misfits gonna be able to fight without they ain't had no time to learn even where they's stations at when quarters is sounded."

"Aye, Jake. I'm with you there, lad, but at least we got mostly a full crew. Though God alone knows where they come from. That bunch from *Constitution* what come over with Tim seems to know what they're about, but this ain't *Constitution*, and I'm guessin' that they gonna be needin' some time to . . ."

"Aloft there! Stations to set stu'ns'ls fore an' main." The bosun's voice floated up to the men perched on the yards as already the necessary spars were being swayed into position. Coleman shook his head.

"Crowding on more canvas so we can close with 'em faster. Seems like this breeze is fadin' on top of it. All right men, let's get that stu'ns'l yard set. They'll be sendin' up the canvas quick as ever they can, you can be sure."

The topman's observation on the wind was right on the mark; it was indeed dropping and the frigate's speed with it. As they finished with the additional sails, the topmen could hear the piping call for dinner and grog and, to a man, as they climbed down or slid down the backstay, each thought there might be a reprieve from what they had feared would be their destiny. Tate voiced it for all of them.

"Mebbe with this wind dyin' off like it be, we ain't gonna be up with 'em afore dark, an' we can slip by without they's seein' us. Get us up toward Nova Scotia an' take some merchant prizes afore we haveta fight one o' they's frigates."

"Have a look, would ya, at them wee vessels what's followin' us out. Lookin' for a show, I'd reckon. Must be three score an' more." The topmen heard their old shipmate, gunner's mate Tim Conoughy, talking to another as they made their way forward to the mess. Tim's Irish brogue was instantly recognizable, and Coleman caught up to him.

"Tim, you old dog, what of the guns? Any of 'em able to fire?" The continuing good-natured controversy between the gunners and the topmen would never cease, even in the face of an upcoming engagement. The comment was tinged with a nervous laugh and a forced smile.

"Well Robert, I surely do hope so, or your arse up yonder won't be worth a tin shillin'. Without my guns, you lot aloft there won't be seein' a friendly face for a while, I'd warrant. If that frigate really is *Shannon* like what the lads say, I'd say you better be prayin' real 'ard that my guns, and the others as well, be workin' right perfect."

The Irish gunner's face split into a broad grin as he clapped a hand on his friend's shoulder. "With all that canvas you got set up there — royals and stu'ns'ls, indeed — we're surely 'eadin' pell mell right into the devil's maw as quick as ever Cap'n Lawrence can take us. I hope 'e don't think 'e's back on *Hornet* takin' on the little *Peacock*. These lads'll fight, but they need time on the guns."

Dinner was a quiet affair; the men finished their meal and grog, and in twos and threes, drifted back onto the spar deck, watching the British frigate draw closer, as the fleet of small craft which followed the American ship set more sail to keep up, not wanting to miss a second of the upcoming action. The men formerly of *Constellation* and before that, the privateer *Glory*, stood at the weather bulwark on the fo'c'sle, each lost in his own private thoughts. Clements looked aloft and spoke for the first time.

"You think Cap'n Lawrence's afraid o' havin' the ensign shot down? He's got three of 'em flyin'. Lookee there, will ya . . . there's one up on the mizzen royal 's'well as one at the peak o' the gaff. And there, even on the main yard he's got one."

"Aye, Jack, but that one for'ard gonna get some attention from them Brits — "Free Trade an' Sailors' Rights." Ain't seen that one afore. Course, I ain't been in the Navy long, neither." Tate pointed at the fore royal masthead as he spoke and his mates followed his finger to the large white flag inscribed with the slogan that had become the battle-cry of the past year. No one else spoke; they, with most of the others on deck, were deep within themselves, and the ship, save for the gentle sounds of the wind through the rigging and the water hissing quietly by below, was shrouded in an eerie silence. The two men-o'-war continued to close.

At a few minutes before five o'clock, Captain Lawrence gave the order to shorten down, and the topmen scrambled aloft to hand the royals, t'gallants and stu'ns'ls. The royal yards and stu'ns'l booms were lowered to the deck. They could see *Shannon* had altered her course to the southeast and also reduced sail to jib, tops'ls and spanker, her fighting sail, a clear indication of what was to come. The ships were some fifteen miles off Boston Light and still separated by more than five miles. *Chesapeake* beat to quarters and ran out her guns. From his station aloft, Robert Coleman heard the familiar beat of "Heart of Oak" drifting faintly across the water as the British frigate followed suit, and he recalled his years in the Royal Navy.

The *Shannon,* showing the effects of long periods at sea without a major refit, looked shabby. Her sides were now a dull black, streaked with salt and a year's worth of crud, the yellow band below her gun ports had faded badly, and her sails were yellowed and stained from countless days patrolling the New England coast. For a brief minute, Coleman hoped that the poor appearance might be an indication of her fighting ability, but quickly realized the opposite would likely hold true; if she had been so long at sea, her crew must be trained and capable and he silently prayed that the Chesapeakes would be up to the task ahead.

A forward wind'ard gun fired suddenly on the American ship, a signal they intended to fight, and *Shannon* immediately answered it, then hauled her wind and hove to, waiting for them to engage. Coleman and Tate, both assigned as breech haulers on the number fourteen gun, jumped as the sound reverberated on the quiet sea. Orders came from the quarterdeck to change sails as the wind backed to the southwesterly and freshened. *Shannon* was now also making a sail change and turned back to the south, paralleling the American's course and just within the range of an eighteen-pounder long gun. After his ship had way on, the British captain ordered the spanker brailed up and again lay to, waiting to the American to make the first move.

"Would you look at that, Jake. That bastard's just waitin' for us." Coleman was incredulous at the action of the British frigate and mentally compared what he saw with what he imagined Captain Winston of HMS *Orpheus,* his last Royal Navy frigate, might have done. Winston, he reckoned, would have gone straight at 'em and begun firing as quick as his guns could find the range. This captain and his shabby vessel were playing at something he didn't understand. And Lawrence held the weather gauge. The topmen returned to their gun posts — and waited.

"Looks like we're gonna bear off some, then round up under 'er stern and rake 'er, by God! Watch, Jake, and you'll likely see something glorious to be'old." Coleman had enough experience in naval battles to recognize what would happen. But it didn't.

At a few minutes before six o'clock, at a distance within easy musket range, a shot from one of the *Shannon* marines in British maintop rang out. And Lawrence's voice from *Chesapeake*'s quarterdeck followed before the sound had faded, heard clearly fore and aft. "FIRE AS SHE BEARS, LADS! *PEACOCK* HER! *PEACOCK* HER!"

Gun fourteen spoke first and put a ball into the stern of their quarry. A cheer rose from the crew as they saw their shot go home.

Lawrence realized as he gave the order to fire that *Chesapeake* was going fast enough to pass by the English ship before he could fire a full broadside. In the next breath, he ordered his ship luffed up some instead of bearing off to pass behind his enemy, to enable the American ship to fire an unanswerable raking broadside. As *Chesapeake*'s sails shivered, a full broadside from *Shannon* rent the air, filling the short distance between the two with dense smoke, splinters and screams. The battle had become general and the ships tore at each other in a deafening cacophony of thunderous claps of cannon fire, shattering yellow pine bulwarks, screams of wounded and dying men, and falling rigging.

With *Shannon*'s second broadside, *Chesapeake*'s jib sheets were cut, her fore tops'l chains shot away allowing the yard to drop into the lifts, and her spanker brails were likewise cut. The spanker billowed out against the rigging and, in combination with the loss of his jibs, prevented Lawrence from passing out of stays and regaining way on his ship. Worse, however, was the loss of his wheel; in a cloud of splinters and blood, the great wheel had simply disappeared, the two helmsmen with it. And the American frigate hung helplessly in stays, her larboard quarter exposed to the *Shannon*'s raking fire. Lawrence's misadventure had enabled the English captain to gain a telling advantage and fire unanswerable raking broadsides into *Chesapeake*'s stern and quarter.

Hopelessly in stays, the *Chesapeake* began to slip astern, her whole deck vulnerable to the deadly, accurate fire from *Shannon*. The British captain had ordered grape and canister shot along with the ball, intending to win the day by decimating the crew rather than destroying the vessel. It told. The carnage was terrible; more than fifty men were killed immediately and over seventy were wounded. Guns dismounted from their carriages along the larboard side of the ship as British shot hammered in bulwarks and then the guns themselves. The American decks ran thick with gore; blood and unidentifiable bits of flesh spattered remaining bulwarks, masts, and gun carriages. The dead and wounded lay where they landed, hands unable to get them below to the surgeon quickly enough. The sand spread around the decks prior to the battle to soak up the slippery blood had become saturated and ineffective; the scuppers and open gunports released a steady stream of crimson into the sea.

Tim Conoughy's number eight gun flew into the air as an eighteen-pound ball scored a direct hit. More than half his crew lay dead with two seriously wounded. Conoughy, spared through pure luck as he stepped away to grab a fresh linstock from the sand bucket, picked up one of the wounded and moved him gently to the foot of the foremast. The words he shouted to the man over the din went unheard; he was already dead. Conoughy saw he was needed on number twelve and moved quickly to help, replacing the gun captain killed by musket fire from the maintop of *Shannon*. He grabbed a sailor standing in stunned immobility by a fire bucket and roughly shoved him toward the after breeching tackle on the gun. He quickly organized what was left of the crew and tried to sight the gun at the bow of the British frigate. It would not bear and the Irishman ran aft, looking to find a gun that would help the American cause. He saw his ship was crippled, in stays, and desperately wounded. He caught up with Lieutenants Cox and Blanchard, both heading for the quarterdeck and spattered with the blood of their gun crews, just as another broadside thundered out from *Shannon*.

The trio reached the quarterdeck where Captain Lawrence, blood running from a wound in his shoulder, was trying unsuccessfully to regain control of his ship just as a marksman's ball fired from the foretop of *Shannon* struck him in the stomach. He fell and Cox, seeing his beloved commander down, rushed to his side. First Lieutenant Augustus Ludlow, himself wounded and bleeding, shouted to Cox.

"Get him below and then get back to your post. See the surgeon gets to him quick as he can. You there, gunners mate, lend a hand with Cap'n Lawrence."

The ship slipped backwards and, with a grinding crunch heard over the now almost continuous British cannon fire, fouled her larboard aft channel and mizzen shrouds in *Shannon*'s starboard bow anchor. The two were joined. Men moved quickly on the fo'c'sle of the British ship to secure the two so the fouled American could not get away.

Lieutenant Cox and Gunners Mate Conoughy carried the twice-wounded Lawrence to the companionway. The captain called out, "Don't give up the ship, lads; fight her as long as she will swim!" They took him below to the surgeons where he repeated again and again his orders, "Never surrender; don't give up the ship!"

On deck, the forward guns of *Shannon* continued to pour a staggering fire into the helpless American; not one of the *Chesapeake*'s guns spoke in return. Those that weren't dismounted either would not bear or had no crew to man them. Aloft, marksmen on both ships fired into the deck of the other, killing and wounding sailors and officers alike. But the men on *Chesapeake* bore the brunt of the punishment, falling dead or wounded like leaves before the gale.

On the American quarterdeck, First Lieutenant Ludlow saw an opportunity. He cried out for seaman Brown to blow the bugle Lawrence had given him and then bellowed, "Boarders, boarders away! Board 'em lads and we'll carry the day!"

Brown was unable to draw a single note from the instrument and Ludlow's command went unheard in the horrendous din of the battle. And the young lieutenant fell, wounded more severely this time by a splinter thrown up from the railing of the quarterdeck. He was carried below as British boarders responded to their captain who was rallying his own boarding party on *Shannon*'s fo'c'sle with the cry, "Follow me who can!"

The British sailors, officers, and midshipmen rallied behind their captain who had leaped onto *Shannon*'s railing and, without a look behind him, scrambled over *Chesapeake*'s shattered bulwark and onto the quarterdeck brandishing his sword and pistol. As he landed on the American ship, he dispatched a seaman who blocked his way and then another with an efficiency born of years with the sword. Nearly fifty Shannons followed, including the first lieutenant and two midshipmen. What remained of the Chesapeakes were driven forward and off the quarterdeck in fierce hand to hand fighting.

Coleman and Tate, freed from their unserviceable gun and with no chores aloft, grabbed up cutlasses from the rack at the foot of the mainmast and ran to the spardeck.

"Jake! Keep an eye out for Mister Blanchard, lad; 'e'll know what to do. Watch to your left . . . oh my God. . . throw me that pike. . . oh God . . Jake, back up, they's more comin' . . ." The scream of wounded men from both sides of the fray, mixed with the ring of steel on steel and underscored by the now sporadic musket firing drowned out most of Coleman's words. He and Jake fought side by side, gradually driven forward along *Chesapeake*'s spar deck.

"Robert . . . I am hit! Oh God, it hurts . . . my arm . . ." Tate screamed for his mate as he fell against the mainmast, clutching what remained of his shattered right arm. His cutlass clattered to the deck as two British seamen, seeing him go down, left him and moved on forward immediately engaging the next American sailors they encountered. Coleman ran to his friend's side.

"'ang on there, Jake. I'll get you below. The surgeon'll take care o' that quick as you please." Robert struggled to pick up his wounded American shipmate with his free hand and dragged him toward a companionway. The hatch was blocked with American sailors fighting hand to hand with British and making heavy weather of it. Robert set Jake down by the starboard bulwark and leaped into the melee. Jack Clements, blood spattered over his bare arms and shirt-front, was in the thick of it, wielding a discharged pistol like a cudgel and cracking British skulls as fast as he could swing. Still, the Americans gave ground.

Suddenly a cheer went up from the quarterdeck, followed almost at once by a thunderous roar of British cannon fire. Coleman, Clements, and the other Americans stopped in mid-stride to look aft. The Blue Ensign of the Royal Navy had been raised to the mizzen peak, below the American flag.

Seeing the visible indication of an American triumph Bosun Clements cried out, "We're carryin' 'em boys, keep it up." He emphasized his words by landing the butt of his pistol on a convenient head and laid out an enemy midshipman who went down without a sound. A cutlass flashed in the rays of the late afternoon sun and Clements let out a mighty roar as the blade neatly sliced off the majority of his right ear; blood poured out and mingled with the blood of others covering his arms and shirt. The bosun whirled, seeking his attacker, and the action saved him from another stroke of the cutlass. He parried with the pistol and kicked out with his left foot. The blow doubled the sailor over and Clements followed his kick with a stroke to the back of the man's head with the barrel of his spent pistol. Suddenly the deafening thunder of the cannonading was gone; the silence gradually became complete to the deafened seamen as even the clash of steel and wood ended as the men realized that the battle was over. The mistake with the flags had been corrected. Now the Blue Ensign of the Royal Navy flew above the American flag.

The Shannons had indeed carried the day. With the Americans

driven forward and below, the resistance died out and the English sailors and officers moved unimpeded about the quarterdeck and spar deck of USS *Chesapeake*, hampered only by the wreckage of what had once been her crew.

Robert Coleman knelt by his friend and spoke. "Looks like you was right, Jake. We couldn't carry 'em. Lookee there, though, would you. Looks like that cove — must be their captain — is down. Aye, and there's another of 'em whats down yonder. I reckon we 'urt 'em some."

Indeed, as the British sailors and officers rounded up the Americans, putting on them the same manacles laid out on *Chesapeake* for the British prisoners, Coleman could see several of the Brits carrying their captain back to the English frigate. He looked about him.

"Oh, Jake. They took a terrible toll from us. They's dead and 'urt Chesapeakes lyin' all about the decks 'ere. Couldn't be more 'an a 'andful of us not 'urt."

"You there, back off a bit. We'll get your friend to the medico, though it don't look like 'e's long for this world to me. Lost a lot of blood, 'e did, it looks. Won't need manacles for you, lad; with that arm busted up like it is you ain't gonna give us no trouble. 'ere, boy, get yourself up then and it's below with you. No trouble now. You lads give us enough trouble already. 'ere — move away now. Your friend's gonna get to the surgeon right quick." The British sailors pushed Coleman away and, taking him by the arms, led him to the hatch. Coleman looked over his shoulder and called to his barely conscious shipmate.

"It's goin' to be righty-oh, Jake. Surgeon'll fix you up quick as ever 'e can."

"What 'ave we got 'ere? A British tar in an American uniform? You get you below, an' no trouble now. 'Ow many more of ya are there, eh? 'Ere now, stick out them paws while I show you 'ow these manacles work." After tightly clamping Coleman's wrists in the iron manacles, the British seaman roughly shoved him down the companionway and shouted to a midshipman nearby. "Mister Littlejohn, lookee 'ere, would ya? We got us a Englishman fightin' on the wrong side, it 'ppears."

Within a short while, the *Chesapeake*'s decks held only Shannons. The American crew had all been herded below and a small cannon, loaded with grape, had been dragged over to the hatch to discourage any who might think it prudent to return to the deck.

*   *   *   *   *   *

All over the grassy hill people strained to see why the firing had stopped, and each sought confirmation of Lawrence's victory.

"They've separated . . . there . . . you see . . . can you tell what happened?"

"Who's got a long glass . . . Tell us what's happening . . ."

"I can't hear any firing. Lawrence must've carried the day quick as he did in *Hornet.*"

"Pass that glass over this way . . . let me have a look."

The same conversations were repeated at each vantage point around Boston. No one was sure what exactly had happened, but they all knew beyond a shadow of a doubt that they had witnessed yet another American triumph. Celebratory dinners were being planned in anticipation of the victory parties that would take place later. In The Presidents' Coffee House, plans were being laid to fete Captain Lawrence and his brave crew in a triumphal parade through the city streets.

Philip and Elizabeth sat silently, young William asleep on his mother's breast. The former *Constitution* midshipman, who had experienced naval battles and indeed, had lost his arm in the action against HMS *Java,* was not ready to celebrate; what he had witnessed did not seem right to him. He again voiced his concerns to his pretty wife.

"I ain't convinced that Cap'n Lawrence carried the day, Elizabeth. I don't think the Brit would have struck as quick as he appears to and it don't look to me like theys much damage to either vessel." He shook his head in consternation. "If only they'd been another league closer in."

A man, who had begun celebrating the American victory even before a shot was fired, staggered by with a long glass under his arm.

"Excuse me, sir. Might I have the loan of your glass for a moment or two?" Philip extended his good arm and took the telescope from the unsteady passerby.

"Shure, lad. Help yershelf. Wounded, eh? You a hero? Can't deny a naval hero the ushe o' me glash. Haven't got a glash o' your own — maybe sompin' wet — to trade me for it, have ye?"

Philip, concentrating on the scene that materialized through the telescope, barely heard the drunk's mumbled words as the man sat on the grass and waited either for the return of his long glass or a glass of grog to be offered. Neither was forthcoming.

"Oh my God, Elizabeth . . ."

"Philip, I have asked you repeatedly not to blaspheme in front of me or the baby. Now if you can't say what you have to without taking the Lord's name in vain, then you may keep your own council." Elizabeth looked at her husband the way one might look at a recalcitrant child who was a little slow.

"Listen to me, woman." Philip's voice was suddenly hard; Elizabeth recoiled involuntarily, her mouth agape. "There are two flags on *Chesapeake*; the British ensign over the American. Means Lawrence has lost his ship. We have not carried the day. Quite the opposite. Oh, what a disaster!" A stunned silence from those nearby lasted only a heartbeat, and then with a rush, dozens of voices began to speak at once.

"Here, lad, give me that glass. You don't know what you're looking at."

"Lawrence couldn't have lost. He's among the best we've got."

"You must have lost your eyesight with your arm, lad. Hand me that glass. Let a man have a look."

"Everyone knows that Brits couldn't carry an American frigate, and certainly not one commanded by Cap'n Jim."

The voices merged into a senseless cacophony of disjointed words and sounds that swirled around the young midshipman's head. He was lost in his own thoughts. Lawrence had lost! He couldn't believe it. His incredulity turned to outrage that such a travesty had been visited upon the American Navy and then just rage, first at the British for taking advantage of an untried, untrained American crew, then at Lawrence, or taking such a crew to sea with the certain knowledge that a seasoned British frigate was waiting for him.

Slowly the realization rippled through the crowd. Conversation died down and the stunned people began to pick up their belongings and head silently down the hill for home and a quiet supper to discuss this ignominy and disgrace in the privacy of their own homes and coffee shops. There would be no celebrations this night.

CHAPTER SEVENTEEN

"Aye, we seen a passel of small craft all around us last night. Real late, it was. Some was yellin' somethin' 'bout *Chesapeake* and a battle, but couldn't make much o' what they was sayin'" Isaac Biggs leaned over the *General Washington's* larboard bulwark along with Bosun Dobson. They were talking with a pair of men drifting alongside in a fishing smack.

"Well, I can tell you this, brother. Me an' me mate here, we was out there, and it was some kind o' terrible. Them Brits just kept a poundin' an' poundin' the *Chesapeake*. Cap'n Jim had his riggin' all cut up and couldn't get the frigate through stays. Seems like it wasn't any time 'tall 'til them British bastards swarmed all over him and, short-handed like he was, he couldn't fight 'em off. Reckon he hadda strike to save his men, an' the ship. Terrible, it were, just terrible." The captain of the fishing boat shook his head. The two privateersmen noticed with surprise that the fisherman actually had tears in his eyes as he recounted the disaster that had befallen the *Chesapeake*.

"That musta been what them two big vessels we steered clear of last night when we was comin' in was, Mister Biggs. Thought they looked too big to be privateers — even in the dark." Dobson scratched his head thoughtfully as he recalled that Captain Rogers had made a wide detour around the two vessels in the early morning hours, as the *General* returned to Salem from another successful cruise. All thought it strange that they were showing lights on their decks, but Asa Rogers wasn't about to close them to investigate, no matter how strange it appeared.

"I reckon we should pass that on to Cap'n Rogers, Bosun. Might be that it changes his plans." Biggs started aft to act on his thought.

The two met Captain Rogers as he unfolded his lanky frame from the aft companionway and, as was his habit, looked first aloft, and then around the deck of his ship before speaking to anyone. All appeared in order.

"What's on your mind, Mister Biggs?"

"Well Cap'n, Dobson an' me just got done talkin' with some coves in that fishin' boat yonder," Isaac pointed to the vessel now full and by in the easy northwesterly breeze and heading past Salem Neck, "an' thought you might be interested in what they had to say. Sounded to us like Cap'n Lawrence took *Chesapeake* out yesterday and got hisself beat pretty bad by some British frigate — HMS *Shannon*, it was. I believe that was the self-same vessel Dickerson an' me run afoul of back in February, bringin' in that Brit merchant from up off Nova Scotia. Didn't think she was still around these waters. Wonder what's gonna happen to Lawrence an' his crew. Guess what's left o' the *Chesapeake*'ll be taken in, prob'ly to Halifax, be my guess."

Asa Rogers looked thoughtfully at the now distant fishing vessel, the bearer of this awful news, and came rapidly to a decision as to his course of action — at least an immediate one. He turned to the bosun.

"Mister Dobson, have my boat put overboard, if you please, and round up enough of a crew to get me ashore. I shall leave directly you're ready."

A quick nod, and the bosun hurried off to find the boat crew and get the boat in the water. Something was afoot; he was sure Captain Rogers didn't go ashore this early, even first day back in Salem after a prize-rich cruise. Why, the crew hadn't even been called to breakfast, and he was certain the captain had not eaten either.

The daylight was gradually getting stronger as the Bosun knocked on the Cabin door, informing the captain all was in readiness for his departure.

"Mister Biggs," called Rogers as he stepped into the waist of his ship. "I should like you to accompany me." He gestured toward the boat as he spoke and the third, his surprise evident but unspoken, stepped over the rail and climbed down the battens on the hull and into the boat. Captain Rogers followed, settled himself in the stern-sheets, and the boat shoved off.

As the boat neared the quay, the captain and his third mate could see a group of men standing in a knot at about the point where the boat would land; from their pointing and gesturing, it was obvious that they were in deep and serious conversation about something. Even before the *General*'s cutter was close aboard, their voices could be heard as the light breeze wafted bits and snatches of their more boisterous exclamations over the water. Rogers spoke to the cox'n and the cutter turned slightly and drifted gently against the pier at the feet of the men. They stopped their debate, and looked at the intruders with unwelcoming glares.

"Jack Criswell! That you?" Rogers spoke to a portly fellow, balding and unshaven, with the red veined, swollen nose of a habitual drinker. Then he stepped out of the boat and into the space the men opened for him, followed closely by his third mate. The man he identified as Criswell broke from the group and made his way toward the captain with his hand out in greeting.

"Cap'n Asa. Good to see you back, sir. I collect you've heard the dreadful news of yesterday?"

One of the others in the group spoke up. "It ain't been established it's 'dreadful' yet, Jack. We ain't got nothin' but the word o' some half blind an' more 'an a little drunk fisherman what claims to been out there. Cap'n Jim mighta took that Brit and'll be bringin' her in this morning. They's a lot what thinks that's the case. You go spreadin' that 'dreadful' news around Salem, folks won't know what to believe."

"Hell's fire, Sam. You saw that blue ensign up over the American one clear's I did. Ain't no mistakin' what that means." He turned back to Rogers and Biggs. "You just come in, Cap'n? You musta come right by them two out yonder."

"Aye, we did that, Jack. Come by 'em in the dark of the night, it was. I give 'em a good berth, bein' as how I was short-handed from sending in a couple o' prizes just last week. So we couldn't tell just what they was; surely two vessels of notable size, they was, and showin' lights like they didn't care who seen 'em. Thought it mighta been a pair of Brits and, with a short crew, I wasn't gonna get in close to 'em. Heard about the battle just this morning from a fisherman headin' out past where the *General* is anchored. Kinda hoped I'd see them two prizes I sent in already here in Salem. Figgerin' on startin' the process to get 'em condemned, collect my lads, and get back to sea. You haven't seen Hardy or Dickerson of late, have you? They'da been the ones brought in the prizes."

He looked at the handful of men and shrugged when he saw

their blank looks. Criswell shook his head and Rogers continued, "Well, maybe they went into Marblehead or Gloucester. By the way, this here's my third on the *General*, Isaac Biggs. A Marblehead lad, and a fine sailor. Isaac, this is Jack Criswell. He runs this dock and the warehouses beyond. Ain't nothing comes or goes without he knows about it. Wouldn't be any trade outta Salem without Jack's help."

Criswell visibly grew in stature, adjusted his soiled vest where it strained its buttons over his ample middle, and beamed at Rogers' praise. He was, in point of fact, barely more than a watchman and occasionally organized hands to help unload a vessel for the Crowninshields' and Derby's. A long career of unreliability brought about by an equally long love affair with rum ended a promising term at sea, and it was through the kindness of several of the Salem merchants, including Asa Rogers, that he held the menial position on the waterfront that he did.

"Cap'n Asa, you be wantin' to know more 'bout that fight yesterday, you might find Dick Waters over to the Anchor Coffee House. He was comin' in yesterday from a trip an' come right by them two durin' the fight. Stayed to watch, I reckon, and came to anchor durin' the middle watch last night, it were. He'd likely give you a better story 'an anyone; be pleased to tell 'bout what he seen, I'd warrant."

"Thank you kindly, Jack. I reckon young Isaac and I'll head over that way and see what's afoot. It's some sharp-set I am anyway, and we can get a bite o' breakfast at the same time." He turned to the boat crew, still bobbing alongside the quay. "Davies, you get yourselves back out to the *General* and be back here at four bells o' the forenoon watch. Tell Mister Coffin to keep a watch out for Mister Hardy and Mister Dickerson, if you please, as they could turn up today."

The boat shoved off from the quay. Without a backward glance, Rogers stepped off for the coffee house and information, both about the possibility of his prizes having come in, and about the outcome of the battle which seemed so uncertain in the minds of his first shore-side contacts. Isaac, watching the boat leave, had to hurry to catch up.

*   *   *   *   *   *

Tate stirred in his swinging cot and rolled onto his heavily bandaged arm. The move brought a groan to his lips and blood to the surface of the cloth binding the wound.

"Easy there, Jake. You're gonna be just fine, I'd warrant. Medico didn't have to take your arm off, after all. Just sewed it up near good's the sailmaker could'a. Ball passed right through, it did. Chewed it up some, an' the surgeon said your bone took a beatin', but it'd heal up righty-oh. Reckon you'll be aloft again afore you know it." Bosun Clements was sitting on a sea chest next to his young shipmate's cot in the crowded and reeking sick bay. Moans and cries of the more seriously wounded could be heard and already the smell of morbidity and wounds turning putrid pervaded the close atmosphere. Combined with the smoke from a pair of whale oil lamps swaying gently from the overhead and the tobacco some of the less seriously wounded used, the fetid air had a palpable quality to it which the open scuttle and windscoop did little to ameliorate. The *Chesapeake* moved easily under plain sail, close-hauled and heading northeast in the company of her captor, HMS *Shannon*. A British crew manned her decks.

Jake Tate opened his eyes at the Bosun's words and looked around. The sight of the crowded sick bay registered slowly, and he looked at Clements.

"We got us a passel o' men hurt, huh, Jack? Guess they took us. What'd you figger gonna happen now? And what happened to your head?"

Clements touched the bandage wrapped round his head and over the place where his right ear had been. "Nothing to speak of lad. Some Brit cove decided I'd be better off with but one ear and got me from behind when I was busy stroking a pistol across th' head o' one o' his damn midshipmen. Likely won't cause me no problem, 'ceptin' lookin' a mite peculiar. Probably won't be as pretty to the women ashore, neither." Clements laughed hollowly at his disfigurement. "Reckon you'll be drinkin' on that arm o' your'n for a while too, lad. As to what happened yesterday; aye, they took us, just like you thought. An' took us hard. I heard over a hunert Chesapeakes was killed, an' damn near as many wounded. Some pretty bad. Cap'n Lawrence was hurt bad and Mister Ludlow as well. Haven't took notice of Mister Blanchard since they boarded us, so I don't know his fate. 'Sides, they put the officers on *Shannon*. Surgeon tol' me they got the British lads from our crew over there's well. Reckon things won't go well for 'em, what with fightin' against they's countrymen." His words were punctuated with the moans of the wounded and the occasional sound of hammering and pounding on deck as the work to put *Chesapeake* to rights continued apace.

"You get you some sleep, lad, an' I'll be by later to have a look at you." Clements stood and saw that the young man was already dozing off, still affected by the laudanum administered by the surgeon. He moved aft, past the canvas curtain rigged to separate the expanded hospital from the gundeck and, nodding to the Royal Marine posted there, he climbed up the ladder to the spar deck.

The bulwarks had been mended and the foremast fished where a ball had taken a bite from it. Knotting and splicing continued and he could see that the jibs and their sheets had been replaced. He shook his head as the recollection of their loss and its impact on the outcome passed through his mind. Had they remained intact, Lawrence might have been able to maintain control of the frigate and raked the British ship as they passed across her bow. Then boarded when the Americans were ready to board rather than as it happened. He looked across the water to HMS *Shannon*, sailing to weather and ahead of their prize. She didn't look any the worse for the wear, he thought, but then recalled the Chesapeakes had only gotten off one real broadside before the British fire had knocked out so many of their guns. And the crews were untrained and unable to recover from the withering grape and canister, not to mention the confusion wrought by the accurate fire from the Royal Marines in the British tops. The bosun remembered seeing his friend Tim Conoughy trying in vain to rally some men to man one of the long eighteen-pounders just as the British came aboard, led by their captain. After that, the confusion of hand to hand fighting with its screaming, shouting, chaotic dance macabre and the overwhelming numbers of enemy on their deck blotted out any specific event, save for his felling a young officer with a blow from a discharged pistol and receiving, in his turn, a cutlass stroke from an unknown assailant. As he relived the horror in his mind, he saw again the decks running red and bodies and parts of bodies lying about as if cast off by a spoiled child. Mostly Chesapeakes, it now occurred to him. He remembered the sudden stunning pain in his head as the cutlass took his right ear and he touched the bandaged wound tentatively, as if to confirm his recollection.

""Ere! What's actin' 'ere? You ain't 'sposed to be up 'ere, sailor.

You'd best be gettin' yourself back below. Don't want any trouble from you Jonathans now, so just get you gone, move it along." The British midshipman serving as first lieutenant on the prize crew nudged Clements with his dirk as he spoke to emphasize his order.

The bosun whirled around and, before he thought, grabbed the hand holding the short blade and twisted it. With a clatter, the dirk fell and the young mid cried out, more in surprise than in pain. Clements realized what he had done almost as soon as he did it and, with a muttered apology, bent and picked up the boy's blade, turned it and offered it to him, handle first.

"You'd be gettin' stripes at the gratin' for what you just did, were you not a prisoner," the boy uttered through clenched teeth as the color returned to his face. "I reckon you'll learn some respect at Melville Island. Aye, they'll teach you your place and no mistake!" He turned and strutted aft toward the quarterdeck, returning the dirk to its scabbard as nonchalantly as he could. Only his eyes, darting about the deck, betrayed his nervousness over his first face to face encounter with an American.

Clements stepped back over to the bulwark, noting that the deck was still a mess and, in spite of the efforts of the prize crew and a few of the unhurt American seamen, still showed dark stains and other signs of the previous evening's carnage. He tried to recall who had been killed and knew that the number was high, very high indeed, given the short duration of the battle. He had heard from the surgeon who dressed his head that from the first shot — he did remember with a smile that it had come from *Chesapeake* — to the raising of the Blue Ensign over the American flag was only a matter of fifteen minutes. That was how the old *Glory* and the other privateers used to do it: sharp and decisive. He had thought the Navy stood off and pounded each other 'til one or the other capitulated.

Guess I still got me a fair bit a learnin' 'bout the Navy, he thought. *Hope I get me the chance. What's this "Melville Island" all about? Must be a prison or the like.*

As his thoughts ran through the gamut of random images, his glance shifted aft and fell upon the mizzen gaff and the blue ensign gently whipping above the American flag; his countenance darkened perceptibly and the scowl that crossed his face caused the pain from his wound to flair.

Damme, he thought to himself, *ain't that a hurtful sight? Just don't sit right, seein' them flags like that.*

He tore his eyes away and turned forward again, gazing absently out over the water at the British frigate sailing quietly along under easy sail. *Wonder if they's any officers still alive.*

His thoughts turned to the British sailors in *Chesapeake*'s crew; besides Coleman and Conoughy, he knew there were at least three others, maybe more. But he had no idea if any survived. He thought he recalled seeing the Irishman carrying Captain Lawrence below just before the British sailors swarmed aboard, but he had not seen Robert Coleman after the action had begun so didn't know whether he was alive, wounded, or dead in the melee. He shook his head slowly. *Gonna go hard on them. Might even get 'emselves hung. Brits ain't gonna take real kindly to their own fightin' 'em from an American ship.*

CHAPTER EIGHTEEN

"So you're of the opinion that Cap'n Lawrence was taken and his ship sore wounded, eh?" Rogers sat with a neatly dressed man, older by all appearances and, from the set of his eyes and the weathered look to his face, a seafaring man. He owned the coastal vessel *Olivia,* brig rigged, and handy as any in the shoal and tricky waters around Massachusetts Bay and Cape Cod. He had been returning to Salem from a run to Cape Cod and had witnessed the entire battle, from the moment that *Chesapeake* and *Shannon* were something more than a league apart to the end, when the British disentangled the two ships and sailed the American frigate away to begin making the repairs necessary to sail safely to Halifax. Dick Waters, his eyes hard and his jaw set, nodded grimly at Asa Rogers. One of his scarred hands rested easily around his cup of coffee, but the other was clenched into a fist so tight as to make the knuckles white.

"Sore wounded, be my opinion, Cap'n. Riggin' pretty well cut up on top of it. Streaks down her sides coulda' only been one thing, too. Wasn't close enough to be sure, but the scuppers was runnin' red by all appearances. Reckon they was a passel o' the crew what passed over to th' other side in the fight 's'well. *Shannon* didn't look like she took much of a beatin' 'tall. Noticed some bulwarks stove in, but seemed like her rig was tight an' serviceable. They was runnin' boats back an' forth 'tween the two for some time, even after it got full dark. I'd warrant they was takin' some o' the wounded over to the British vessel an' mebbe some prisoners 's'well. One thing other that I recollect: one o' my lads said he saw a' explosion near the quarterdeck o' *Chesapeake* just afore them Brits boarded, but I didn't see anything like that. Mighta been one o' them hand granadoes the Brits got a fondness for. Don't seem quite fair, you ask me. But I reckon no one did." Waters smiled slightly at his own remark, but his eyes remained flinty. He continued. "Damn shame, losin' that vessel and all them men. But I reckon . . ."

He didn't get to finish the thought; a boy ran into the coffee house, breathless and hot. He had apparently run a fair distance and had news to share, but it was nearly a minute before he could stop gasping and make coherent speech. Most of the men in the coffee house watched him struggling for his breath; some offered encouragement for him to deliver his message, but most sat patiently and waited. Finally it came.

"They's goin'. The Brits is sailin' northeast. *Chesapeake* with 'em. They ain't comin' into Boston or here . . . they's goin' away."

"Well, I reckon that answers the question 'bout who carried the day. Had Lawrence beat 'em, he'da been headin' into either here or Boston." One of the patrons in the restaurant spoke aloud, obviously referring to a previous discussion. The silence that greeted first the boy's announcement and then this man's comment was complete; to have the stunning news confirmed was more than the people wanted to hear. Gradually, talking in subdued tones, they began to leave the establishment in twos and threes, walking out and onto the quiet streets of a somber Salem.

Asa looked at his third mate, swallowed a mouthful of coffee, and said, "I got a few people to see and some things to check on, Isaac. Should you be wantin' to pay a visit to your folks for a day or so, be all right with me. You figger on bein' back here in no more'n two days. We'll likely be headin' out again quick as ever we can unless Hardy and Dickerson got into some trouble bringin' in them prizes. They oughta be showin' up today, tomorrow latest; by my reckonin' they're already a day an' more longer than I thought they'd be. I figgered to give the lads a run ashore for a day or so, anyway, and this looks like a good chance for that." He paused and looked off into the distance, ruminating over the recent turn of events. Then he went on.

"This loss of the *Chesapeake* frigate gonna put a new slant on things right quick, by my lights, and I'd warrant the folks up here gonna be more willin' to take a part in this war than ever they been. Might even stop tradin' with the Brits now. We'll have to see."

"Aye, Cap'n. I reckon my folks would be happy to see me. Been six months an' more since I been in Marblehead, so I thankee most kindly for the chance to get there. What do you think is gonna happen here-abouts now? I mean . . ."

"Well, for one thing, I'd warrant people'll stop callin' the *Chesapeake* a 'bad luck ship'. Sometimes a passel o' minor things'll build up in folks' mind that ties a ship or person to bad luck, but then when something like this happens, folks'll get behind that same man, or in this case, ship, and make 'em into a hero. And Jim Lawrence was damn near a deity to these people, 'specially after that run he had with the *Hornet*. Navy thought so too. Folks ain't gonna believe he got beat by anything short of foul play . . . you heard that Waters cove sayin' they was talk of the Brits usin' hand granadoes against the *Chesapeake*. Whether it's true or ain't, folks ain't gonna take kindly to it and they gonna figger that they's fine British friends maybe ain't so fine after all. I'll tell you this though, lad, after this shock and sadness wears thin, folks gonna be some mad — this bein' the first beatin' we've taken on the sea — and they'll be wantin' to do something about it. You mark me well on that; they'll be lookin' to hurt the Brits however they can." Rogers sincerity and conviction was telling, and Isaac figured he was likely right.

The two men stood, Rogers dropped a few coins on the table, and they stepped out onto the street. Isaac turned southward and followed the coast road, heading for Marblehead and his home, while Captain Rogers headed off to the warehouse and office complex his company maintained on the Salem waterfront.

As the *General Washington*'s third mate stepped along the road he kept a weather eye out for a passing wagon or coach on which he might catch a ride and he thought on what he had just heard from his captain and the events of the past few days.

To be sure, the loss of the frigate was serious, but his time in the Royal Navy had taught him that it was certainly not the end of the world; one ship would not make that big a difference to the final outcome of the war. On the other hand, this was the first time America had suffered a naval defeat and most of the folks he'd seen were surely stunned by the news. Acted like the war was lost just acause the frigate was taken — even in this anti-war, pro-British part of New England. Maybe Cap'n Rogers was right; maybe they'd be upset enough by Lawrence's defeat to stop tradin' with the enemy and start helpin' out with the American side of the war. Maybe some might even sign onto warships or privateers.

He thought about that, and it put him in mind of his friends from the British Navy and the American privateer, that beautiful sharp-built schooner *Glory*, that they all sailed on. "Wonder whatever happened to Coleman, Clements, and that Irish gunner, Conoughy? Probably down in the Indies, takin' British merchants and warships and gettin' rich on prize shares.

"Course," Isaac said aloud to no one — he was totally alone on the road — "I ain't doin' too bad my own self on that score. Cap'n Rogers' luck holds, an' we'll all be pretty well set." He smiled at the thought and picked up his pace some.

In time, a wagon slowed as it came upon him striding purposefully along the road. The driver looked down at the sailor, sized him up and offered him a ride. Isaac accepted with a smile and climbed into the back where two other men, obviously sailors in the Navy, sat amid coils of nets and rope. The odor wafting out identified the wagon and its owner as being in the fishing trade and, as Isaac settled himself in a corner opposite the other two, it brought back memories of his days as a lad, fishing on the Banks with his father and Mr. Rowe. It seemed so long ago and so much had happened to him in the intervening years. He was so lost in thought that he missed the words of one of the Navy men with whom he shared the bed of the wagon.

"Hey . . . I'm speakin' to you, lad." The older of the two poked Isaac in the leg, getting his mind back to the present.

"Oh, sorry mate, I didn't hear you. My mind was full and by in a fresh breeze. What was it you said?"

"I was askin' you where you was bound and what ship you come off'n."

"I'm headin' down to Marblehead to see my folks. Been out o' Salem six months an' more, an' ain't seen 'em in that time. On the *Gen'l Washington*, a private armed brig. I collect you coves are Navy?"

"Aye, got us a leave while *Constitution* gets herself refit in Boston. Headin' back now. Hope she's comin' along right smart; every man jack on her's likely ready to get back to sea, I'd warrant. When we left wasn't no decks on her, so most o' the crew'd been moved into the Navy Yard. What was left of 'em anyway. More than half had been shipped off to New York or to other ships. Reckon a passel of 'em's on *Chesapeake* with Cap'n Lawrence. Guess they'll be seein' some action long afore we do. Cap'n Lawrence's just chafin' at his lines to get to sea, I'm told. Workin' even the officers and mids, he was, to get that ship ready for sea. An' he'd only been aboard for less'n a week. Heard that from some wharf rats afore we left Charlestown."

"You ain't heard this, then: *Chesapeake* went out two days ago and got took by *Shannon*, right off'n Cape Ann. Terrible loss, it were, an' from what I heard, they was a passel what got killed — or leastaways hurt bad." Isaac shook his head and realized by the looks from the two Navy men that they must have had friends aboard. This impression was confirmed with their next words.

"Oh hell's fire, Bill, I wonder who got it. Gunners more'n likely. Poor old Hocker — he probably got hisself kilt. Wasn't none too bright, neither. Probably stood up to see what was happenin' and looked right into a British eighteen-pounder."

"Your likely right 'bout that, Sam," responded Bill. "Wasn't that Irish cove a gunner s'well? He got took over to Lawrence's ship. I recollect him sayin' he was gonna get him some action finally. Said the only action he'd seen was from the deck of a British ship 'gainst the Frenchies. He'd had a run o' bad luck, bein' on that ship down to the Chesapeake what couldn't get beyond the Capes on account o' the blockade. Kinda funny, you think on it, that he went from being in th' Chesapeake to on the *Chesapeake*, an' didn't have much in the way of luck with either one!"

"Aye, though I'd doubt he thought it funny, his own self. Cap'n Stewart just come up from Gosport. He left command o' the *Constellation*, tied up in the blockade for the quarterdeck o' the *Constitution*, what's tied up in a refit. Don't reckon he's gonna be seein' action any time soon, neither. Hell, ain't none among us gonna, what with that damn British fleet standin' off an' on day after day. Heard Decatur's got three or four blocked into New London by a seventy-four and a couple o' frigates."

The two continued to chat idly about the state of the war, while ignoring their fellow passenger. Isaac listened idly to them and it suddenly dawned on him who it was they had been talking about earlier in the conversation.

"You coves mentioned an Irishman — a gunner, you thought — come up from the Chesapeake. Do you recall his name, by chance? It couldn't have been Tim Conoughy could it?"

"Aye, that'd be the one. Tim Conoughy. Fine fellow, he seemed, the little time I got to know him. Seemed to want to fight the Brits real bad. Thought it a mite strange for an ex-Royal Navy man to be wantin' to fight his own kind." The sailor paused as he thought further, then continued, "But I reckon he wa'n't no different than any o' the other Brits fightin' in the American Navy, upon thinkin' on it."

"Wasn't a topman — 'nother Brit, in fact, named Coleman, Robert Coleman— in that crew, was there? What about an American name o' Clements?"

The two seamen looked at one another silently as each searched their memories for the names Biggs mentioned. Finally, one, the younger of the two, responded.

"Don't recollect anyone o' them names, Brit or other. Course, coves was comin' and goin' quick as ever you please. Ordered in, then moved out — either to the fresh water Navy up to the Lakes or off to *Chesapeake*. Musta been more 'an fifty sent over to Lawrence after he come aboard to see the Commodore. Most hadn't been aboard us a month. An' we been gone a few days now on top of it. But I reckon they figgered you ain't got a need for a crew on a ship what ain't got a rig — or even a deck!"

The two laughed at their joke, then continued their conversation, largely ignoring the privateersman who shared their ride. Isaac leaned back and thought about his friends. *If Tim somehow found his way from Baltimore to Boston and then to the Chesapeake, why not Coleman and even Clements?*

*   *   *   *   *   *

"Charity . . . that you? Glad . . . mmmmphhh . . . back . . . Sorry . . . Baltimore . . . I . . . no, sweet Charity, don't . . . never . . ."

"Jake, lad, wake up. You're dreamin' again. You ain't in Baltimore. You're on the British frigate *Shannon*. And I surely ain't your 'Miss Charity'." Clements gently shook his young friend's shoulder. Tate's eyes snapped open, darting around feverishly as he tried to locate himself and identify the moans, cries, and shouts he heard as well as the stink of the 'tween decks area on the British man o' war turned temporarily into a hospital. He tried to sit up in the swinging cot he occupied in the sick bay. Clements put his hand again on Jake's shoulder, gently pressing him back down. The young topman's eyes finally focused on his shipmate and friend.

"Lay still, lad. It's me, Jack Clements. You got moved over here to the *Shannon* when the surgeon saw that arm all turnin' putrid

— showed signs o' morbidity, he said." Tate's eyes widened somewhat, and his hand moved instinctively to his right arm. A panicked look came into his eyes as his hand found nothing below what had been his elbow. The former bosun of *Chesapeake* continued in a voice gruff and louder than it needed to be, but it was as soothingly quiet as he could manage.

"Aye, it's gone, Jake. Medico hadda take it afore the putrefaction spread and killed you. An' here's the first time you come to since. Looks like your fever's broke — or at least eased a bit."

"Feel like I fell from the t'gallant yard an' hit ever' spar an' line on th' way down." The young topman mumbled, still disoriented. He frowned, making the effort to think, his eyes closed, and his head filled with the screams and shouts of men in hand to hand combat punctuated with the clash of steel blades and the crack of pistol and musket shots.

"I 'member the fightin' and then the damn Brits comin' aboard an' someone haulin' down *Chesapeake*'s colors right about the time I reckon I got myself shot. Someone drug me over to the mast, I think. Guess I cain't recall much after that. How'd we get took over here? Whyn't they jest leave us in *Chesapeake*? An' what about the others? What of Coleman and Johnson? How 'bout Tim? He here too?"

"They bundled up all our Brits — Conoughy and Coleman and them others — an' took 'em out o' *Chesapeake* soon's the fightin' quit. Took 'em in manacles, they did. Reckon it'll go hard with 'em once we get to Halifax. Ain't seen 'em since. Brits got 'em locked up somewhere apart from the rest o' the crew. Couple o' days back some o' the other lads got they's dander up and made the Brit prize crew think they was gonna take back the ship; hove to both vessels, they did, an' run 'bout half the crew over to the *Shannon*. Some more o' the wounded 's'well. That's when they took you over. I guess cause I'm a warrant, they let me have run o' the ship below. An' that's better than most got it; they's still wearin' the iron. An' they got a pair o' nine-pounders loaded with grape an' canister aimed down the scuttles over to the *Chesapeake*. Reckon they ain't gonna take any chance that the ones left over there might start some trouble. Heard from one of the surgeon's mates just last night we been off Halifax couple o' days now and just waitin' on the fog to lift afore we go in. Said it'd likely be this morning. Cove said they was still tryin' to put *Chesapeake* to rights — knottin' an' splicin', patchin', fishin' a mast. Decks still all ahoo; lines ain't been made up, an' gore still ever'where. Reckon they got some work on *Shannon* yet to do, 's'well. Been some poundin' goin' on topside an' yellin'. They's some scuttlebutt makin' the rounds that Cap'n Lawrence is bad off — still alive though, last I heard. Lieutenant Ludlow too.

"Jake? You still with me, lad?" Clements moved closer to his friend. Tate's eyes fluttered and he looked at the bosun briefly and fell back to sleep. "Reckon I gone on long enough. You sleep an' I'll check you later on." Clements stood, as much as the low overhead would allow, and made his way between the hammocks and swinging cots of the crowded hospital, careful not to bump any of the occupants. The moans and cries of the hurt sailors could still be heard as he stepped past the hung canvas and into the even more cramped berthing space where the American sailors were confined.

Sam Johnson, a bandage stiff with dried blood around his head, was sitting on the deck with his legs out in front of him and touched the bosun as he went by. Clements stopped and squatted down beside his former shipmate.

"How's your head, Sam? Course, any other part o' your body what took that hit likely woulda kilt you dead, quick as kiss your hand."

"I reckon it'll take more 'an some Brit musket ball to put me in a shroud — 'specially one aimed at my head. An' what about your own head, Bosun? You feelin' any better?"

Clements nodded and smiled, wincing some. He put a hand up to the bandage on his head. "I'll make it all righty, Sam. You don't need to worry 'bout me."

"Aye, Jack. That's good. But this ain't: I just heard that Cap'n Jim died. Ludlow ain't doin' much better, but he's still alive. Mister Blanchard come through a bit ago and tol' us. Said we was headin' in to Halifax Harbor, *Chesapeake* right astern of us. Sure am glad I ain't got to watch that. That, more than a ball, might put me into the sight o' the devil. More than any of us could take, I'd reckon."

"Mister Clements . . . what do you figger gonna happen to us, we get in?" Another of the Chesapeakes spoke up, voicing the concern most of the men, including Jack Clements, felt.

"I ain't got any idea 'bout that. Reckon they'll put us into some kinda prison or other — maybe a hulk. Then what, only the Almighty knows." He turned back to Johnson. "Sure am sorry to hear 'bout Cap'n Lawrence. He oughta get a decent burial. Sure hope they don't just throw him over the standin' part o' the fore-sheet. Wouldn't be right, you ask me."

A round of "Ayes" went through the space and the men continued to talk quietly about the uncertainty facing them and the fate of their shipmates still on *Chesapeake*. Clements found a space and made himself as comfortable as he could, listening to the noises emanating from both the gundeck over their heads and the spardeck above that.

Cheers, running footfalls, and the sudden discharge of a cannon that made them all start, told them that they were nearing their destination. The cannon shot was echoed, apparently by a gun ashore, and followed by others, both aboard *Shannon* and from the shore batteries. Tension among the Americans increased; worried looks and a few murmured words passed between several. A hatch in the gundeck was opened above their heads and the cool fresh air that filtered down to the captives, along with the slight increase in light made them all look up. A face looked down at them, then turned and disappeared.

The noise increased, now heightened by the open scuttle, and further running footfalls gave testimony to the efforts of the crew to bring the frigate to anchor. Muffled commands could be heard and the rattle of blocks and the other trappings of the rig as the sails were clewed up and finally, but only for a moment, the air was filled with the absence of sound, as the water ceased its constant murmur along the side of the British ship.

The Americans soon could hear the sounds of boats that now circled the triumphant frigate and the barely discernible sounds of their occupants yelling and shouting congratulatory slogans. A distant thunder signaled the Citadel, high above the Dockyard, had joined in celebrating the British victory and, over that, the peal of church bells provided a higher pitched counterpoint to the cacophony which, though muted by the thick hull and decks of HMS *Shannon*, brought an increased burden of sadness and uncertainty to the Chesapeakes as they waited to realize their fate.

Quite without warning, a half dozen Royal Marines appeared in their midst — they had come forward in the 'tween decks — and now stood with bayonet-tipped muskets at the ready, while an additional six climbed awkwardly down the ladder from the gundeck; their muskets, unslung as each landed, were also leveled at the American prisoners. Their sergeant moved quickly into the Americans' midst.

"All right, you lot. Listen 'ere. Any trouble from the least of yers, an' ye can count on feelin' the steel o' th' Royal Marines. Up with ye now, an' lively about it." In the dim light that filtered through the open scuttle and around the bulkhead aft and canvas forward, the Chesapeakes could see their tormentor and his colleagues watching them much the way a fox might watch a coop of chickens and, without a murmur, they rose slowly to their feet and shuffled, bent by the weight of their ignominy as well as the low overhead, in the direction of the ladder.

They emerged onto the gundeck blinking and squinting in the stronger light that came through the gangways from the spardeck and now the sounds of celebration, muted from below, assaulted their ears and added to their misery. The sergeant gave them no time to consider their position.

"Keep it movin' there! Up ye go, we got boats awaitin' to take ye on a merry ride. Ye'll soon be feelin' the solid soil o' Great Britain under your feets, an' no mistake. An' then a fine place where you can lay about an' consider your luck at bein' safe an' sound from th' dangers ye faced on th' 'igh seas. Aye, ye'll find me colleagues at Melville Island fairly leapin' to make you comfortable. Har har har. An' some other coves what thought they might take up arms against 'is Majesty 's'well, though bein' Frenchies, ye'll likely not find 'em much for conversation. Har har har."

The sergeant poked a few of the Americans with his bayonet, receiving no response save a step toward the ladder leading to the spar deck and the waiting boats.

As he came out into the light of a summer afternoon in Halifax Harbor, Bosun Jack Clements squinted down his eyes and cast them quickly around the British ship. Coming to anchor and looking quite the worse for wear was *Chesapeake*, a cable astern. The Blue Ensign flying tautly above the American flag in the moderate breeze brought a scowl to his face and his fists balled without his conscious thought. Milling small craft, decorated in bunting in apparent haste and filled to capacity and beyond with well-wishers, circled the two frigates. Their passengers, still dressed for the church services interrupted by the arrival of *Shannon* and her prize, pointed and commented excitedly on the obvious punishment received by the American, while countless others, also liberated from Sunday services by the excitement, lined the nearby shore cheering and waving, delirious in their joy at this first naval victory and the capture of an 'impregnable' American frigate. All around the harbor, and as far as Clements could see from his vantage point were ships: British men o' war, transports, and what were apparently prizes, formerly American and a few French merchants, awaiting adjudication. His eyes moved closer: around the deck of *Shannon* an unrepaired bulwark and a pair of dismounted cannon were the only evidence he could make out of the fight that took such a desperate toll on the American vessel. No gore remained on deck, if indeed there had been any five days previous, and the rig, what he could see of it, was taut and unscathed.

As they shuffled by one of the spardeck eighteen-pounders, Clements could make out semi-circular markings on the deck behind it; he recalled that he had noticed the same at each battery on the gundeck. He was a bosun, not a gunner, but his instinct told him that this ship had reached a level of efficiency in gunnery to which most, in either the British or the American Navy, could only aspire. On taking a second look, he discovered rudimentary iron sights on the top of the gun barrel; no doubt these contributed as well to the deadly accuracy of their fire. He made a mental note to talk with one of *Chesapeake*'s gunners about these improvements to the British cannon.

Small wonder, he thought, *that our rag-tag bunch what ain't never fought together was whupped so quick.* The marine nearest him prodded him with a bayonet and he moved toward the waist where the boats waited to take the prisoners ashore.

CHAPTER NINETEEN

"Hands to braces and sheets; let fall the tops'ls. Mister Coffin, we'll have silence fore an' aft. See to it." Captain Rogers' form, visible only as a shadow darker than the surrounding darkness, glided to the wheel and, in words indistinct to any but the men at the helm, ordered the *General Washington* brought to an easy reach.

Only the hands nearest the quarterdeck had heard the hoarse whispers and, of course, Starter Coffin. The mate immediately moved forward and, in his distinct gravelly growl, enjoined the hands to silence and speed as they carried out the orders which would enable the brig to get out to sea, having just won her anchor from the sandy bottom of Salem Harbor.

The nor'easter had moderated; no longer was the warm rain being blown horizontal. But even with it eased, the rain and the profound darkness of the late June night would be their allies in slipping past the tightened British blockade. Word on the waterfront was that the Brits had strengthened their choke-hold on the American coast with the addition of several more brigs, sloops of war, and a frigate all sent down from Halifax. Since the success of HMS *Shannon*, the Royal Navy had nearly sealed the Massachusetts coast from Cape Cod to Portsmouth and any vessel desiring to take to sea waited for a night such as this — dark and dirty — with squalls that would drive the lions from the gate as they sought sea room to ride out the weather. Asa Rogers. and indeed all hands, had been aboard the privateer for nearly two weeks, watching and waiting for such an opportunity. Tension rose as the glass fell and finally, the northeast storm came through allowing them the chance they had awaited. And they all, to a man, clambered for the chance to right the wrong their country had suffered at the start of the month.

"The tide's still makin', Cap'n. 'Ppears to be settin' us to th' south a mite. Be more comfortable comin' a trifle higher." The second mate, well known to Rogers and, indeed, most of the seafaring community, was new aboard the *General* and offered the suggested course correction quietly and with some trepidation. He waited silently, a shadow, as the Captain watched his ship's progress against the barely visible smudge of land to starboard.

"I quite agree Mister O'Mara. Your observation is astute. You may make it so; about a point to weather should answer nicely. Mister Coffin, you may trim her close hauled. And I need not remind you to do it quietly."

The *General Washington* eased up, her tops'ls and reefed courses trimmed without a single shiver at the hands of her adept crew. As she breasted the rolling ground swell forcing its way into the confined waters of Salem Harbor, the brig began the familiar and easy motion her crew knew so well. The northeaster, docile for the moment, would return with a vengeance soon enough, but now with the temporary lull, the officers needed only to watch the action of the tide to get the handy little brig to sea.

Tom O'Mara, his face and deep-set eyes shrouded under the weathered tarpaulin hat pulled down low on his forehead, watched the ship carefully even so and stood close by the helm where he could watch the compass in the dim glow of the binnacle. Tall, his long arms hung at his sides, his wrists showing out the bottom of his sodden canvas coat. Had it been only slightly lighter, one might have noticed his fists clenching and relaxing as he conned the vessel out of the harbor. It weighed heavily on him that he had a large berth to fill and knew also that many of the crew sorely missed Jared Tompkins, his predecessor, a kindly, easy-going man, and fine sailor killed by a splinter in an action during the last cruise. He had been buried at sea.

O'Mara, ashore and without a berth, had run into Captain Rogers shortly after the disastrous *Shannon/Chesapeake* duel. When Rogers had suggested he might fill the second's berth on the *General,* he fairly leaped at the opportunity. Salem-born to immigrant parents and named in lofty tribute to his antecedents, Thomas Francis Xavier Ignatius O'Mara had sailed on both Rogers' and Crowninshield ships for many years, but never with either of the great men personally. He was well-known by most of the sea-farers between Salem and Boston as a fine seaman with an abnor-mally low boiling point; in fact it was his quick temper and even quicker fists which accounted, yet again, for his current availabil-ity. And he had promised himself, should he find a berth as a mate, that he would make every effort to control his temper.

"She seems to be responding nicely, Mister O'Mara; you may keep her as she is. I am going forward for a spell." Without a back-ward glance, Captain Rogers stepped off the quarterdeck and dis-appeared into the darkness.

"Who's that there? Oh, Cap'n, I didn't see you comin'. Every-thing all right?" Third Mate Isaac Biggs was standing in the bow, a foot on the butt of the bowsprit and his head pulled into his can-vas jacket, dull with the soaking rain. He leaned forward over his raised knee, both arms resting easily on his leg as he peered intently into the dark ahead of the privateer.

"Just dandy, Isaac. Just come forward to have a look around and see that we're keepin' a sharp weather eye out. Wouldn't do to find that one o' them frigates was pokin' 'round out here. I am hopeful they and their associates have headed well offshore dur-ing this spell of weather. No sir, wouldn't do at all to discover one still on station."

"Amen to that, Cap'n. I got two aloft at the crosstrees and I'll be changin' 'em every hour. Likely not gonna see much in this rain, but like you said, they won't likely be anything to see. An' I got Davies just aft o' the chains there with the deep lead."

Almost as if on cue, the two men heard Davies quietly announce the depth as he hauled in the ocean leadline; they were still on soundings and would be until they passed below Great Misery Island.

"Good thinking, Isaac. Wouldn't do to find Harding Rocks on a night such as this." With that, Captain Rogers disappeared aft and Biggs continued to peer into the dark ahead of the *General Wash-ington* as the brig shouldered aside the growing swells generated by the storm that rolled in from the open expanse of the Atlantic.

It was about halfway into the middle watch when Biggs stepped onto the quarterdeck, found the captain among the dark shapes, and announced quietly, "Cap'n, we're off soundings. I have secured Davies since he ain't found a bottom with the deep lead for the past fifteen and more casts."

"Very good, Mister Biggs . . . Mister Coffin: who has the watch?"

The growl emanated from the leeward side of the quarterdeck, "Be Biggs, an' the starbowlines, Cap'n. You figger we can go to a reg'lar watch now?"

"That will answer nicely. I'll be in the Cabin, should you be needin' me, Mister Biggs." With that, the men watched as the tall form of Asa Rogers appeared to sink into the deck as the captain went through the scuttle and down the ladder to his cabin.

"You'll do well to keep men aloft, Isaac. Wouldn't serve no purpose at all to get took by surprise should there be a Brit lurkin' out here. Be sure to change 'em right often and keep your lads quiet. Even in this weather sound'll carry more'n you'd think." The deep gravelly voice resonated out of the dark, raised somewhat now to be heard over the rising wind. Periodically, as the vessel got further into the Atlantic seas, a gout of spray would fly down the deck, causing the men on deck, even those as far aft as the quarterdeck, to hunch down into their already-soaked jackets. The weather would likely continue to worsen through the next day or so and that was fine with the men and officers of the *General Washington*. With every mile of open water they gained, they lowered the chance of being detected; along shore, the British had little to do but watch the harbors for shipping, but at sea, there was just too much area to cover and the attitude on the blockading ships was that the frigates, sloops, and brigs escorting the merchant convoys would have to deal with any of the United States vessels that slipped through.

That night and the next several days passed uneventfully; the weather did in fact, get worse and, to the straining eyes of the lookouts, the sea was empty, save for the American brig. *General Washington* continued under shortened canvas in a southeasterly direction, handling the now heavy seas in her comfortable, albeit wet, manner. Every man knew that with each day, the likelihood of detection grew less, and by the fourth day out, they were all breathing easier. It was during the afternoon watch one day in early July that contact was finally made.

"Sails . . . I got two ships o' sail, hull down, and showin' a point off the leeward bow. 'Ppear to be under easy sail." The lookout in the foremast crosstrees was alert and there wasn't a man on deck who didn't stop what he was doing to cast his glance to the horizon. Of course, from deck there was nothing to see, which sent the officer on the quarterdeck into the forward rigging with a glass to see for himself what was out there. A messenger had been sent for the captain, and, by the time Third Mate Biggs returned to the deck, Rogers was waiting impatiently by the foretopmast backstay.

"Well, Mister Biggs. What do we have?"

"Looks to me like a pair of Bermuda sloops, Cap'n. Or possibly one an' a schooner-rigged vessel. They're headin' to the north under easy sail, an' on the larboard tack. Might be ahead of a convoy or might just be on they's own. Wasn't nothing else in sight, even with the glass. Probably out of St. George's in the last couple o' days or more."

"Thank you. We'll harden up a trifle, if you please, an' have a look. I doubt they've seen us yet, though I 'spose it's always possible. When they're hull up from aloft, we'll clear for action, but keep the gunports closed until we know what's actin'."

With a quiet "Aye," Biggs headed for the quarterdeck, giving orders to sail handlers, Gunner Hogan and Bosun Dobson, each as he passed them. The ship was brought to a course that would intercept the two potential prizes while maintaining the weather gauge. Word spread throughout the ship that something was afoot and the off watch section began to filter up on deck to discuss what might be. T'gallants were set and two additional stays'ls to close the distance before dark. Rogers could use the cover of night to disappear should the pair prove to be more than he felt the *General* could handle safely, but he would also have the opportunity to engage them if they turned out to be a couple of merchants, or even lightly-armed Royal Navy vessels. The wind was holding nicely at west-northwest and could be expected to do so at least until dark, still some five to six hours distant. Plenty of time to close — and even take them. The men watched and waited impatiently.

*   *   *   *   *   *

"Step along, there, you God damned turncoat. You start laggin' and you'll feel my steel, an' no mistake. Wouldn't be no one grievin' over your bloody arse, neither. Keep steppin' along with them other traitors. I'd warrant you'll wish you'd never been born an Englishman by the time you face the gibbet or the lash, by God. A floggin' 'round the fleet would be too good for ye — 'angin' is what ye deserve. Aye, a 'angin'." A Royal Marine brought up the rear of the small procession of prisoners, and was flanked by an additional three on each side of the column; a marine subaltern led the group of British deserters through the back of Halifax, past the Citadel, and onto the road that would take them around the end of the Northwest Arm of Halifax Harbor.

The five British sailors, late of USS *Chesapeake* and still stiff from their confinement aboard *Shannon*, struggled to keep up the pace set by the young officer. Most showed some physical manifestation of their part in the battle, either before or after *Shannon's* sailors and marines had boarded *Chesapeake*. Two limped horribly; their bloody bandages, one around a thigh and another covering most of the calf, still seeped from wounds not yet closed. They were helped by shipmates, one with a head wound wrapped in a dirty bandage, brown with dried blood, and another with most of one arm wrapped in a blood-soaked bandage. Only one among them was unhurt, and he brought up the rear, helping his wounded comrades as they faltered. It was while he struggled to help up his long-time friend who had stumbled — weak from the serious wound in his thigh and from loss of blood — that he provoked the Royal Marine's impatient encouragement. He didn't stop moving, but turned to look at the Redcoat after the wounded man was back on his feet and once again stumbling along. His look was blank; it held no animosity or rancor, but it inspired the marine to more invective.

"'Ere, what're you lookin' at, you filthy turncoat? Leavin' a nice Navy vessel to join up with them American upstarts and takin' up arms against the King and country what birthed you — you orta be 'ung. An' I'll warrant you will be. Har har. Unless me colleagues yonder at Melville Island 'ave an accident with ye. Har har." The Royal Marine poked at the sailor with his bayonet, encouraging him to move faster. The pace remained unchanged.

"I can manage, Robert; by me own mother's eyes, I can. You step along like the cove wants. You topmen got the luck o' St. Patrick on you, comin' outta that scrape with nary a drop o' blood spilt. Hidin' up aloft, were you? Tol' you all the excitement's at the guns. Next commission we're gonna see that Mrs. Conoughy's boy gets 'is young arse up there in the clouds." Tim smiled thinly at his friend, maintaining the long-standing rivalry between the topmen and gunners. Through teeth clenched in pain, he continued. "I coulda stayed down there in Gosport on *Constellation*, but it was action I was cravin' and I guess that's what I got, eh, Robert lad? An' now a chance to have a wee visit with some of me countrymen on top o' it."

"Don't waste your breath talkin', Tim. I'd warrant we'll find time enough for that whenever we get to wherever it is we're goin'. An' your 'countryman' back there ain't likely to . . ."

" 'Ere now. Shut your gobs, you two. Ye'll be needin' all the breath you got for our little walk in the woods. Gotta get you over there afore it gets dark or I don't get me wee dram of good Jamaica rum."

As the cart track they were on fed into a wider road, the British seamen, formerly of USS *Chesapeake*, could make out the end of the long line of the American prisoners marching ahead of them. They too were flanked by Redcoats on either side, as well as ahead and astern. Many were wounded, but could walk; those that couldn't had been taken to the British Naval Hospital in Halifax along with the more seriously wounded officers, American and British. According to one talkative marine guard, the other officers — 'the ones what wasn't 'urt bad' — would be given their parole across the harbor in Dartmouth or Preston. And would be free to come and go within certain limits until exchanged.

As the road ran down a hill and emerged from the woods, the men, first the Americans and then the British, could see ahead of them the water of the Northwest Arm where it dead-ended in the inland shallows and, looking to their left, they could see it extending through the woods for some distance, but the open end of the Arm was not visible. Instinctively though, most knew that the open sea and freedom, should they make it there, lay in that direction. Directly across the narrow band of water was a pretty cove — or would have been but for the blight of the island set in its opening. On the eastern end of the island was a house perched high on a knoll, partly covered in scrub grasses; the rest of the island was surrounded by a fence, high and with pointed tips. The men could see part of the prison itself now; barracks of wood and stone, wooden storehouses, and other buildings all painted blood-red, and glowing ominously in the late afternoon sun. A signal mast stood next to the house on the knoll, apparently for communicating with the fort on Citadel Hill. It seemed to the prisoners a dismal and formidable place to behold; even the golden glow of a late Sunday afternoon in early June, and the clear water, dazzled with the low sunlight and reflecting the deep blue of the Nova Scotian sky, could not soften the ugliness of the red-painted buildings on the rocky island. Behind the island were dense woods, similar to the forests that covered much of the area between Halifax and the Northwest Arm.

"There you are, lads, 'ave a good long look at your new 'ome. Ye won't be seein' it from this place again, I'd warrant. Har har." The Redcoat allowed the men to stop for a moment to take in the sight of the prison that covered nearly all of the little island. But not for long. "Awright, then, let's get movin' right smart."

Tim Conoughy leaned heavily on Coleman's shoulder, more to talk quietly than for the support it offered; but the wound in his thigh now bled freely, and putting any weight at all on it caused him to flinch and, on occasion, grunt in pain.

"What of the others, Robert? Did you get a chance to see Jack or young Tate? I 'eard one of the lads mention that Sam Johnson was 'urt sore bad, but not a word 'ave I 'eard of our other mates that come up from Gosport."

"They wasn't bringin' me the news regular, Tim. But I did 'ear that Cap'n Jim passed over just afore we come into 'Alifax. An I seen Mister Blanchard on deck as we was gettin' into the boats; didn't 'pear to be 'urt that I could make out. Maybe Clements and the others is up ahead there. Blanchard'll likely be given 'is parole, not locked up. They don't do that with the officers."

"What of young Isaac, Robert? 'ave ye seen 'im? Did he come through . . . as good . . . ohhhhh."

Coleman's head whipped around to look at his friend. His jaw muscles tightened and his brow furrowed. "Tim, Isaac ain't with us; 'e's somewhere in Massachusetts, remember? We ain't seen 'im since last winter, 'e didn't stay in Baltimore to join the Navy with us. You all right there, Tim? Tim?" Coleman realized he and another were supporting the entire weight of their shipmate. The Irishman's head drooped, his chin resting on his chest. The topman called to the guard.

"Hey, you. Redcoat. 'ere . . . give us a 'and 'ere. Me mate's passed right out. Musta lost a lot o' blood." As he spoke, Coleman eased Conoughy's inert form to the ground and knelt over him. The Irishman was deathly pale.

"Look's like 'e's dead to me. No bother there. Just leave 'im be.

Too bad 'e cheated the 'angman, though. Move along now."

"'E ain't dead, damn it. Just passed out, 's'all. Give us a minute and we'll carry 'im the rest o' the way. Ain't right to just leave 'im, even if 'e is dead, which 'e ain't."

Coleman and the least-wounded British sailor, a man named Edward Tingley, picked up the form of the Irishman and staggering slightly, rejoined the procession now heading around the end of the Arm, following the water's edge.

Less than an hour later, all the prisoners, American and British, marched or were carried through the gate of the prison on Melville Island. Mr. Walton, the camp doctor, met the procession, checking visually each of the men as they arrived. One look at the Irish gunner, one of the last he saw, caused him to shout at the Marine subaltern who had led the group.

"'Ere now, Mister Marine. What's actin' wi' this one? Why 'aven't you left this cove in the 'ospital at the Dockyards, then? You must think I got time 'angin' 'eavy on me 'ands, me an' them sorry excuses for surgeon's mates what's assigned 'ere. You two, carry 'im right over there with them others and don't tarry. Poor sod's likely enough to die without you delay any more." Several others among the wounded sailors had already been taken to the hospital and two of the British seamen with them. The Irishman groaned as Coleman and Tingley followed the outstretched arm of the doctor to the entrance of the hospital building, also painted blood-red, located across the yard from the barracks building, and carried Conoughy inside.

When they rejoined their shipmates, all hands were being lectured by the warden, a paunchy florid-faced Royal Marine, with a bulbous nose tracked with the red and blue veins of a serious drinker. He was stuffed into a uniform that may have fit him ten years earlier and showed the markings of a major. As they took the places opened for them by their mates in the rear of the group, Coleman and Tingley stood with their American shipmates and listened as the warden touched on what their lives would be like going forward; it was apparent to the most casual observer that this officer had never seen a shot fired in anger, except perhaps at the back of an escaping prisoner.

" . . . roll your 'ammocks daily and ye'll be washin' an' holystonin' the decks twice a week, an' make no mistake, it'll be no different than when you was at sea; I run this island just like a man o' war, an' them decks'll be clean an' white. Ain't no worries 'bout 'ow long it takes ye; you got time — plenty o' time, as none of ye'll be goin' anywhere soon. Har har har. An' then after your breakfast, ye'll be free — it's not like ye'll be free, what I mean to say is, ye'll 'ave time — to do what ye will. Some of our French visitors use the time to make gewgaws to sell on Sundays to the folks what come over to gawk and point at ye from 'Alifax an' Dartmouth. You could do the same, if ye've any talent. An' I 'ope ye do, as ye'll be needin' spendin' money to buy the things what ain't supplied by the Transport Office for its prisoners." After a pause for this news to register, he continued. "An' I own the store. Just there, right by the gate. Sells everything a body might need. Wool for your feet in the winter, flannel for next to your skin, an' a host of other necessaries. We got the occasional wee dram o' spirits, an' all of it cheap; you ask any of them Frenchies. You'll see."

He stopped, looked at the guards waiting for the men, and said, "Issue 'em their 'ammocks and blankets, then take 'em an' show 'em to their quarters. Keep 'em away from the Frenchies for now." And he turned to walk back up the hill to the officers' quarters on the top of the island. It was immediately apparent to all, prisoner and guard alike, that the warden, Major Ian Gilpatric, was less than sober, as he stumbled onto the first step of the walk and wove his way up.

The guards herded the sailors inside a stone storehouse where they drew hammocks and blankets, and then into the long, two-story, wood and stone building and to what would be their homes for some time to come.

A narrow hallway, illuminated by some lanterns augmented by half a dozen "purser's glims," stretched out for some distance in front of them; wooden doors with heavy iron hardware opened at frequent intervals, and a stone stairway disappeared up into the darkness to their right. The men could see that the wall by each cell was pierced with a small opening leading to a shelf in the inside. "That's for your food," one of the taciturn guards explained unnecessarily. As each four men reached a doorway, they were pushed inside of the six-by-nine-foot cells.

Inside, they found a metal basin, a wooden bucket in the corner, and a window high up in the end of the narrow wall. Iron hooks protruded from the wall, obviously for the hammocks. The light, what there was of it in the fading daylight, filtered in through a glassless, barred window set deep in the stone wall. The door slammed shut behind them and they heard the bolt being shot home with a depressing finality.

"Ain't as much space in here as they was on the barky, by God."

"Aye, an' a damn sight colder I'd warrant, once the weather turns. Ain't no stove or nothing."

"Now what, I ask ya. We gonna be here 'til the war ends, like he said?"

"I didn't sign on to be locked up in a cage. I ain't no animal. I'm tellin' you coves right here an' now, I aim to get me out o' here quick as ever I can, an' no mistake."

"Did you catch a glimpse of that battery on t'other side of the bridge comin' into the island? Aimed right at the gate, it were, like they was expectin' all hands to bust out at once."

And so it went; each group of four Chesapeakes were shut into a small stone cell. The reaction was mostly the same, save for a few who set up such a caterwauling that even their mates told them to shut up.

It would not be long before they met their French neighbors, many of whom had been residents of Melville Island prison since the fish factory that originally occupied the island was experimentally used for the prison. The current facility was erected in 1808, after the Crown — in the person of the Transport Office Agent for Prisoners — had determined the shoreside prison would be an improvement over the hulks in Bedford Basin. The health of the prisoners had improved, and while the escape rate was up considerably, more the result of using the healthier prisoners to build roads around the area, the majority of the escapees — all from the work parties — were usually rounded up within a fortnight. And not a one had escaped from the island prison itself — ever.

Jack Clements, even though a warrant officer, received no special treatment and, since young Jake Tate had been deemed fit for the island instead of the Naval Hospital in Halifax, they had been put into the same cell along with Sam Johnson, who was not hurt as badly as some had thought, and Ike Massey, a waister from northern New York and a transferee from USS *Constitution*. He bemoaned his ill-starred luck as the four of them sat on the cool stone floor and waited for what might come next.

"I hadda want to go to sea. Coulda stayed right in New York and fit with them coves what come up to the woods. Course, they didn't fare so good with the Brits what come down from Canada, I reckon, an' I coulda been sent out to Fort Detroit with the army. Likely woulda got meself kilt out there. Them coves got so bad beat they wasn't but a couple lived to tell the tale, an' from what I heard, they run away. Leastways, here we sit honest an' straight, an' we're still breathin'. . ."

"Shut up, Massey. You got no call to complain. You wasn't hurt that I kin see an' you're still alive. Lookee yonder at young Tate; he ain't said a damn word an' ain't got but one arm thanks to them damn Brits, an' what's he gonna do, a topman what's missin' a arm." Johnson paused for breath, and Jack Clements cast a glance at the young topman with 'but one arm' to see how he was taking his shipmate's remarks. Tate stared straight ahead, his eyes unfocused. It didn't appear that he even heard them. Drawn deep within himself, Jake was barely aware of his surroundings.

Johnson continued, "We're all pretty lucky, even Jake. I heard Mister Blanchard tellin' one of the Brits that more 'en a hunnert Chesapeakes got kilt in the fightin' an' more died afore we got to Halifax. An' we left nigh on to fifty at the hospital. So I figger them poor coves ain't got nothin' to look forward to; we're still alive, an' gonna get outta here sooner or later. An' we ain't goin' back on that damn jinx ship. I didn't believe all them tales 'til now, but looks like they was righty-oh. We had ourselves a good crew, an' as fine a cap'n what ever sailed, fought less'n fifteen minutes, an' here we sit in a Brit prison like common thieves or somethin'."

"They don't think of us as common thieves, Sam. And they get treated a damn sight worse'n us, I heard tell. 'sides, we might get ourselves exchanged for some Brit coves they got in the United States. Thief ain't gonna get exchanged, but prisoners of war likely will." Clements was standing, straining to see out the window which was somewhat over his head. The light was fading quickly now and, as the gloom of the small cell deepened, the men lapsed into silence.

By early July, the routine had become ingrained and the prisoners were now allowed to wander around the yard within the high palisades and the stone walls topped with shards of glass, giving them the opportunity check on their mates and get the lay of the island prison. Most had accepted their fate and waited to see which of their mates would be sent over from the hospital — and which would be sent to Deadman's Island and an unmarked grave in that aptly named pile of dirt and rock in the little cove immediately to the south of Melville Island.

CHAPTER TWENTY

"Another day or two, three at most, and we should be seein' the Massachusetts coast, less'n we see one o' them Brit blockaders. Reckon we'd be sunk then; not much we could do 'bout it if'n they chose to fight us." Dobson looked aloft as he spoke to the third mate, taking in the *General's* fished foremast and the bowsprit with its jury rig holding it together.

"Our prizes would surely be easy pickin's 's'well for 'em; jury-rigged an' with short crews trying to sail 'em and hold 'em together 'til we get back to Salem. I don't think them Brits locked up below would be likely to help out much, should we be boarded," Isaac agreed with a smile. "Let's just hope this breeze holds nice an' easy from the sou'west an' keep the men alert — the ones standing lookout aloft."

After spending two full days hove to, mending spars and replacing sails holed in the taking of the two prizes off Bermuda, knotting and splicing the rigging, the small flotilla got under way in calm seas and an easy sou'west breeze. The eight Americans and twelve British seaman killed in the action had been buried together shortly after the battle, and a half dozen General Washingtons, three British sailors and one officer were resting in a make-shift hospital under the privateer's fo'c'sle.

Three days into making their westing, one of their prizes, a schooner, disappeared during the night and the privateer and the prize sloop hove to to wait what turned out to be half a day for the schooner to catch up; the repaired main topmast had failed and the prize crew spent an uneasy night drifting and jury-rigging a spare main boom to replace it. Otherwise, their passage had been, so far, unremarkable. All hands fervently hoped it would continue that way, all the way into Salem Harbor, two or three days distant.

"I'll tell you this, Dobson," said Isaac while the two watched the Bermuda sloop and the schooner following along, one on either quarter of the *General Washington*, like obedient children, "I don't reckon this comes close to evenin' up the score for what happened to the *Chesapeake*. Half a hundred Brit sailors, a few officers, and a couple of British privateers — not even Royal Navy — don't signify on that 'count. I heard before we left Salem from some coves off'n *Constitution* that one and maybe more of my old shipmates was on *Chesapeake*; I collect, from all the accounts of the action I heard, that they either got 'emselves kilt in the fight, or lacking that, they've got locked up in someplace called Melville Island up in Halifax. Hard to fathom that I'll likely never see 'em again."

"Aye, Isaac, I can un'erstand that. Lost a passel o' my own friends over the year an' more o' this damn war. Ain't nothin' for it, though. You just hope the ones you ain't sure of're still upright somewhere, sailin' or yarnin' in some tavern, an' that they'll turn up someday. I'd reckon you don't know whether your friends was kilt or no, or even if they was on the frigate. They could still be holed up somewhere on another ship, blocked into a harbor by the damn Brits and wonderin' what became of you."

"Well, that's something, I guess. Just have to wait and see what . . ."

"Sail . . . sail fine on the larboard bow! Hull down, she is, and 'pears to be but one. Showin' tops'ls and t'gallants that I kin see."

Once again, the lookout's cry stopped all human motion on the brig; O'Mara, who had the watch, leaped into the rigging with a glass and yelled at the messenger to "Fetch the Cap'n, quick as ever you can." Biggs glanced at their prizes to see if by chance they had seen the sails also; all appeared serene from what he could see and, he guessed correctly, that Captain Rogers would be taking action to deal with this most unwelcome visitor.

"Mister Coffin, Mister Biggs, we'll bear off a point, if you please, and smartly. Until Mister O'Mara returns with his report, I'll be taking no chances."

The two mates moved men to sail-handling positions and the brig headed off, making her course nearly north and, hopefully, away from the stranger. By the time the lines were again coiled down and the ship full and by on her new course, the second jumped off the bulwark and stepped to the Captain's side, his long glass still slung by its leather strap from his shoulder.

"I'd stake my life on that bein' a Crowninshield vessel, Cap'n. In fact, I'd bet a fair piece o' change that she's the *Henry*, the brig Mister Crowninshield favors for his own use. Armed with eight six-pounders and a pair of eighteen-pounder carronades, she is — or was when last I seen her. She ain't showin' no flag that I could make out from aloft, but the way she carries her fore tops'l and jibs is — well, they just ain't any others I ever saw what look like that."

"Mister O'Mara, you bring most welcome news and pray you are right in your assessment of that vessel, as you are indeed betting your life and, I might add, all of ours on it. None-the-less, we shall continue on this course until we are sure. Make a signal to Mister Hardy and Mister Dickerson to bear off and stay close, if you please. We shall watch, and wait."

"Mister Biggs?" The voice behind Isaac was quiet — almost a whisper — and filled with concern and without turning he knew at once to whom it belonged.

"Yes, Dunn. Everything all right with our passengers?" Butterfingers had been given the chore of tending to the British captives confined below.

"Yes sir . . . that is, I reckon it is, sir. I just come from forward and looks to me like Smith ain't doin' so good. Rantin' an' ravin' he is and thrashin' around something fierce. Sweatin' like a horse on top of it. Could you come an' have a look, sir?" The concern in Dunn's voice caused Isaac to turn and look hard into the seaman's eyes; the big man's whole posture, from the look in his eyes to the wringing of his great hands, and the repeated licking of his lips, mostly hidden behind the bushy brown beard, spoke of a genuine fear about his shipmate. Without further words, Biggs started forward to the improvised hospital where Tight-Fisted Smith, cruelly hurt in the action, still remained along with the other sailors.

As they neared the scuttle, open and with a wind sail rigged for ventilation, both men could hear someone crying out and making a host of unintelligible sounds, interspersed with a string of curses. Biggs dropped down the scuttle and was greeted first by an unpleasant pungent odor — the smell of decay and mortification — and then, as his eyes adjusted to the gloom, by the sight of Smith. The topman was half in and half out of his hammock, his face flushed and glistening with sweat in spite of the comfortable temperature, and the bandages had been ripped off his chest. The deep gash which showed there was grisly, and the raised lump alongside the wound where the six-inch splinter still remained was red and angry. Yellowish fluid oozed from the wound, and the red streaks radiating across Smith's chest indicated putrefaction of major proportions. Captain Rogers had not dared remove the splinter with the limited implements available to him and his limited skills as a surgeon. It was obvious even to Isaac that the morbidity from the wood lodged in his chest was growing worse and, if left untreated, would likely kill Smith before the brig reached Salem.

"Fetch Cap'n Rogers, Dunn. Quick as you can. I'll stay here with Smith." Biggs eased the topman's contorted form back into the hammock and spoke quietly to him while he found a cloth in a bucket of tepid but fresh water. He wrung out the cloth and laid it gently on Smith's forehead, then wiped it down the man's face cooling his fever and easing his discomfort. Smith's eyes fluttered and opened, fixing on Isaac's face. A spark of recognition was there and Isaac continued speaking soothingly to his friend. As fast as Isaac wiped away the sweat it would reappear. His friend's eyes had sunk into his head and were bloodshot, ringed with dark smudges. He rinsed the rag in the bucket and turned back to the patient as the lanky form of Captain Rogers materialized on the ladder.

"What's the problem, Mister Biggs? Dunn said something about one of the topmen. I can't be spending my time down here; we got a situation topside what's gonna need my attention sooner than later, I'm thinkin'." Rogers covered the deck between the ladder and Smith's hammock in one stride and looked at the man's face. After a moment, his gaze shifted to the suppurating, fetid wound.

"I was afraid of this. Not takin' that splinter out's what's responsible for the wound becomin' putrid like it is. I ain't sure I can get it out now, but maybe if I open this up some, I can relieve some of the pressure and let out some o' that pus. I reckon a medico would want to bleed him, too." Rogers' voice was barely audible; he was talking mainly to himself, hearing how his diagnosis and plan of attack sounded. He stood and motioned to his third mate.

"I fear we may not be able to stop this spreadin' fester. You can see how the morbidity's spreadin' down his belly and up toward his neck. Them red lines there. That splinter must have been. . ." His ruminations to Isaac were cut off by a renewed outburst and thrashing from Smith. Rogers looked at the sailor and, with a shake of his head, made up his mind.

"Mister Biggs, get him onto those sea chests and tie him down. Wouldn't do to have him bouncing around while I'm trying to open that thing up. I'll be back quick as ever I can." With that, the captain turned and ran up the ladder.

When he returned, he bore the medical box. His brow was furrowed and his eyes had a worried cast to them. Isaac assumed the captain's concern was over Smith's condition; he was only partly right.

"That ship yonder has borne off and appears to be makin' for us. I got to get this done quick and you'll have to help me." He opened the large box and pulled out a stoppered glass bottle, about half of which he poured into Smith's mouth. He stepped back and looked around. "Where's Dunn?"

The big seaman appeared from the gloom. "Here, Cap'n."

"All right, then. You and Mister Biggs're gonna have to hold Smith down. I've given him as much laudanum as I dare, but it'll be a bit afore it takes aholt of him." He stepped back and, reaching into the medical box, produced a thin-bladed knife, which he tested on his thumb. The blade winked in the flickering light of a lantern Biggs had hung over the sea chests where the hapless sailor was stretched out.

"Make sure them bonds is tight and then get hold of him." Rogers looked up at his third and the seaman and received a nod that they were ready. His hand hesitated a moment, then moved with a deceiving steadiness to the raised, angry welt on Smith's chest. Carefully, he cut a long, deep incision down the length of the splinter, then around one end. The wounded sailor gasped as the knife cut into his flesh, then lapsed into silence — either passed out or in the drifting world of a laudanum-induced delirium.

Lifting the flap of skin he had created, Rogers peered into the wound. He straightened up, sighed, and again pressed the knife into the new wound. After cutting more, he again stooped and studied what he could see inside the cut. The smell newly emanating from the putrid wound was overpowering, but the Captain ignored it and, continuing to stare into the opening in Smith's chest, muttered under his breath.

"I can see that lump of wood in there plain as day. Haulin' it outta o' him ain't gonna be easy. Likely tear up half his chest . . . nothing for it . . ." He straightened up and set down the knife, picking up a pair of long forceps from the box. Turning back to the patient, he was poised with the forceps to enter the wound when Smith suddenly and with unexpected strength, struggled to sit up, crying out in pain. His face, now pale even in the yellow light of the whale oil lantern, glistened with sweat. The sweat mixed with the blood from the incision and ran down his chest.

"Hold him steady, lads. This here's the tricky part." Rogers waited a moment for the man to quiet down and then carefully poked the forceps into the wound. His face showed the strain of concentration and responsibility. He muttered unintelligible sounds as, gently, he moved the tool around, feeling for the wood, his eyes closed. Suddenly they popped open and a look of satisfaction passed across his face; it was gone quick as the splash from a wave disappears on the sea.

"There it is . . . just gotta get this . . . blast it. . . steady lads. . . I can feel it now . . . there . . . got it . . . now just ease it out." With his other hand, he lifted the flap of the wound and, working the splinter back and forth with the forceps, gradually moved it out of Smith's chest. The sweat beaded on his brow, reflecting the light of the lantern like little jewels, as he concentrated on the task at hand. "Don't break now . . . hold him still now, lads . . . just a little more . . . easy now . . ." Rogers, with a deft movement of his hand, pulled out the six-inch lump of yellow pine soaked with blood and pus. The wound bled freely now that the splinter was out. Rogers held the splinter up into the light for scrutiny.

"Don't look like any broke off in there. Here, Isaac, pour some o' that blue stuff outta the bottle yonder in there . . .that's it. Right into the opening. Oughta clean it up some, maybe stop it from gettin' any more putrid, though with that tops'l yard outta there, the mortification ought stop of its own." The captain picked up a roll of bandage and began applying it to Smith's chest, finishing with a round turn behind the sailor's back to hold the dressing in place.

"Ain't as pretty as a medico woulda done it, but it'll have to do. Reckon I oughta bleed him some, but I'm damned if I know how much to let out. Hold that pan there, Dunn. That's it, right under his arm." The knife blade twinkled in the lantern light and a stream of blood spurted into the basin in Dunn's hand. After a moment, he put another piece of bandage on Smith's arm and tied it securely. The flow of blood stopped and Dunn moved the pan away.

"Well, I can't do better than that. It's all I know to do. Get him back into the hammock and we'll hope Smith is strong enough to survive both whatever mortification is left and my doctorin'. Gotta get back on deck. If that turns out to be a Brit, what we've done here'll probably be for naught anyway, less'n they got a real surgeon aboard. Mister Biggs, I'll be needin' you on deck quick as you can get there. Smith'll likely be quiet for a good while with that laudanum I gave him." Rogers stepped onto the ladder and disappeared into the daylight on deck.

∗　∗　∗　∗　∗　∗

The steady drizzle showed no sign of easing; indeed, if anything, it seemed to rain harder frequently, adding to the already dismal conditions at Melville Island Prison. Many of the men stood in small groups in the walled yard, blankets or scraps of canvas over their heads and shoulders, and chatted quietly about life as a prisoner with the long term inmates of Melville, the French.

Most of them had been captured in the Indies and had been brought to Halifax, the only British base in North America, with their ships. The ships were condemned and sold; the seamen were condemned and locked up. Most had accepted their fate with calm resignation. Some tried to escape from the road-building or wood-cutting gangs that daily left the confines of the island. Most of them were quickly caught; some took longer, but any that survived the recapturing had only the Black Hole on water and ship's biscuit to look forward to. They accepted the risk but, after they again saw the daylight from the Hole, the "runners" lost the right to join the work parties and, with it, their source of income, regardless of how meager.

Almost all of the nearly six hundred French prisoners on the island knew of the supposedly successful runners: names, dates, and where each wound up. No one knew for certain that any had made it, though some certainly must have and struggled across Nova Scotia to the Acadian settlements where they were accepted and protected. Some, the Frenchmen related, had stolen boats and sailed across the Bay of Fundy, with its dangerous currents and riptides, to America. The American prisoners listened attentively to the tales and mentally made their own corrections in each failed attempt — corrections that would enable them to succeed.

"I'd reckon that water right there'll get a body into the Atlantic, easy as kiss my hand, on an ebb tide. All you'd have to do is steal a boat and you could even drift out." An American prisoner had already formed a plan, but he had no idea of the tides or the length of the Northwest Arm, or how he'd secure a boat, or get past the various batteries along the shoreline which were always manned with Royal Marines. The two French with whom he spoke merely shook their heads and said in French, "Another tenant for the Black Hole."

Elsewhere in the yard, other Frenchmen shared survival hints with the American sailors. There were few Frenchmen who spoke English with any expertise and none of the Americans spoke more than a few words of very bad French. Conversation was difficult at best, with both sides raising their voices in the hope that by so doing understanding would come. Arms flailed, heads bobbed, and some even resorted to drawing pictures in the mud in an effort to make themselves understood.

Clements and young Jake Tate, his arm now almost healed and only occasionally painful, had been fortunate in meeting with a French prisoner who had been on the island since it was a fish factory and had learned English from a guard during that time. He leaned carelessly against the stone wall of their barrack, staying out of the rain by staying under the overhang of the roof; the Americans stood facing him, standing in the rain.

". . . you catch zee rats and moles, you must eat zem quickly, or zee guard come an' take zem from you. Eef zey catch you wit' zee rats, zey cut your rations zee next day. Also, zave the bones for using in zee sewing, you are un'erstan' me?" Georges Fragard watched his new friends expectantly and smiled when they nodded.

"I sailed with a cove, back in the year two it was, what had been caught up by the Brits in the fightin' in '79. Spent nigh onto four years in some pest hole. He not once got hisself flogged though. Said the Brits only flog their own sailors, not prisoners. What about that, Georges?" Clements cast a glance at Jake, who was listening attentively.

"Zees ees *verité* — I mean, 'ow you say — trut'. Not once 'as zee prisoner 'ere been give' zee lash. Eef you try to escape and zay catch you up, after you come out of *le cachot* — zee 'ole, as you say — zay take zee clothes and you wear zen only zee blue suits wit' POW on zem all over. Zere, you see 'eem zere." Fragard pointed to a group of French prisoners, all attired in faded blue denim trousers and shirts, much like purser's slops, but each labeled

"POW" in scarlet on front and back and on each leg of the trousers. There would be no mistaking someone off the island in those clothes as anything but a prisoner.

"Zee turnkey, Major Gilpatric, ees very, 'ow you say eet, proud? *Oui*, I t'eenk zat ees it, proud, zat no prisoner has ever escaped from zee island. But 'e ees not a bad man; he arranges for zee butcher een Alfax to save for us zee bones of zee beefs — for zee carving, you know?"

"I collect that's how the coves here amuses their 'selves, eh?" Tate was beginning to take an interest in the conversation.

"*Non*, eet ees, 'ow zay, make zee money for zee extra food an zee *vin* — wine, you know? Zee store. Some of zee men make zee little *voiliers* — model *bateaux* — an' zay sell zem to zee peoples from Alfax who come to zee bazaar, which ees on Sundays. Zay pay many dollar an' zen zee mens, zay don' 'ave to eat zee rats, you know?" Fragard smiled at his students, obviously relishing his role as their mentor. He went on. "Other of zee mens, zay make zee knitting of wool, you know? An' others make zee 'ats of straw. But zee biggest is zee knitting — zay make all t'ings, from *la chemise* — excuse, I mean zee shirt, to zee gloves an' stockings. Zee people from Alfax pay moneys, an' we eat from zee turnkey's store. Ees better zan zee *merde* from zee galley, you know?"

Several of the Chesapeakes had joined the group now and had been listening attentively; all nodded enthusiastically. Some quiet talk among themselves identified various areas of expertise and several were mentally counting their profits already.

"Guess I'm gonna be eatin' 'zee *merde* from zee galley' — whatever that is. Ain't much carvin' or knittin' I kin do with but one arm. Mebbe I kin sew shirts an' such. Any o' the coves doin' that, Georges?"

"*Oui*. Zere ees a — how you say — tailor. 'e was zee *corsaire*, you know, zee . . . em . . . privateer. 'E makes zee shirts an' trousers, but 'e ees always busy. Maybe 'e needs zee 'elp, an' 'e shares with you zee moneys."

"All righty now, Georges — you been here long enough — how's a body get out o' here . . . off'n this island?" Clements voiced what many had on their minds. Furtive glances bounced around the yard, taking in the stockade fence and walls and noting the location of the few guards in evidence.

"From zee work parties only, *mon ami*. One can not get from zee island because of zee sharks. An' from zee work parties, you will be catch, an' then eet ees the *cachot* — zee 'ole, an' zee blue shirts."

"What sharks? Ain't sharks up here in this water. Too cold by half for 'em this far north. Who told you they was sharks yonder?" Johnson, just joining the group in time for the 'sharks' comment, wasn't convinced a bit.

"Oh, zee guards. Zay feed zem zee meat, you know? I 'ave nev-aire seen zee shark wit' my own eyes, but I 'ave 'eard zem splash-ing in zee waters of zee cove — when zee guards, zey feed zee meat to zem. I would not try to sweem from 'ere, my frein', eef you value your 'ide." Georges was certain of the existence of the sharks, right here in the cove at the end of the Northwest Arm.

"I was watchin' one o' the guards fishin' — jest the other day, it were — an' he was pullin' in fish right smart. They was sharks yon-der, there wouldn't be no fish gettin' caught — leastaways not with-out gettin' et in the pullin' in." Clements agreed with Johnson's original thought and was as certain of their absence as Fragard was of their presence. The other Americans nodded in agreement. And the conversation endured, until the ringing of a bell called the men to their evening meal.

CHAPTER TWENTY-ONE

Captain Rogers' concern grew. The strange ship was making an obvious effort at maintaining the weather gauge and now was closing. And they were staying just beyond the range of Rogers' nine-pounders.

"Mister Coffin, we'll go to quarters, if you please. And break out the arms chest. Battle sail now, Mister Biggs. Mister O'Mara, take over the conn." The captain stepped forward to the rail of the quarterdeck to watch the progress his crew made as some of them unlimbered the main deck carronades and the primary battery below. Others of the crew were already in the rigging to furl t'gallants, royals, and reef the courses. Reports flowed into the quarterdeck indicating readiness for battle, as Rogers thought about the fine crew he had and hoped they could survive yet another meeting with the British. Their last, while profitable for the Americans, had taken its toll and now the prizes he had in company were a liability rather than a help. He turned to a quartermaster.

"Show a signal to the prizes to bear off downwind and make all possible sail. Rejoin upon hearing my gun, or head for Salem independently tomorrow."

As the flags fluttered to the cro'jack yard conveying his orders, he watched the approaching stranger, still to wind'ard and bearing down even sharper on them. His intentions were clear.

"Open the gun ports larboard side. Pass the word for Mister Coffin." Rogers gave the orders without shifting his glance from the larger brig bearing down on them from wind'ard. He put his glass to his eye and studied her intently. The two ships were separated by just over a cannon shot and Rogers knew they would open fire — at least with a ranging shot — sooner than later.

"Sir?" Starter Coffin was at his elbow, a pry bar from one of the long guns in his hand, the other scratching his beard. He too watched the approaching vessel, his eyes squinted down more than usual as he looked toward the late day sun. Rogers turned away from the rail.

"Mister Coffin, since we'll be firing to weather, I want half the battery loaded with . . ."

Boom!

Both men turned as one in time to see gray smoke drifting over the closing brig's bow. They watched the water for the splash. None came.

"Cap'n, I think that gun was fired to wind'ard. He either wants us to heave to, or he's lettin' us know he's gonna engage us."

"There surely was no splash that I could see, Mister Coffin. As I was about to say, load chain and bar shot in the after guns; since we'll be firing high anyway, we might as well try to wound his rigging. Have the larboard battery stand ready to fire on my command."

"Cap'n, signals on that ship, sir. Showin' an American flag now, too." The quartermaster studied the brig through the long glass. Again, Rogers turned to the rail and raised his own glass to his eye.

"By the Almighty, you're right, sailor. And he's comin' around. Helmsman, bring her up two points." He faced forward and raised his voice. "Mister Biggs, we'll be hardenin' up some. Mind your sheets and braces."

"Sir, them flags is in our book. Says 'Heave to and identify'. Shall I put up the flag, sir?" Davies had his hand on the halyard and Rogers noted that the American flag was already bent on.

"Hold on a moment, son. I've seen this ruse afore. Brits'll show the American flag and maybe even the right signals from some captured signal book. By the time we smoke what's afoot, it's too late to do anything, and they got 'em a prize without firin' a shot. Lookee, they've got their ports open and the battery run out. I'd warrant they're ready to shoot quick as kiss my hand." He studied the brig, now almost within range of a musket shot, with the glass.

"Cap'n, I am sure as I can be that she's Crowninshield's *Henry*. I'd reckon he just wants to make sure who we are afore he decides we're friendly." O'Mara watched the brig close. She had not shortened down as had the *General*, and the American brig, now under her battle sail plan, stood little chance of outsailing their antagonist should she prove unfriendly.

"All right, Mister O'Mara; we'll show our colors now, if you please." Rogers continued to keep his glass on the other ship. He was aware of the snapping of the American flag as it whipped to the gaff. He half expected to see the other ship replace its own flag with the British battle ensign and open fire. He bellowed forward to the first mate in the waist.

"Mister Coffin, stand by the larboard battery. I will bear off to open the after guns as soon as I see what this cove is about. Mister Biggs, men to sail-handling stations, if you please."

As the idlers picked up braces and sheets, ready to trim for the eased course, the stranger bore up herself, backed the main tops'l and with a speed that impressed even Asa Rogers, furled her other sails and hove to. A figure climbed into the lower mizzen shrouds with a speaking trumpet.

"We are the *Henry* out of Salem. George Crowninshield, commanding. What ship are you?" The voice floated across the water easily, carried as it was by the wind. The response would have to be shouted to windward.

"Asa Rogers, George. Private armed vessel *General Washington*. We are bound in with some prizes. Come aboard if you like."

"I shall Captain. I have some information that might be of interest." As he spoke, the General Washingtons could see a boat being swung out on a double whip from the main yard. The *Henry*, hove to, but still making way, closed another 100 yards or so, and then splashed the cutter.

The crew was down the side of the ship and the boat away and pulling toward the *General* with military precision. It was only a few moments before it bumped alongside, and the waisters on the brig threw down the man ropes.

George Crowninshield, the third, climbed the battens up the side of the brig, helping himself with the man ropes. His hollow cheeks, giving his face a pinched look, made Rogers remark silently, "He looks even more like his father than I had recalled." The young man smiled, showing his teeth, but his eyes held no mirth. As he swung a long leg over the bulwark and landed on the deck, he took the proffered hand from Rogers.

"A pleasure to see you again, sir. I'd reckon the last time we met was in my father's office before the war. I had just taken command of the *Henry* and was about to leave for a cruise to the Indies. Father had her fitted out as a privateer in September of '12. Took her out once and turned her back over to me." His pride and an evident feeling of self-importance salted his words, and Captain Rogers bit back a leveling remark, instead greeting the oldest son of his main competitor cordially.

"I trust you saw your father well when you were in? I missed him the past several times I was in Salem, though his presence was surely felt, and it was only some four or five months ago I crossed tacks with Jack Leighton's *Salem Lady* outbound." As he noticed the young Crowninshield looking around the *General,* it occurred to him that they were still at quarters. "Mister Coffin, you may secure the men from quarters now. I don't think we need worry about *Henry* firing at us. Mister O'Mara: a signal to Dickerson and Hardy to rejoin, if you please, and fire a leeward gun. They're still in sight."

"I apologize for causing you concern, Captain. Seeing that Bermuda sloop and the schooner sailing in company with you caused me some concern myself. Thought you all might have been British privateers looking for some opportunities. But I collect you took 'em as prizes your own self." Seeing the older man nod, the young Crowninshield smiled wanly. "Looks like a profitable voyage for you then, sir; I give you joy of your success." An undercurrent of insincerity flowed just below his jovial tone.

"Well we ain't in yet, George. And as you said, there's a blockade hereabouts. If you're just out, you might be tellin' me where you think the Royal Navy's sailin' these days."

"Aye, sir. That's exactly what I had I mind to tell you. We left Salem just the day before yesterday, it was, and we saw one o' their frigates . . ." The two men went aft to the Cabin, and their voices trailed off, leaving the waisters and idlers wondering just what was in store for the *General* when she returned.

*　*　*　*　*　*

"Well, lookee 'ere. Back from the dead, it 'pears." Coleman, sitting outside with his fellow Chesapeakes nodded toward the hospital building and the figure, leaning heavily on a crutch, slowly making his way toward them. In Robert's hand was a scrap of driftwood from which he was fashioning a passable likeness of a whale. The others with him, Bosun Clements, Jake Tate, Johnson, and Tingley, were likewise engaged in various pursuits that they hoped would become a source of income at the Sunday bazaars.

Each looked up as Coleman spoke and their faces split into broad smiles all around.

"'Bout given you up for dead an' buried in one o' them holes over to Deadman's Island. Been a regular detail o' the Frenchies, carryin' the bodies from th' hospital into the boat an' then yonder to bury 'em. Glad to see you wasn't in one o' them." Clements set down his bit of wool and needles from which he was knitting a scarf and stood to greet the Irishman.

"Aye, they tried, I can tell you, they did, but Mrs. Conoughy's boy's tougher than old leather. No English medico's gonna put me into the ground, by all the saints." His grimace with each step, the sweat beading his brow, and the pallid tone of his face told the men that his wound was still a source of considerable pain. But he bore it with outward nonchalance and bravado; wouldn't do for his shipmates to know he still hurt something fierce.

"Give you a stick to lean on, I see. That was mighty kind of 'em. Are you healed up then, Tim? An' what happened to your clothes? Them prison slops s'posed to be only for 'runners' . . . an' God knows, you ain't gonna run nowhere for a while." Clements put out his hand and the Irishman took it, leaning more heavily on it than either of them expected; both staggered slightly, causing Tim to wince, immediately covering it with a smile. And then, keeping his still painful leg straight, he sat down on the proffered stool which the bosun had just vacated.

"Thankee for th' seat. And ain't the clothes grand, though, Jack? Just what I'd in me mind so as not to call attention to meself should I get the chance to take leave o' this place. I reckon they likely burned me other clothes — cut and ripped they was, and not a little bloody, they held no special attachment for me. Wasn't fit for wearin' even by some bilge rat, I'd warrant. An' as to the 'ealin', I reckon they figgered I was 'ealed enough to give up me bed to some poor cove who'll likely be dead sooner than later."

Conoughy, realizing that his friends likely saw through it, gave up the charade that his leg was not painful. He admitted, "Still 'urts some powerful lot, though — 'specially when I bend it. Feels like all the 'ealin' it done gonna come undone when I move it more 'an a little. Reckon that's why they give me the stick, so's I don't 'ave to move it much, least for a while. But it sure is nice to get out o' that hospital. What a misery that is — coves in there caterwaulin' all night they are. Fever an' dysentery, men dyin' near every day.

And the smell — powerful 'orrible it were; putrefaction and mor-bidity and just wouldn't quit. Hard to get a breath without near pukin', I'd warrant. Reckon they musta took out more than a few this past month an' more."

"Aye, that they did, Tim. Carried 'em in a wee boat over yonder to that little pile o' rock an' dirt they call Deadman's Island. A cove can see the trees on it from the second deck o' the barracks. One o' the Frenchies what always seems to go on the burial details told me they ain't no markers an' it's a shallow grave for each load. Ain't none o' the Chesapeakes got picked for that detail yet; must be duty for senior men. I'll tell you, though, I wouldn't mind doin' it, just for the change o' scene from inside." Tingley smiled at his com-rade, glad as the others to see him alive and back with them.

"What of the others, then, lads? 'Ow many of us're still around? Mister Blanchard an' Mister Ludlow — what of them. Did Cap'n Lawrence make it? I recollect 'e was sore wounded in the shootin', 'e were, an' me an' Mister Cox took 'im below to the surgeon while we was still fightin'. Come back up on deck, I did, an the whole quarterdeck was full o' *Shannon*s an' a Redcoat, damn 'is eyes, stuck me with a bayonet quicker 'an ever I could get outta the way. Went down like a sack o' fine Irish potatoes, an' they left me alone after that. Figgered I wasn't no worry then, I reckon. Just carried on all 'round me. Cutlasses swingin' over me 'ead, pistols goin' off, people yellin', an' them damn sharpshooters in the foretop sprayin' balls at everything that moved. They was blood flyin' everywhere, an' more 'an once, I seen some go down, theirs or ours, just from slippin' on that bloody deck. Some cove in a fancy uniform fell on top o' me — didn't know whether he just slipped or was shot 'til 'e was on th' deck an' I seen th' blood on 'is 'ead. Deep cutlass wound it was, an' 'is brains was comin' out th' side o' 'is 'ead. Decided 'e was an officer, I did, from the look of 'im, an' then I musta passed out, cuz the next thing I can recall was comin' to below — on *Shan-non*, it was, an' I 'ad manacles on me wrists. Recollect you was there, Robert, and Tingley too. Didn't see none o' the others o' you coves, though 'til we took our little walk through the woods, an' precious little o' that comes to me mind. Don't recall seein' any o' the officers either." Conoughy stopped, and looked around at his former shipmates, obviously glad to be back in their company, and anxious for news. His eyes fell on Jack Clements, and he frowned. "What 'appened to your ear, Jack? Ain't natural, 'avin' but one."

"Well, ain't that just so. Reckon the same thing what happened to your leg, 'ceptin' mine come clean off." Clements filled in the details of his wound for the Irishman and finished his tale with "but I don't pay it no mind; got me another what works just fine, long as people talk into that side o' me head!" He laughed ruefully and sat down in the dirt. "As to the officers, well, I guess you ain't heard that Cap'n Lawrence been dead since afore we come to anchor in Halifax. Didn't hear nothin' from any o' the lads 'bout buryin' him at sea, so I reckon they took him ashore to bury. Seen Mister Blanchard an' Mister Cox goin' ashore from *Shannon* 'bout the same time as the rest of us, but I got no idea what happened to 'em then. They ain't here, though, I can tell you that. Heard Mister Ludlow was cruel hurt; he'd likely be in the hospital at the dockyards in Halifax — or dead."

"Zee 'ospital sends out anozer, eh? An' zees one, he ees alive, not for zee, em, 'ow you say, bury on *la petite isle, oui?* Georges strolled up to the group and stuck out his hand to the Irish gunner. "I am called Fragard."

Tim looked up at the Frenchman, smiled, and took his hand. Johnson spoke up for the first time. "This cove's Georges, Tim. Speaks English pretty good for a Frenchy an' he's been some helpful to a few of us, what with showin' us the ropes an' all. Been here a while, so he knows most o' what's doin'." Johnson held up the piece of bone he had been whittling on. "Showed us 'bout makin' gewgaws for the bazaar they hold ever' Sunday. Ain't sold nothin' yet, but these Frenchies ain't doin' bad at it, near as I can figger." He smiled at Fragard, who nodded.

"*Mai oui.* In time, *mon ami*, you will be selling to zee peoples from Alfax too. When you 'ave something to sell, I think." He looked back to Tim and continued. "I esplain you. Most of my countrymen 'ave been 'ere since zee beginning. After all, consider; *les Français* 'ave been at war wit' the British for many more years than *les Americains.*" He puffed up a little, and continued. "I myself 'ave been 'ere after one year an' more on zee — how you say, *les bateaux* — zee sheeps without zee masts in Bedford Basin — *oui*, zee 'ulks. Thees island was still zee fish factory when first I bring 'ere, you are un'erstand me? I think my *Anglais* ees not so good."

"Aye, Georges, I understand you just fine. But 'ow's a cove get 'imself off this island, eh? No interest 'ave I 't'all in stayin' 'ere more time 'an it takes to figger out a way off . . . and get me leg to work proper." Tim grimaced as he shifted his weight on the little stool.

"You, I zink, will not be leaving soon, *mon ami*. Even if zere was — 'ow you say, *le rue* — zee street to lead you over. Per'aps, when zee leg can walk, zen you get on zee work party, an' maybe zen you see a way. You must have zee patience, you are un'erstan' me?"

"Patience, aye. Got me plenty o' that, by all that's 'oly. An' me leg be 'ealin' right quick. Won't be long afore I'm . . . 'old on there. Why ain't you coves got your own selves on a work party?" He looked sharply at his former shipmates and was greeted with sorrowful looks.

"They ain't givin' the Chesapeakes any work parties, Tim. I reckon they figger we might try to escape. An' they got us under they's eyes most o' the time — 'ceptin' at night and then we're locked into the barracks. An' there's a long gun — eighteen-pounder I'd guess from the size of it — right outside the gate an' aimed in. Heard it was loaded with grape, case anyone opens the gate when they shouldn't. 'Cordin' to Georges here, ain't no one ever got off the island without they was on a work party." Jake shook his head. "Don't mean we ain't been thinkin' on it, though. Couple of the lads got some ideas workin', but no one's tried to make it yet. One of them even thought o' bustin' the head one o' the dandies what comes in on Sundays for the bazaar an' takin' his clothes an' walkin' right out with the rest of 'em when they leave. Might happen, too."

The conversation was interrupted by a commotion at the main gate. They watched as it opened, allowing a work party to return under the watchful eyes of three marines with muskets held ready. Through the opening in the palisades they could all see the Royal Marines outside on the mainland, attentively manning their artillery piece. Indeed, as Jake had mentioned, it was aimed right into the compound. At the end of the work party, a tall man, not in uniform and obviously not part of the work gang, walked up to the turnkey, held a brief conversation, and entered the compound. The gate swung closed behind him and he stopped, as if getting his bearings. As he turned toward the Chesapeakes, his face broke into a smile and he walked confidently forward.

"By all that's holy, lads, would you lookee there. Mister Blanchard, over here!" Clements was on his feet again, and waving his arms toward the approaching figure. Indeed, it was Midshipman — still Acting Lieutenant — Blanchard, and in civilian clothes. He looked older than any remembered him, even though it was something less than two months since they had parted company on the deck of *Shannon* in Halifax Harbor.

"Are you lads doing well? Do they take care of you? Bosun, how's that head, eh? Tate, sorry about your arm, lad. Reckon you'll be out of all this once we get ourselves home. Gunner, when last I seen you, you could barely walk, and no mistake there." He nodded at the others. "I reckon you'll want to know that Cap'n Lawrence died from his wounds afore we got to anchor an' they give him a captain's burial, right in Halifax. Turned out a host of Royal Navy and Marines, an' the senior-most captains in the harbor was his pall-bearers. Let what was left of the American officers an' midshipmen march in the procession. Buried him with full honors, they did. Mister Ludlow too." He saw the surprised looks and hastened to explain. "I reckon you know the first lieutenant was sore wounded during the fightin' and, while he lingered for a week an' more after we come in, he didn't survive his wounds. The Brits gave him a fine funeral as well and buried him right next to the Cap'n. Most o' the townfolks turned out for it, well as for the Cap'n. Had a church service an' procession with honors befittin' his rank all the way to the graveyard. I was right there with Mister Cox." He stopped, as if thinking, for a moment. The bosun filled the brief silence and was joined immediately by the other Chesapeakes in a rush of questions.

"Where they got you, Mister Blanchard, an' why ain't you locked up?"

"What happened to your uniform? They take it away from you, or what?"

"Who else 'sides Mister Cox an' you is still alive?"

"Can you get us outta 'ere?"

"What of the ship, sir?"

The young lieutenant laughed and held up his hands. "Haul short there, men. I'll tell you what you want to know." He looked at the expectant faces around the group and tried to give nothing away with his own expression. One of the men jumped up to offer Blanchard his seat, and the lieutenant sat down. The men gathered around him; even Conoughy leaned forward, the better to hear his officer. And Georges Fragard, after a brief introduction to the American officer, hunkered down with the others to hear news of the outside world.

"The Brits give all — ha, 'all', indeed; there wasn't but two of us an' a handful of mids still alive — or out of the hospital." The young officer laughed ruefully and began again. "They gave Mister Cox and me our parole and took us across the harbor to a town called Preston. There's a bunch of Frogs — *pardon, m'seur* — officers all, who been livin' there for some years. Seems like that's where they put all the captured officers, seein' as how there ain't but little chance to run off — and we all gave our parole on top of it. Anyway, the place's just farms and poor folk who put the officers into spare rooms, or in their barns, I reckon, at times. The Agent for Prisoners gives us an allowance of half pay, most of which goes to the farmer for the room and what little food they can spare us. I borrowed some money from one of the French officers to buy some clothes so I didn't have to wear the uniform all the time. The *Chesapeake*'s still to anchor in the harbor, and when I come across in the ferry from Dartmouth just this morning there was a passel of boats still around it, like they'd never seen a frigate afore. As to gettin' you out of here; that's . . . well, I don't know . . . you see, there's talk of exchanging the officers for some Brit officers bein' held in Boston, but nobody has said anything about exchanging you men. I don't know what will happen there, but I'll speak to the Agent for Prisoners when next I see him and inquire."

Their faces, hoping for good news, fell, and even though most knew, or guessed before they heard it that they were here for the duration, despaired at hearing the words spoken aloud. They would be here until the war ended. Whenever that would be.

The conversation drifted on, with little of consequence being said, until the lieutenant stood, saying "Well lads, it's back to Preston for me; wouldn't want to get picked up by our 'hosts' wandering around the streets of Halifax. You watch yourselves, and I'll get back when I can."

With that, he shook a few hands, and strode purposefully toward the gate, which was opened by the guard. The Chesapeakes watched his departure silently; one lifted a hand and waved to the officer's back, unseen, and then the gate was closed.

CHAPTER
TWENTY-TWO

Asa Rogers looked around the room; quite impressive, he thought. *Certainly fancier than the meetin' room in my place. Likely impresses anyone comin' in to make a deal with the Crown-inshields.* He had been shown into the room by a mousy clerk, whose appearance was not in the least enhanced by the threadbare and dingy shirt showing above the equally worn waistcoat which lacked several buttons on its front. The young clerk had asked him apologetically to "Have a seat, sir, while I fetch the misters."

Before he sat, however, he had a look around the room; surprisingly, Rogers had not before been entertained in this room by his sometimes-friendly competitors. *Must be something important, to be summoned here,* he thought.

Around the room was a variety of paintings of men and ships; many bore labels on the ornate frames indicating the subject and the date. Some ranged back to the pre-Revolution days, he noted, and depicted the hard-eyed stares of former Crowninshields, obviously masters and deep-water men; no pallid paper shufflers in this group! He studied closely a brilliant image of a ship, a brig of some considerable draft; it looked familiar to him, but he couldn't place it. *Well, I likely seen it more'n once comin' or goin' from the harbor. Guess it would be strange for it not to be familiar-looking.* He was still studying it when he sensed, rather than saw or heard, a presence behind him. He turned, as George Crownin-shield, Jr. spoke to him.

"She sails as good as she looks and I agree, she's a handsome vessel, by all the stars! Hullo, Asa, and thankee kindly for comin' by."

"Hello George. I didn't hear you come in, so intent was I on this fine lookin' brig. She looks mighty familiar; reckon I've seen her in person more'n once comin' or goin'."

George looked at his guest with a bemused expression. "I should hope; she's young George's command — the self-same one what met you t'other day when you was bringin' in those prizes. You recollect the brig *Henry*, I 'magine. Accordin' to George, you two give each other quite a scare. Good thing neither of you turned out to be what the other thought — surely woulda come out different, I'd warrant." The senior Crowninshield smiled, albeit thinly, and, while his eyes crinkled with mirth, his thin lips barely curled upwards to show a glimpse of yellowed teeth.

"Fine young man, young George is." Rogers deflected the conversation away from his memory lapse. "Hadn't seen him in some time, until the other day. Almost didn't recognize him when he came aboard. Half expected you when he hollered across the water that he was 'George Crowninshield'. A competent seaman, I'd warrant, as well."

"Aye, he is that. I gave him the *Henry* upon fittin' her out as a privateer, and right pleased I am, indeed, with what he's done with her. More'n a half dozen prizes he's brought in, some with fine cargoes that turned the firm a tidy sum. But you ain't interested in our successes. And that's not what I asked you here for, either. Something more serious by half, I'd warrant, and something I'm bettin' you'll want to join with, if I know you, Asa."

Rogers looked hard at his friend. They were competitors and unlikely it was that George Crowninshield would invite his longest and strongest competitor to 'join with' anything of commercial benefit. Rogers' firm was still considered by the Crowninshield family to be 'upstarts'; it had only been in business for one generation, coming into the second with Asa's sons, while the other's history went back well into the days when Massachusetts was still only a colony. Even so, next to George's enterprise, there was none with a longer history, nor more successes, than the Rogers' firm. He sat down in the offered chair and George walked around the long table to sit opposite him.

The silence hung heavily in the room as Crowninshield collected his thoughts. He steepled his fingers in front of his face, his elbows resting on the highly-polished table. Piecing blue eyes under bushy gray eyebrows stared at his competitor, his mouth a thin line.

Suddenly, he dropped his arms to the table and folded in all but his index fingers; still steepled, they pointed at Rogers like a long gun poking out from a gun port.

"Young George'll be with us in a moment, but I reckon we can start. Let me tell you some background and then I'll lay out my plan to you.

"Two months past, back in June, the first it was — a dreadful day, by all the stars — Jim Lawrence took the *Chesapeake* out to meet HMS *Shannon* right off the harbor down to Boston. I believe you mighta missed the horrible event, bein' as how you had the *General Washington* at sea, if the memory serves."

"Aye. That's a fact. Come in the day after the battle — passed the two of 'em during the early morning afore we made port. Found out later it was them we passed knotting and splicing and makin' repairs afore they headed up to Halifax, I guess."

"Well, as you read in the papers, Cap'n Jim was cruel hurt during the battle and died afore even they raised Halifax. The Brits, from all accounts, give him a splendid funeral with all the trappings fittin' a captain — even a Royal Navy captain." He paused again. Rogers nodded, his face giving nothing away, and his friend pressed on.

"Problem is, Lawrence got buried up there in Halifax along with his first lieutenant, a Mister Ludlow, who passed on some days after they was in. Some of the folks hereabouts don't think that's right, an American frigate captain — a hero, in point of fact — bein' buried in British soil. I aim to go get him — and Ludlow."

At that point the door opened and young George strode in, his pinched face and close-set eyes darted around the room and took in Asa Rogers sitting opposite his father, to whom he spoke first.

"Sorry I kept you waiting, sir. Had some pressing matters that needed takin' care of right quick. Nice to see you again, Cap'n Rogers. I collect you made the harbor without difficulty?" Again, his lips smiled, but not his eyes.

"That we did, George. And thanks in no small way to your well-informed advice on the blockaders. Woulda' been mighty inconvenient to meet up with one or more of them, what with the *General* not totally fit and them other two jury-rigged just enough to get 'em home. I thank you again."

The younger Crowninshield formed his mouth into what might pass for a smile and nodded once in acknowledgment. The pleasantries done with, his father continued.

"Sit, George. I was just about to tell Asa about my plan to bring Lawrence and Ludlow back to Salem and give 'em a proper funeral and a monument right here in town." He turned back to Rogers and smiled thinly; the tip of his tongue, startlingly pink against the pale skin, poked out and wet his bloodless lips. "I got a letter of truce signed by Mister Madison down to Washington which I 'spect'll let us sail to Halifax without bein' bothered by the Royal Navy; and should they wish to board, the letter'll likely provide us with passage into and then back out of Halifax Harbor. I aim to sail the *Henry* right up to their dockyard and get the two of 'em and then sail back out again. I reckon that what with them Brits bein' civilized folk, they oughtn't to have any difficulty with us carryin' home our dead. What do you think?"

"I think that's fine, George. Reckon the Brits got enough decency in 'em to let you pass through their ships. But what is it you want me to do?" Rogers was mystified as to why he had been called here to learn of the plan and it came through in his voice.

"I was just comin' to that, exactly. The *Henry* brig ain't going to be crewed like a privateer, Asa; I got together a dozen and more masters from hereabouts and down to Marblehead and they're going to crew the vessel. Reckon it's a proper tribute to Cap'n Jim and oughta be mighty impressive to the Brits to see the regard we hold him in. I'm askin' you to join us." Crowninshield looked hard at the man across the table and waited for his answer. Again, his fingers steepled in his folded hands, forming the familiar long gun aimed at his guest.

Rogers looked back at him and raised his eyebrows. "What about the ones what's still alive up yonder — the other officers . . . and the sailors? We gonna get them as well?"

Young George responded. "Likely the officers'll be traded back to us for some Brits we're holding here, Cap'n. And the men . . . well, nobody seems to know what's afoot there. Asides, gettin' 'em back is rightly the Navy's responsibility. And that damned jinx ship is still in the harbor, I'm told. Likely . . ." He was beginning to get thoroughly exercised when his father interrupted.

"Now George, don't start with that 'jinx ship' bilge again. You know 's'well as anyone, ain't no jinx on the *Chesapeake*. Though I'll admit she's had more'n her share of bad luck. From her launching when she stuck on the ways to that terrible incident with the Brits back in ought seven to right up when she come in from her last cruise afore Lawrence took her out. An' the fact he lost out that day was on account o' the Brits usin' some kinda explodin' device — like a granado. I got that on good authority. But jinx? No, some bad captains combined with some bad plannin' and some ungentlemanly tactics, you ask me. As to the men, Asa, I collect they're held in a prison on some island — can't rightly recall the name just now — in what they call the Northwest Arm. 'Ppears to be a narrow cut up the back side o' the city. I might even have an old chart of it somewhere. But that's not my aim; as young George just said, that's the Navy's problem. Mine, and ours if you'll sign on, is just gettin' Lawrence and Ludlow and bringin' 'em back here for a proper burial, as I said. What say you, Asa? Are you comin'?"

"Just the one vessel, George? You're puttin' a powerful lot of faith in a piece o' paper, you ask me. The Brits don't care 'bout Madison signing a 'truce' document, less'n it's for the whole shebang. They could board you and take you in as a prize yourself; and all them masters you got signed. You oughta consider goin' up there in more'n one ship and armed well, should there be some trouble. I might bring the *General* to help you should something unforeseen occur. Can't think it would hurt none." Rogers smiled disarmingly across the table.

Both father and son frowned. They didn't expect to have the very essence of their plan questioned. But Asa Rogers was a successful businessman and privateersman. Maybe there was merit to what he said. The two Crowninshields looked at each other.

Asa leaned back in his chair and looked around the room. He noticed the exquisite molding around the ceiling and the dentalling under it. The oil sconces and the chandelier were obviously costly and probably came from England well before the current hostilities; maybe even before the previous war. Likely made of crystal, he deduced from the way they caught the window light and bounced it around the room in miniature rainbows. More stern-countenanced men stared down at him, further testimony to the longevity of the company and, from the unsmiling, hard eyes on each, evidence that these men were responsible for the early successes of the shipping firm; Asa could imagine that these coves would brook no nonsense and each had probably seen his share of difficulties. Likely to have been privateers during the War of Independence 's'well, he thought, just like the current owners and their captains. His mind went from the portraits of the iron-handed — and willed — forebears of the Crowninshields to the men who likely were languishing in some pest-infested and foul hole in Halifax. He looked back at George.

"You propose to take this risk — the risk of one of your best vessels and the lives of a dozen and more ship captains — just to bring back a couple of bodies what're already buried? Doesn't sound smart to me, George. If you was goin' after the men, I'd be more inclined to join you; after all, they're alive, I reckon." As he spoke, the two Georges' frowns deepened, and the senior Crowninshield furrowed his brow in consternation, his jaw muscles clenching, giving his cheeks an unnatural, hollow look.

"Asa, Jim Lawrence was a hero and he fell in battle defending our country. It just ain't right that his remains should spend all eternity in some God-forsaken place like Halifax. The folks here need to be reminded of what a hero he was and I aim to do that with a monument markin' his grave — right here in Salem. If'n you don't want to tell me you're with us right now, you can think on it for a while, but I'm goin' whether you come or no — and within a week from right now."

"George, I think what you're doin' is admirable by any man's measure. I surely do. But I got no need to risk my life for a couple o' bodies. You can put up any number o' monuments without puttin' a body under 'em. And I'd think that if it was so all-fired important, the Navy would be takin' care o' this, not leavin' it to the local citizenry. I'm thinkin' more on what's goin' to happen to the sailors from that ship — the live ones? They just gonna be left to rot in some prison in — what'd you call it? the Northwest Arm, aye, that's it — or is somebody goin' after them?"

"Lookee here, Asa." The senior Crowninshield's frustration was beginning to get the better of him and he had difficulty understanding Rogers' reticence to participate in what he considered a grand gesture. "The Navy can't go get anyone, alive or dead; they can't even get their ships to sea. The damn blockade got 'em bottled up all the way to the Virginia Capes. Decatur's on the *United States* with a couple of others — the old British *Macedonian*, the one Decatur sent in last year, and *Hornet* — all tied up in New London, likely grounded on their own beef bones by now so long have they been blocked in. *Constitution*'s just finishin' a refit down to

Boston, but it ain't lookin' like Cap'n Stewart's goin' to get out anytime soon. They's more in New York can't get out past Sandy Hook and I reckon the Chesapeake Bay's closed up tighter'n a Scotsman's purse with whatever ships're there. No sir; ain't goin' to be a Navy ship goin' anywhere for a good while, I'd warrant. Which leaves it up to the privateer fleet, which seems to come and go as they will, and I ain't got to wait to be told what to do here. As to gettin' the sailormen, I reckon that'd take a damn army to accomplish; the Brits up there ain't goin' to let me or anyone just sail in there and gather up those men. They're holdin' 'em in a prison, as prisoners of war, Asa. No, I don't reckon gettin' them out can be done — not with a piece o' paper from President Madison, by all the stars. But gettin' Lawrence and Ludlow, I reckon the Brits could understand that and not make a big fuss about it. We're goin'. Now how about it; you joinin' me — or no?" George glared at his friend and, feeling some spittle that had collected in the corners of his mouth, wiped it away with a well-manicured hand in a gesture that was both angry and impatient. Young George had not seen his father so exercised since he quit commanding ships in the fleet. He tentatively put a calming hand on his father's sleeve. It was rudely shaken off.

"Well, George, I certainly do appreciate your offer to join you, I do. But I got to think on it for a bit afore I make any rash judgments. I thank you for your hospitality and, should I determine not to go with you, I wish you the best of successes. I'll take my leave now, if you please." With that, Asa Rogers calmly unfolded his lanky frame from the chair and rose. As he opened the door to leave, he heard young George comment under his breath, "You surely don't need him, Father. I doubt he has the courage to sail into Halifax Harbor. I heard on the waterfront that he won't engage even a merchant if they's an escort anywhere under the horizon. I reckon . . ."

"Hold your tongue, George. You don't know what you're talkin' about. Asa Rogers is one o' the best and boldest sailin' out yonder; he'd be a worthy addition to the crew — that's why I asked him."

Rogers had tensed initially as heard the young man's comment. Now he again relaxed and allowed himself a small smile, closing the door behind him. *Nice to know at least one of the Crowninshields has some regard for him.*

CHAPTER TWENTY-THREE

"You may set t'gallants, now Mister Coffin, if you please, and have someone bring that Frenchman — what's his name . . . Faitoute, I believe — to my cabin. And keep the lookouts sharp. Another close call with a Brit ain't gonna do us any good; we can't expect to have a convenient fog bank today. Now the wind's changed, the weather's too clear by half for that. It was only through the Grace of God that we didn't get ourselves caught by that frigate. That and the inattentiveness of their lookouts." Rogers smiled, recalling the sight of the Royal Navy frigate still hull down and to seaward, and oblivious of them. Had it not been for the fog lying just to leeward that he sailed into, the *General* would most likely have been smashed to matchwood or taken as a prize. This blockade was becoming a source of constant aggravation, not only to him but to all the privateers operating in the North Atlantic.

He listened as the watch was ordered to stations for handling sails and, hearing Third Mate Isaac Biggs send his topmen aloft to let fly the t'gallants for'ard, stepped into his Cabin. Moments later the Frenchman, a former naval officer and captain, knocked at his door.

"Captain Faitoute, when we met in Salem last week, you outlined a plan you thought might get us into the Northwest Arm and more specifically, to Melville Island with little or no trouble. I am glad you were willing to join us and I apologize to you for not being more hospitable for the past two days since we got underway. You will understand, I think, the necessity of my being on deck which left little time for the niceties." Rogers smiled at his guest; he had begun to like this Frenchman.

He recalled their earlier meeting in a coffee house in Salem, introduced by a privateer captain who happened to be in port that day. Faitoute, the skipper said, had been given his parole and transport to Massachusetts earlier in the year after being held by the British in Halifax for nearly twelve months. After chatting for a while, Rogers learned that while the former French officer had given his promise not to take up arms against England, advising an American privateersman would not, in his own mind, constitute a breech of that promise.

And so had begun a relationship. Captain Rogers wanted to know if it was possible to get into the Northwest Arm — essentially under the Royal nose — and out again without getting caught; Faitoute had an ax to grind and was more than willing to help in any way he could. And he had knowledge of the area from first-hand observation that was unavailable elsewhere.

"*Oui, Capitan.* I 'ave no difficulties wit' your need to sail your sheep t'rough the blockade. I am mos' 'appy to 'elp you and, as you Americans say, 'wipe the eye' of the British. The memory of HMS *Orpheus* pounding my beautiful little brig *Toulon* wit' 'is 'eavy cannon an' then doing not'ing to stop the fires except . . . well, thees ees no' your problem, sir. But I will remember until my last breath the sight of my fine brig in flames and then exploding as the fires touched the magazine." Faitoute shook his head, as if to dislodge the memory that had been his constant companion for a year and more.

He looked at the American captain and smiled ruefully. "As I said, *Capitan,* thees ees not your problem. I will again show you on the chart exactly how you might get to the prison, but I will have to draw for you the final part of the journey, as it will not be on the chart." Faitoute stood and leaned over the desk where Rogers had laid out a chart — old to be sure, but the Royal Navy wasn't making current ones readily available to Americans — that showed the coast of Nova Scotia and the entrance to Halifax. Rogers joined him, a pair of brass dividers in hand, and the two began talking intently, devising a strategy to carry out Rogers' self-assigned mission.

On deck, Isaac and Second Mate O'Mara, who had the watch, stood at the taffrail astern of the brig's wheel and watched as the handy little Bermuda sloop kept pace with them, a cable to leeward and just off the *General's* starboard quarter. The day before, both men recalled, the fleet sloop had been first to make the safety of the enshrouding fog bank.

"She swims right nice, eh, Isaac? For a little fellow, she's keeping right up with us. Hardy's doin' right well, I'd warrant — for never havin' sailed somethin' like that. Must be on account o' that ketch we're draggin' along behind us. Any idea what all this is about? Cap'n ain't told none of us much, that I can figger. Even Starter Coffin ain't been told nothin'.'"

"Well, Tom, first off, Hardy's sailed 'bout everything what'll float and hold canvas; that's why he's a prize cap'n. Never know what he's gonna have to sail or in what kinda shape. As for what's gonna happen next, Cap'n don't exactly confide in me neither. But I reckon he'll be tellin' us what we're about soon's he figgers we need to know. It's that French cove I cain't figger. I know I seen him somewhere afore. He an' I crossed tacks sometime, but I surely cain't recollect where. Well, mayhaps it'll occur to me afore this cruise is done." Isaac stared off into nothingness for a moment before he shook his head and continued.

"But I'll warrant this ain't gonna be no ordinary cruise. We ain't never gone out — least since I been aboard — with a vessel in tow and a prize alongside. That don't happen 'til we're headin' in. And it ain't normal for Cap'n Rogers to hang on to a prize. Heard ashore the other day he snatched it right out o' the auctioneer's hand, he did. Said he decided not to sell it, even after it'd been condemned as a prize. Strange doin's, you ask me." Biggs paused and looked at the ketch following obediently on her long tow line. "And Starter tol' me just afore we claimed our anchor the other night that that ketch astern is full to th' gun'ls with explosives and rockets. Can't figger what for, for the life o' me."

The second mate watched the ketch on her towline with a renewed interest, armed now as he was with the knowledge that her cargo could, if handled carelessly, turn them all into scrap in the wink of an eye. No wonder Hardy was keeping his distance at a cable and more.

With their course generally northeasterly, O'Mara was guessing that they were heading toward Nova Scotia or the coast of northern Massachusetts, probably to teach those royalist bastards a thing or two about tradin' with the enemy like they been doin' since the war began. As he understood it, their continued trade wasn't so much a statement against the war as it was a desire to increase their wealth. The war had severely hampered the loyal American traders who dealt only with neutrals or that long-term enemy of

Great Britain, Napoleon Bonaparte. And even honest trading was becoming increasingly difficult in light of the ever-tightening blockade along the eastern seaboard of America. Their conversation was interrupted by Ben Stone, captain of the foretop, who sought the third mate.

"Beggin' your pardon, Mister Biggs. I'm wonderin' if I might have a word with you?" Stone stood a respectful distance from the two mates so as not to be within easy earshot of their conversation. He had spoken during a lull in their words.

"Aye, Stone. What can I do for you?" Biggs turned, leaning his back on the rail behind him and smiled at his topman.

"It's that cove we took aboard to replace Tight-Fisted Smith, sir, that I ain't sure 'bout. Had him aloft earlier while we loosed the t'gallant for'ard, an' he froze up on me. Don't act like he never been aloft afore, you ask me. Gonna kill hisself or someone else, there's a problem."

"Cathcart? Recall he said he'd been a topman in the Navy just last year. Said his ship was paid off an' here he was. Thought it mighta been a touch off the mark at the time, since I don't think the Navy pays off when they come in. Too hard to find more crew — an' train 'em. Brits only do it when they put a vessel in ordinary — and then only when they's in home waters. But he claimed to know his work. I ain't much concerned 'bout whether he's a deserter from the Navy — or somethin' else — but I surely ain't happy to hear what you're tellin' me now. What's your thought on what to do 'bout him?"

"Sure wish ol' Smith hadda pulled through. Butterfingers tol' me 'bout what the Cap'n did — diggin' that lump o' wood outta Smith's chest; thought when he done that that he mighta had a chance. I know we had our fallin' outs from time to time, but I couldn't ask for a better topman. Aye, he was one to have next to you when the weather was up."

"Aye, I reckon he'll be missed, Stone, but the medico ashore couldn't get all the putrefaction outta him — even bled him two, three times after we brought him in. Said they was more'n likely pieces of cloth an' dirt in the wound aside the splinter an' even if Cap'n Rogers hadda took the splinter out right off, they'da still putrefied in there. A loss to be sure. But that don't answer my question; what do you aim to do about Cathcart?"

"He freezes again up there, I'm gonna throw his no-good arse over the side. He ain't no use to me. How 'bout we put him on hauley-pulley and see if they's one of the waisters what wants to go aloft?"

"I'll check with Mister Coffin on it, Stone. See what we can do. If'n we don't get you a replacement, though, you'll have do with what you got. Either make Cathcart a topman, or work the yards short-handed."

Stone acknowledged the mate's remark and returned forward, clearly unhappy. O'Mara commented on it and added that he sensed a general undercurrent of tension aboard; not like the last cruise when the men were all eager to get to sea and take prizes. "I'd reckon ever' man jack of 'em knows they's somethin' afoot here — somethin' different 'bout this time," he added with a frown. They would not have to wait much longer to discover just what it was that was going to be different this time out.

Toward the end of the first dog-watch, Captain Rogers, accompanied by their French supernumerary, called all hands to the break of the quarterdeck. The men gathered by watch in two loose groups, led by their petty officers. The mates joined the captain and the Frenchman on the quarterdeck and for a moment or two, they listened to the murmurings of their crew as they guessed and wagered on what they would hear. All had assumed that "Now we're gonna find out what all this is about." They were right.

"Men, I reckon most of you figgered out this ain't to be an ordinary cruise; and it ain't, not by a long shot. We wouldn't be goin' out with that little sloop yonder, nor with a ketch towin' astern loaded with explosives." A general rumbling of surprise went through the crew, though to Rogers, it didn't sound negative — a good sign, he thought. He waited while the mates restored quiet, then continued in the same low voice in which he had started.

"You all recollect that when Cap'n Lawrence took the navy frigate *Chesapeake* out at the start of June, he got himself beat pretty bad by the British frigate *Shannon.* A lot of men on both sides was killed, it said in the newspaper accounts of the battle, but they's a lot of Chesapeakes, men and officers, what're bein' held in a prison not far from Halifax." He stopped when the Frenchman touched his sleeve and turned. Faitoute spoke under his breath and Rogers turned back to his crew.

"Cap'n Faitoute, here, tells me there are no officers held in prison with the seamen, but there likely are all the survivin' seamen held in a place called Melville Island. I aim to use *Dancer* and that ketch astern to get 'em out and bring 'em home." He pointed first at the Bermuda sloop, still sailing neatly about a cable to leeward, and then the smaller ketch tugging at her tow-line as the beam waves slid her first to one side and then the other of the *General.*

"We got us a plan that's as good as I can make it based on what we know and what Cap'n Faitoute, here, can provide about the lay-out and customs of the Brits in Halifax. I reckon we're gonna have to sail by the seat of our pants once we get in close, but it won't be no different from takin' on some of the Brits we took on together goin' back to the start of this war. Most o' you men was aboard when we took the boats into a fleet o' merchants in a snow storm last winter. That took a lot of courage; this'll likely take the same. If this fine tops'l breeze we got holds, I 'spect we'll be heavin' to durin' the morning watch tomorrow to get ready and make some changes, both to the *General,* and *Dancer.* And once it starts, it's gonna have to keep actin' 'til it's either over an' we're out with the men, or they catch us an' lock us up with the Chesapeakes." The silence that greeted his words was complete. The groan of the spars in their jere tyes and quiet whistle of the breeze through the mile and more of rope rigging, the rattle of the occasionally unstrained block, and the whoosh of the sea as it parted and slid past the sleek hull were easily heard — and totally ignored, by all hands.

Suddenly, a voice from the larboard watch cried out, "Three cheers for th' Cap'n . . . huzzah . . . huzzah . . . huzzah!"

Before the first 'huzzah' was done, the rest of the crew, to a man, joined in lustily and voiced their complete approval to Rogers' daring plan — even though none, including the captain himself, knew what they might encounter in its execution. Such was their confidence in Asa Rogers.

CHAPTER TWENTY-FOUR

Ding ding, ding. Five-thirty in the morning watch. The crew had been piped to breakfast, but few could eat, the anticipation being what it was. The privateer and the Bermuda sloop were hove to in calm pewter seas under an ominous sky. The brief but fiery sunrise of earlier in the watch foretold ugly weather moving in, but many expected it as the night before had become increasingly overcast. And then the wind had died, just after it clocked into the east. No rain yet, but the day was far from over; in fact for much of the American crew, it had barely begun. And most knew they would see rain sweeping in from the open expanse of the North Atlantic on the crest of a growing gale. It was only a matter of when.

By the middle of the morning watch *Dancer* was secured alongside the *General Washington* and a steady stream of men moved back and forth between the two vessels. They carried munitions, arms, cutlasses and pikes to the little sloop and then, curiously, burlap sacks filled with they knew not what, but happily not heavy. The sacks were stowed in the sloop's hold on top of the weaponry and when the task was finished, a casual look would reveal the hold filled almost to capacity with sacks of unmilled grain. While *Dancer* was being loaded and fitted out as a merchant trader, a meeting was going on in the Cabin of *General Washington*, to detail the plan.

Jeremiah Hardy, Prize Captain and skipper of the Bermuda sloop, would sail her into the outer harbor of Halifax and hopefully be able to convince any Brits who might stop him that he was only an American trader bringing grain to Hosterman's Mill in Purcells Cove. The sloop's crew would consist of a landing party of privateersmen under the direction of Third Mate Isaac Biggs. And

Second Mate Tom O'Mara, along with half a dozen more seamen, would stand into the shore in the bomb ketch towing a pair of the *General*'s boats. What happened after that would be decided on the spot and depended in large measure on the weather (hopefully bad), Hardy's ability at playacting (hopefully excellent), and the manning level of the various batteries along the shore of the approaches to the harbor (hopefully weak and inattentive). Captain Rogers would sail the privateer undetected into the shallows behind MacNabb's Island, called the Eastern Passage, and wait for his men to carry out their part of the mission, but ready to assist with the *General*'s guns if he deemed it necessary.

"*Oui*, American sheeps sail into the 'arbor all the times, I think. And never 'ave I 'eard of them being detained. When you pass the battery at York Redoubt, if they see you, you may 'ave a visit from a Royal Marine at Point Pleasant, right 'ere at the — 'ow you say — *la bouche?* — *oui*, the mout' of the Northwest Arm." Jean Faitoute stabbed his finger at the chart and the prize captain, third mate, and second mate all peered attentively at it. Captain Rogers stood to one side, having already been through it with Faitoute several times. Each time some small change had been made to strengthen the plan. Neither felt they could further improve on it.

"How're they gonna know we ain't lookin' to be hostile? I don't reckon they gonna let just any ship sail in easy as kiss my hand, now, eh?" Hardy was not totally convinced that this Frenchman had all the answers.

"You'll be flying a Brit flag in addition to the American; that's what Cap'n Faitoute says all the traders do when they come in. And if this weather continues to thicken, it ain't likely they'll see you anyway. Accordin' to the cap'n here, it's an easy league twixt this York Redoubt and Point Pleasant; they ain't going to be seein' signal flags sent one to t'other — or lights, for that matter — in the teeth of a gale." Captain Rogers spoke for the first time since the briefing had begun and Biggs, O'Mara, and Hardy nodded in unison, hoping the weather would be as bad as they needed. "And," he added, "even if they should see a signal, they ain't likely to be comin' out to have a look-see in a small boat in that weather. Not the Royal Marines, I'm thinkin'."

"*Oui*. Purcells Cove, she is right 'ere, and 'osterman's Mill 'ere." Again Faitoute's long tapered finger touched the chart at a point more than halfway into the Northwest Arm. "That's where you must anchor your vessel and go ashore. I can not . . . there might be. . . *oui, je suis sur*, there is a dock 'ere, and with an anchor down, you can make fast to it. It will look like you are unloading the grain sacks more that way. Then you will go t'rough the woods to the island." Faitoute looked at Isaac and smiled. "You will 'wipe the eye' of the English, no?" I am sorry I will not be wit' you to see it, but your Capitan Rogers, 'e wants to me stay 'ere, on this sheep." Isaac didn't feel as confident as the Frenchman that he would 'wipe the eye of the English'.

"Mister O'Mara, you'll sail the ketch to the shallows to the east of Point Pleasant, there either to ground her, or anchor her within hail of the beach. Accordin' to Cap'n Faitoute, they ain't nobody what can see you there, an' you'll leave two men aboard to light the fuses when they get the signal. Course, you'll have to leave 'em a boat 's'well. Wouldn't do to make 'em swim for it. Ha ha." The mates smiled, albeit thinly. Rogers continued. "When you got her into position, you'll take the other boat and sail right 'round the point and into the Arm. With a bit o' luck, you'll be able to sail right to the prison dock, help Isaac, here, with his task, and sail back out again. I am told that small craft sail around the point and into the Arm continually, so it should arouse little suspicion. It might be easier gettin' back out — leastaways for the boat — 'cause the Brits'll be lookin' t'other way." Rogers then detailed more of the plan to his mates and Jeremiah Hardy. It would be up to them to pick and brief their crews.

Before the meeting ended, there came a knock on the Cabin door. Upon instruction, it opened and a seaman, one of *Dancer*'s, apologized for interrupting, then said, "Sir, Mister Coffin sends his respects and all the cargo's been shifted an' the crew's standin' by." He stood there, hat in hand and obviously uncomfortable at being not only in the Cabin, but surrounded by two captains, two mates, and an important foreigner.

He fidgeted for a moment while a final point was made by Captain Faitoute, then Rogers said, "You may tell Mister Coffin we'll be up directly and he may have the men stand ready to get *Dancer* underway." The sailor could not get out of the Cabin fast enough.

Isaac stayed behind for a moment when the others left the Cabin. "I'm thinkin' I know you from somewhere, Cap'n Faitoute; you look real familiar. Been gnawin' at me since we was underway."

"I do not know where it might be, young man — Mister Biggs.

oui? I 'ave been in the service of France since I was barely more than a boy, beginning my service as *le aspirant* — 'ow you say . . emm . . . midshipman, *oui?* And until t'ose English sank and burned my beautiful little brig, *Toulon.* That was in the Indies somet'ing over a year ago. We an' t'ree other vessels was escorting a — 'ow you say . . . convoy? *Oui,* convoy, I t'ink — back to France. Barely 'ad we left Guadeloupe when a squadron of British frigates attacked us. We fail mos' terrible at protecting our merchants. But never can I forgive that Capitan Weenston for destroying such a beautiful vessel as my petite *Toulon.* Then they send me to this God-forsaken place, 'ere, in the North Atlantic — instead of they give me parole there, in the Indies. Such barbarians!"

"Winston? Did you say Cap'n Winston? On the frigate *Orpheus,* he was. Now I recollect. I was aboard when we took your brig and I 'member how she took fire and burned. Right up 'til the fire touched the magazine. They wasn't nothing to be done for it, Cap'n. I got no reason to have any regard for the Brits, neither — I was pressed into that frigate off'n an American merchant my own self. Escaped from a prize crew when they was took by some American privateers. I heard the Brits took all they's prisoners up here to Halifax, bein' the only place they got over here."

"Many of the French officers were released in the Indies, after they gave t'eir parole, a promise not to take up arms against Britain. Ptew!" Faitoute spat angrily as he recalled more of the events of that unpleasant time. "Now I am free. I give my parole in Preston, and because I am gentleman I will not take up arms 'gainst England. But I will do all I can to 'elp you get your men from that prison. And if an Englishman dies while you do it, I will not be sorry." Faitoute turned and mounted the steps to the quarterdeck, his anger and frustration still evident when he reached the deck. But habits die hard and, as he emerged, the hard gray eyes of a former commander in the French Navy gave nothing of his emotions away, instead they flicked expertly over the entire ship from masthead to deck, taking in everything before him, each element registering in his brain without conscious thought.

Isaac appeared moments later and one glance around the decks of the privateer, a look at the sky and the pewter, oily calm water told him all he needed to know. *Dancer* had to be got under way soon, before the wind piped up and a sea started running. And he aboard with the men who would make up the shore party once they got into the Northwest Arm. As he started forward to collect the men he would take, he heard the captain's voice behind him.

"Mister Biggs, you'll be wantin' to step lively now. Once the wind comes back, you and Hardy will be off on *Dancer*." Captain Rogers voice was even and unemotional; there was no tension evident in spite of the fact that they were embarking on a most perilous undertaking and one he was sure no private vessel had attempted before. Even though there was no profit to be gained from the adventure, it was abundantly clear to all that he would brook no delay in getting started.

Within the hour, Biggs' men and gear were aboard, the sloop cast off, and the wind was beginning to fill in from just a little south of east. The ground swell of rollers became first riffled with the breeze, then a short chop formed as the wind continued to increase. Within another hour, it had begun to rain, though not yet as hard as it would, and the wind was moaning in the rigging. From the privateer's quarterdeck, *Dancer* could be seen on a close starboard reach under shortened sail as she labored through mounting seas.

Indeed, the *General* was working for her weathering as well as she sailed close-hauled under tops'ls, a reefed forecourse, and the spanker, also reefed. Forward, a single jib balanced the mizzen. The second saw that the helmsman was not struggling with the brig, a good indication that the ship was well-balanced. In fact, despite the worsening weather, she was having a much easier time of it than her smaller consort to leeward.

He heard the crew called to their supper and wondered where the day had gone; it seemed like only an hour ago that they came out of the cabin after learning the details of the rescue plan. Rogers stood by the helm watching his ship sail; "Mister O'Mara, we'll have a reef in the foretops'l, if you please."

The second nodded and said "Aye" as he stepped forward to see to the reef. Starter Coffin chose that moment to step onto the quarterdeck and pointed his chin at the ketch working hard at her towline astern.

"She's makin' some water, Cap'n, looks like. Mebbe a shorter line would answer. Wouldn't do to get all them munitions soaked through."

"Aye, Mister Coffin. You may be right. See to it, if you please."

As he spoke, a sharp gust heeled the *General* suddenly and, catching the helmsmen unawares, caused her to round up as the ketch yawed, heading down on a wave. The hemp towline went bar-taut, giving up half its girth in the process. The ketch jerked back into the wake of the brig and coasted forward, slackening its tether. But the damage had been done. Where the line crossed the transom, it showed a large frayed section and, in fact, of the three strands making up the line, only two remained.

Coffin grabbed two men, idlers, and together they dove for the failing line. Six hands struggled to find room to hang on, while Rogers himself went to the bit where the line was secured to take it in and make it fast again outboard of the damaged section. As the brig pushed her way into a particularly large wave and slowed momentarily, the ketch surged ahead, slackening the towline. All three of the men hanging on sat down suddenly as the strain was eased; scrambling to their feet, they hauled in. The captain took the turns on the bits, making fast the line with the ketch at the end of it, loaded with powder, rockets and oil. They pressed on to the northeast and the coast of Nova Scotia.

"Make a signal to Hardy that we are hardening up now, and good luck," said the captain as the lookout in the foretop announced the appearance of the highlands just behind the Nova Scotian coast. It was after supper, though not yet evening, but it might well have been, so dark was it. With the heavy overcast of scudding cloud, it was quite unlikely that even if seen, the vessels would be construed as a threat. The ordered flags whipped out straight from the leeward end of the cro'jack yard, and were matched by lights in an appropriate pattern. In moments, they were acknowledged by the sloop to leeward which bore off slightly in a physical confirmation of understanding, and Rogers called out, "Hands to sail stations. Mister Coffin, we'll be coming close-hauled, if you please." As the ship pointed her bow closer to the wind's eye, he spoke to the helmsman. "Keep her hard on it, lad; give nothin' to leeward."

CHAPTER TWENTY-FIVE

Isaac stood with Jeremiah Hardy on *Dancer*'s quarterdeck; three men labored at the tiller as the little ship leapt over the sea, heading for Chebucto Head, the promontory that marked the southwestern end of Halifax Harbor's entrance. The vessel was reefed down and reaching, but still labored in the heavy swells capped with breaking waves. It would not be too difficult to maintain the agreed upon ruse of making *Dancer* look like a merchant coaster running in from the foul weather, should any on shore happen to notice her arrival.

"Deck there . . . on deck! I got breakers larboard bow . . . an' mebbe a light above 'em," the lookout in the larboard rigging cried out. Instantly, a dozen eyes swiveled to the leeward side, squinting through the dark, hands thrown up to shelter faces from the lashing rain.

"Silence! I'll have silence fore an' aft." Hardy's voice was louder than necessary and cracked as he momentarily lost control of the strain he felt. But he needn't have spoken; the two men forward whose voices prompted his order had already been quieted by their mates. Everyone peered into the wet night to see the breakers so as to gauge their distance. Putting *Dancer* ashore now would not only scotch the plan, but would likely get all hands drowned into the bargain.

"There, Jeremiah, just abaft the larboard shrouds; you can see the line o' white." Biggs had his arm up, finger extended, and spoke quietly to the sloop's captain.

"Aye, I got it, I do. And I can hear 'em 's'well. Probably oughta bring her up a half a point. No sense in cutting it too fine. And I ain't relyin' on that chart Cap'n Rogers give us. No siree. Not one eight years an' more old. The Devil himself only knows what mighta changed — or what them Brits mighta done 'round that point."

In response, the three men eased their grip on the tiller and *Dancer* came up, closer to the wind. A brief luff in the sail was quickly corrected and the little ship forged ahead, cutting through some waves and over others, true to her name.

"Aye, we'll hold that for now. Looks right good for gettin' round them rocks." Hardy was satisfied, but the tension came through in his voice. Had there been more light, Biggs and the others would have seen his clenched fists and rigid posture.

"I'll see to gettin' some flags ready, Cap'n. Hope we don't need to show lights. Reckon they wouldn't see 'em any more 'an they'll see the flags, but don't hurt none to be ready." Isaac stepped to the scuttle and disappeared, only to re-emerge minutes later with two large red, white, and blue flags clutched to his chest. He bent the American one onto a halyard and the English flag to another that ran to the larboard end of the maintops'l yard. "Ain't gonna see these, I'd warrant. They'll be lucky to see the vessel in this weather. Probably all asleep on top of it." Isaac muttered hopefully as he hauled the two ensigns aloft.

Dancer swept around Chebucto Head, easily clearing the point and its protecting rocks. Hardy bore off some to accommodate the shoreline as it curved inward to the west toward the mouth of the Northwest Arm. He knew that York Redoubt with its Martello tower, some six nautical miles in, would be their real first test. At the rate they were moving, it would be only slightly more than a half-hour until they were in position to be challenged. And it would seem like only a few scant minutes.

The rain continued intermittently, switching between a sullen drizzle and a wind-driven deluge and then stopping altogether for minutes at a time. Not a star was visible and the shoreline showed only as a darker smudge in the black night. The opening into the Northwest Arm would likely not be visible until they were nearly in it. The tension built on the little sloop's quarterdeck and indeed, throughout the ship the men were edgy, talking quietly in clipped tones and clustering amidships near the stout trunk of the mast. Now that they were in the lee of the entrance, the seas had calmed and the sloop rode more easily, though still with her lee rail awash, as she tore through the darkness. As they drew near the position of the battery at York Redoubt as marked on their out-dated chart, no one spoke; all eyes fixed on the shore barely visible through the darkness, watching for the first sign of a light, the flash of a gun, or the shouted hail from the shoreline.

"There, Jeremiah, right abeam. See? Up high on the hill there. You can see the tower. Just like Cap'n Faitoute said it'd be. Leastways, I think it is. Don't seem to be much goin' on. Reckon the weather's keepin' most of 'em inside. Probably oughta get most o' the men below; a trader would likely be short-handed." Isaac stood close beside the prize captain and hoped that his voice sounded calmer than he felt. This surely was more dangerous than cutting out that merchant last winter; aye, more dangerous by half. If this went wrong, he'd wind up right next to the men he was sent to rescue. If he didn't get hung, that is, him and all of the men with him.

Unbidden, the image of his parents flashed into his mind's eye. His mother, the spotless apron perennially wrapped around her ample middle, her face, wreathed in graying hair, trying to be cheery to cover her concern at her only son's return to sea in the midst of a war, and his father; he stood beside his wife and spoke softly to his son, returning to a life the senior Biggs knew well with all its dangers and uncertainties. The lines in his face seemed to deepen as Isaac's mental picture focused on his father's unsmiling eyes and his lips compressed into a tight white line. This vision swam with the snug house they maintained — the one in which he grew up — with its comfortable rooms and big fireplace, the crane holding a pot from which emanated delicious smells; he could almost smell his mother's fish chowder.

Isaac shook his head, banishing the images, and forced himself to focus on the immediate future. He again reviewed their plan, mentally checking off the weaponry he would need, the men he could count on and, most importantly, the sketch Captain Faitoute had drawn for him of the layout of the island and its prison. This would be something he could tell his grandchildren about — if he survived to tell anyone!

"Only the watch stay on deck. The rest of you get below and stay there, 'til I or Cap'n Hardy calls you back up. No tellin' what we gonna find gettin' in there. I don't reckon they's any Brits gonna be out an' lookin' at us tonight, but no point in gettin' caught up if they are." Isaac spoke to the men in a whisper, trying to ensure that none of the uncertainty he felt came through in his voice. It was easier in a whisper to hide it and it was important that the men knew that both he and Cap'n Hardy had figured out all the things that might go wrong and were confident in the plan. And its success.

With only a handful of men on deck, a few boxes and crates placed before *Dancer* left the side of the privateer, and most of the lines and sheets lying in an unruly tangle — or so it would appear to a landsman — on deck, the sloop gave every indication that she was just what would be expected by the British Marines guarding the entrance to the Northwest Arm, an American trader who had sailed across the Bay of Fundy from the northern coast of Massachusetts with grain for Mr. Hostermann which would be ground into meal for the good people of Halifax and the military stationed there.

"Isaac, Isaac come here." The hoarse whisper emanated from the quarterdeck and, even barely heard over the sounds of the ship racing through the water and the wind whining through the rigging, the urgency was apparent.

In two bounds, the third mate was by Hardy's side. "There, there. Do ya see? On the shore just off the starboard shrouds there. The light . . . do ya see it?" Hardy was pointing and gesturing wildly, his voice rising.

"Aye, I got it, Jeremiah. Reckon it's that battery Cap'n Faitoute tol' us 'bout at Point Pleasant. Said they didn't often have an officer there, just enough conscripts to man the guns. Recollect he said if we got past York Redoubt without no trouble, we wouldn't likely get it here." Faitoute had said no such thing, but Isaac hoped it would calm his skipper. He needed him to get into Purcells Cove. And to wait while he went over land to Melville Island.

The rain had started again with a vengeance. Visibility dropped to barely beyond the bowsprit so hard did it come down. And now the wind was easing a trifle. Still east though. "Thank the Lord for that," thought Biggs. It would make it easier to get into the cut of the Northwest Arm — and out again. Suddenly, a crashing boom rent the night. Everybody on board *Dancer* started and some cringed, waiting for the splash of the ball from the shot they heard. Then came another boom. And another. Long guns, most thought, some aloud, others silently, but none the less fearfully. The sleeping Marines at Point Pleasant Battery had obviously spotted them, though God only knew how in this weather, and were seeking the range with their big guns. There must be a signal other than the two national ensigns and their lack of it . . .

"It's thunder. It's only thunder. They ain't shootin' at us. It's jest thunder." Butterfingers Dunn had figured it out first and his words were a great comfort to all hands, particularly Captain Hardy.

"Thankee, good Lord above. Now just get us safely in there without no more surprises." The captain prayed openly, but quietly. Only Isaac, standing nearby on the quarterdeck heard the muttered request to the Deity.

"The good Lord's got enough on His mind, Jeremiah, without havin' to worry 'bout us'n. I reckon we'll do better takin' care of our own selves." Biggs had been brought up with a gracious Lord, but not one to be bothered with trivialities. Time enough later to call on the benevolence of the Lord, should they really need it. Almost as in agreement with Isaac's words, a great flash of lightning rent the darkness, throwing everything, the ship, the water, the opening of the Northwest Arm, and land at Point Pleasant into an eerily still image. It was burned onto their eyes. The crash of the thunder following brought everyone back to their senses.

"Did you see that, or did I just imagine it?" Hardy was pointing to windward into total blackness; there was nothing at all to be seen.

"See what? I seen we're headed fair for the cut yonder, if that's what you're sayin'." Biggs strained to maintain the image the lightning flash had shown them, but it faded almost as quickly as it had appeared.

"No, I seen we're headed into the opening. That ain't what I seen to weather, though. Seen a boat, headin' this way; comin' downwind right for us. Didn't you see it, Isaac?"

"Musta missed that, I reckon. Where'd you say you seen it? How big was it? Could it have been a warship?"

"Small, I think. Aye, small it were. No bigger 'en the ketch you was towin' astern o' the *Gen'l.* Might be comin' out from the battery there at the point to have a look at us. Probably oughta have some o' the men load one o' them carronades to starboard, just in case, I'm thinkin'."

"I don't think it was comin' from the battery yonder if'n you seen it where you said, Jeremiah. Might be just some poor soul what got caught by the weather who's tryin' to get home. 'Sides, what's some little boat gonna do to us? Likely they cain't catch us up, the way we're sailin', and they cain't have much of a battery aboard, the vessel's small as you say. Let's not look for things to worry us. They's enough ahead to think on, I'm thinkin'.''

Another streak of white light lit the sky and this time, Isaac saw the small boat himself. Not only was it not coming after them, it was in fact the bomb ketch from the privateer, heading to the place east of the point where O'Mara had been instructed to leave it.

"Looks like the *Gen'l* musta made her anchorage, Jeremiah. That's O'Mara in the ketch, headin' into the point. Hope they don't see him with all this lightning. I reckon he seen us, though. Least-aways, I hope he did. Let him know we're where we s'posed to be."

The sloop shot into the opening of the Northwest Arm; dark shapes loomed on either side, reaching up into the sky. In the next flash of lightning, they saw the shore was lined with huge pine trees and at the water's edge, boulders that would tear the bottom out of anything unlucky — or unskilled — enough to run afoul of them. Protected from the easterly gale, *Dancer* slowed to a moderate, more sedate pace; the water was completely calm and the quiet was broken only by the wind, now reduced to a whisper, and the gentle splash of the bow wave returning to the sea. They were past the battery at Point Pleasant and into the Northwest Arm.

"Isaac, you better get some men for'ard with the anchor. No tellin' how far that cove is where we're s'posed to tie up. The Frenchy said a league, but he was guessin'. Better to be ready, case it's less."

Hardy was regaining some of his self-confidence, now they'd made it actually into the cut without discovery, and Isaac smiled inwardly as he went forward to get Dunn and a few others rigging the best bower for letting go on a moment's notice. Hardy was right; no telling how quick they might need it. After only a moment, it seemed, it was ready, hanging only by a stopper to the cathead.

"Goddamn it, Dunn. What the hell do you think you're doing?" The voice cut like a knife through the silence and was answered immediately by the bark of a dog on shore. Isaac turned and went back to the bow at a run. He found Butterfingers Dunn with a sailor's neck in his hand. The sailor's toes just touched the deck and his arms flailed in front of him. Isaac's arrival stopped the flailing, but Dunn continued to hold the man almost off the deck.

"What's goin' on here, Dunn?" Isaac grabbed the big seaman's arm and peered into the face of the other. It was Cathcart, the top-man afraid to go aloft. "What was that shoutin' about, Cathcart?

Don't you realize we're tryin' not to get noticed here? Dunn, put him down. All right, tell me what's the story." The dog ashore continued barking unabated.

"He was throwin' papers over th' side, Mister Biggs, an' I tol' him to knock it off. He didn't, an' I grabbed him up so's he'd stop. Don't know what the papers was all about, but didn't look right to me."

"How 'bout it, Cathcart? What about the papers you was throwin' overboard?"

"You damn fools ain't gonna get in here, an' out again without you're gonna get caught. Brits ain't stupid, you know. They'll be on to you in a flash an' locked up you'll be — right up yonder with your mates off'n th' *Chesapeake*. I don't aim to let . . ."

"Dunn, take him below and figger some way to keep him quiet and out of trouble. Stone was right. Man's not what he said he was. Might be some kinda spy for the Brits or something. Better make sure he cain't cause any more trouble."

"Hey, ashore, there, wake up you Brits . . ." A crushing blow across the back of Cathcart's head ended the shout. No one moved for a minute, waiting to see if anyone had heard. The silence was undisturbed.

Even the dog had quieted and *Dancer* continued up the Arm toward Purcell's Cove as Butterfingers Dunn, after returning the belaying pin to the rack, dragged seaman Cathcart in a strong grip below to a stores room, picking up a short coil of rope as he passed.

CHAPTER TWENTY-SIX

The thunderstorm moved off to sea, leaving the air heavy and sodden. Distant crashes and the occasional flash of lightning called to mind a naval battle being fought just over the horizon. A damp breeze, still mostly east and a reminder that the storm still lingered, filtered through the trees across the Arm and ruffled the water alongside the pier at Hosterman's Mill, set well back in Purcells Cove. No dog barked, no light showed, no one challenged them; the place appeared deserted. The mill building sat near the pier, dark and empty, but likely would be a-buzz come morning. The American seamen planned to be long gone before the first mill worker showed up.

Dancer lay partially alongside the pier, but with a bow anchor down in the middle of the cove. The leadsman's whispered calls coming in had shown three fathoms as the anchor splashed, held, and the sloop swung around, her stern neatly contacting the pier; Hardy may not have an abundance of courage, but he was a fine seaman and ship handler.

Quietly, with orders given in whispers, the bags of grain were brought on deck, then onto the pier, where they would stay while Isaac led his men through the forest to the bridge at Melville Island. The weapons came up and were neatly stacked on deck; cutlasses, pikes, and half pikes. A few muskets and pistols were added to the collection and Isaac gathered his sailors, a dozen and more strong.

As the men stood in a tight circle on deck with the privateer's third mate in its center, the only sounds were the creak of a deck plank, the infrequent groan and squeak of the lines holding the stern of the sloop to the pier, and the scratch of callused bare feet shuffling nervously on the deck as the men waited.

"You'll each get a cutlass and a pike, or half pike. Some will have a musket or pistol, but them what do, hear me good; they ain't to be fired less'n I tell you. We ain't lookin' to let 'em know what's afoot here. And when we're on the island, each of you are gonna have something to do." He went on to describe in some detail the assignments for each smaller group and to impress on them the need for silence. He looked at the large pocket watch Jeremiah Hardy had loaned him for the mission with the admonition to ". . . be sure it gets back to me, with or without you" — just past midnight. The British watches ashore, both on the island and at the batteries around it would have changed. In another hour, the new watch would be comfortable and hopefully dozing. It was time to go.

The path from the pier into the woods was well trodden and, even in the all-encompassing darkness, easy to follow. After a hundred yards, however, it veered sharply inland, forcing the men to break a trail along the water's edge. Wet branches slapped at faces, sometimes pushed away by groping arms, sometimes not. Wet undergrowth thick with brambles entangled and tore at trouser legs; rocks and roots caught at unprotected feet, tripping, bruising, and cutting even the hardened feet of the seamen. The men, in spite of these difficulties, remained silent, each following the man in front with only the occasional stifled grunt as someone tripped over a rock or root, or a branch caught an unsuspecting face. The cutlasses the men carried, as well as the pikes, helped push back the heavier branches, but hacking them off as they passed was too noisy by half; they just couldn't risk announcing their presence, especially when they had little idea of how far they had to go before they would find their first obstacle.

The rain had softened the ground and the undergrowth; there was no cracking of twigs or rustling of dry leaves. But there were puddles, some surprisingly deep with unseen stones and twisted roots hidden in their depths. Isaac led, taking the worst of the branches and pushing them back; he followed the rocky shoreline, with all its undulations and deep cuts and coves. From time to time he stopped, both to check his bearings if they got out of sight of the water, and to let the men catch their breath. He was followed by Davies, the cox'n, and then the others. Butterfingers Dunn brought up the rear, his massive body moving with surprising agility and quiet through the woods. So far, the men knew of nothing that might have given away their presence on the peninsula. The light breeze and their own breathing seemed to be the only sounds. Not even did they hear animal noises as they moved carefully toward the British battery outside Melville Island Prison.

"Oof . . . watch it . . . shhhh . . . damnation . . ." Whispered exclamations as the line stopped moving, and each man, concentrating on where he put his own feet, gently collided with the man in front of him. As they peered through the darkness, they could make out a light that twinkled dimly through the trees, casting a pale yellow glow and dark, dancing shadows that by contrast seemed even darker than the surrounding gloom. With silence restored, the men gathered closer to Isaac and Davies.

Pulling Davies close, Isaac whispered, "That's likely the battery what's s'posed to be aimed at the main gate of the island. Cap'n Faitoute said they manned it all the time. Gotta get in there and secure the men an' spike that gun. No blood on some of 'em; need the uniforms."

Davies signaled some of the men forward. With gestures, he passed on their instructions and, in perfect silence, they followed Isaac toward the Royal Marine camp. A sentry leaning up against a tree next to his musket was half asleep; this boring duty numbed the mind. Davies moved silently around behind him and reached around the tree supporting both the Marine and his weapon. A muffled grunt followed the thud of the pistol butt as it landed on the man's head; a second later, a small clatter as his unconscious form collapsed to the ground, knocking over the musket.

The cox'n looked around fearfully; had the noise, small as it was, been heard? Were they given away? The men held their collective breaths; after what seemed an interminable interval with no stirring from the camp, Davies motioned them forward and they crept toward the sleeping forms of the Marines sprawled around the cannon. The lantern, dim and small as it was, cast a light that, to men who had spent their last hour and more in total darkness, was shockingly bright; it made their task easier and one by one, they took up positions by the sleeping Marines, belaying pins, pistols, and pikes ready in their hands.

A man named Russell, moving through the sleeping men, tripped over one; he caught himself before he fell, but the Royal Marine awoke with a start, having been kicked soundly in the backside.

"'Ere. Who's there? That you Stokely? A little care, man. Mind where you put your feet. 'Ullo, who the 'ell're you? What's actin' 'ere? ALARM. . . ALAR . . ." The cutlass stroke turned his final word into a gurgle and the Marine's head, now barely attached to his neck, lolled to one side as his lifeless body fell back with a faint thump and the blood poured from his neck, forming a black puddle that glistened in the dim light.

Others began to awake from the shouted alarm of the dead Marine and the night suddenly filled with the sounds of pistol butts, cutlass handles, and pikes making contact with heads.

"Oooh . . . umph . . . *thwack* . . . *thud* . . . oooof . . ." Then silence, punctuated by the panting of the American seamen as they stood stock still, looking around in the dim light. Had they missed any? Had any stolen away to make a head visit before the privateersmen arrived? What now? Isaac moved around the camp, talking quietly to the men. They had performed flawlessly for the most part at their first test; but the hard part was yet to come.

"Get some o' them uniforms off 'em. The ones what ain't dead, gag 'em an' tie 'em up good. You four, get the uniforms on, an' pick up a musket. An' keep your mouths shut. Davies, see about spikin' that long gun there. Wouldn't do at all to be greeted by that fellow when we're comin' out. Hopefully, I can still sound enough like a Brit to get the gate opened. Once we do, you all know what to do." Isaac's hoarse whisper galvanized his men into action.

In just a few moments, the American seamen had struggled into Royal Marine uniforms. They laughed and giggled at each other, albeit quietly, until Isaac and Davies shushed them, their smiles giving lie to their harsh words. Leaving the lantern burning where they found it, Isaac adjusted his red coat where it strained across his broad shoulders and led his men to the bridge and the gate beyond it. The sailors not in British uniforms remained just off the path in the trees, while the ersatz Royal Marines marched straight up to the gate and stood arrayed behind Isaac while he pounded on the it and shouted impatiently for entry in an accent befitting the uniform he wore.

"'Old your 'orses. I'm comin'. You blokes ain't been relieved yet. 'Ere, now, you just took the watch an 'our an' more ago. Whot's your troub . . . Who the 'ell are you? Whot's the . . . ummph . . ." The turnkey collapsed where he stood just inside the open gate, a cutlass clean through his chest. Quickly, two men dragged his body outside the gate and into the water next to the bridge. When they finished, they waved their shipmates into the prison.

The men moved into the yard as they had been instructed, heading to the hospital, the main barracks building, and the hill where the officers' quarters were. A uniformed "Royal Marine" accompanied each group.

Isaac led his group to the nearest of the barracks; two men pulled the bar locking the lower door and opened it. The half-asleep guard sitting on a stool collapsed cooperatively when the pistol butt stove in the back of his head. Isaac and two more men quietly mounted the outside stairs, repeating the move with the locking bar in the hasp. This time the marine was awake and when he heard the door open, he stepped forward, a lantern held high. The redcoated Marine in front of him did not surprise him and his last words were "Early now, aren't you, for my relief?" The bayonet on Isaac's musket pierced his heart quickly and cleanly, and he collapsed into the waiting arms of Russell, who had been standing just to one side of the door. Quietly, the Americans dragged the guard's body into a corner and, taking the lantern from where it landed on the floor, started down the passageway lined with solid red doors. None were secured with padlocks; iron pins went through the hasps keeping the doors closed and the men inside.

At the first door they opened, nothing stirred; snores, grunts, and the occasional groan greeted them. Along with the smell of unwashed bodies and an open waste bucket. Russell went to the nearest hammock and, putting his hand over the mouth of its occupant, shook him gently.

"Mooomphh . . . oooph . . ." The hand was removed. "What? What now? The bottom deck flooded again? Hey, who in blazes are you? You ain't a Brit." The man in the hammock looked wide-eyed at Russell standing over him, finger on his lips.

"Shhhhh. We're gettin' you outta here. You off'n the *Chesapeake*?" The man nodded silently. "Wake your mates and keep 'em quiet. Stay in the building 'til someone gets you. Bring nothin' but what you can wear. And keep quiet!" Russell left the man staring and followed the other General Washingtons out of the cell and down the hall, where the process was repeated, until the four privateersmen, accompanied by a few of the Chesapeakes, reached the other end of the barracks. Noises coming up from below indicated similar progress from the other group handling the ground floor.

A British voice filtered up from below as Isaac led his men onto the inside stairway at the opposite end of the building. He hurried down, musket in one hand, cutlass in the other. A figure was standing by the stairs inciting the others to speed. His accent was clearly English, but his words, and the lack of a uniform suggested he was not a Royal Marine. The accent did not cause Isaac concern; he knew there were a large number of British seamen in the American Navy. The man was unaware of Biggs' approach from behind until Isaac spoke.

"You don't shut your mouth, you gonna have the guards down from the hill on us, sailor. Jest gather your mates an' wait yonder 'til we tell you to come out." The man with the accent turned and, seeing Isaac in a Royal Marine Uniform, paled, looked again, then guffawed quietly at the sight.

"By all that's 'oly, would you 'ave a look at this! Never thought I'd be seein' the likes o' you in that uniform — tryin' the Marines, now are ye? What are you doin' 'ere, Isaac?" Coleman stood smiling at his old shipmate and waited while the American found his voice and collected his wits.

"Come to get you out, Robert. Didn't know if'n you was in here or no, but since Cap'n Rogers come up with the plan to get the Chesapeakes freed, I figgered I'd find out. Heard Conoughy was on that frigate; thought you might have been too. But right now we ain't got time to gam. Help us round up the others and be ready to come out of the building when we tell you. And keep quiet! Where the devil are all the guards? We've only come across a few around the barracks and o' course, the ones at the battery outside the gate." His concerned expression gave way quickly to a smile when he heard that the officers were up in the house on the hill and the others in the guard barracks next to the hospital. Isaac, decidedly more than pleased to have found his friend alive, placed a hand on Coleman's shoulder, giving it a gentle squeeze. "Get your lads together; we'll be back quick as we can."

"You people're makin' enough noise to wake the dead, for God's sake. Ain't you been told to keep quiet?" A harsh whisper from behind them startled Isaac and his men. They whipped around and came face to face with Second Mate Tom O'Mara, a cutlass in a hanger from his shoulder, a pistol in his hand, and blood all over the front of his shirt. It shone in the dim lantern light, black and wet.

"You made it! We seen you sailin' in just afore we come into the Arm. That your blood?" Biggs motioned his men to go on down the hallway while he talked quietly with his superior.

"Not on your life, it ain't! Some Brit that was down on th' dock behind the hospital didn't want us to come ashore. Opened him up like a sheep, I did, an' the bastard sprayed blood all over the place. Boat's at the dock there; couple men with it. And there's another boat there too — a bigger one, might serve better. How you doin' here?"

"Doors is all opened in here. Reckon same goes for the other barracks — that stone building to the west. I was about to send these lads and some o' the Chesapeakes to have a look into the guards' barracks. And there are some of the men in the hospital checkin' for Americans. Noticed a lot of Frenchies here, 's'well as the Chesapeakes. I been just leavin' their doors open; Cap'n Rogers didn't say nothin' 'bout them. Neither did Cap'n Faitoute, come to think on it. Rest o' my lads went up the hill to the officers' quarters. Mebbe we oughta get up there."

At a nod from O'Mara, barely visible in the dim lantern light, Biggs turned and started out of the building. But before either could take another step, a shot rang out, splitting the quiet so suddenly both men visibly jumped. Voices, muffled but clearly angry, came down from the hill and a flickering light showed in a window in the house perched atop it.

After the briefest of pauses, both men went at a dead run toward the hill; past the long, low, blood-red storehouse, the blacksmith's shed, also red, and on to the steps ascending to the officer's quarters, racing up them two at a time. The light still flickered in the window, but the voices had quieted and no further shots were heard. When they reached the house, they saw the door flung open and light spilling out from within — that same flickering light, but much brighter than an unshielded candle. Simmons, one of Biggs' men in the red-coated uniform stepped out into the darkness; even with the light behind him, the uniform showed clearly for what it was. O'Mara drew his cutlass and charged straight for him, ready to separate head from neck with one swipe. Isaac shouted.

"Hold on, Tom. That's Simmons. He's one o' mine. Stop." O'Mara, his sword arm still raised over his head, stopped his mad rush and stared. By God, it was one of the Gen'l Washingtons.

What was he doin' in a Marine jacket by all that's holy? He turned, the confusion apparent on his face, as his arm lowered the cutlass back to the hanger and looked at the third mate. And noticed for the first time that he also was wearing the red coat and white trousers of a Royal Marine. His confusion grew.

"It's how we got in here, Tom. And with luck, how we'll get out 's'well. Didn't you notice I'm wearin' the same rig? I got a few others in 'em too." Isaac looked at Simmons, his eyes still wide from his brush with decapitation by his own second mate. "It's all righty, Simmons. What's afoot here. Who fired the shot and why is the place all lit up?"

"Markham fired the shot, Mister Biggs. At one o' the Brits what tried to run down the backside o' the hill for the water. Don't know whether he got him or no. As to the light, well, that would be the fire the lads is tryin' to put out right now. Lantern got knocked over and . . . well, a desk and chair caught the flame. Spread into the wall. No water up here, 'ceptin' some pitchers an' chamber pots. Lads're doin' the best they can." Simmons shuffled his feet as he spoke, aware that his team had created a potentially disastrous situation. In the reflected flickering light, his thin form seemed to shrink and his drawn face, with an overlarge nose and deep-set eyes, colored. A shouted curse came from behind him and, grateful, he turned and went back inside followed closely by the two mates.

The situation was not as desperate as it might have been; there had been six officers in residence, including Major Gilpatric who still hadn't figured out "what was actin' 'ere" — he'd again fallen into bed blind drunk — and five of them were tied securely to chairs in a central parlor. The sixth, a lieutenant apparently, was the one who escaped; that had been ascertained now, and in fact, one of the General Washingtons had heard him splash into the water at the foot of the hill.

The fire was small and, while not yet out completely, was well in hand, though it had caused significant damage. Isaac smiled at the competent job done by his crew and watched as Second Mate O'Mara looked over the befuddled officers, checked the desk for any intelligence that might be found, then nodded in concurrence when O'Mara complimented the sailors.

"Sir, I think there may be some trouble yonder in the yard; sounds like the men might have their hands full." Simmons had come from the window; the men could hear the sounds of fighting and yelling floating up through the night. If they could hear it so plainly, who else could as well?

Biggs and O'Mara ran to the front door of the house and stared open-mouthed; the guard's quarters had apparently emptied and the General Washingtons were struggling with them. So far, no shot had been fired, but the yelling and clanging of cutlasses was enough to wake the less fortunate souls resting on Deadman's Island in the cove. The mates, followed by most of the men on the hill, ran down into the melee.

Isaac, instead of joining the fray immediately, ran up the steps to the prison barracks and bellowed for Coleman. "Robert. Get all the Chesapeakes rounded up and get 'em outside. We need a hand here." Without waiting for an answer, Biggs ran back down the steps and unsheathing his cutlass, headed for the nearest red coat he saw in the darkness. Suddenly he remembered, *by the Almighty, I'm wearing a red coat my own self.* He stopped, dropped his weapons and pealed off the offending garment. In the seconds it took him, Coleman had reacted and Isaac heard the American prisoners pouring out of the barracks, carrying whatever weapons they could find. With his former shipmate at their head, they waded without hesitation into the fight with all its swinging cutlasses, slashing pikes, and air of utter confusion. The air rang with the sound of steel on steel and the angry epithets hurled from both sides.

Isaac had no time to watch the American prisoners as they grappled with the guards, shoulder to shoulder with the General Washingtons, all fighting like badgers in the confines of the prison yard.

Isaac ducked as a musket swung past his head and came up with his own musket, bayonet first, into the center of an amorphous form looming at his side. He was rewarded with a surprised grunt and a gurgle and watched as the form crumpled to the ground.

"Zees way, 'ere. *Allez, allez vite!*" The French prisoners had joined the brawl. Isaac looked; a group of them were herding the guards back toward their barracks and Tom O'Mara was right in the middle of it.

"General Washingtons! Here, lads. Damn . . . oooof . . . watch it . . . Push 'em this way. Move lively, now." The second kept fighting, swinging his musket like a club, first this way, then that way. At the other end of it, the bayonet cut and slashed, cutting a swath in the ranks of the British Marines. The French had formed on him and widened the opening he had made. O'Mara's voice rang out over the yelling, cursing throng and soon the American privateersmen had rallied to him. With the French and Americans working together, the British Marines had little choice but to give ground and they fell back, seeking shelter in their barracks where they likely expected to make a stand.

One of the French prisoners leaped up the stairs behind the last Royal Marine and, as the door slammed in his face, he dropped a musket, barrel first, into the great iron hasp, effectively locking the guards into their own barracks. At a command from O'Mara, two of the Americans ran around the building securing the other doors in a like way. Suddenly, all was again quiet, save for the panting of the exhausted seamen.

"It's time to go, lads. No tellin' what we mighta missed. You General Washingtons what come with me round up the Chesapeakes what can walk and get over to the gate. Mister O'Mara's lads and the hospital cases get to the dock and the boats. If you cain't take both of 'em, burn one — or sink it." Isaac had restored order for the moment and felt they had accomplished what they had set out to do. But they weren't out yet and there was no telling what they might have to deal with before the broad swells of the Atlantic welcomed them back.

CHAPTER TWENTY-SEVEN

"Better cut them little boats loose, Tom. Don't want to have to deal with 'em if'n we need to make haste gettin' outta here." Hardy was ready to leave and no mistake, though the third mate had yet to return with his sailors and the rescued Chesapeakes.

The half-dozen men who had remained aboard *Dancer* had not been idle while the rest were ashore; the sacks of "grain" had been soaked in whale oil and laid end to end up the pier all the way to the mill building itself and a trail of black powder led back down the dock to where the sloop was rocking slightly in the rising breeze. A slow match burned in a tub of sand on the pier. More cutlasses stood in racks on deck and the four carronades which graced the deck of the sloop were charged and double-shotted.

Isaac and his now greatly enlarged group emerged from the forest, ghostly figures floating out of the fog — an aftermath of the storm — and onto the dock; he noted the preparations for the destruction of the pier and mill with a smile, and hurried his charges along the dock to the waiting sloop.

"Get them men below, for now, Davies. Put 'em in the hold. Tom, you have any trouble gettin' out? I thought I heard a passel o' shootin' that sounded like it might be comin' from your direction." Isaac spoke to the second as the latter cast off the British boat and watched as it drifted with the tide into the dark ruffled waters of the Northwest Arm. A few of O'Mara's men had rigged a single whip to the sloop's mainyard and were just about ready to hoist onto the deck the cutter which they had towed astern of the larger British boat as they made good their escape.

"I reckon that Brit lieutenant what run down the hill from the officers' house musta swum across to the other side and run to the fort there in Halifax. If not him, then some son-of-a-bitch got a whole host o' so'diers what turned up at the water's edge just after we got the sail up and headed fair down the Arm. Chased us on foot 'long the shore for maybe a mile 'til they realized we was outstrippin' 'em and they was just wastin' they's lead. Don't reckon I ever seen that much lead fallin' — all around us, it was, by God. Caught a few o' the ones already wounded and Simmons took a ball right through the head. Killed him on the spot, I'd warrant. One o' the other lads took one through the leg when he stood up to help Simmons, damn fool. An' the boat ain't worth much but cuttin' loose like Hardy wanted. Cutter likely can be patched up; bein' it was astern of us, it only took a few shots what holed her some. You have any trouble?"

"Let's get them lines in, lads, lively now. Be light right quick, an' if'n you want to see your wives an' sweethearts again, best be quick about it. An' man them guns." Hardy was anxious to be gone. The privateersmen moved around the decks of the Bermuda sloop, stepping over the rescued and wounded Navy men who had not found room in the small hold. Most were quiet and after a few were shushed by their shipmates, all were. Except for a whispered curse or command and the click of the pawls on the capstan as the anchor was claimed, *Dancer* made a ghostly image indeed as she slipped away from the pier and out of the fog that clung like a hangover to the wet shoreline. She left a legacy; the eerie glow of the powder train burning up the pier toward the oil-soaked sacks would soon tell all and sundry that the Americans had been a-visiting.

The men with no duties watched the glow as it grew and crept toward the mill. The fog caught the tiny fire and magnified and softened it as the powder train was consumed. The sloop, clear of the cove, was now headed south and down the Arm toward the battery at Point Pleasant. Suddenly the sky behind them lit up as the gun powder reached the oil soaked bags; they burst into flame which raced hungrily toward the mill structure. As it began to burn, the sky brightened as the flames from the growing fire reflected off the fog and low clouds.

"Looks like they won't be usin' that mill for a spell, Hardy. Your lads did a fine job o' settin' that blaze." Isaac smiled appreciatively at the prize captain. "Reckon all we got to do now is get past them two batteries and join up with the *Gen'l*."

Tom O'Mara joined the two on the little quarterdeck, having supervised the stowing of the cutter amidships. "We still got a little surprise for them Brit bastards at the Point; Jeremiah, where'd you stow that rocket I give you? Time's gonna be right pretty quick now to be shootin' her off."

"I got it right below, Tom; left it right where I said I would. You think it's gonna be real smart to announce ourselves like that? It's still pretty dark and there might be fog out at the point like they was back yonder; them coves might not even see us. They didn't when we come in — or you, I'd reckon, either."

"After I shoot that rocket, I'd wager them Brits at that battery gonna be so busy they won't even be lookin' this way. Leastways, that's the idea, accordin' to Cap'n Rogers, anyway. Reckon it just might work." The prize captain and the privateer's third mate watched as O'Mara's dim form slipped down the scuttle to the sloop's aft cabin. Moments later, he emerged with a bundle wrapped in oiled cloth which he carried to the taffrail at the stern.

"Where you reckon we are, Hardy?"

"'Bout half a league or so from the entrance, I'd guess. This wind holds like it is from the east, it won't be but a few minutes 'til that point's abeam." *Dancer* was making a nice turn of speed through the protected water and her wake showed dimly behind them as a trail of white speckled with the glow of some surface-dwelling phosphorescent creatures.

"Isaac me lad, would you be so kind as to find me a lit linstock so's I can prepare this little present for our friends yonder?" O'Mara was ebullient with the anticipation of what was about to happen. Biggs caught his mood and responded in kind.

"Why of course, Mister O'Mara. It would be a pleasure. One lit linstock comin' up." He left the quarterdeck to return moments later with his hands cupped around a glowing slow match. Hardy watched the two with reserve; he was not yet sure whether announcing their presence to the Royal Marines manning the battery at Point Pleasant was such a great idea.

O'Mara propped the rocket up on an upturned bucket and held the slowmatch to its fuse. The powder-impregnated hemp glowed and gave off a small shower of sparks as it caught the fire. With a great whoosh, the rocket left the deck and soared aloft; the men watched as it climbed leaving a fiery trail, then burst in a brilliant display of light.

Almost immediately a dull boom thundered out from the land to larboard, followed by an audible splash, fortunately some distance to wind'ard.

"Well, now you've done it, O'Mara. I tol' you firin' off that rocket wasn't real smart. Them coves sure hadda see that — an' now us. Musta been one o' them marines that was shootin' at you run down an' tol' 'em to watch for us." Hardy was not happy and could not rid his mind of an image he had thought of earlier: his handy little sloop being blown to matchwood as they attempted to make good their escape. He bellowed forward. "Davies, Dunn! Get them carronades aimed at th' point. Give 'em something to think on 'stead o' shootin' at us." Hardy would not go down without a fight.

Moments later the sky to the east took fire, silhouetting the trees on Point Pleasant, the point itself, and the Marine battery. Streaks shot through the night, as rockets went off indiscriminately and explosions echoed off the water and nearby land.

"Well, I guess that oughta 'give them bastards something to think on, 'sides shootin' at us!' Them rockets I hung in the riggin' o' that little boat went off just like I figgered they might. " O'Mara was practically dancing with glee at the display he had arranged.

"That was the bomb ketch, I'd reckon, eh, Tom?" Isaac watched appreciatively as some of the rockets and the burning shards of the explosion landed ashore. "Too bad it rained so hard last night. Mighta started them woods burnin' were it a little drier." Biggs clapped the second on the shoulder in congratulations of a fine job setting the ketch in the right place. Even Hardy overcame some of his reserve and was catching the spirit, smiling broadly, but still cautious and not about to give in entirely to the celebration until they were safely back at sea.

Boom! All eyes squinted into the still-bright light, trying to see the fall of shot. "Guess them Brit marines ain't as dumb as you thought, O'Mara. Looks like they's still shootin'." The captain's doubt was apparently justified.

"Aye, they's shootin' but not at us. Looks like them guns is trained around toward the other side o' the point — where we put that ketch. Must think they's gonna get invaded. God alone knows what they's shootin' at; cain't be much o' anything left of that little vessel we put on the hard." O'Mara was quite right; no shot splashed in the water anywhere near *Dancer* and, her reef shaken out and under a press of canvas, she continued unscathed past

Chapter-Twenty-Seven

Point Pleasant and into the more open water of the outer harbor.

Hardy brought *Dancer* closer to the wind, easing the vessel to the east toward MacNabb's Island and a rendezvous with the *General Washington* which having seen the fireworks, should even then be coming around the north end of the island to escort the sloop out to sea.

"One down, one to go." Hardy muttered to himself as he strained to see the outline of the privateer against the slowly-lightening eastern sky. Aloud he said, "What you got planned for the battery yonder, O'Mara, up on the York Redoubt?" His tone provided some insight to his concern.

The second just looked at Hardy, his lips a thin line, and said nothing. He turned to weather to see if he could spot the familiar rig of the *General.*

The eastern sky was light enough now to show clearly the silhouette of the island. The storm clouds were breaking up some, allowing the rays of the rising sun to peek through. It should be easy to spot the privateer with the brightening sky behind her. All eyes, not just those on the quarterdeck, scanned the far shore beyond the north end of MacNabbs watching for the brig to appear.

"There . . . on deck . . . there she be! Just now roundin' the end of that island yonder." The seaman hanging in the larboard rigging was first to spot the ship and the others quickly picked up the sight.

Under reefed tops'ls, a forecourse and spanker, a bone in her teeth and her guns run out on the starboard side, *General Washington* rounded the northern end of MacNabb's Island and bore down from windward, a vision that caused all hands to smile and some to laugh in glee.

"We're as good as outta here now."

"What a sight she is!"

"Would you have a looksee at that!. Ain't that just beautiful!"

The comments flew around the deck. What could possibly go wrong now? The men shared with each other the joy of seeing the powerful brig with her significant weight of metal bearing down to accompany them out, knowing it would now be a matter of minutes before she was close aboard and an hour, give or take, until they were safe in the broad reaches of the North Atlantic. Even if the Brits could get a warship under way from the Dockyards, it would be too late; *General Washington,* given the headstart she had, could outrun virtually anything that might come after them. They were as good as home!

Boom! Heads swiveled to starboard seeking the source of the shot, as a hole appeared in the mains'l just below the peak. The marines manning the battery at York Redoubt were awake and *Dancer* was silhouetted against the eastern sky, making her just as easy to spot as had been the *General Washington.*

Boom! Another shot thundered across the water. The aim was just as true as the first shot; the ball went through the mains'l slightly higher, ripping away the top foot of the mast and with it, the main halyard. The sail came down with a crash, enveloping the midships area of the sloop in heavy canvas, lines and blocks. Confusion on deck was rampant and *Dancer* slowed noticeably without her primary canvas, providing an even easier target for the guns ashore.

"Man them carronades, damn your eyes!" Hardy's bellow spawned instant action and the starboard side guns fired almost at once. To little avail; the guns could not be elevated high enough to land their shot above the cliff and the balls thudded harmlessly into the earthen face well below the British position. Isaac and O'Mara ran forward. Captain Hardy headed the sloop higher in an effort to increase his distance from the guns of the York Redoubt.

Without warning, the forward carronades thundered again, belching fire and smoke and a pair of twenty-four-pound iron balls. They hit higher on the cliff, but still frustratingly below the battery on its top. And the British battery responded. Hardy, from his position on the quarterdeck, could see the flashes as two of the big guns fired almost simultaneously. He cringed, waiting for the fall of shot. He saw the splash from one, but before he could even let out the breath he held, the second round plowed into the forward bulwark of the sloop; had it been two feet higher, it would have dismounted the forward carronade, likely killing both mates and the gun crew. As it was, a two-foot hole opened in *Dancer*'s side and the spent ball still had enough carry to lay waste to the forward part of the hold, killing or wounding a half dozen of the Chesapeakes sheltering there. *Dancer*'s other starboard carronade spoke now and again, the men could see a gout of wet soil leap out of the cliff in the weak morning light.

"Bear off! Head straight for the shore." Booming from the weather side came what could only be the voice of God. Hardy started, then turned and looked to wind'ard; there was *General Washington* bearing down on them, the Captain standing on the bulwark by the mainmast, a speaking trumpet held to his mouth. Hardy didn't react and Rogers repeated the order.

"Hardy. Head straight for the shore; get under their guns!. Now man. Do it!" Realizing it was probably his only chance to escape the accurate fire, Hardy threw his weight into the tiller along with the two men already there. The sloop, her square sail forward and two jibs billowing in the still-favorable breeze, bore off, picked up speed in spite of the lack of the big mains'l, and raced for the cliffs. *General Washington* followed, her forward guns firing at the clifftop, but with only slightly more effect than *Dancer*'s had had earlier.

Boom boom! Two more shots thundered from the British battery. Hardy's turn had not been quite quick enough to escape another salvo and both balls found their marks in the scudding sloop. One went home with a resounding crash in the side, abaft the beam, midway between wind and water, while the other seated itself firmly in the mast, head high. Splinters flew and the rent timbers complained convincingly, providing a higher pitched counterpoint to the screams and curses from the Chesapeakes in the hold. The mast wobbled, but remained upright, held aloft only by its shrouds and stays. More than half its girth was gone.

"Hands topside! Lively now!" O'Mara was yelling down the hatch into the faces of the Navy seamen sequestered there. They didn't need to be told twice; with a rush, everyone who could walk piled out of the hold. Some of the more experienced men saw immediately what was needed and began cutting away the still-billowing mains'l, part of which was dragging overboard to leeward. Others were helping wounded comrades up from the confines of the hold.

Boom boom! This time, the thunder came from astern, and Isaac and O'Mara looked toward shore in time to see the *General*'s iron find a home in the Martello Tower on the top of the cliff. Others saw it as well, and a weak cheer went up from the Dancers. Even Captain Hardy was encouraged; it looked as if the sloop was now close enough to the cliff that the British guns could not depress enough to hit them. Relief flooded through him with the realization that they were safe — for now anyway — from the devastatingly accurate fire. The privateer, having fired a final salvo with her forward guns, was heading for them, closing the distance quickly.

"Cap'n . . . that mast ain't gonna . . ." Isaac never got to finish the sentence warning Hardy of the unstable mast. With a rending crash accompanied by the popping of shrouds and the back stays, the mast collapsed, falling forward slowly, as the nearly severed lower part failed, sending fragments and splinters flying. The majority of the spar remained aboard, but the larboard end of the yardarm went over the side, acting as a break and causing the sloop to round up, helpless and within a few hundred yards of a lee shore. The two men near the mast suffered in the extreme; one took a long leaf pine splinter through his neck and the other was lifted off the deck by the broken end of the spar as it fell forward, catching him just under the chin. Both were dead before their shipmates had time to contemplate what had happened.

"Cut that away! Get that yard free of us. Get it clear!" O'Mara's voice overshadowed Hardy's as both saw instantly what was needed. A further command from the quarterdeck: "Forward there, Isaac. Get some men on the anchor. Don't let her go less'n I tell you, but get it rigged out." Hardy was still in command and not about to let his ship go ashore.

Dancer had stopped; all her sails were gone and she wallowed slightly in the increasing beam sea rolling in from the Atlantic. She made leeway slowly toward the rocky shore as the waves and wind conspired against her. The men worked frantically to clear the mess on the main deck, Chesapeakes pitching in with a will alongside the privateersmen. Within minutes, the yard had been hacked off and was gone over the side. The sail was gathered and contained, lashed securely to the broken mast. Order was being restored and the four carronades were clear and serviceable; it mattered little as there was no chance of elevating them sufficiently to hit the battery on top of the cliff. To the good, there was no chance that the guns ashore could be depressed enough to hit the helpless sloop.

"Lookee yonder, lads! Here she comes, hell bent! That sure is. . ." The seaman crumpled where he stood, his last vision that of the privateer, a bone in her teeth, coming to their rescue. A red blossom formed on his chest as the musket ball that had entered his back went through his heart and then his chest. The crack of the weapon had been so faint as to be unheard on the ship.

"Down! Everybody get down behind something. They's come down the hill with muskets." Isaac had been next to the hapless sailor and it took him a moment to figure out what had happened. The men responded quickly and ducked behind the starboard bulwark. Still the deadly lead balls thumped into the deck, the stump of the mast, and the outside of the bulwark.

And the brig stood on, now backing her reefed tops'ls and clewing up the forecourse. As she turned behind the sloop, a thunderous roar from her starboard broadside loosed a hail of grape shot into the shore line and the Royal Marine sharpshooters who had taken up a position there. The small arms fire stopped.

"Hands to the larboard rail. She's comin' alongside. Lively now, afore them bastards start shootin' again." Hardy saw exactly what Captain Rogers was about and correctly positioned his men to receive the lines from the brig.

With a rending crunch and a jerk that caused the men on the sloop to grab hold of something to keep their footing, the privateer drew side by side with the wallowing sloop; lines were passed and secured. Rogers bellowed, louder than necessary given the proximity of the two vessels. "Hardy, get your men aboard quick as ever you can. If you got any powder left, set a keg in her bilge and blow her bottom out. No sense in givin' 'em back the sloop, even as hurt as she be."

The men didn't need to be told twice; that lee shore was still looming, and the marines would begin shooting again any minute. The wounded were handed across the bulwarks to willing hands on the *General*; the others jumped across to the decks of the privateer. Soon her decks were crowded and hands were sent below to allow the General Washingtons to fight their ship should it again become necessary. Hardy watched his men and the Chesapeakes leave *Dancer* and when all but the mates had left, he grabbed the two and they disappeared below.

Biggs was first back on deck, only to disappear again down an aft scuttle. O'Mara and Hardy emerged moments later expecting to see the third waiting for them. He was nowhere in sight.

"Musta gone over to the *Gen'l*, Tom. Better get our own selves over. Them ain't the longest fuses I ever set. Not by a long shot, they ain't." Hardy and O'Mara made for the bulwark and climbed across to the waiting deck of the brig.

"Cast off them lines. Fuses're lit." O'Mara bellowed to his men on deck, and hands rushed to obey. As the last line was hauled back into the privateer, Isaac emerged from the aft scuttle, smiling.

In less than a heartbeat he took in the scene before him, hearing shouted orders to make sail. And the smile vanished.

"Braces haul. Man your sheets. Loose the tops'ls. Lively now." The gravelly voice of Starter Coffin accompanied by some pushing and cursing moved the crew to work quickly in getting the brig underway from the doomed Bermuda sloop. He did not see his third mate on the deck of *Dancer*. Hardy however, did and yelled.

"Isaac! Jump for it, lad! Fuses're lit. Come on son, you can make it!" Hardy's shout caused the others on the brig to look up from their work and they saw the popular third mate running across the doomed sloop's deck, headed for the bulwark just abaft the stump of the mast. Without hesitating, the young man mounted the waist-high bulwark and threw himself across the widening expanse of water between the two vessels. Eager hands reached out from the privateer and caught him, as he half fell across the brig's bulwark, and hauled him roughly aboard.

"Damn near didn't make it, lad. What ever the hell was you doin'? Hardy and me both thought you'd already left, comin' top-side afore us as you did. Where did you go?" O'Mara's concern was hardly masked by his gruff manner with the third mate and his grip of Isaac's shoulder didn't slacken as he waited for an answer.

"Figgered to set another charge back aft, Tom. Didn't reckon that one we set for'ard'd do the job. When she goes off now, they won't be nothin' but matchwood for the Brits to make use of." Isaac smiled and gently removed his superior's hand from his shoulder.

"By the eyes o' me sweet saintly mother, ye'll never learn to let them what knows 'andle that sort of job, will ye now? A job for a gunner, if ever they was one."

At the sound of the Irish accent, Isaac turned and stared wide-eyed at his old shipmate. Then with a smile that lit his whole face, he grabbed the gunner by both arms.

"Conoughy, you rascal. I heard from a couple o' your mates you was in *Chesapeake*; just couldn't stay put could you. Glad to see you alive and well. I seen Robert on the island. Who else was in that crew?"

"Clements' 'ere 's'well, Isaac. And Jake Tate too." At Biggs' blank look at this last name, Conoughy paused, then continued. "Reckon you won't know young Jake; he joined the *Constellation* frigate in Baltimore last winter and come up with us to Boston. Got 'isself assigned into *Chesapeake*, same as the rest of us. Lost an arm, 'e did, against *Shannon*. Clements ain't got but one ear now. Don't know where 'e's got 'isself off to; seen 'im only just now, I did." The Irish gunner looked around the deck, seeking his friend. Then he continued. "But it sure is a wonder to see you, Isaac. I'm given to understand you was the cove what got us out o' that pest 'ole, an' if'n you was, you've saved me sorry arse yet again, ye have, lad. I for one am mighty grateful to ye. By all that's 'oly, I am that, indeed."

Boom! All conversation stopped and heads turned back toward the privateer's wake as the charges set in *Dancer* went off; the little ship raised herself up in the middle as the first keg of powder exploded. The deck lifted and while she was up, the after charge, the one set by Isaac, detonated. It separated the stern from the rest and a cloud of splinters filled the air. When the smoke cleared, nothing but loose timbers floating in the rising chop was visible; there would certainly be nothing left for the Brits to salvage.

"Mister Biggs, you did a fine job with them explosives, lad. And I'd reckon you'll have ample time in Salem for catching up on your mates' doin's; right now we need to get some sail on her so's that frigate standin' out don't jest sail right up to us an' invite us to join 'em in Halifax." The unmistakable voice of Captain Rogers, even as gruff as it appeared to be, was a welcome sound to Isaac's ears.

"Aye, Cap'n. We'll get the *Gen'l* flyin', by the Almighty we will." Isaac started forward, rounding up his topmen as he went and occasionally casting a wary eye astern where the entire rig of a Royal Navy frigate passing Georges Island could be seen easily in the full light of morning. Under other circumstances, it would have been impressive, set as she was to the royals with stu'ns'ls aloft and alow. Right now, it served to galvanize the third mate and his topmen to get sail made as quick as ever they could.

And quick it was; within minutes, the brig was fairly flying, heading for the point at Chebucto Head and the open Atlantic, her stays and shrouds groaning under the strain of the enormous press of canvas she carried. The buntlines were stretched across the bellies of the billowing sails and the chop hitting the wind'ard side of her bow sent a stinging spray half the length of the ship, making a standing rainbow as the sunlight shone through the drops. The ship heeled further to starboard as she gained the more open water and the full force of the easterly half-gale was felt. Two more men were added to the wheel just to keep her head down. The brig was in a race for her life when she turned the point at Chebucto Head and bore off. And she was winning it.

The mood on deck was jubilant; faces were wreathed in smiles. A few of the Chesapeakes remained topside to help the privateersmen handle lines and sails, grateful to be at sea again — and as free men. Clearly, *General Washington* was outstripping the English frigate, which, still in the lee of MacNabbs Island, would not feel the strength of the breeze for some time yet.

"Well, Isaac. Reckon you done it. A fine job o' work it was. Davies tol' me all about it." Starter Coffin's eyes were squinting more than ever, a sure sign he was smiling. His beard hid his mouth almost completely, thus there was no indication of his joy in that quarter. There was, however, a trace of jealousy in his voice; young Biggs would be drinking on this tale for some time to come. But his praise for the former Royal Navy topman was genuine. He walked with Biggs aft where the third had the watch.

"Reckon I got the watch, Cap'n. I can take her if you want." Biggs looked at his captain, realizing suddenly how tired he was. He swayed slightly, standing there, and noticed that suddenly, his eyes felt as if they were full of grit. His wiped a hand across them and shook his head. Rogers noticed.

"I'll take her for a while, Isaac. Why don't you get yourself below and get some sleep while you can. If'n that frigate catches us up . . ." Rogers didn't need to finish the thought. Isaac smiled, mumbled "Aye, sir," and turned from the quarterdeck to go below.

CHAPTER
TWENTY-EIGHT

"I heard what you done, Asa. Word's all over Salem. Musta been quite an adventure, getting those men out of that prison. Did you suffer many losses?" George Crowninshield had asked the privateer skipper to join him at his table in the American Coffee House. He couldn't help but notice when the tall man entered; a murmur went through the room as the other patrons recognized Rogers as the man who did what the Navy wouldn't — or couldn't. The senior Crowninshield and his crew of masters had successfully retrieved the bodies of James Lawrence and Augustus Ludlow from Halifax under a letter of truce. The *Henry's* return to Salem with its prestigious crew and esteemed cargo had created a stir, albeit a somber one. But yesterday, when the privateer *General Washington* sailed in and made fast to the pier, it took no time at all for the word to race through Salem that she was back and what she and her crew had accomplished. The whole town lined the streets to welcome back the men of *Chesapeake* as they left the dock in an impromptu parade. Cheering and shouting, waving and flags; it was a sight to stir the heart of even the most jaded. And the General Washingtons found that people gathered 'round to hear the tale again and again in public houses and coffee shops. They gloried in the notoriety and drank deeply at the wellspring of fame. Rogers, however, remained taciturn and outwardly unaffected.

"Not too bad, George. A few in the fighting on the island and a few when we was leavin'. Had a few more hurt and lost that pretty little Bermuda sloop I brought in a few weeks back. But she served her purpose well, and my lads did themselves proud." Asa smiled as he recalled how the two crews had blended together to get the best speed out of the *General* and outrun the British frigate that chased them for two days out of Halifax. "*General Washington* done right fine, 's'well. An' that French Cap'n, Jean Faitoute turned out to be a real asset to the endeavor, he did. Knew them waters right well and, more important, knew right where the Brit batteries was. Hope he makes it back to France all right like he said he was gonna do. Aye, a fine fellow, he was."

Meanwhile in a tavern much less distinguished and catering to the lower-level denizens of the waterfront and fo'c'sle hands, a noisy table of sailors were bringing each other up-to-date on their lives over the past ten and more months. A young man at the table smiled, but kept his own counsel; he had his sleeve cut off at the elbow and roughly sewn closed. He had experienced many of the tales being told by the Irish gunner and English topman. But the realization that that part of his life was over was beginning to hit home and silently he pondered what the future would hold for him now.

"Isaac, you surely did miss some 'igh times, by all the saints. But I reckon you 'ad some your own self, chasin' around on that brig like you was. Jack 'ere was talkin' 'bout goin' back to the private navy just t'other day. Reg'lar navy cost 'im an ear, it did. Righty oh, Jack? . . . Jack?" Conoughy was unable to resist poking a little fun at the former bosun, still a little sensitive about his disfigurement.

"Aye, Tim. I heard you the first time. Just payin' you no mind, is all. He's right though, Isaac. I don't aim to go back aboard a Navy vessel; most of 'em bottled up somewhere and cain't get to sea anyway. Be just like bein' on the *Constellation* down there in Gosport. Figgered I'd head back down towards the Bay and see about a berth on one o' the private vessels still sailin'. Reckon you was the smart one way back in November, stayin' in the privateers." He paused, a thoughtful look on his face; it gave way to a smile. "You know, I just thought o' something. Ain't Mister Blanchard gonna be some surprised when next he comes to visit us over to Melville Island? We ain't gonna be there! Mebbe ain't no one gonna be there, 'ceptin' a bunch o' Brit guards what ain't got nothin' to guard!" Clements laughed.

"Aye, reckon 'is face'll be a picture, all righty. Too bad we couldn'a brought 'im out with us. For an officer, 'e ain't a bad sort, an' I'd reckon to sail with the cove again." Coleman smiled at his former shipmates who knew the young lieutenant; they nodded in agreement.

"I heard when we come in yesterday that the officers was bein' traded for some Brit officers we got here; that or given they's parole and sent back to America. Reckon they likely take more care with the officers than you common seamen on an enlistment." Biggs hadn't thought he knew any officers in the American Navy; when he had heard the comment a day ago about trading the officers back it didn't signify. His friends brightened visibly at the good news.

"Jack, I'll likely regret sayin' this, but maybe they might find a berth for a topman and a gunner on those wee ships. I reckon you're righty oh 'bout the Navy not goin' to sea, an' I don't know what else I'd do. 'Sides, like Isaac says, they care more about the officers than us fo'c'sle coves an' I don't reckon I want to get locked up again." Coleman looked hard at first Tim Conoughy, then at Jack Clements. They broke into smiles simultaneously and Isaac laughed.

"You coves just cain't be satisfied with where you are. They's privateers sailin' right here — Salem, Marblehead, an' on up towards Portsmouth now I hear. Whyn't you just stay here? They's berths aplenty right here. 'Sides, what makes you think you can just walk away from the Navy? Navy might have something to say 'bout that."

"Ain't the need for men now, Isaac. Ships ain't sailin' and I heard once you been captured, Navy'll let you go if'n you're of a mind. As to stayin' put, we stayed where we was when we paid off from the ol' *Glory* and look where it got us — locked up in some God-forsaken prison in Nova Scotia. You come north and done pretty good, sounded like. 'Ceptin' for the cold. Not sure I'd like that much. 'sides, changin' home ports might be lucky, aye, lucky like it was for you." Clements had made up his mind.

"But we're 'ere now, an' mates once again. May'aps we oughtn't to ship out separate, might be that's the bad luck." Coleman raised his tankard in a mock salute to his words and all followed suit. Including Jake.

"'Ow 'bout you, Chauncey Tate. What'll you be doin'?" Tim smiled at the young man, encouraging him to join in the conversation.

"Been thinkin' about just that, Tim. You boys been good to me, takin' care o' me when I got hurt an' all, but I don't think they's a place for a one-armed topman aboard any vessel, private or navy. Reckon I'll head on back to Maryland and look up Charity. See if'n she'll have me for a husband, even though I'm lackin' an arm.

Less'n she's done run off with some other cove. So when you head back down toward the Bay, reckon I'll ride along with you, you don't mind. Aye, it's likely time for me to swallow the anchor." Tate smiled, almost as if hearing himself say the words had solidified the idea for him. "Aye, that's just what I'll do." He repeated, just to hear the sound of it. Still pleased, he raised his empty tankard and his voice. "Another round, barman."

The End

Author's Note

In the first nine months of 1813, privateers operated with impunity from the New England ports, as the British had not yet enough naval resources to blockade all of them as well as the southern ports. The *General Washington*, while a creation of the author's imagination, is characteristic of the northern private armed vessels and her operations and crew, typical.

The frigate *Constellation*, commanded by Charles Stuart, did get trapped in Norfolk/Gosport by the blockade at the Virginia Capes after completing her refit at Baltimore in February of 1813. Many of her crew were transferred to other Navy ships. Ultimately her commanding officer was transferred to USS *Constitution* as the frigate was completing her refit in Charlestown, Massachusetts, in May of that same year.

Of course, James Lawrence, fresh from his successful cruise in USS *Hornet* and feted as a hero by the American people, took out his new command, USS *Chesapeake*, whose checkered past concerned him not at all, to meet HMS *Shannon* on that fateful first of June, 1813. He had been aboard barely two weeks. Lawrence's ego demanded that he continually 'prove' himself and, to his mind, his less than glorious career would get a further boost from a successful meeting with the crack frigate of the Royal Navy.

Conversely, *Shannon*'s Captain, Philip Broke, had commanded the British frigate for more than six years when she met *Chesapeake* and maintained a superbly trained crew. He was known for his innovations in gunnery. As Bosun Clements noticed when leaving *Shannon* in Halifax, some of Broke's innovations included train marks on the deck around each gun and the iron sights he saw mounted on each barrel. It has been said that *Shannon*'s gunnery was the fastest and most accurate in the Royal Navy.

And so a desperately ill-prepared American frigate and the most capable one of the Royal Navy joined battle with an outcome that could only be pre-ordained. They met just a few miles off the coast of Cape Ann, Massachusetts, watched by spectators in small craft as well as from every high vantage point ashore. The ensuing battle is well-documented by both English and American sources and the surviving American prisoners were, in fact, incarcerated on Melville Island, Halifax.

Of the three hundred eighty-two souls who went out in *Chesapeake* that day, sixty-two, including six of the eight officers, died and eighty-three were wounded. In *Shannon*, forty-three were killed and thirty-nine wounded, one of the highest butcher's bills of the times; and all in a thirteen-minute engagement.

There was no raid on the prison at Melville Island staged by an American privateer or any other vessel; that action is entirely the product of the author's imagination. The Chesapeakes who survived the battle with HMS *Shannon* and were sent to Halifax were repatriated in September of the same year. There actually were five British seamen on *Chesapeake*, but they were not to be so fortunate; in October of 1813, they were brought back to England in, ironically, HMS *Shannon* and court martialled. One was hanged; the other four were flogged 'round the fleet. The United States frigate *Chesapeake* was sailed back to England, but never saw action again. Ultimately, around 1820, she was broken up, and her timbers used to construct a mill, known as the "Chesapeake Mill." It is reported to have survived well into the twentieth century.

Remnants of the British prison still exist at Melville Island, today the home of the Armdale Yacht Club. Parts of the wall, the storage building, and one of the barracks can be seen; the latter is used today by the sailors at Armdale Yacht Club for storage and is well-maintained as an historic site. The bridge has been replaced by a causeway and the warden's home on the hill now serves nicely as the warm and comfortable clubhouse and a repository for some marvelous photographs of the prison as it looked early in the twentieth century.

In the story, McNab's Island, named for Peter McNab of the Scottish Highlands who settled there in 1754, is referred to as Mac-Nabb's Island in conformity with the navigational charts of the early nineteenth century. Hosterman's Mill and pier did exist at the time of the story and were not, of course, burned by the Americans. The York Redoubt and the Battery at Point Pleasant can still be seen today, complete with some of their guns. National parks have been built around these sites, favorites for locals and tourists alike for picnicking on pleasant summer days.

Licensed trade between a variety of northern New England merchants and the port of Halifax did exist in large measure; indeed, records indicate that in 1813 alone, 107 American vessels entered Halifax to trade under license agreements. They became a quite routine sight for the Royal Marines guarding the entrances to Halifax Harbor. As the blockade tightened and more of the New Englanders supported the American war effort, this number fell precipitously; in 1814 there were only 28, and in 1815 (even though the war was officially over) there were none.

On August 7th, 1813, George Crowninshield, a dominant Salem merchant and captain, did sail the brig *Henry* into Halifax under a letter of truce signed by President Madison, and returned to Salem with the bodies of James Lawrence and Augustus Ludlow, First Lieutenant of *Chesapeake*, on August 22. They were interred there the following day. Sometime thereafter, Lawrence and his first lieutenant were again exhumed and their coffins taken to New York City, where they rest today at the foot of Broadway in the cemetery at Trinity Church, not far from the water.

While not mentioned in the story, the Derby family of Salem were, in fact, the dominant merchants of the period and built piers, warehouses, and other buildings, many of which can still be seen today in that charming and historic town.

Naval historians debated the action taken by James Lawrence for years. Early "whitewashing" and hero-worship, coupled with his death in the action, served to cover his massive blunder and turn it into an act of "desperate heroism." His two surviving officers, Acting Lieutenants Budd and Cox, became scapegoats and were court-martialled for their imagined fault in the loss of *Chesapeake*. Current opinion is justifiably harsh toward Lawrence; many senior officers of the United States Navy maintain, albeit quietly, that had he survived, he should have been court-martialled and shot.

Regardless of which camp one might favor, it is undeniable that Lawrence did become a symbol for courage in the face of overwhelming odds. And he gave us one of the greatest and long-lived slogans in history, "Don't give up the ship!"

William H. White
Rumson, New Jersey

About the Author

Photo by Tina/Visual Xpressions

William H. White, a life-long sailor and amateur historian, has been a commercial banker, professional photographer and served as an officer in the U.S. Navy during the 1960s. He is involved in both sail racing and cruising, primarily on the East Coast in one-designs and offshore boats. He resides in New Jersey with his wife of thirty-four years. They have three grown sons. *The War of 1812 Trilogy* was born out of his love for history and the sea. More information on the author and his books can be found on his website: www.1812trilogy.com.

About the Artist

Paul Garnett began drawing before he could write his name. He was a shipwright on the vessel *Bounty* built for MGM's 1962 remake of "Mutiny on the Bounty" and his paintings have been published twice by the foundation which now owns the ship. His art has also been showcased on A&E's television program "Sea Tales" and the History Channel's "Histories Mysteries: What Really Happened on the 'Mutiny on the Bounty'," and by *Nautical World* magazine.

Following is a selection from

The Evening Gun

the third book in the War of 1812 Trilogy
by William H. White
Look for it in Fall 2001

The black-hulled sloop ghosted around the point and into the small bay. The men on deck were silent, unmoving; in fact, they were barely breathing. Standing next to the helmsman, Isaac Biggs strained his eyes through the darkness. Even though he had cut the point as close as he dared, few aboard had been able to make out any details of the land; it was merely a dim smudge in the surrounding night. Those aboard took some comfort in knowing they in turn would be difficult to spot should anyone be looking. Now they had to find the object of their late-night foray without themselves being seen.

A whispered voice, hoarse with excitement, floated aft. "I think I got her, Isaac. Lookee there, just off'n the wind'ard bow. Looks like there might be a light showin' for'ard on her." Jake Tate hunkered down at the butt of the slender bowsprit, just inside the bulwark. Even with only the scant light from a few stars peeking through the overcast night, his shaggy straw-colored hair seemed to glow, disembodied and suspended in the dark. He had the sharpest eyes aboard and, though he had only one arm, had made himself indispensible on the little vessel.

Biggs strained his eyes to penetrate the darkness, wondering how Jake managed so effortlessly. Standing as tall as his five-foot-four-inch frame allowed, he peered resolutely into the night to see what the young Bayman had spotted. He pushed a hand through his curly hair and, with his sleeve, mopped the beaded sweat off his narrow forehead. Chesapeake Bay's oppressive heat had begin early this year and even nightfall did little to cool the air or ease the heaviness that made it hard to breathe.

As the sloop eased into Tavern Creek, the air stilled; all breeze seemed to be caught and held by the freshly-foliated trees lining both banks. A faint glimmer caught his eye.

"I got her, Jake. Good eyes." In the next breath, Isaac whispered to the helmsman to "bring her up a point" and felt, rather than saw, that the black-dyed sails were trimmed properly as the sloop made her way silently toward a cove about halfway into the creek. He knew that there was little chance of any but the most alert watchman on the British frigate seeing them; the arrogance of the Royal Navy and their certain knowledge that they had successfully cowed all the inhabitants of the region virtually assured him that the watch would be sloppy at best. More likely would be someone hearing them, and he had admonished his men to "be quiet as the dead, or we stand a fair chance of bein' dead." The only sound was the gentle rush of water as it parted before the rakish sloop's hollow bows.

A few minutes later, the shoreline suddenly appeared. Isaac, having taken the tiller himself, eased the sloop into a spot Jake had described to him before they left Kent Island. He brought her head to the wind, now barely a whisper of a breeze, and the crew handed the big mains'l silently at the first sign of a luff. The sloop, barely moving, coasted less than her length and stopped. The anchor was eased carefully into the still, black water. Any who might have heard the faint splash would have thought it a fish jumping. The stays'l and jib dropped noiselessly and were lashed down on the deck. The square tops'l had been furled to its yard even before they entered the creek.

"Everyone below now, quick as you please, and not a sound." Isaac didn't have to remind his crew how critical was complete silence; mostly Maryland watermen, each was more than familiar with how easily sound carried across water, especially on a still night. They'd been through this drill many times before, and the American sloop was building an enviable success record harassing the British. With each little triumph, the British grew more determined to capture the little sloop, but Biggs and his small crew had managed so far to disappear in the confusion they created.

The six men crowded into the small hold and waited silently for their captain to join them. A few shifted their feet, leaning on the bulkhead or the mast. One or two mopped their faces but, for most, the sweat ran down their necks unnoticed in the close quarters. The shirts of those who still wore them were dark with sweat. The hatch closed over their heads as Isaac appeared on the ladder. The heat built instantly; someone lit a small lantern which cast long shadows and a dim yellow light reflected on the glistening faces. It gave them an even more sinister look than they already had.

"I ain't gonna tell you how important what we're doin' is; you all know that since we started doin' these little raids we been drivin' the British crazy. Commodore Barney ain't got no plan to stop, an' gettin' caught up by them surely wouldn't be part of anyone's plan. Less'n a mile into the creek there's a British frigate. 'Ccordin' to the commodore, it's the self-same one what's been sending parties ashore to burn farms and steal livestock. I don't know that we can stop 'em, but we surely can let 'em know we're here. And mayhaps get us a little payback for the trouble they been causin'." He then outlined the plan again and, after putting out the light, climbed up and opened the hatch. The night air, hot though it was, flooded into the hold, smelling like the woods so nearby, and the men silently followed their captain onto the deck.

With practiced, economical moves, a boat was launched quietly. Isaac and five of his raiders nestled between the casks of powder and other supplies needed for their mission. Oars, their mid-sections wrapped where they rested between the thole pins to muffle the noise, were wetted, and a hissed command from Biggs moved the boat away from the sloop and into the darkness toward the British frigate.

Jake Tate, now alone on the sloop, waved unseen as the boat quickly disappeared into the night. He listened intently, straining to catch the splash or creak of an oar; the silence of the middle watch hours was broken only by the rustle of the trees and the peeps of the frogs that had emerged from the mud to fill the night with their rhythmic sounds.

Good luck, men, This one ain't gonna be easy as them others — not against a frigate, by God. Jake thought about the task his mates had before them, and wished he were with them instead of minding the sloop. *Well, reckon I couldn't be much help to 'em anyway. That surgeon on* Shannon *took care o' that. Course, I could be dead or settin' with Charity an' her folks at the farm. Ugh!* The one-armed sailor shook his head at the though of being stuck ashore and, worse, with those high-minded in-laws of his who thought this war was all a waste of time and money. And it interfered with their importing business. Bad business indeed to be on the "outs" with England. Tate spat over the side and sat on the hatchtop to wait, a pistol and cutlass in easy reach of his good left arm. He had managed to become adept at handling both weapons with what had been his 'off-side'. In fact, in the almost twelve months since he caught the ball that led to its amputation, his missing limb had become little more than an inconvenience to him.

The sloop had been swallowed by the darkness

within moments of shoving off. Isaac now steered up the creek close to the shore, a dark, broken backdrop that made it difficult for anyone watching to notice the small craft. Part of his mind concentrated on keeping the boat headed fair, watching for low branches and stumps as the shore slipped past; the other part of his consciousness reviewed their plan and, more importantly, their escape back to the sloop. Satisfied with the plan he and Jake had worked out with Commodore Barney, whose local knowledge was as great as Jake's, that part of his mind turned to the recent past and how he and Jake wound up in the Chesapeake sailing small boats against some of the best of the Royal Navy.

Shortly after Oliver Perry's September triumph in USS *Lawrence* on Lake Erie, the Navy recognized that a greater need for sailors existed inland than on the coast. Hundreds were detached from blockaded frigates, brigs, and sloops and marched to New York state where their services were in desperate need. Robert Coleman and Tim Conoughy, Isaac's two formerly Royal Navy mates, now seamen in the American Navy, had been included in the group sent inland. Biggs had remained with the Salem privateer, *General Washington*, and Captain Asa Rogers for another successful cruise after their harrowing rescue mission to Halifax.

Jack Clements, former Navy warrant bosun, who had been with Captain James Lawrence aboard the frigate *Chesapeake* in June of 1813, had been released from further obligation to the Navy in recognition of the injury he received when the *Shannon* had boarded and taken the *Chesapeake.* His ear had been cleanly, almost surgically, removed by a cutlass stroke during the brief but fierce hand-to-hand fighting on *Chesapeake*'s deck and his wound was treated by the British surgeon while the American survivors were on route to Halifax and the Melville Island prison.

There was little chance that any shipping could

escape the tight stranglehold the Royal Navy now maintained on the entire coast, from the Carolinas to northern Massachusetts; if a vessel was in, it stayed in, and, if offshore, her master had to find another port from which to operate. trade suffered and, with very few exceptions, the deep-water Navy and most of the privateer fleet remained harbor-bound.

This was the driving force that drew Clements and Isaac, accompanied by Jake Tate, back to the Chesapeake. Jake had also been in the Navy and, like Clements, had been released from further service due to the wound he received during his service on *Chesapeake*. He was headed, reluctantly, for married life ashore, feeling that there was little chance of his finding a berth afloat.

The three left Boston a month after their friends marched inland, arriving in Baltimore just ahead of winter. It had taken them no time at all to find useful employment with Commodore Barney's small "navy." Jake, grimly anticipating a life ashore with Charity, was understandably delighted to find that his services would also be needed — even with only one arm. He and Isaac had been sailing this sloop together for close to three months, and Jack Clements, along with a wall-eyed waterman named Frank Clark, skippered a similar vessel. So far, both the former privateersmen and the Navy bosun, late of the *Chesapeake*, had enjoyed only success and the two seventy-foot sloops and Barney's gunboats, like biting flies around a horse, had become anathema to the ships and forces Captain Robert Barrie regularly sent out to find and destroy them. The gunboats, based south in the Patuxent River, had almost been caught twice, but the sloops had operated unchallenged.

"Isaac! Lookee there, ain't no one watchin' out," Sam Hay whispered where he crouched next to Isaac and poked him sharply in the ribs, bringing his whole attention to the present.

Isaac grunted and peered through the night. "Aye,

'ppears so, Sam."

They could make out no watchman or indeed any other on the frigate's deck. A dim lantern showed near the foremast, and Isaac detected the faint aroma of tobacco in the still air. The watchmen must be hunkered down near the foremast having a smoke.

"Easy now, lads." Isaac's whispered command took the boat alongside the towering, sheer wall of the British frigate. The oars were silently boated. He steered to a position under her starboard main channel where they were unlikely to be seen and where they would set the first surprise for the Royal Navy.

A stout line was heaved around the shroud lanyard and secured in the boat. One of the Americans stepped barefoot over his boated oar and shinnied up to the channel. A small cask filled with black powder was handed up to him, and he placed it carefully between the hull and the lanyards, affixing a length of slow match to its top. After a brief pause, the powder-impregnated cord flared suddenly, then dimmed to a glow. The sailor slid down the line and back into the boat. The forward starboard channel received the same treatment. All remained still.

Silently, Isaac moved the boat still farther forward, until his men could reach the anchor cable. A hatchet made short work of the heavy hawser, and, still unnoticed by the watchmen, the frigate floated free in the confined, shallow water of Tavern Creek.

"Isaac! What the hell is that?" one of the men whispered frantically, pointing ashore. A glow was building above the trees, lighting the blackness and silhouetting the trees. True to form, the British raiding party ashore had probably fired a building belonging to an uncooperative farmer and would soon be returning to their ship.

"We best be gettin' ourselves outta here, lads. I 'spect them Brits'll be headed back quick as you please now they done their dirty work. Reckon they'll be some surprised." Isaac smiled unseen in the darkness and, as the oars were shipped, steered the boat back toward the shoreline and their sloop.

A sharp crack, a musket shot, rang out from the deck of the frigate, followed by a loud cry. "Alarm, alarm! Starboard side. Small boat 'eadin' off!" One of the frigate's watchmen had finally looked their way.

"Row, men! They've smoked us!" Isaac steered closer to shore, hoping the boat would blend into the shadows, but the light of the burning building beyond the trees silhouetted them for the Royal Marines firing at them. More shots rent the night, then a crashing boom as one of the swivel guns fired from the frigate's fighting top. Falling shot pocked the water around the little boat.

The oarsman immediately in front of Isaac sighed and slumped over his oar. Isaac grabbed the man by the front of his shirt and pulled him to the deck. He then took the dead man's seat and pulled his oar, his hand sticky with the man's blood. An explosion lit up the warship's rig briefly in its flare.

"That's the first of 'em, lads! Keep rowing. It ought to take their minds off'n us!" Isaac was delighted to see one of their charges had done its job. The other should be going off any moment now. And, as more British sailors and marines came on deck, someone was bound to notice the frigate drifting with the ebbing tide. The more determined Royal Marines maintained their musket fire. Their missed shots splashed around the boat and the thump of balls hitting the hull kept the crew rowing hard, not in a panic, but with the steady, rhythmic strokes of seasoned professionals.

Clive Billings, rowing the forward shore-side oar, suddenly screamed and dropped his oar, clutching at his chest and shoulder. His normal voice sounded like a stuck door being forced; his scream penetrated the senses. His mate picked up the other oar, barely missing a stroke, and resumed pulling, handling both oars until Sam Hay, crouched in the bow, shoved the stricken Billings aside and took over the oar.

"Get you aft, Clive, and take the tiller!" Sam said sharply. "You ain't hurt so bad as you cain't steer. Isaac's pullin' an oar. Get goin'. And stop that hollerin'! You're giving the Brits somethin' to shoot at."

The thought that the Marines were aiming at the sound of his voice immediately caused Clive to cease his noise and stumble aft to the tiller. In an effort to remain silent, his lips pressed into a thin line across his face; his head swiveled back to the warship, and his eyes darted wildly around, bouncing from the frigate to the dark shoreline, trying to see who had, and might again, shoot at him.

Isaac maintained the pace of their rowing while seeking the source of the shot that wounded Billings. It couldn't have come from the frigate; the angle was all wrong. Besides, the sailors on the frigate, now brightly lit by the fire amidships, were likely too busy now to worry about escaping Americans.

Then he heard crashing through the underbrush and, ahead of them, muffled orders and the sounds of men running, breaking branches and splashing through shallows. As he twisted his head around, a muzzle flash flared dazzlingly for a second, then another, and another. The air hummed as musket balls flew close to the now desperately-rowing raiders.

"Steer away! Get farther from the shore!" He spoke sharply to the wounded man at the tiller, and the boat swerved toward the middle of the creek. More shots came from shore, but at least the Marines on the frigate were silent now, busy with the fires. Isaac realized the small boat could well be out of their range by now, getting close to the sloop and the limited sanctuary it offered.

"Isaac! Larboard, man! Steer to larboard!" Tate's voice rang out over the water, and Billings, his pain momentarily forgotten, pulled hard on the tiller. The boat responded instantly, and immediately a thunderous crash filled the night. Screams and curses erupted from the trees along the shore. It took the crew a moment to realize what had happened.

"Good job, Jake! Hit 'em again if you can!" Isaac bellowed at the sloop and its sole occupant, who was manning the falconet mounted on the forward bulwark. The boat was suddenly alongside, and again the little flared swivel gun crashed. No return fire came from the shore.

The men scrambled up on to the sloop's deck; Isaac helped the wounded Billings, and then two men handed up the body of their dead shipmate. They cut the boat loose and the men rushed unbidden to their stations for making sail. In a trice, the black sail went up and the anchor cable was cut with the same hatchet used on the frigate's cable. A light breeze filled the sail, soon aided by the jib and stays'l, and the sloop gathered way. Isaac steered her clear of the shore and headed for the turn in the creek which would lead them to the Bay. The sloop quickly picked up speed, and soon they were safely hidden in the dark night. Isaac could still see the glow in the sky from the burning farm building and the lesser fire on the British frigate. And behind both, the faint orange and red harbingers of sunrise.

Also available now

A Press of Canvas
the first book in the War of 1812 Trilogy
by William H. White

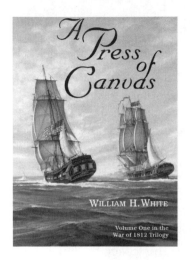

W. H. White's novel, *A Press of Canvas*, introduces a new character in American sea fiction: Isaac Biggs of Marblehead, Massachusetts. Sailing from Boston as captain of the foretop in the Bark *Anne*, his ship is outward bound with a cargo for the Swedish colony of St. Barts in the West Indies in the fall of 1810. When the *Anne* is stopped by a British Royal Navy frigate, Isaac and several of his shipmates are forcibly pressed into service on the *Orpheus*, actively engaged in England's long-running war with France.

The young Isaac faces the harsh life of a Royal Navy seaman and a harrowing war at sea. His new life is hard, with strange rules, floggings, and new dangers. Then the United States declares war on England and Isaac finds himself in an untenable position, facing the possibility of fighting his own countrymen.

Written from the aspect of the fo'c'sle rather than an officer's view and through the eyes of an American, *A Press of Canvas* provides new perspectives and an exciting story of this often neglected period in American history.

"Sailors everywhere will rejoice in the salt spray, slanting decks and high adventure of this lively yarn of the young American republic battling for its rights at sea."
Peter Stanford, President, National Maritime Historical Society

"A great read . . . a very engaging story with believable, honest charac-ters . . . taught me a lot about this period of history . . . just fabulous!"
John Wooldridge, Managing Editor, *Motorboating and Sailing*

Excerpt from *A Press of Canvas*

"Biggs, find Mr. Clark, if you please, and ask him to step aft." Captain Jed Smalley continued his pacing of the quarterdeck of the bark *Anne*, casting an occasional glance at the sails hanging limply aloft, reflected almost perfectly with the image of the ship in the brilliant, but dead calm sea. Isaac Biggs, Captain of the Foretop, had been taking his ease with some of his fellow topmen in the scant shade offered by the vessel's deck house when Smalley sent him to find the first mate.

"Aye, sir." He said aloud, and to himself, *Something must be gonna happen. Maybe the Cap'n figgers we gonna get a breeze o' wind. 'Bout time, I'd reckon.* He stood and walked forward, squinting as he left the shade, and the full force of the Caribbean sun, low in the sky and bouncing off the quiet sea, hit his eyes. He noticed with pleasure, and some relief, that the deck no longer burned his bare feet as he made his way forward, and the tar caulking the seams no longer oozed from between the long leaf pine boards.

As he gained the fo'c'sle, he could smell that Cook was getting close to having the evening meal prepared. Isaac could only imagine how hot the galley must be, and the air around the Charlie Noble stack shimmered as the cooking heat rose from it. First Mate Sam Clark was sitting with some of the foredeck hands on the butt of the bowsprit, and Biggs watched for a moment as the jib boom on its outboard end described lazy circles in the air from the gentle rolling of the ship.

"Mr. Clark, Cap'n wants you on the quarterdeck, if you please. Sent me to get you." The mate looked up at the young topman. He stared for a moment at the curly dark hair, the earnest penetrating eyes, and the easy smile that always seemed ready to expand into a full grin. The mate smiled in spite of himself and stood.

"He say what he wanted?" There hadn't been anything requiring the mate's attention for the two days they had been becalmed, and even though he knew it would be unlikely for Captain Smalley to have shared his thoughts with a foremast hand, his curiosity got the better of him. He could see the tall, whip-thin form of the captain some 130 feet away, still pacing his domain, and he wondered how he stood the black frock coat he habitually wore at sea, regardless of the weather.

"Not to me, sir. But then I guess he figgered it wasn't none o' my business. He ain't been off'n the quarterdeck since the breeze quit, though, 'at I've noticed. Probably concerned 'bout gettin' into St. Bart's afore someone else gets our cargo for the return." Isaac watched the sails overhead as he spoke; they still showed no signs of life, not even the t'gallants some 140 feet above the deck. Not a breath of air was stirring.

The two stopped as they passed two of the bark's longboats, lashed down tightly, and covered with taut canvas, bleached white by the tropical sun. Isaac, seeing his friends still taking their ease, rejoined them in the shade as Sam Clark continued to the quarterdeck.

"Think we're gonna get us some breeze, Cap'n? The men been scratching the backstays and whistling until they's lips hurt. You'd think we'd have more wind 'en we could handle from all o' that. I cain't recall them nor'east trades droppin' fer this long down here. Might be gonna change. Mebbe get some weather."

Smalley had stopped his pacing, and stood at the larboard rail staring at the horizon to the east. He continued watching the horizon, while his first mate stood patiently behind him, waiting. Clark could see the sweat running down the captain's neck and the queue in which he habitually wore his gray hair was damp from it, the black ribbon drooping. Hatless, the tall, almost gaunt skipper suddenly turned, squinting at his mate with deep-set pale eyes that most took as blue, but were in fact gray, in a weathered face that had seen the sea in all her moods over the nearly forty years he had been at sea. His jaw line showed a stubble of white bristles — not from slovenly habits, but from an inability to see close at hand without his spectacles. And he did not feel that wearing spectacles while he shaved was appropriate. He had been captaining vessels for 25 of his 48 years — everything from small coastal vessels to a few brigs, schooners, and this bark, *Anne*, his favorite, and also the largest.

"Yes, Mr. Clark, I think we might get a breeze this night. And from the look o' them clouds startin' on the eastern horizon, mebbe even some rain inta the bargain. You can let the men enjoy a song after supper if they's a mind, as I figger we'll be workin' with no time for gaiety and cavortin' soon enough." Smalley's baritone voice was quiet, as always.

Underscoring his words in an ironical counterpoint, the silence of the day was broken only by the slatting of sails and the slap of unstrained sheets and halyards as *Anne* rolled in the gentle swells. Sam Clark knew better than to doubt this man's sea-sense; he had sailed with him for five years now and had yet to see him err when it came to anticipating the weather.

"Aye, sir. I'll give the second the word; it'll most likely be his watch that's shortenin' sail later."

Clark left the quarterdeck and the captain continued pacing, glancing from time to time at the eastern sky. Absently, Smalley watched Clark's compact form head forward, not thinking about anything in particular, but aware of everything going on aboard his ship. One part of his brain again gave thanks that he had this strong leader and excellent seaman as his second in command. He noticed, without thought, that Clark stopped and spoke with a few sailors, his powerful arms gesturing aloft, and, as he turned his face eastward over the larboard side, his light-colored beard glowed as the lowering sun shone through it. The captain expected that the wind would come in more from the east than the north, and said to himself, *Be nice if'n we might could get them steady half gales back we been enjoyin' since Boston. This don't look like it to me, though. Reckon they might just be some weather over yonder. Be takin' in a passel o' this canvas before long, I'd warrant.*

The *Anne* had all her canvas set — courses, tops'ls, t'gallants, and the spanker on the mizzen; all hung as slack as wash on a Vineyard clothesline. The stays'ls and jibs forward and the sprits'l under the rakish bowsprit were motionless and it might seem to the casual observer, and certainly to some of the landsmen aboard, that thinking about shortening sail was, at this point, a waste of effort — indeed, even foolish.

The rattle of the pumps brought his mind back to the immediate present, and he looked up the deck where he could see, just abaft the capstan, two men working the handles for the pumps, manned for about an hour during each watch to keep the holds and bilge as dry as possible. He noticed that Clark was now deep in conversation with Second Mate Joe O'Malley and Third Mate Ben Jakes, both good sailors, but only the second was the kind of leader Smalley wanted in his ship. Jakes was a smarmy little man with a scraggly beard and a mean cast to his eyes. Even in the heat of the day, his tarpaulin hat was pulled low on his narrow brow, hiding his eyes as they darted everywhere but at the person with whom he spoke. He did not inspire trust from anyone, least of all the captain. Snippets of conversation drifted aft.

". . . Aye, if Cap'n Smalley's lookin' . . . breeze, I'd bet on it. Seen . . . before . . ."

"Thinks . . . men need sompin' to do . . . shorten down? My maintopmen surely don't need no practice . . . tell Biggs . . . his crew aloft . . . ain't no wind yesterday, ain't none today and ain't none tomorrow, neither. Man's gotten . . . sun, you ask me."

"I'll let you know when . . . later . . . supper . . . jest lettin' ya know . . . get yer boys together."

Biggs stood up and stepped over to where the mates were talking. After waiting for a break in the conversation, he looked at Clark. "Did I hear something 'bout shortenin' down later?" At a nod from Clark, he continued "I'd best get my boys fed if . . ."

Clark cut him off. "Ain't no rush, Isaac. Cap'n said be after supper and mebbe a song. No need to rush none."

Smalley smiled to himself; that young foretopman was always ready to work, and eager to advance himself. *Reckon he'll make a fine mate — mebbe even a master — someday. Good man, that. I could use a dozen like him.*

He watched as Biggs, dismissed by the first mate, joined one of his foretopmen and moved over to sit on one of the 24-pounder carronades, straddling the short barrel. Biggs rested his large, scarred hands on the bulwark in front of him, unconsciously flexing the muscles in his forearms as he stared out to sea, watching the horizon. So intent was his gaze that the fellow with him remarked.

"Isaac, what's that you're lookin' at so hard? Ain't nothin' out there 'ceptin' flat calm water."

"Cap'n thinks we gonna pick up a breeze o' wind here soon enough, and I'm tryin' to see what it is he sees makes him think that. Stuff I need to learn my own self, if I'm gonna ever sail as mate. Must be them low clouds over yonder. Looks like it could rain, you ask me." He leaned over the rail, looking at the water and the black sides of the ship with the white painted gunports.

The ship had been painted before leaving Boston for this run to St. Bartholomew and he knew she still looked Bristol. The gunports, mostly there to deceive, did include four that opened to reveal the 24-pounder carronades, short barreled and with a range of scarcely more than a pistol shot. They were lethally effective when properly served and loaded with bits of iron, nails and chain; unfortunately, there were few aboard save Mr. O'Malley who knew how to handle them, and the owners, New Englanders all and parsimonious to a fault, felt there were far better ways to spend money than on powder and shot for practice. Let the Navy handle that. Besides, if a French privateer or British man-of-war really wanted to cause trouble, those four carronades would not slow them down much.

There seemed to be little defense against the British "right of search" boarding parties which could strip a ship of vital crew members in a trice. The British had been busy with the French for the past several years, but instead of that ongoing war distracting the English Navy from American ships, it focused the attention of any short-handed Royal Navy vessel squarely on American merchant vessels. The conflict required a constant supply of seamen to sail the king's ships. And in the eyes of the British, a supply of skilled sailors existed for their pleasure on American ships like *Anne*. A cry from the masthead of "Sail ho!" could mean an opportunity to speak a homeward bound American, or the potential for the British to board them on the premise of looking for British subjects avoiding service in His Majesty's Navy. This had become an increasingly frequent occurrence in the past several years, and a problem that many ship owners and captains felt should be handled by the American Navy. If it led to war, so be it.

Smalley, while not having experienced the British "right of search" first hand, agreed with his fellows that something must be done, and soon. Already ships that had been regulars on the Indies run were heading off to Europe or Russia where there was less likelihood of problems with the Royal Navy. Smalley had captained a score of successful trips to the Indies for his owners, but still felt the uncertainty that always showed up about two or three days before the anticipated landfall. That landfall this time would be St. Maarten, just to the northwest of his destination and occupied by both the Dutch and the French. The likelihood of crossing tacks with a French privateer leaving or returning to port was a consideration, but he was more concerned about a British ship, and this was, in part at least, why he had been on the quarterdeck for most of the past two days.

Designed to carry cargo in many forms, *Anne's* deck areas and holds were packed with a variety of barrels, casks, crates, and puncheons filled with goods for the market in St. Bartholomew, a Swedish colony and free port. Some contained fish, beef, and butter; others were in fact empty — the clean barrels were themselves the trade goods. From time to time, the cargo included boots, shoes, and hats. The return trip would find the holds filled with barrels of molasses for the thriving rum distilleries in New England, and brown sugar for both American consumption and re-shipment to Europe.

"Dingding, ding." The ship's bell called the captain back from his reverie, and he watched his men appear on deck for supper and their evening ration of rum. The heat was beginning to tell — or maybe it was the boredom from being becalmed — but small fights and arguments were breaking out; it was only a matter of time before one or another of the men brought forth a knife. The men of the larboard watch were eating so they could relieve their mates in the starboard section at 6:00. Smalley looked at the eastern sky for the hundredth time in the past two hours and saw his suspicions were about to be confirmed.

"Mr. Clark," he called to the mate. "We'll hand the t'gallants now, if you please. And trim for an easterly."

The mate glanced at the horizon, and saw that once again Smalley had anticipated the weather accurately. "Aye, sir. And don't look to me like they'll be any singin' this night, 'ceptin' mebbe the wind." His brow furrowed in concern.

Indeed, even as the captain spoke, the water had begun to stir; little ripples and ruffles disturbing the reflected image of the ship which appeared in the molten glass of the still sea. The temperature reacted to the cooling easterly breeze as it started to fill in, and the men on deck moved as one to the weather rail, to feel the relief on their sweat stained faces and arms. Hats off, and the sweat drying on their faces, they stood with their shirts pulled open, feeling the cooling gentle breeze on their skin; a few laughed, while others just enjoyed the sensation quietly. Captain Smalley had a reputation for being conservative, and the preliminary shortening sail prior to a blow instead of during it was one of the manifestations of his conservatism, and one appreciated by his sailors.

"Mr. O'Malley," hollered the mate as he started forward, "Let's get all hands on deck, if you please. We'll be shortening sail directly." Seeing Third Mate Ben Jakes, who had neither opened his shirt nor doffed his hat, loitering near the 'midships capstan, he nodded and spoke.

"Mr. Jakes, have your topmen stand by to go aloft — and see if per chance you might be able to keep up with the foremast hands. The only topmen slower than your crew are the bunch on the mizzen, and Jackson's landsmen are afraid to let go of the jackstay and beckets."

Jakes bridled at the remark, but said nothing save "Aye," tugged his hat brim further down, and went to ensure that his men were ready at the weather shrouds when the word to shorten was passed. The traditional rivalry between the hands working aloft on the three masts had transcended normal competition, resulting in several fist fights and more than a few incidents involving the ever-present seaman's knives which, fortunately, resulted in only minor wounds. The other mates, of course, were well aware of this contest of the seamen's skills, and used it constantly to their advantage; a certain benefit to the ship was that sails were usually smartly handed, furled, and set.

The hands had begun to break off from their pause at the rail and take their positions when the order to shorten sail went out. The waisters gathered amidships to handle halyards, sheets, and braces, pulling the big square sails around either to fill them, or spill the wind from them so the men aloft could furl them. As O'Malley and Clark saw that the "heavers" were in position at the foremast, he signaled Biggs and his men aloft. The t'gallants, being the highest sails on *Anne*, were usually first to come in when the weather started — not only did the yards have to be lowered and the sails furled to the yards, but the masts had to be either housed or struck down into the lower rigging. This was frequently difficult and dangerous. When non-emergency shortening was being accomplished, it was often done from the foremast to the mizzen, one mast at a time. This generally was quicker as enough men were available as 'heavers' at each mast when done individually, as opposed to breaking up crews for halyards, sheets, clew tackles, and braces at each mast.

Biggs' men were at the topmast cap and on the rope ladder leading to it from the top of the lower mast. Seeing this, Clark blew his whistle and shouted for clew lines to be hauled up and halyards to be let go. As the yard moved down the t'gallantmast, the sail drooped from its clewlines. Immediately the yard came to rest on the top mast cap, the men jumped onto it to haul up great handfuls of sail, securing it along the spar. As soon as the sail was securely furled, the order came to "ease jumper stays, standby to house the t'gallant mast." Biggs' men watched below to ensure the necessary lines were in hand, then, on order from Biggs, pulled the dog from the topmast cap and the t'gallant mast slid down the lubber hole in the topmast, coming to rest against a stop so that only a few feet of it showed above the topmast. There it was made fast securely.

The foremast jacks were then released by Biggs to go below, and most slid down the backstays to the deck. Even before they reached the deck, the maintopmen had started to perform the same tasks on the main t'gallant mast. Biggs watched for a few minutes as Jakes continually harangued his men, more often distracting them than inspiring them to greater speed. As the clewlines for the main t'gallant were hauled up, the sail's middle moved up toward the yard producing a "draped" effect which made it easier for the men on the yardarm to haul up the canvas and secure it. It seemed as though the job was going smoothly, in spite of the third's "encouragement." Biggs knew that Jakes had a great deal more deep water time than he, but he also knew that most on board thought Biggs was a better sailor.

As he made his way forward with his mates for supper, Isaac Biggs recalled the men who had taught him to hand, reef and steer. Of course, his father, a Banks fisherman who had taken young Isaac to sea at the tender age of eight, had been the major influence. Isaac remembered the skipper of that schooner, Mr. Rowe; a real sailorman he was who had sailed the deeps, and had only taken up fishing later in life. He had found in the lad a willingness to learn and an enthusiastic pupil who eagerly absorbed all that he saw and heard. It was he who had arranged for the boy to secure a berth as ordinary seaman on a brig out of Salem bound on the coastal route south. A bully mate had convinced Isaac that minding his business and staying out of reach was the way to not only stay alive but also to advance, and within a short while, Biggs had been made an able seaman.

Still youthful and unwelcome ashore with the older men, Isaac, while becoming a most competent sailor, was sadly lacking in worldliness. His Methodist upbringing had taught him taverns were no place for a young Marblehead sailor, and aside from the half rations of grog provided him due to his youth, he had yet to taste the sweet potions of the ale houses. A succession of coastal ships added to his education, and ultimately to his current berth as captain of the foretop here on *Anne*. Watching others over the years, men he respected, had taught him that it was easier to lead men from in front, than by pushing from behind with a starter and shouts. The men liked his easy-going style and instinctive leadership and bent to their tasks with a will.

Captain Smalley, with whom Biggs had sailed for almost two years, had noticed his development and natural ability aloft as well as with his men, and was waiting for the opportunity to find him a berth as a third on a sloop or brig. To that end, Smalley had encouraged Sam Clark to instruct the topman in the art and science of navigation, and the reports he received from the mate confirmed his hopes for the lad's potential.

The third on *Anne*, Ben Jakes, was a poor leader of men and weak of character. Any man who felt regular use of a starter necessary would not, in Smalley's opinion, ever rise to command. Smalley also suspected that Jakes was involved in some underhanded dealings aboard, and did not trust him. Jakes was, however, an excellent seaman, and for that, the captain found him useful.

The wind was rising steadily now, and it was obvious to even the landsmen aboard that some dirty weather was indeed afoot. The t'gallants were in their gaskets and their masts struck down. The ship was responding to the trimming of sheets and hauling on the braces; she moved quickly now through the still calm sea as gradually, the wind's song in the rigging rose from a whispered caress to an insistent whine. The sky became darker — an ominous darkness which was beyond the growing dusk. Heavy clouds were beginning to move rapidly across the sky, increasing the gloom of twilight. The main topmen were back on deck, and were headed for the galley and their evening meal, debating the relative rapidity of handing their respective sails. In all likelihood, they'd be back soon — either to relieve the starboard watch or to reef tops'ls and courses if the wind continued to build. *Anne* began to heel to the wind, and the occasional burst of spray from the now building seas wet the decks.

Second Mate Joe O'Malley made his way aft toward the quarterdeck, moving his lanky form down the now canted deck in a rhythm dictated by the seas as they attacked the windward bow of *Anne* and rolled down the side of the ship. He noted the men working under the direction of First Mate Clark securing the carronades against the bulwarks. This action would be justified by the deteriorating conditions; a loose gun could wreak havoc on a tossing deck. The men had shortened the gun tackles and the barrels were slanted up against the bulwark and tied in place with heavy hemp line. Once secured in this manner, it would take more severe weather than they expected to move them.

O'Malley stepped onto the quarterdeck and headed for the wheel, where the helmsmen's stance and concentration provided a marked contrast to their inactivity earlier that day. O'Malley considered adding another pair of seamen to the wheel, then decided it could wait awhile. As the leader of the starbowlines, he was responsible for ensuring that the ship was properly manned while his watch was on deck. He checked the slate on which were recorded the regular casting of the ships log; after a string of "0"s and "1"s, it was good to see an "8" written on the slate just a few minutes previously. He estimated the wind at about thirty knots already, and knew that if it continued to increase, sails would again have to be shortened.

Spray was now blowing across the quarterdeck, making the watch turn their faces away from time to time when a heavier gust carried the spume over the deckhouse. It would surely get worse before it eased any. He watched the ship's boy turn the glass and move forward to the bell; five strokes could be heard before the wind carried the sound to leeward and away. The larboard watch was on deck and taking their positions at lookout, and at the sheets and braces, ready for the inevitable commands necessitated by the rising storm. O'Malley saw Ben Jakes, late yet again, heading for the quarterdeck to take over the watch until eight bells when O'Malley would return to manage the ship until midnight. Jakes relieved his superior with few words exchanged in the face of a rising wind and their mutual antipathy.

Having assumed the watch, Ben felt the ship shiver slightly as a larger wave shocked the windward bow, and a burst of green water flew down the deck. The door to the deckhouse closed as O'Malley disappeared inside, narrowly avoiding a surge of water down the companionway. *What a night this is going to be*, thought Jakes, buttoning the top button on his oiled canvas jacket, and jamming his hat even further down on his head. *This is only going to get worse.*

He was right; the storm continued to deepen as he alternately stood by the helmsmen and paced up and down the quarterdeck. The captain had apparently decided to hold the sails currently deployed, at least for the time being, trying to make up some of the time lost in the calm; his orders to the watch were quite explicit and woe to the mate that countermanded them without damn good reason! Shortly before he was scheduled for relief, Jakes saw two of his maintopmen appear by the covered area abaft the deckhouse where the waisters and idlers were allowed to shelter in bad weather. Watching them for a minute or two, he realized they were arguing about something; hearing what was out of the question. Then he saw one of the men turn toward him and shout something; the wind carried the words away as soon as they were out of his mouth, but their implication was clear.

Ben Jakes had some unsavory characters in his watch and had found them useful in carrying out some of his less-than-honest chores. Those same men also found that Jakes could be helpful to them on occasion as well, and the resulting symbiotic relationship was usually at cross purposes with the goals of the captain and the owners. On a ship the size of *Anne*, many of these "deals" and goings-on were known throughout the fo'c'sle and mates' mess, but it was often better to ignore things that didn't affect you if you wanted to avoid an "accident." The captain and first mate suspected that Jakes was behind some of the problems they had experienced in the six months since he joined the ship, but none were as yet serious enough to override the fact that he was a very good seaman, and could be counted on to act properly when the situation required it. So far, his primary "business" appeared to be selling ships' stores and extra equipment ashore and, while it certainly was not desirable, it was common enough practice in both the merchant fleet and the Navy that it could be overlooked for now. If it developed into a greater problem, he could be paid off and put ashore.

Raising his voice over the increasing whine of the wind as he moved toward the two, Jakes shouted, "What are you two lubbers doin' hangin' about back here? You're s'posed to be for'ard."

One of the men, an older topman with a natural sneer to his face shouted back, " We can get there quick as ever you please should we be needed there, but we wanted to have a word with you."

They stepped into the deckhouse to continue the conversation at a more moderate tone. "Well, here I am. Have yer word."

"Biggs is gettin' to be more of a problem than ever. He was mentioning again to the first this afternoon that a lot of his spare line and blocks was gone missin' and that idler, Billy, 'at works as the captain's steward was standin' right there with his ears flappin' like wings. We wouldn't want our "business" to get snuffed by a nosy mate. If Billy happens to mention it in front of Cap'n Smalley, Clark mightn't have a choice but to close us down and God knows what else. What do ya think?"

"I think Biggs might have an accident aloft. There's some dirty weather makin' up tonight and my guess is the tops'ls and courses will have to be reefed during the evening watch. I'll . . . " Before he could finish the thought, Joe O'Malley appeared on the ladder, heading for the quarterdeck where he expected to find Jakes awaiting relief from his watch. A look passed between Jakes and his men that said, "He heard it all — now what?"

O'Malley instead spoke up and said, "I figgered you'd be aft, Ben. What are you doin' in here? A little weather botherin' you?"

"Just chasin' these two back up for'ard, Joe. And you needn't worry 'bout me and weather; I seen more than most. You here to take the watch now?" The menace in the third's growl was clear.

Ignoring the tone, O'Malley moved on, speaking over his shoulder to Jakes. "Aye. Let's get on with it before it gets any worse out there. I wouldn't want you to have to stay out in this any longer than necessary." They stepped outside, Jakes ignoring the jibe, accompanied by the two topmen who, with a look at Jakes, disappeared forward. O'Malley led the way to the quarterdeck, and turned when he got to the binnacle. "What was that all about?" he said. "You doin' 'business' at sea now? I thought you only traded in port. I would mind me ways at sea; there's no place to lay up if it gets stormy, if you get my drift."

"I would keep me nose in me own damn business, were I you, Joe O'Malley" snarled Jakes. "You gonna relieve me or stand there spoutin'?"

"You're relieved. But I'll warrant I see you again before the middle watch. We'll be shortenin' down, way this wind's risin', is my guess."

Jakes turned and moved forward, going around the deckhouse to the pin rail at the foot of the mainmast where his two sailors waited. "Well?" asked the older of the two, who had assumed the role of spokesman for these two miscreants.

Jakes studied his crony for a moment before responding. "He's thinking he knows more 'n he does. Don't worry about him. I think that foretopman, Biggs, is going to have to be taken care of though. Maybe I should have a word with one of his men later. If this weather holds, it's just possible that Biggs might have an accident while he's out on the foretops'l yard. That'll ease his sheets and at the same time cut us some slack with Clark. O' course, we'll be ashore in a couple of days, and sometimes men have trouble when they're drinkin' and carousin'; anything might happen."